PRAISE FOR *THE CLOSER I GET*

'A sucker punch of a twist that took my breath away! Absurdly gripping, and enough to unnerve anyone who has ever spent any time online' Angela Clarke

'A brilliantly twisty book' Lisa Jewell

'A chillingly recognisable dissection of the toxic interconnections the internet can produce. A delicious tour de force' Alex Marwood

'A great thriller, taut and tense, with a truly unexpected ending' Russell T Davies

'Absolutely sensational' Elly Griffiths

'*The Closer I Get* is as perfect a thriller as you'll read all year. A creeping sense of dread that never lets up' Caz Frear

'Dark, devious and with a growing sense of dread that bleeds from the pages, *The Closer I Get* is bloody brilliant. Clever, twisty, immersive' Neil Broadfoot

'Beautifully written, with rich and deliciously flawed characters, tense and compelling from first page to last' Amanda Jennings

'This book will make you rethink your social-media obsession. Dangerous from page one, lit by bursts of black humour, ultimately honest about the frailty of ego and the masks we all wear. Terrifically readable' Sarah Hilary

'A real page-turner with engaging characters, scary, dark themes and some surprising humour!' Alex Reeve

'A terrifying portrayal of the online world. The characters are top notch, the writing sublime, and the storyline chillingly plausible. This is dark, twisty fiction at its very best' SJI Holliday

'Compelling, creepy and completely believable ... I Loved it' Mel McGrath

'Frighteningly good. One of the best books you'll read this year' Ed James

'Effortlessly readable, intensely chilling. That ending just floored me' Chris Whitaker

'An absolute stunner, with a deliciously twisted ending' Lisa Hall

'Unsettling. Taught. Menacing. Unnerved me and had me gripped right till the end, when Burston puts the killer into killer twist. His best yet' Jonathan Harvey

'Brilliant, chilling, totally awesome writing' Miranda Dickinson

'Dark, thought-provoking and totally riveting' Matt Cain

'The kind of book you read in one breathless gulp' Cass Green

'A gripping, chilling tale of obsession' Katerina Diamond

'Dark and creepily addictive. Certainly makes you think about your online connections' Jane Isaac

'I devoured this book. The last forty-odd pages were read from between my fingers. The tension is almost unbearable. The twist is gut-wrenching. The book is a masterpiece in sustained suspense and smart, literate contemporary horror. Bravo Mr Burston' Derek Farrell

'A deliciously unsettling read that will make you think twice about that sesh on social media. It made me want to move to Hastings though' Lesley Thomson

'This is unlike anything else I've read recently. Clever, tense, bang-on-the-moment, thrilling, and, God, it makes you think about how social media invades our lives ... A totally gripping thriller that I'll be thinking about for a long time' Louise Beech

'A witty and insightful novel, filled with mischief and compassion' Susie Boyt

'Very easy to read, certainly keeps you hooked in with plenty of twists. I suspect it will be a big read this summer' Fiona Sharp

'A gripping ride through the heartlands of need and hurt. Even at his most thrilling, Paul Burston never loses his sense of real pain and suffering' Philip Hensher

'A curious and unsettling novel that makes you think twice about ... everything. Beautifully written, dark and compulsive. I devoured it' Syd Moore

'Gripping and terrifying' Rowan Coleman

'Intelligent, well written, funny, dark and relevant' SJ Lynes

'A dark, twisting tale that shines a light on the murkier side of human nature, social media and fame' Adam Hamdy

'A thought-provoking social-media thriller about fear, fanaticism and the psychological legacy of harassment. Written from differing perspectives in alternate chapters, this is the story of a formerly successful author and an increasingly hostile online fan ... The best work of fiction yet from the novelist, journalist and literary salon host' *Attitude Magazine*

'Brilliantly written, it's compulsive and twisty and the final reveal will unsettle and startle the reader ... Intelligent, gripping and compulsive. This is incredible writing that challenges the reader; complex, subtle and incredibly powerful' Random Things through My Letterbox

THE CLOSER I GET

ABOUT THE AUTHOR

Paul Burston is the author of five novels and the editor of two short-story collections. His most recent novel, *The Black Path*, was longlisted for the *Guardian's* Not The Booker Prize 2016 and was a bestseller at WHSmith. His first novel, *Shameless*, was shortlisted for the State of Britain Award; his third novel, *Lovers & Losers*, was shortlisted for a Stonewall Award and his fourth, *The Gay Divorcee*, was optioned for television. He was a founding editor of *Attitude* magazine and has written for many publications including the *Guardian*, the *Independent*, *Time Out*, *The Times* and the *Sunday Times*. In March 2016, he was featured in the British Council's #FiveFilms4Freedom Global List 2016, celebrating '33 visionary people who are promoting freedom, equality and LGBT rights around the world'. He is the founder and host of London's award-winning LGBT+ literary salon Polari and founder and chair of The Polari First Book Prize for new writing and The Polari Prize for established authors.

Follow Paul on Twitter *@PaulBurston* and visit his website: www.paulburston.com.

THE CLOSER I GET

PAUL BURSTON

**ORENDA
BOOKS**

Orenda Books
16 Carson Road
West Dulwich
London SE21 8HU
www.orendabooks.co.uk

First published in the United Kingdom by Orenda Books, 2019
Copyright © Paul Burston, 2019

A catalogue record for this book is available from the British Library.

Paperback ISBN 978-1-912374-77-9
Hardback ISBN 978-1-912374-89-2
eISBN 978-1-912374-78-6

Typeset in Garamond by MacGuru Ltd
Printed and bound by CPI Group (UK) Ltd, Croydon, CR0 4YY

For sales and distribution, please contact: *info@orendabooks.co.uk*

For V.G. Lee, my partner in crime in many ways.

'There is always some madness in love. But there
is also always some reason in madness'

—Friedrich Nietzsche

PART ONE

1

It was great seeing you today. You probably don't believe me, not after everything that's happened. But it's the truth. I'd never lie to you, Tom. I never have. Not once. I'm not like the others. Sometimes I think I'm the only truly honest person left.

We live in an age of such deceit, don't we? People lie all the time. It's second nature to them. Everyone is so afraid of appearing stupid, or saying the wrong thing and offending someone. Everyone's so keen to make a good impression – virtue signalling and boasting about their perfect lives on Facebook, posting artfully posed selfies and filtered photos of their dinner on Instagram. Social media has made liars of us all.

Not me, though. If anything, I'm too honest for my own good. Maybe if I'd learned to hold my tongue more, we wouldn't be in this mess. But then I wouldn't have been true to myself. I can't change the way I am, Tom. Even for you. Even if there's a price to pay.

You used to admire my honesty. 'Refreshing' you said. 'A free thinker'. Did you change your mind? Or were you humouring me when you said those things? I'd hate to think that you lied to me from the outset. That would make you a hypocrite, my darling.

I probably shouldn't tell you this. I probably shouldn't be writing to you at all. But before we go any further and our words are twisted and taken out of context, I want to make one thing clear: I don't blame you. Honestly. I don't think you knew what you were getting yourself into. I don't think either of us did. Maybe if we had, we'd have done things differently.

But life's not like that. You don't wake up one morning knowing that today's the day you'll meet the person who'll change your life forever. You don't go into these things with your eyes wide open. They just sort of creep up on you. And that's how it was with us.

'We don't decide when we fall in love. We don't choose it. It chooses us. We have no more control over it than we have control over the weather.'

Do you recognise those words? You ought to, because you wrote them. That's a direct quote from your second novel. I wonder if you knew then how true those words were, or if you were just trying them on for size, the way some writers do. I suppose it's what literary critics would call style. I've never been a big fan of style, myself. I prefer my writers to say what they mean and mean what they say. But as I think we've established, I'm not your average reader.

I remember the night we first met. I don't wear makeup as a rule, but I'd made a special effort that night – eyeliner, lipstick, a bit of blush. It's not every day a girl gets to meet the man she's admired from afar. I remember the crisp white shirt you wore and the slightly cocky, slightly nervous smile when you walked into the crowded bookshop. I remember thinking that your author photo didn't do you justice, that you were far better-looking in the flesh. Never did I imagine that this would be the start of something life-changing. I'd only come to hear you speak and get my book signed. Emotional attachments were the last thing on my mind.

Contrary to what you might think, I didn't plan any of what happened after. Grand passions really aren't my thing. I'm not one of those women who sit around dreaming of being swept off their feet. I've never needed a man to complete me. Not like my mother. She was never happy unless she had a room full of male admirers, yet never tired of boasting about her feminist credentials. But we both know what hypocrites feminists can be.

In fact, that was one of the first things we agreed on, that night at the bookshop when I stayed behind after the crowds had dwindled. Some dreary woman was complaining about the lack of positive female role models in your books, as if your first responsibility as a novelist isn't to tell a good story but is to make her feel validated.

I could see you needed rescuing, so I spoke up. 'That's the trouble with certain kinds of feminists. What they lack in imagination, they make up for in self-righteousness.'

You feigned shock. 'And what kind of feminist are you?'

'The recovering kind,' I replied, and you laughed, flashing those perfect white teeth of yours.

You asked my name and I handed you my business card.

'Evie,' you said. 'That's a pretty name.'

I watched you slide the card into your breast pocket. Then you took my book and signed it: 'To Evie, a kindred spirit. Best wishes, Tom Hunter'.

Imagine: me and Tom Hunter – kindred spirits. If only you'd known how thrilled I was. But I hid it well. I've always been good at hiding things.

And that was just the beginning. I'd been following you on Twitter for a year by then. But despite tagging you in several posts that praised your work, you hadn't followed me back. Clearly you had a change of heart that night. Did you check my profile before you went to sleep? Did you lie awake, counting down the hours until you made your next move? Because at 6.12 a.m. the next morning, there it was – a notification informing me that you were now following me on Twitter.

I tried not to read too much into it. But I couldn't help myself. 6.12 a.m. is an intimate time to be expressing an interest in someone. Most of us are barely awake at such an early hour. I pictured you lying in bed, wiping the sleep from your eyes and looking at your phone, already thinking of me. It's no wonder my mind was racing. A girl could be forgiven for thinking you had designs on her. And as this girl soon discovered, she wasn't wrong.

But back to today. I spotted you long before you saw me. You were climbing out of a black cab. You had the collar of your jacket turned up and a red scarf tied loosely around your neck. You looked good. A little tired around the eyes perhaps, but I suppose that's only to be expected. It can't have been easy for you, keeping up appearances all this time. No wonder the strain is starting to show.

I assume that was her with you. Emma Norton. The one I'm obliged to refer to as 'the other woman'. I must say she looks nothing like her profile pic. She's obviously not a natural blonde – not like me. Dad says my hair is the colour of honey. The sweetness starts at the top of my head and runs through me like letters through a stick of rock.

Was Emma the reason you blanked me today? I won't pretend I wasn't hurt by that. My lawyer said I shouldn't talk to you. But we're both adults – we can still be civil to one another. And just because someone studied law, it doesn't mean they're always right. I've had injury lawyers cold calling me about car accidents that never happened. That's how much faith I have in the legal profession. Remember when Morrissey wrote that song describing lawyers as liars? As a fellow fan, I'm sure you'll agree that he had a point.

Listening to all the legal arguments today, I was struck by a number of things. One: what a mess we've made for ourselves! Two: what clever bastards those lawyers are. They twist everything, don't they? And three: wouldn't it be easier if we just sorted this out between ourselves?

I know we tried before, that night I waited for you outside your flat. Maybe if you'd invited me in instead of freaking out and calling the police, we could have resolved our differences there and then. We still could. It's not too late. Why make this any harder than it needs to be? I'm willing to forgive and forget if you are.

Promise me you'll think about it. Sleep on it and email me in the morning. And if I don't hear from you, at least I'll know where I stand. And I'll see you tomorrow in court.

Yours

Evie

2

EIGHT MONTHS EARLIER

'I'm a writer,' Tom said. 'I write novels.'

This was usually the point at which people asked 'Anything I'd have read?' For most of the authors Tom knew, the honest answer would be 'Probably not'. But he was one of the lucky ones. His first novel had been an international bestseller. Rights were sold in forty countries. There was even a film adaptation starring Ryan Gosling, which ensured that while Tom Hunter wasn't exactly a household name, he did enjoy a certain amount of brand recognition. He also had a level of financial security rare among his peers, and a flat overlooking the river in an area of Vauxhall largely populated by hedge-fund managers.

Success had come easily to Tom. Too easily, his detractors might have said – and there were plenty of those. The critics hadn't been kind about his second novel, and it had struggled to repeat the success of his first. Truth be told, he was still struggling – though this was something he was barely willing to admit to himself, let alone anyone else.

None of which was of the slightest interest to the woman looking at him from behind the reinforced glass partition. 'And you're here to give a statement?' she said. 'Perhaps you could start by telling me what happened?'

Tom had thought about this a lot on his way to the police station. Where to begin? What to say? He'd given a brief account to the two officers who visited his flat three days ago. But this was more serious. This woman was a detective. What he said now would determine what further action, if any, was taken. He'd never given a police statement before. He didn't know what was expected.

He loosened his shirt collar and leaned forwards in his plastic chair. 'I went through this with the police on Tuesday.'

'I know. But if you wouldn't mind going over it again, just so I'm clear.'

Was this a test, Tom wondered – a way of checking whether he had his story straight?

'I'm being harassed,' he said.

The detective nodded. 'I'm aware of the nature of your complaint. The person you say is harassing you – is this someone you know?'

'Not really.'

'I'm sorry, I don't understand.'

'It's someone I met online,' Tom explained. 'A woman, on Twitter.'

The detective gave him a look which suggested that social media wasn't her favourite topic of conversation. Tom wondered how much police time was wasted investigating complaints made about comments posted on Facebook or shared on Twitter. Quite a few, he imagined. He was aware, also, that Detective Inspector Sue Grant worked for the hate-crime unit, and was probably used to dealing with cases far more serious than this. Online harassment was one thing. But it was nothing compared to a man who'd been queer-bashed or a woman whose husband was using her as a punch bag.

'That's where it began,' he said, fidgeting in his chair. 'But pretty soon it started spilling over into other areas of my life – emails, blogs, comments posted on Amazon and various online forums.'

'And you've never actually met this person?'

'No. Yes. Kind of.'

The detective gave him a quizzical look. 'Well, which is it?'

'We met once, I think. At a book signing.' Tom smiled modestly. 'I do a lot of book signings.'

'And do you recall meeting her at this book signing?'

'Vaguely. I meet so many people. And it was quite some time ago.'

'How long ago exactly?'

Tom thought for a moment. 'About a year.'

The detective looked surprised. 'This has been going on for a whole year?'

'More or less.'

'Why didn't you report it earlier?'

Of course, he'd known that she would ask him this. He'd been going over it in his head since he made the initial phone call to the police, trying to think of how best to explain himself. 'I thought I could handle it. I thought she'd lose interest. And to be perfectly honest, I was rather embarrassed.'

'Embarrassed? Why?'

He shrugged. 'A man being bullied by a woman – it's a bit pathetic, isn't it?'

The detective looked at him. 'Men can be victims, too. Domestic abuse, harassment – it can happen to anyone.'

'That's good to hear,' Tom said, then quickly corrected himself. 'I mean, it's good that you take this stuff seriously, Detective.'

'We take all crime seriously.'

Tom smiled and nodded. 'Yes, of course.'

The detective tapped at the keyboard on the desk between them, rolled her eyes and rose from her seat. 'I'm afraid we're having a few problems with our computer system. So, if you'd like to follow me, we can go and make a start on your statement.'

She instructed the officer at the reception desk to buzz Tom through, and escorted him into the interior of the police station, opening each successive door with a swipe of her security pass. As they waited for the lift, Tom's eyes were drawn to a poster on the wall. A woman's bruised and battered face stared back at him. 'Domestic violence is a crime', the text stated. 'Report it!' Not for the first time, he wondered if he was doing the right thing.

Then he recalled Emma's stern words on Tuesday evening: 'She won't stop, Tom. She's made that perfectly clear. And for all we know she could be dangerous. She's already affecting your health. You have to do something now, before it gets any worse.'

It was Emma who urged him to call the police and waited with him until they arrived. She'd offered to accompany him tonight, too, but Tom had insisted that it really wasn't necessary. There was no way of knowing how long this would take. Some things he was better left doing alone.

The lift groaned as the doors closed, prompting a sharp spike of anxiety. Tom wasn't good with lifts at the best of times – a hangover from the days when he first moved to London and lived on the ninth floor of a tower block in Kennington, where he once found himself trapped in the lift for over an hour. At least this lift didn't smell of urine, although there was the familiar whiff of fast food. He wondered about the eating habits of the woman standing next to him. She caught his eye and he quickly averted his gaze.

The lift stopped on the third floor, where she led him along a windowless corridor with harsh strip lighting and into a large open-plan room with carpet the colour of weak tea and rows of desks and computer terminals, most of them unoccupied. As they entered the room, the detective exchanged greetings with a couple of uniformed officers and a tall, stern-looking man in plain clothes with his shirt sleeves rolled up – her sergeant, she explained in a hushed voice.

She led Tom over to an empty desk, pulled up an extra chair for him to sit on and took out her pocketbook. 'Perhaps you could start by telling me what you know about this woman...' she checked her notes '...Evie?'

Tom nodded. 'Eve Stokes. She calls herself Evie.'

'When did you first become aware of her?'

'She's someone who started following me on Twitter.'

'And you said this was about a year ago?'

Tom shrugged. 'More or less. It's hard to be exact. I have a lot of Twitter followers.'

'I see. What else?'

'She started by tweeting me, saying she was a big fan of my work. She has a blog where she writes about books. She's clearly educated and often quite insightful. But there's a lot of anger and frustration there. Some of her blogs are quite extreme.'

'Extreme in what way?'

'There's a lot of upper-case invective.'

The detective looked at him blankly.

'She uses capital letters a lot, for emphasis. And she can be quite vicious. She writes like a disaffected teenager who's read a few books on literary criticism, but she's in her thirties. She clearly hasn't done as well in life as she thinks she ought to have, which is probably why she spends so much time on Twitter, sniping at newspaper columnists and other writers. She lives in East Dulwich with her father. He's not very well, or so she says.'

The detective raised an eyebrow. 'For someone you've barely met, you seem to know rather a lot about her.'

Tom smiled grimly. 'Well, you know what they say – know your enemy.'

'I thought you said she was a fan.'

'She was, yes. But fandom is a funny thing. It's never really about you – it's really about them. Fan is short for fanatic, you know.'

The detective gave him a look that said she wasn't born yesterday.

'It really is a form of fanaticism,' Tom continued. 'Almost a disorder in some cases. Certainly so in hers. That's the thing with social media. All sorts of people have direct access to you. And when you're in the public eye...' He paused and gave a modest smile. 'When you're known, even in a small way, you're bound to attract a few oddballs. Twitter can be a real vipers' nest at times. But it's good for book sales, so...'

'And you run your Twitter account yourself?' the detective interjected.

'I do.'

'You don't have someone who could do it for you?'

'I can't afford staff.'

'But presumably your publisher can?'

Tom coughed. 'I'm between publishers at the moment.'

'A friend, then?'

'There's nobody I'd really trust to do it properly. It's a lot to ask of someone.'

'But it would give you a break. Sometimes these things die down when the person realises they're not getting through.'

Tom shrugged. 'If only. If you ask me, she needs sectioning.'

'A person can only be detained under The Mental Health Act if they're deemed to pose a threat to themselves or others.' The detective consulted her notes. 'You say you met Ms Stokes at your book signing. Is that the only time you've seen her in person?'

Tom thought for a moment. 'There was one other occasion – at the farmers' market at Oval. At the time I put it down to coincidence. Now I'm not so sure.'

'But you recognised her?'

'It was more a case of her recognising me. She looked over and waved.'

'And did you speak?'

'I acknowledged her and moved swiftly on. I didn't wish to be drawn into a conversation.'

'Why was that?'

'I don't know her. My gut instinct told me that something wasn't quite right.'

'I see. And has Ms Stokes ever made direct threats against you?'

'It depends what you mean by threats.'

'Has she ever threatened to cause you physical harm?'

'Not directly, no. But she's hinted at it. After she turned on me, she made veiled comments on Twitter about getting back at me in some way. "Don't get mad, get even" – that sort of thing. I don't know what she's capable of. She could be a knife-wielding maniac for all I know.' Tom smiled weakly. 'What I do know is that she's obsessive and relentless, and clearly very angry with me.'

'And why do you think that is?'

'Honestly? I think she developed a crush on me, and she can never have me.'

'Because you're attached?'

'Because I'm gay.' Tom searched the detective's face for some reaction, but her expression remained impassive.

'I see. And was she aware of this?'

'I didn't lead her on, if that's what you mean.'

'I'm not saying you did. I'm just after the facts.'

Tom sighed. 'I don't make a secret of it. I'm not one of those professional gay types. I don't shout it from the rooftops. But it's not something I'm ashamed of. It's part of who I am. It's not all that I am.'

'But if she knows you're gay, surely she—'

'We're talking about someone who isn't quite right in the head,' Tom said, more irritably than he'd intended. 'In her mind, she probably thought it was some minor obstacle to overcome. There are women like that, you know. They see gay men as a challenge.'

The detective smiled tightly. 'You say she turned on you. What did she do exactly?'

'Her emails and tweets became more aggressive. She started using homophobic language.' Tom paused. 'That makes this a hate crime, doesn't it?'

'Possibly. First we need to establish that a crime has been committed. Do you have copies of these emails and tweets?'

'Some of them, yes. I deleted a lot of the emails. And some went into my spam folder.'

'Can I ask why you deleted the emails?'

'Just out of instinct, I suppose. They disgusted me, so I deleted them.'

'Well the more you can find – the stronger the weight of evidence – the better the chances of the CPS pursuing the case.'

'Do you think it's likely that they will?'

'It really all depends on the weight of evidence. I believe my colleagues asked you to bring in as much supporting evidence as you could find?'

'They did,' Tom said. 'And I have.' He reached into his leather messenger bag and took out a manila folder bulging with sheets of A4 paper.

The detective looked slightly taken aback. She logged onto the computer in front of her and opened up a template headed 'Witness Statement'.

'Right,' she smiled professionally. 'Why don't we make a start?'

✖

For the next two hours, Tom described the events that had brought him here. As he talked, the detective typed, then invited him to read back what she'd written. Progress was painfully slow. Tom lost count of the number of times he had to correct her spelling, or rephrase something to make the meaning clearer. At regular intervals he was asked to describe the contents of one of the many printed emails and screenshots of tweets he'd bought along as evidence. Each was given a reference number and slipped into an exhibit bag, which he was then asked to sign.

The statement described how the woman Tom knew as Evie Stokes first started following him on Twitter.

'At first, her tweets were either flattering or innocuous. "I loved your last book" or "What do you think about this author?" I didn't reply, though I may have "liked" the odd tweet here and there. This continued for several months.'

'And you didn't think to block her?' the detective asked.

'I didn't see any reason to. There was nothing to indicate that she wished me any harm. She was just another overeager fan on Twitter.'

Then came the night they supposedly met at a book signing at Waterstones in Piccadilly. Tom couldn't recall meeting anyone called Evie that evening – 'I'm sure I'd have remembered' – but he'd signed a lot of books for a lot of people, and as he explained to the detective, it was some time ago. He vaguely remembered a woman tweeting him later that night to thank him for signing her book and congratulate him on a successful event. Out of courtesy he may have followed her back. He realised later that this woman must have been Evie Stokes.

From this point on, the volume of tweets increased considerably. Sometimes he'd receive four or five in the space of an hour or so. Some days there was as many as twenty or thirty. Most were fairly innocuous in tone, though he did start to find the woman's persistence a little irritating. He replied once or twice, but as the quantity grew, he stopped responding – so as not to encourage her any further. Gradually the tone of the tweets changed. She became more aggressive, demanding to know why he was ignoring her. It was at this point that she started using words like 'prick', 'gaylord' and 'pansy'. It was then that he blocked her from his Twitter account.

'Why did she suddenly become aggressive?' the detective asked. 'Was there a particular incident that may have prompted it?'

Tom shrugged. 'She got it into her head that I'd agreed to read her book.'

The detective looked surprised. 'So she's also an author?'

'God, no!' Tom shook his head. 'That's precisely the point. She isn't published but she seemed to think I could help. People often assume that. They think that because you're published you hold some secret key to the kingdom, and if you'd only agree to help, they'd be bestselling authors in no time.'

'And did you read it?'

'I've had neither the time nor the inclination.'

'I see.'

'I'm not sure you do,' Tom said. 'This sort of thing happens a lot. People ask you to read their stuff, and you try to avoid causing offence by saying something noncommittal. If they then send it to you and you don't respond, they assume you weren't keen and just leave it at that.'

'But not her.'

'No. She was just getting started.'

He described to the detective how Evie started bombarding him with emails, demanding to know what he thought of her book. He blocked her email address, but each time he did she'd open another account with another provider. Then, when he checked his Twitter account, he discovered that she'd found a way of contacting him despite him having blocked her.

'Her trick was to tag me into tweets, along with half a dozen people I regularly interact with. If any of them replied to her unwittingly, her tweet would then appear in my feed. She even boasted about it, saying it was a triumph for free speech.'

'And you have proof of this?'

Tom handed over a printout of her tweet. 'If that's not a clear statement of intent, I don't know what is.'

The detective examined it for a moment.

'I know these may seem like small incidents,' Tom said. 'But it's the continuous, repetitive nature of it that gets to you. There's no respite. It's every day.'

'I understand the nature of harassment,' the detective replied. 'And what was the content of her tweets at this point?'

'Some were just playground insults. Gaylord. Pansy. Sissy. But some were calculated to cause as much upset as possible. "You're the AIDS generation! You're lucky to be alive!"' Tom's voice faltered. 'I had friends who died of AIDS. I don't need reminding of the fact.'

The detective looked sympathetic. 'I can see why you'd find that upsetting.'

Tom continued. On the advice of a friend, he tweeted Evie Stokes asking her to refrain from tagging him. He showed a screenshot of this tweet to the detective and she entered it into evidence. He also informed his Twitter followers of what was happening and asked them to either block her, not respond or not include him in their responses. Again, he hoped that things would finally die down.

Instead, they escalated. Stokes posted comments under reviews on Amazon, claiming co-authorship of the book he was currently working on. She made a series of amendments to his Wikipedia page, deleting links to his official website and inserting hyperlinks to her blog, where she repeated her claims and accused him of plagiarism.

'All completely untrue, of course,' Tom said. 'But potentially very harmful to my career.'

'Why?' the detective asked. 'If there's no truth in her allegations, how could they harm you?'

'People believe what they read. And there are plenty of lazy journalists out there who rely on Wikipedia or Twitter for background information. All it takes is for someone to repeat what's written there, and suddenly the claim has credibility. Soon it's part of the official narrative around me and my career. Which is exactly what she wants, of course – for our names to be linked in people's minds. She's a succubus, feeding off my reputation.'

The detective's expression suggested that she didn't know what a succubus was, but Tom decided to let it pass. Instead he described how the volume of emails continued to rise, sent by Stokes from a variety of different email addresses, either repeating the same allegations or apologising for offending him and suggesting that they meet to 'talk it over'. No sooner had he blocked one email than another would appear.

'And you didn't think of changing your email address?' the detective asked.

'I thought of it,' Tom replied. 'But why should I? I've had the same email for years. I'm self-employed. I rely on it for work.'

'I see.' The detective scribbled something in her notebook. 'What about phone calls? Does she have your number?'

'Not as far as I know. I mean, she's never called me.'

'And there've been no silent calls, nothing of that nature?'

'None I can think of.'

'You might want to consider changing your number anyway, just in case. So, what happened next?'

Tom continued with his story, describing how the daily bombardment of tweets and emails began to grind him down. His work suffered. He found it hard to focus. For the first time in his life, he developed writer's block. He began drinking heavily – a bottle of wine a night, sometimes more. He started smoking again – a habit he'd picked up in his teens and quit when he turned thirty. He was unable to sleep, lying awake all night or drifting off for a few hours before being jolted back to consciousness. Each morning, he approached his desk with trepidation. He dreaded checking his emails or logging on to Twitter. Finally, on the advice of a friend he went to see his doctor, who told him he was suffering from acute anxiety and prescribed a course of antidepressants.

Tom's voice cracked. He lowered his eyes and took a deep, steadying breath. 'Sorry. I didn't realise it would be quite so hard, going over it all again. I've never taken antidepressants in my life. But it's been incredibly stressful. There've been days when I thought I was losing my mind.'

The detective's face softened. 'I understand. And we don't need to talk about that now. You'll have an opportunity to talk about the impact of the crime at a later date. This witness statement is simply about gathering the facts.' She glanced up at the clock on the wall. 'But I'm aware that you're tired and it's getting rather late. Would you prefer to stop now and finish this another time?'

'No. I'd sooner get it over and done with.' Tom cleared his throat and wiped his eyes with the back of his hand.

'There is help available,' the detective said, taking a box of tissues from the desk drawer. 'Have you spoken to victim support?'

Tom took a tissue and blew his nose. He smiled weakly. 'I've never really thought of myself as a victim. It's not something I'm entirely comfortable with.'

'You're doing really well. This shouldn't take much longer.'

In fact, it was more than an hour before the statement was complete. The detective printed off a copy for him to sign and date, and as they waited for the lift, she handed him a card with her direct line and other contact details.

'What happens now?' he asked. 'Will she be arrested?'

The policewoman's expression was inscrutable. 'From what you've told me, it appears that a crime may have been committed. But we'll have to see what Ms Stokes has to say for herself. And then it's up to the Crown Prosecution Service.'

Tom knew the odds weren't good. He'd read somewhere that only sixteen percent of harassment cases reported to the police resulted in prosecution. For stalking, it was even fewer – a measly one percent.

The detective must have read his mind. 'We will look in to your complaint,' she said firmly. 'That's really all I can say at this point. But I can assure you that it will be investigated thoroughly.'

The lift arrived and they stepped inside.

'So you'll be putting her under some sort of surveillance?' Tom asked as the doors closed.

The policewoman smiled tightly. 'I'm afraid it's not as simple as that.'

'But someone will monitor her activity online?'

'We'll certainly take a look at her Twitter feed. That's all I can say at this point.'

'I see,' Tom said, although he didn't really see at all. Surely it was up to the police to gather evidence now, or what was the point in him having spent the best part of three hours stuck in this grim excuse for a building? 'One last thing. When she's arrested, I assume you'll seize her computer?'

'Again, that really depends on the CPS.'

'But what if someone was accused of distributing child pornography?'

As the lift shuddered to a halt, the detective met his gaze. 'That would be a very different case.'

The doors opened and he followed her out into the corridor.

'What should I do in the meantime?'

'If she contacts you again, report it to the police, quoting the crime reference number you were given on Tuesday. If you think of anything else that might be useful, let me know and we can make an additional statement. All my details are on the card I gave you. And please, if she emails you, don't delete her emails. Forward them to me and we can add them to your file.'

She swiped her security pass to open the door, and shook Tom's hand.

As he turned to go, a thought occurred. 'What if she turns up at my flat?'

A flicker of alarm crossed the detective's face. 'Does she know where you live?'

'I don't think so. But I can't say for sure. She might.'

'If she approaches you in person, call 999 immediately.'

3

What was that stunt you pulled in court today? A screen? Seriously? You requested a screen between us while you gave evidence. What am I – some sort of wild animal you need protecting from? What did you expect me to do, Tom? Leap across the room and go for your throat? A little woman like me and a big man like you? Don't make me laugh.

When they first told me, I thought they were joking. I was in one of the consulting rooms with my lawyer when a court official came to break the news.

'But why does he need a screen?' I demanded.

My lawyer shrugged and replied, 'It's within his rights.'

Your rights? What about my rights? I'm the one on trial here. Surely I should have the right to see my accuser?

Apparently, you'd made a request to the Crown Prosecution Service, insisting that you found me intimidating and didn't want to 'feed' my 'fixation' by giving me the satisfaction of looking at you.

Really, Tom, you don't half flatter yourself. And we both know that not a word of this is true. If you ask me, it was more a case of you not wanting to look me in the face when you lied. It's harder to lie convincingly when the person you're lying about is standing right in front of you. That's the real reason you asked for that screen, isn't it Tom? Not so that I couldn't see you. So that *you* couldn't see *me*.

Earlier in the day we'd heard from your policewoman friend – the one who came to arrest me the night this whole nightmare began. Do you have any idea how distressing that was? The police turning up at my door, barging into my bedroom, accusing me of all sorts? You know my dad hasn't been very well lately. He's the reason I moved back home.

How do you think he felt, seeing his only daughter led away by the police like a common criminal? That's a cruel trick to play on a man with a heart condition.

I was charged under the Malicious Communications Act. Me! A woman who doesn't have a malicious bone in her body. Who has only ever wanted what's best for you. Who stood by you when the critics trashed your last book. How many times did I leap to your defence, Tom? How many hours did I spend reassuring you that the critics were wrong, that they weren't fit to pass judgement on a book so original and so brilliantly written, it was beyond their comprehension? 'Ignore them,' I said. Then, when you insisted that reviews that bad were impossible to ignore, I did everything within my power to soften the blow. I've lost count of how many reader reviews I posted on Amazon, how many critics I took to task in the comments sections, how many Wikipedia pages I corrected. I was your biggest supporter. And then you send the police round to accuse me, of all people, of malice?

Anyway, there she was again this morning, my arresting officer, standing in the witness box and looking very pleased with herself, as if she'd apprehended some major offender and not a woman whose only crime was to fall for the wrong man. From the way she described you, I could tell that you'd obviously worked your charms on her, too. That's a real gift you have there, Tom. Pulling the wool over people's eyes. Getting them to do your dirty work. Playing the victim when really you're the one pulling all the strings. How clever you are, my darling. And how deceitful. Even the criminal justice system's finest minds are no match for you.

Not that I consider Detective Inspector Sue Grant an intellectual giant. If anything, she seems a bit thick. She has one of those faces that suggests lower intelligence – fleshy cheeks, a short nose, hooded eyes and a fat chin. I can easily picture her sitting at the back of a classroom, unable to complete her assignment, chewing on a ballpoint pen, oblivious to the blue ink staining her lips. And nothing she has said or done during this whole sorry affair leads me to believe that I've been remotely harsh or hasty in my judgement. On the contrary, each encounter has only served to reinforce my initial impression of her as someone who isn't quite up to the job.

You'll be pleased to hear that she stuck to her script – the one I'm sure you had no small part in writing – and was helped along by the prosecutor, who looked suitably stern with her severely arched eyebrows and dark hair in a French pleat. It hasn't escaped my attention that the people lining up to help you destroy my reputation are mostly women. So much for the sisterhood, eh? But I did find myself wondering how much say you had in all of this, and whether there was a reason for it, other than to provoke me. Is a female prosecutor more likely to curry favour with a woman judge? It certainly seemed that way today.

When they first told me there'd be a district judge presiding, I took it as a good sign. According to the government website, judges are only called upon to try cases in magistrates' court when a case is deemed too complex or sensitive for mere magistrates to handle. What could be more fitting in our case? I'm complex and you're far too sensitive. So I had high expectations of Her Ladyship's mental faculties. Here, surely, was someone of great learning who would cut through the crap and get right to the heart of the matter.

From where I was standing, there were plenty of holes in DI Grant's evidence. And she came unstuck a few times under cross-examination, getting her dates and times confused and failing to explain why, if I posed such a threat to you, it had taken her so long to secure an arrest warrant.

It's a shame you weren't there to see it – the great detective, fumbling with her notebook, fluffing her lines. I know the system forbids you from hearing another witness's testimony until after you've given evidence, but this whole trial is such a farce anyway, I doubt it would have made any difference. To me, it was perfectly clear that Ms Grant fell a long way short of making a convincing case. But for some strange reason, the judge seemed willing to take her at her word. It's at times like these that one's faith in the system is put to the test – and on this occasion it failed miserably.

They actually called in a Twitter expert next. Can you believe it?

The CPS have people to explain how social media works. I'm assuming the judge isn't a big fan of Twitter, because she looked a bit confused and needed some things explained to her several times. The poor man did his best, but I could tell from her responses that she wasn't entirely sure where all this was going.

Finally, after a lot of waffle about hashtags and tagging and Twitter interactions, the prosecutor got to the point. And the point she was trying to make is that my interactions with you on Twitter were tantamount to harassment. Honestly, it was all I could do to stop myself from laughing out loud. I'm sure the thousands of women who've experienced real harassment will be delighted to hear that their experience has been equated to someone sending a few tweets!

By the time this ridiculous charade was over, it was time for lunch. Her Ladyship glared at me over her spectacles, telling me in no uncertain terms that I would be on bail during the lunch break and was legally obliged to arrive back at the courtroom no later than five to two. What did she expect me to do? Do a runner? And miss the rest of the day's entertainment? As if!

There aren't a great many options for a girl looking for a nice spot of lunch within easy walking distance of Camberwell Green Magistrate's Court. To be honest, I wasn't that hungry anyway, but my dad said I ought to eat something and escorted me to a local sandwich bar. In case you've forgotten, that's my dad who has a weak heart and is now forced to sit through this sham of a trial. As we sat eating our sandwiches, he assured me that he didn't believe a word of what people were saying about me. I was so touched, I almost broke down and cried. He looks so frail these days, and yet here he was, putting on a brave face for my benefit. Remember what I said yesterday, about not blaming you for any of what's happened? I'd like to revise that statement. I do blame you for the impact it's having on my dad. If anything should happen to him as a result of this, I'll hold you personally responsible.

After lunch it was back to court for the star performance – the one I was permitted to hear but not see. My objections to your request for a screen fell on deaf ears, and I was forced to hold my tongue as you took your place in the witness box. As it turned out, the screen wasn't a fixed screen, but a curtain. Part of me wanted to leap across the court, pull back the curtain and expose you for the fraud you are, like Dorothy in *The Wizard of Oz*. But that would have only played into your hands. I could still feel your presence, though – the way the curtain moved in response to your body, the faint smell of your cologne. (Tom Ford Noir, if I'm not mistaken. How like you to wear your namesake next to your skin. Could you be any more narcissistic?)

And then of course there was your voice. I have to ask: did you spend hours perfecting that voice you used as you gave evidence today? Because it's not one I've ever heard you use before. That tremulous way you spoke, the slight catch in your throat as you told the court of your ordeal; it was so totally out of character. Whatever happened to the experienced public speaker, the great orator who can hold a room with his sharp wit and piercing insights? Today you sounded like someone who's never been on stage before, who finds the whole thing nerve-wracking. At first I thought you must be ill or coming down with something. And then it struck me. This was your 'good victim' voice – another of your ploys to win sympathy. Honestly, Tom. These cheap tactics of yours. Anyone would think you had something to hide.

I could see Emma in the public gallery, her features carefully arranged into a look of deep concern, like an overprotective mother watching her precious child tread the boards for the first time in the school play. That's quite a double act you have there, though of course it was clear to me that parading her in court like that was a provocation. Were you hoping that her presence would unsettle me somehow? Well, I hate to disappoint you, but I don't fall for your tricks that easily. I watched her watching you, hanging on your every word. And on the rare occasion that our eyes met, I beamed at her as if she were an old friend and not someone I would gladly slap across the face if she came within three feet of me. I figured since we're all so busy acting...

The prosecutor began by asking you how it all began and referring you to sections of your witness statement. What a ridiculous situation.

Surely if you were telling the truth, you wouldn't need prompting? But prompt you she did.

'And when did you first become aware of the defendant?' she asked, as if I was the symptom of some mysterious illness and not a person. That's the worst part about the whole court process, I think. It's so dehumanising.

Not that you seemed to care. Secure behind your safety curtain, you told the court how I 'stalked' you on Twitter and 'bombarded' you with 'harassing' emails.

'And did you at any point encourage the defendant to maintain contact with you?' the prosecutor asked.

'No,' you replied, shakily. 'I asked her to stop, but she kept on. I blocked her on Twitter, but that only made matters worse. She started tagging my followers, so if anyone replied, her tweets would appear in my feed. I blocked her email address, but she kept creating new accounts.'

Lies, all lies, right down to that phoney victim voice of yours. What you didn't say, and ought to have said, is that you revelled in the attention. You led me to believe that what we had together was something special and worth holding on to. 'A meeting of minds,' you called it. 'Kindred spirits,' you said. I know that we were never really lovers, not in the traditional sense. And that never bothered me in the slightest. Physical love is so overrated anyhow. Passion soon burns itself out. What we had was so much more than that. Or what I thought we had. But you encouraged me to think it, Tom, whatever you told the nice lady judge today. You encouraged me, right from the start.

It was only when you were cross-examined that I heard a voice I recognised as yours.

My defence lawyer is an Asian chap, painfully polite, with a strong sense of social justice and a firm belief in freedom of speech – both qualities I once associated with you, ironically enough. He began by stressing that he was only here to do his job, and that nothing he was about to say was in any way personal. He then asked if it was fair to say that you're an oversensitive man.

You didn't like that suggestion at all. 'Not especially,' you replied, sharply.

'So you're seriously telling me that you find these words offensive?' He then read out a list of words I'm alleged to have used to describe you.

I could feel you bristle, even with that heavy curtain between us. 'Yes,' you said. 'I find them offensive.'

'Really?' My lawyer's tone was incredulous. 'You find the word "pansy" offensive?'

'I do,' you snapped. 'Just as I'm sure you find the word "paki" offensive.'

What I'd have given to have seen your face then! You realised, I'm sure, that he'd tripped you up good and proper, that he was tearing off that mask of yours, exposing you for who you really are. And he was just getting started.

'You've told the court that you wanted no contact with my client,' he continued. 'And yet you chose to follow her on Twitter. Why was that?'

'I follow lots of people,' you replied.

'Not nearly as many as follow you. I took a look at your Twitter account this morning. You're currently following a few hundred people, compared to the tens of thousands who follow you.'

Again, I could feel your anger rise. 'So?'

'So it seems to me that you're quite choosy about who you follow on social media. And yet you chose to follow my client. Despite your claims that she was harassing you.'

'The harassment came later,' you snapped. 'If I'd known then what I know now, I'd have blocked her immediately.'

'Yet at the time you were perfectly happy to exchange pleasantries on Twitter and even reply to her emails.'

'I'm not sure what point you're making.'

'My point is that you actively encouraged contact with my client, before turning around and accusing her of harassment. You're an intelligent man. Surely you can see how confusing this must have been?'

You didn't have an answer for that. How could you, when we both know he had you bang to rights?

'I'd like to turn to the issue of my client's book,' my lawyer said. 'We're aware, of course, that you yourself are a published novelist. You've told the court that you did everything you could to discourage my client from contacting you. And yet you offered her your professional guidance and agreed to read her manuscript. Why was that?'

'I didn't agree to read it. She sent me an email with two attachments. One was a Word file that I presumed to be the manuscript and the other was a video of her talking about the book.'

'Mr Hunter, we have an email from you to Ms Stokes in which you expressly agree to read her work. How do you explain that?'

'I was just being polite.'

'So you haven't actually read the book in question?'

'I didn't even download it.'

My lawyer smiled. 'But that simply isn't true, Mr Hunter. As the files were large, my client emailed them to you via a file-transfer service. Records show that the files were downloaded.'

You hesitated before replying. 'Then they must have downloaded automatically when I opened the email. Yes, I remember now. They were saved to my downloads folder. I deleted them shortly afterwards.'

How did it feel, Tom, knowing that you'd been rumbled? Looking across the courtroom, I could see from Emma's face that she wasn't too impressed with your performance. There was definitely a flicker of doubt there. And that smug smile the prosecutor wore was beginning to fade, too. She knew, I'm sure, that your story was starting to unravel, that you weren't the reliable witness she'd been led to expect.

But the best was yet to come.

'I'd like to refer you now to the emails dated February twenty-third this year,' my lawyer said. 'The ones sent after my client was first taken in for questioning. The ones you say you found alarming and distressing.'

'I did find them alarming and distressing,' you replied. 'She was threatening me with violence.'

Lies, Tom! All lies! I never wrote those words and we both know it!

'You're aware, of course, that my client categorically denies sending you those emails. Just as she categorically denies making similar threats to you the night she was arrested outside your flat.'

'I'm aware of that, yes.'

'You're aware, also, that these dozen or so emails came from a Gmail account with no proven link to my client.'

'She used various email accounts to harass me. As soon as I blocked one, she'd open another.'

'But you didn't block this one, did you? You received numerous emails from the same account; emails you say you found distressing and alarming, and yet you didn't block the address. Why was that?'

You didn't answer.

'Isn't it the case, Mr Hunter, that we have no real way of knowing where those emails came from or who sent them? Gmail accounts are notoriously hard to trace. For all we know, you could have sent those emails to yourself.'

You laughed then, a hollow sound that echoed around the court-room. 'Don't be so ridiculous! Why would I do that?'

'To further incriminate my client.'

At this point your prosecutor friend interjected, reminding us that you weren't the one on trial. More's the pity.

'I'd like to return to the question of hate speech,' my lawyer continued. 'We've established that there are certain words you consider offensive. And yet you've used some pretty offensive terms to describe my client. You've called her a troll. You've told the court that she's mentally ill.'

'She is a troll,' you replied. 'And I believe she is mentally ill.'

I could really hear the arrogance in your voice now. You who must not be challenged, who refuses to consider the possibility that he might sometimes be wrong. How furious you must have felt.

'And are you qualified to make that assessment?' my lawyer asked. 'You're not a mental-health professional.'

'I don't consider her behaviour to be that of a normal person,' you said, haughtily. 'She's obsessive and relentless. And the fact that she refused a psychiatric evaluation suggests to me that, on some level, she knows she's mentally ill.'

'And yet you encouraged your thousands of followers on Twitter to attack a woman who, by your own estimation, is somewhat fragile. You told her to drop dead. Not very noble of you, was it?'

He certainly had you there. Hoist by your own petard, as they say. I couldn't wait to hear you try to wiggle your way out of that one. And wiggle you did, Tom – like a worm on a hook.

'I didn't encourage anyone to attack her,' you said. 'I simply asked them not to include me in their replies to her. Telling someone to drop dead is just a figure of speech. She'd been harassing me for months. I was at my wit's end.'

'You called her a troll and made jokes about her mental health on a public forum where you are followed by tens of thousands of people. Surely you don't seriously expect us to believe that you didn't wish her any harm?'

'All I wanted was for her to stop contacting me,' you replied. 'That's all I ever wanted.'

I must have laughed out loud at that point – an actual 'LOL' – because the judge called for order.

'But he's lying!' I said, and was immediately threatened with contempt of court.

I think I'm beginning to see how this whole thing works now. And more to the point, I now have the full measure of you, Tom. I know the lengths you'll go to and what's required of me if I'm to stand any chance of winning this case. And that's good to know. But I can't pretend I'm not disappointed.

If there's one thing I've learned in life, it's that people don't really change. Who you are in your twenties is pretty much who you'll be for the rest of your life. Your appearance will change – whatever the manufacturers of those age-defying face creams tell you – but your personality remains the same. A person's belief system, values and code of conduct remain pretty much fixed for their entire adult life. Politically, they might move to the right as they grow older and feel they have more to lose, but even then they're often quite embarrassed about it and will lie to pollsters before elections. Their world view remains essentially the same.

I didn't know you when you were twenty, or even thirty. We don't go back that far. Still, I find it hard to believe that you've really changed so much that I can barely recognise you. Which leads me to the unpleasant conclusion that I never really knew you at all, that the person I heard but wasn't allowed to see in court today is the person you've always been. I've been had, basically. And what really makes me angry is that I should have seen this coming. The writing, as they say, was on the wall. Because you're a professional liar, aren't you, Tom? You make up stories for a living. And today in court you told a load of stories about me.

But here's the thing. Everyone has their own story to tell. And tomorrow I'll have an opportunity to tell mine. It won't be as melodramatic as yours. I won't put on a strange voice, or hide behind a curtain or a screen. I'll stand before the court and speak plainly for all to see. I'll tell them everything.

All men have secrets, Tom, and I know yours. I know the truth about you. So be warned. Tomorrow I'll expose you for the liar you are. And heaven knows you'll be miserable then.

Yours

Evie

4

FOUR MONTHS EARLIER

Lucinda King was seated at her usual table in the dining room at the Groucho Club, fiddling with her phone. Her familiar black bob was tucked behind one ear, and she appeared to be frowning, despite the widely held belief that she was no stranger to Botox.

She didn't look up as Tom entered the room, which irked him more than he cared to admit. Through no fault of his own, he was at least fifteen minutes late. Cabs were a luxury he could no longer afford, so he'd been forced to take the Northern Line from Oval, experiencing the kind of delays that had earned it the nickname The Misery Line. Were Tom in Lucinda's place, he'd have been scanning the entrance by now, wondering where on earth he'd got to. There was a time, not so long ago, when she'd have displayed more concern than this. A lot had changed since then.

Tom had dressed for the occasion in a Zegna suit and Hugo Boss shirt, purchased with the advance from his first book and currently feeling rather damp around the back and armpits – another of the indignities of tube travel. His attire was possibly a little formal for a lunch meeting, but the suit gave him confidence – something he'd been rather lacking of late.

He coughed as he approached his agent's table and she leapt to her feet and greeted him with a disarming smile. 'Tom, darling! How have you been? Has that ghastly woman had her comeuppance yet?'

There wasn't a lot about Tom's life that Lucinda didn't know. She'd been his agent for the past seven years – and for the first four of those she'd been very attentive, parading him at book awards and publishing house parties, taking him out for long, boozy lunches and opening chilled bottles of champagne whenever he visited her office to sign contracts or just catch up.

But that was then. Apart from a chance meeting at last month's Costa Awards, he hadn't seen Lucinda in person for the best part of a year. She was rarely available to talk on the phone and sometimes took days to respond to his emails.

The reason, of course, was that Tom Hunter was no longer her golden boy. She had other, younger, more marketable clients these days – all those photogenic blondes fresh from their MA courses, each hailed as the most exciting new voice in fiction by the same critics who used to shower him with praise and were now rather less effusive – if they bothered to review him at all. He wondered if the exciting new blondes had all this to look forward to, or if it was a fate reserved for those, like him, who'd enjoyed such enormous success with his first novel that anything less than a film tie-in was now seen as failure.

'I'm fine,' he said, and planted a kiss on his agent's proffered cheek. 'And no, she hasn't had her comeuppance yet. But I refuse to let it get me down.'

'That's the spirit!' Lucinda exclaimed as they both took their seats.

Around them, the cream of London's creative industries radiated self-importance with their booming voices and company expense accounts. Tom spotted a few familiar faces and a knot of anxiety tightened in his chest. He used to love coming to the Groucho. That was before his last book bombed and his nemesis began her campaign of public humiliation. He wondered whether many of those exchanging nods of recognition with him were secretly enjoying his fall from grace.

'Now, tell me everything,' Lucinda said. 'How's life in Vauxhall? How's the new book coming along?'

'Shall we order first?' Tom asked, reaching for the menu. He hadn't eaten properly in days. His mouth watered as he considered the options – fillet steak, Dover sole; even the liver sounded appetising.

'Of course, darling,' Lucinda cooed. 'The lamb sounds good. Or are you veggie? I forget.'

Of course you do, Tom thought bitterly. He wondered when his agent last entertained one of the exciting new blondes. She probably knew everything there was to know about their dietary requirements – assuming they ate anything at all.

'The lamb sounds perfect,' he said, and pushed the menu away.

'Are we drinking?' Lucinda asked.

For a split second Tom took this as a reproach about his recent alcohol intake. Then, seeing her inspect the wine list, he relaxed. 'I'm game if you are.'

'It is Friday,' Lucinda said, adopting an uncharacteristically girlish voice, the kind less authoritative women often used to excuse their indulgences. 'I'm sure this calls for a bottle of something. And red wine does have its health benefits. All those lovely tannins!'

She gestured to the waiter, who took their orders and complimented them on having chosen so wisely.

'I think we'll be the judge of that,' Lucinda quipped when he was out of earshot. 'So tell me, darling – how's the new book?'

Ah yes, the new book. The one Tom had been working on for the best part of three years. The one he was writing out of contract, having been unceremoniously dropped by his publisher. The one he was still no closer to finishing. That new book.

There were a million excuses he could pluck out of the air. He was depressed. His back was playing up. He was suffering from writer's block. There were far too many other commitments and simply not enough hours in the day.

But unlike just about every other writer he knew, Tom had no excuses. He had the one thing they would all kill for – the luxury of time. He didn't need to hold down a job to support his writing. He didn't have to juggle childcare or other family responsibilities. He didn't even have a significant other who could complain of feeling neglected while he devoted himself to his novel. He lived – and usually slept – alone. He hadn't had a meaningful relationship in years and had no intention of settling down any time soon. He had all the time in the world – and a dozen chapters he wasn't really happy with. That worked out at four chapters a year, or one every three months. There were authors who churned out a whole book in less time. The fact that his chapters weren't much better did nothing to alleviate his feelings of self-loathing.

'The book is coming along,' he said, and was grateful for the interruption when the waiter arrived with the wine.

Lucinda held up her wine glass in one perfectly manicured hand. 'To you,' she said. 'And your wonderful new book. Now, when can I see some pages? Have you brought some with you?'

Deep down, Tom knew there was little point in delaying the inevitable. He should just come clean and admit that there was no wonderful new book – certainly not yet and probably not for the foreseeable future. But his pride got the better of him.

'It still needs a bit of work,' he said. 'Another edit, then it'll be in much better shape. I'd hate for you to see it before it's ready.'

His agent studied him over the rim of her wine glass. Lucinda was famously tough. She always got the best deals for her clients – and she usually got the best work out of them, too. She knew when to push, how to cajole, and what was required from all parties if a book was to succeed in an already saturated market. Publishers were intimidated by her, and authors were awed by the mere mention of her name. Of course, these were the very qualities that attracted Tom to her in the first place. But right now, they terrified him.

'So,' she said, fixing him with her forensic gaze. 'Tell me what's troubling you. It's this dreadful woman, isn't it? What's happened now?'

Tom grimaced. 'More emails. Only now she's threatening to get back at me if I go ahead and testify against her in court. I thought once they'd arrested her, she'd pipe down. If anything, she's getting worse.'

'I assume you've been back to the police.'

'I've given so many statements to them, that building feels like a second home.'

Lucinda shuddered. 'You poor thing. But this won't look good for her in court – breaching her bail and intimidating a witness. Have they set the trial date yet?'

'Not yet. I'm told it could be another six months.'

'Bloody ridiculous! And what are you supposed to do in the meantime?' Lucinda bared her teeth in what could pass for a smile. 'Apart from finishing your book, of course.'

✄

Before Lucinda took him under her wing, Tom Hunter was just another aspiring novelist with plenty of ambition but no real game plan. His career to that point had been unremarkable. He'd studied English and drama at university, and toyed with the idea of becoming a playwright. But the collaborative nature of the theatre put him off. He didn't want to entrust his words to the interpretations of actors and directors. He wanted total control.

Before turning to fiction he'd served an apprenticeship of sorts, writing feature articles for the weekend supplements. He travelled widely, stayed in some of the world's best hotels, and interviewed a lot of famous faces. He made a decent living and developed a taste for a certain kind of lifestyle – comfortable, expensive and usually charged to whoever he was commissioned to write for. Of course this was back in the days before digitalisation – before the notion of 'free content' cut great swathes through the industry, slashing budgets and expense accounts and reducing word rates to such an extent that, these days, the only people who could afford to go into journalism were those with wealthy parents.

Tom's parents weren't wealthy. His father was a builder and his mother had worked as a nurse before retiring a few years ago. His older brother, Mark, was a lot like his father – practical, good with his hands; a man who knew his place in the world and didn't need to look very far to find it. And Tom – well, Tom wasn't. His father's disappointment in him had been obvious from an early age; and his mother's love was conditional at best. He'd always felt like a stranger in the family, a dreamer whose dreams didn't match those of the couple who raised him, and whose achievements were viewed with a mixture of suspicion and what sometimes felt like resentment. He was the first in his family to go to university, the first to move more than twenty miles from the town where he grew up, the first to make it in a profession widely considered both middle class and not quite professional. Yet somehow this was never enough. 'You can always teach,' his mother said when he left university with plans to become a writer. 'People will always need teachers.'

Tom owed his parents a lot. He had his father's lean, muscular build, strong jaw and thick head of hair, coupled with his mother's even features and soulful brown eyes. It was a killer combination and one that caught the attention of both men and women. Tom wasn't so naïve as to think that his good looks hadn't played some part in his good fortune. But the greatest gift his parents had bestowed on him was far simpler. Without his upbringing he would never have developed the thick skin and sheer bloody-mindedness necessary to turn his dreams of a life less ordinary into reality.

Self-sufficiency and a sense of his own worth could only get a man so far. If there was one person who contributed to Tom's success more than any other, that person was Lucinda King. They first met when he proposed a profile of her to the books editor of a Sunday newspaper, insisting that readers would be just as interested in her as they were in the authors she represented. She'd graciously agreed to give him an hour of her precious time, and the interview took place at her office in Bloomsbury. It was only as the hour was drawing to a close that Tom casually mentioned the novel he'd been working on.

Lucinda didn't take the bait immediately. But when the profile appeared the following weekend and she was able to see for herself just how good a writer he was, he received an email thanking him for his kind words and inviting him to lunch. Soon afterwards, and on the basis of three sample chapters and a synopsis, he had a two-book deal with a major publisher and an agent most authors would kill for.

The first novel was an immediate success. *Boy Afraid* was inspired by a lyric from a Smiths song and told the story of a young man struggling to make his way in a world where masculinity was in crisis and male suicide claimed more lives than gun and knife crime combined. Critics compared its author to the likes of Nick Hornby and Jonathan Coe, the *Daily Mail* named the book 'novel of the year' and *The Times* said simply 'destined to be a modern classic' – a quote that found its way onto the mass-market paperback.

As it turned out, the predictions were entirely accurate. The novel topped the *Sunday Times* fiction chart and was selected for inclusion in the Richard and Judy Book Club. Foreign rights soon followed, and round upon round of author tours, across the UK and beyond. It was while Tom was on tour in America that he received news of the film option. By the time he delivered the second book, the first was on the big screen and he was walking down the red carpet in Leicester Square with the cast and director, scarcely able to believe his good fortune – or the fact that he was now on speaking terms with Ryan Gosling.

Those were the days! When the flush of success was still new and the rewards so great that even his parents stopped asking when he'd get a proper job. When the money from the film came through, he paid off their mortgage and traded in his small studio flat in Stockwell for a luxury apartment overlooking the Thames. He splashed out on designer clothes and vowed never to spoil his shiny new kitchen by doing anything so basic as cooking in it. Instead, he took a New Yorker's approach to life – dining out at every opportunity and not simply when it was time for dinner.

Tom had a lot to thank Lucinda for – and thank her he most certainly had. In the acknowledgments to his second novel, *Little Man*, he expressed his gratitude to his 'superstar agent' for 'steering me in the right direction' and 'believing in me before I believed in myself'. This last part wasn't true. Tom had always believed in himself. But it looked good on paper, and he hoped the compliment would make her feel beholden to him in some small way. As for the 'superstar' part – well, it didn't hurt to remind people about the calibre of your greatest supporters. Superstar agents didn't represent just anybody.

Unfortunately for Tom, few readers made it as far as the acknowledgements. The second book bombed. Fans flocked to Twitter to express their disappointment. The critics waded in with glee. No longer was he hailed as 'gifted' or 'a genius'. The book was denounced as 'lazy', 'dull', 'a crushing waste of time, trees and a once promising talent'.

One reviewer suggested that the first novel had been a fluke. Another advised him to stop writing immediately, before he destroyed what little credibility he had left. For the first time in his life, Tom knew the full horror of those three little words 'one hit wonder.'

The question now was whether his agent still believed in him, or whether today's lunch date was a precursor to her letting him go.

✴

'I don't want to pressure you,' Lucinda said, in a tone which Tom took to mean that she was about to do just that. He wasn't wrong.

'Your last book wasn't quite the success we were all hoping for,' she continued.

Tom smiled wryly. 'Difficult second-novel syndrome.'

'Possibly. Or maybe it was more than that.' She paused for effect. 'Perhaps it's time you thought about branching out a bit.'

'Branching out?'

'Try something a bit different. The market has moved on. People aren't buying sensitive male fiction anymore, certainly not in the numbers they were five years ago. Have you ever thought about writing crime?'

Tom pulled a face. 'And destroy what's left of my reputation? I don't think so.'

'A few years ago, I'd have agreed with you,' Lucinda said. 'But things have changed. People aren't nearly as snobbish about it these days.'

'I'm not a snob,' Tom replied, though deep down he suspected that he probably was. 'I just don't think I'm capable of writing a decent crime novel. My imagination isn't nearly dark enough.' Again, he wondered if this was strictly true.

'We could always try changing your name,' Lucinda suggested.

Tom was aghast. His first instinct was to say that he'd never been so insulted. But he had been. The sales figures for his last novel were about as insulting as it got.

'I didn't realise things were quite that desperate,' he said. 'I'm quite happy with who I am, thank you. I'm not about to start pretending to be someone else.'

'Lots of authors do it,' Lucinda insisted. 'Don't take it so personally.' She smiled. 'A rose by any other name...'

'I'm familiar with the quote. And unless I'm very much mistaken, Romeo doesn't smell half as sweet by the end of the story. Possibly because he winds up dead.'

Lucinda allowed herself a little laugh. 'See! I knew you had a dark side! But don't think of it as an ending. Think of it as a new beginning. A fresh start. We can reposition you in the market and—'

'No,' Tom said firmly. 'I'm not changing my name.'

'Fine,' Lucinda snapped. 'But if we're to move forwards, I strongly suggest that you deliver something very different.'

This was it – the ultimatum he'd been bracing himself for since the moment he arrived. Part of him wanted to tell his agent where to stick it. But another part wanted to prove to her – and himself – that he was capable of rising to any challenge she or anyone else put before him.

'I'll give it some thought,' he said. 'I may have something that would keep my existing fans happy and still allow me to take my writing in an exciting new direction.'

He didn't really. He was bluffing. But as he said the words aloud, the seed of an idea rooted itself in Tom's head. It germinated over coffee and continued to grow as he thanked Lucinda for lunch and they walked out onto Dean Street, exchanged air kisses and went their separate ways.

By the time he arrived back home in Vauxhall, Tom knew what he had to do: forget the book he'd been working on – he'd lost faith in that months ago. And, as his agent had made abundantly clear, she wanted something different. So he'd give Lucinda her crime novel. The protagonist would be a version of himself. Tom had been excavating elements of his own life in fiction for years and saw no reason to stop now. And he already had his antagonist. That obsessive, relentless woman had given him more than enough material to work with. The solution to his writer's block was staring him in the face.

He went into his home office, sat at his computer and got to work.

5

DAY 3

I'm surprised you weren't in court today. I thought you of all people would be there. This was it. The day you've dreamed of for so long, the moment this whole sordid affair has been leading up to – your chance to see me standing in the dock like a common criminal. At the very least I thought you'd have come to admire your handiwork.

But when I looked out at the public gallery, there was no sign of you. At first I thought you'd been unavoidably delayed – car trouble, a traffic jam, a person under a train. But you never showed up. Your dear friend Emma was there, briefly. But where were you? Did you have something more important to do today? What could be more important than watching me being grilled alive by your stern-faced prosecutor? I'd love to know.

My lawyer suggested that, because you'd requested a screen yesterday, you'd probably been advised that showing up today would weaken your case. How would it look to the judge if one day you couldn't bring yourself to look at me and the next day you were sitting in the gallery, gloating? Was that it – another of your cheap tactics? Were you secretly wishing that you could be there to see me squirm? Was it a pleasure you were forced to deny yourself – you who never denies himself anything? How did it make you feel, Tom? What did you do to fill those long, lonely hours?

Did you start the day with a run? I know how much you love running, the hours you spend pounding the pavements down by the river where you live. How nice for you, that you can afford a riverside apartment when most writers are struggling to survive. What does the average author earn these days? Ten thousand a year? There aren't many who command the big advances you're used to. Do you wake up each morning and count your blessings? Or are you up and out of the door without a moment's thought?

I often picture you in your running gear – face flushed, hair wet with sweat as you push yourself to go that extra mile. I imagine your heart racing as you follow the Thames Path past the bridges – Vauxhall, Chelsea, Albert, Battersea – all the way to Wandsworth, Putney, Hammersmith and back again. What is that – a two-hour run? That's a long time to be away from your desk. How do you justify that to yourself, I wonder?

You once told me that you get some of your best ideas when you're out running. Or maybe I read that in an interview somewhere. In any case, I don't believe for one second that the reason you run is to feed your muse. Things are never that simple, certainly not with a man like you. It's largely vanity, of course. You're not getting any younger, and I'm sure you'd sooner die of a heart attack than give in to middle-age spread. But there's more to it than that, isn't there? You're like the runner in that old song by The Three Degrees – you run but you don't show love. What is it you're running from, Tom? Is it me, or is it yourself?

It's a shame you weren't there to hear me give evidence today. But then you've never been much of a listener, have you? You love the sound of your own voice. But you rarely listen to what others have to say. I wouldn't describe you as rude – you'll smile and nod when someone else is talking. You might even ask the odd question now and then. But really you're just waiting for them to finish so you can steer the conversation back to your favourite subject – the life and works of Tom Hunter.

I've often thought that such a lack of curiosity must be quite a handicap in a novelist. But it's one you make up for somehow, like a deaf person who learns to lip-read or a blind person whose hearing becomes more acute. Do you ever listen to music when you run? Something to drown out the traffic noise or the burble of the river? Or do you prefer to be alone with your thoughts? Are the only other sounds you hear your own footsteps, heavy breaths and the beat of blood in your brain?

I'm not expecting an answer, but it may interest you to know that while you were out running I was being sworn in at court and preparing to give my side of the story. I wish you could have seen me, Tom. I wore that blue dress – the one you commented on the night we first met. My hair was tied back and I even went to the trouble of applying a little makeup. None of that heavy contouring girls are going in for these days – just a bit of lipstick, a little mascara, a touch of eye shadow. My dad said I looked most ladylike and very professional, and we all know how important appearances are at times like these.

You might be wondering why I'm going to the trouble of telling you all this. Why, when you couldn't be bothered to show up today, should I show you such courtesy? It's really quite simple. I'm keeping a detailed account of everything that happens in court because when I'm exonerated – which we both know I will be – I want there to be a record of what you've put me through. Every false accusation, every twisted lie, every time you or one of your supporters came unstuck in the witness box – it will all be there in black and white, preserved for all to see. Who knows? Maybe when this is all over I'll sell my story to one of the newspapers.

Speaking of which, I'm assuming you saw that scurrilous piece in last night's *Evening Standard*? It says a lot about the state of modern journalism that an article no longer than a few hundred words could contain so many inaccuracies. Don't reporters bother to check their facts anymore? I am not and have never claimed to be a 'book blogger'. Yes, I occasionally review books on my blog. But I also write about other things that interest me – music, current affairs, sexual politics. I am not an 'aspiring journalist'. Who in their right mind would aspire to a career in an industry in such steep decline it's practically dying before our eyes? It's just a pity some of its practitioners don't hurry up and die a little sooner.

I wonder if the hack responsible was back in court today, or if they only came to hear your side of the story? You media types tend to stick together, don't you? I see this every day on Twitter. Some journalist shares a link to their latest opinion piece and a load of their media mates retweet the link and compliment them on how brave and well argued it is. Dare to voice a dissenting opinion and they turn on you like a pack of wolves, tearing you apart, calling you a troll. I've lost count of the number of times I've been blocked on Twitter, usually by so-called commentators who say they believe in free speech but only have time for those who pander to their egos and agree with everything they say.

It's a funny word, troll. In 'The Three Billy Goats Gruff' by Hans Christian Anderson, a troll is a hideous creature who lives under a bridge and threatens to gobble up anyone who attempts to cross. The first two billy goats trick the troll by appealing to its greed, each insisting that if they are allowed to pass, the next goat along will provide an even bigger meal. The story ends with the biggest billy goat pushing the troll off the bridge and into the water below, where it's carried away by the current and presumably drowns. I'm sure you're familiar with the story, Tom – but it's worth thinking about before you toss such words around so lightly.

As I explained to the court this afternoon, these days people use the term 'troll' to silence anyone who happens to disagree with them. It's a nasty little word, as dehumanising in its way as those insults you claim to find so distressing. Why should some insults be classed as 'hate speech' and others not? Surely it's for those on the receiving end to determine how offensive or upsetting a word can be. And as I asked the court, why should your feelings be such a cause for concern and mine be disregarded so blatantly? It's not as if you even denied using your enormous social-media platform to hurl insults at me.

'Perhaps not,' your prosecutor replied. 'But let me remind you that Mr Hunter isn't the one on trial here. You are.'

As if I needed reminding of that! I suppose she thought she was being clever, when really all she did was highlight the injustice of the situation. It's you who should have been in the dock today; you who should have been asked to justify his actions; you whose account of our relationship should have been ripped apart like the tissue of lies it is.

But I'm getting ahead of myself. Your prosecutor friend didn't get her claws into me until after lunch. The morning session was a far more civilised affair – just me telling my story in my own words, without constant interruptions or hostile questions. My lawyer helped by taking me back to the night we first met and talking me through our subsequent correspondence. He paid particular attention to the emails you sent – proof, he told the court, that you weren't being harassed at all, but had actively encouraged me to maintain contact. Several times he asked me to read sections of your emails aloud.

I won't pretend that I didn't find this part of the proceedings upsetting. How could I not, remembering the pleasure those emails brought me at the time, and the pain that followed when you suddenly decided that our relationship was over? But unlike you, I didn't resort to histrionics. My voice didn't falter. There was no catch in my throat. I spoke plainly and from the heart.

There was so much I wanted to say, Tom. So many things I wanted the court to know. But I followed my lawyer's strict instructions and kept my answers short and to the point. Yes, we had been in regular contact for a period of several months. No, I was never given any reason to believe that my emails and tweets to you were likely to cause distress. Yes, you had replied to me on a number of occasions. No, I was not seeking to harass you. Quite honestly, I'd have thought that much was obvious. But apparently these things need spelling out in court, so spell them out we did.

A strange thing happens when you're standing in the dock, reliving the events that brought you here. You lose all track of time. It's as if the world suddenly starts listening and the words just pour out of you. I'm not used to being the centre of attention, not like you, but I can see how easily one might become addicted. I don't know where the hours went, but before I knew it my lawyer was thanking me and telling the court he had 'no more questions', and the judge was calling time for lunch.

Despite feeling a little overdressed for Camberwell Green, I made my way with Dad back to the same sandwich bar as yesterday and I ordered the exact same thing– tuna salad on granary and a Diet Coke.

My dad said I was doing well, and reminded me that things would be a lot tougher this afternoon, when it wouldn't be my lawyer asking the questions but yours. I must remember to stay calm, he said, and think carefully before I open my mouth. I told him he needn't worry. I knew exactly what to say and how to handle myself. People have been underestimating me all my life. It would take more than some jumped-up crown prosecutor to get the better of me.

I looked for you again after the lunch break. Surely by now the temptation to see me squirm would be too powerful to resist? But still there was no sign of you. And here's the thing – I didn't squirm. I'm not saying your prosecutor didn't give it her best shot. She tried, Tom. She tried really hard. But what chance did she have, when the case against me is a pack of lies?

Let's start with the biggest lie of all. Yesterday you told the court that we didn't really know one another, that the only time we ever met was that evening at Waterstones when you signed my book. Of course you couldn't deny that this meeting took place – the signed book is proof. But that wasn't the only time I had the pleasure of your company, was it? Remember that day at the farmers' market? Or how about that night at that gastropub in Kennington?

'You're aware, of course, that Mr Hunter denies ever arranging to meet you on those occasions,' the prosecutor said. 'And that by placing yourself in the same locations as him at the times you say, you're only incriminating yourself further.'

I know why you lied, of course. You can't admit to yourself that what we had was special. You're afraid of intimacy. I get that. But I can wait. You'd be surprised at how long I can wait. I've had a lot of practice. I have the patience of a saint.

'But he wanted to see me,' I insisted. 'He called me.'

'Unfortunately, we only have your word for that,' she replied. 'And as the case against you has repeatedly shown, your word is hardly reliable.'

Of course it was far harder for her to dismiss the evidence provided by your emails. As my defence had already made clear, those emails demonstrate beyond any reasonable doubt that you were every bit as invested in this relationship as I was. I offered to send you examples of my writing and you readily accepted. You even agreed to read my book. How could anyone in their right mind conclude otherwise?

I can only assume, therefore, that your learned prosecutor friend is not a reasonable woman and is not of sound mind.

'It's not unheard of for authors to respond to unsolicited fan mail,' she said haughtily. 'The fact that Mr Hunter took the time to reply to your emails is simply a sign of his good character and in no way indicates that the two of you were involved in any kind of relationship.'

'Then why did he take my business card?'

'Again, we only have your word for that. The word of a woman who continued to bombard Mr Hunter with emails long after he stopped responding. A woman who used multiple accounts to ensure that her emails reached their target, despite his best efforts to block her. A woman who breached her bail conditions by turning up outside his home, making threats and leaving him with no choice but to call the police.'

'I didn't threaten him!' I said.

'Mr Hunter has already told the court that you did. And this is entirely consistent with the tone of your emails and the aggressive, harassing nature of your interactions on Twitter.'

Ah yes, Twitter – where the seeds of our relationship were first sown and where it ended in insults and bitter recriminations. Having called in a social-media expert to help the poor judge make sense of this brave new world of ours, I suppose it was inevitable that much of the crown's case against me would depend on their interpretation of 'evidence' gleaned from Twitter. My lawyer had told me as much, and had given me an opportunity to explain myself earlier in the day. I did pretty well, I thought. But, boy, did your prosecutor make a song and dance about it!

I won't bore you with the details – who said what and when. What's the point? We're both familiar with the facts. We both said things we regret. We both have the screenshots of those tweets in our case files. But if you'd only seen the way she carried on. To hear her talk, you'd think I'd sent you death threats. Me, who has gone out of my way to support and defend you whenever necessary. Me, who wouldn't hurt a fly unless the fly really hurt me first.

I know you're a sensitive soul, Tom. I know you don't take criticism well. But am I seriously expected to believe that those tweets I sent had such a devastating effect on you that you were forced to seek medical attention? This is just another of your stunts, surely? I know you have a statement from your GP, describing your fragile emotional state and confirming that he felt it necessary to put you on a course of antidepressants. But doctors can be bought like anyone else, especially when you're paying for their services. How many times has your Harley Street doctor been persuaded to prescribe you sleeping pills, I wonder? How many courses of antibiotics have you been on in the past few years? A damn sight more than those of us who rely on the NHS, I'll bet.

What really irritates me, and what I tried to explain to the court today, is that social media isn't like real life. Nobody walks up to you in the street and shows you a photo of their dinner or their cat, the way they do on Facebook. Conversations aren't conducted in person the way views are exchanged on Twitter. There's no room for pleasantries when your thoughts are squeezed into a few hundred characters. We're both adults, Tom. We both know how easily things said on Twitter can be misconstrued and blown out of all proportion. For a short time, there we were, at the centre of our own little Twitter storm. But it wasn't a storm entirely of my making, whatever the prosecution claimed today.

As I told the court, I'm perfectly willing to hold up my hand and say that, yes, I did some things I regret. I shouldn't have sent some of those tweets. It is a truth universally acknowledged that things tweeted in the haze of a drunken hour are often regretted in the cold light of day. But who among us can honestly say that they've never said something they shouldn't have? I'm sure your prosecutor friend has lost her temper on occasion. I know for a fact that you have. And as I tried to explain to the judge, tweets taken out of context can be made to appear threatening when really, they were just playful banter between friends.

All things considered, I think I gave a pretty good account of myself. And I told them everything, Tom. I told them how you charmed me and used me and lied to me – as well as the police and the whole damn lot of them. I could have gone on for hours. But the judge in her infinite wisdom decided that I was tired and had probably had enough for today. Her concern for my welfare might have been touching had it not seemed so insincere. If you ask me, she just wanted to slope off early and be home in time for *Real Housewives*.

So, the show's not over yet. I'm back in court again tomorrow, when I'll be made to answer a few more questions and the judge will return her verdict. My lawyer has advised me to hope for the best and prepare for the worst. I'm sure this is the same advice they give everyone – 'managing expectations', I believe it's called. Personally, I think he's being overcautious. I'll be very surprised if I'm found guilty of anything, given the weakness of the case against me. It'll be like the Twitter joke trial all over again. Another wrongful arrest. Another waste of police time and resources.

Will I see you in court tomorrow? I do hope so. It wouldn't hurt you to take a little more interest in what happens to me, given that our fates are now so intertwined. You do realise that, don't you? Whatever the outcome, whatever the judge decides, our names are now linked forever. Tom Hunter and Evie Stokes. Tom and Evie. I hope that makes you as happy as it makes me.

Yours, always

Evie

6

FOUR WEEKS EARLIER

'How was it?' Emma asked. 'More to the point, how are you?'

Tom shook his head. 'Grim.'

He'd come straight from the police station, where he'd spent the last hour and a half giving an impact statement to DI Sue Grant. It was the fourth time he'd been back to the station since giving his original statement seven months before. Familiarity hadn't made him any fonder of the place. Thankfully, it was only a short walk from the station to Emma's flat off Brixton Hill. It had taken him less than fifteen minutes and he'd barely broken a sweat.

'You must be worn out,' Emma said. She embraced him quickly, giving him a kiss on the cheek. He returned the gesture clumsily and with rather less enthusiasm. She pulled away. 'Someone's tense.'

'Sorry. But I have wine.' He handed her the bottle he'd bought at the off-licence. 'It's nothing special. The choice was pretty limited.'

'It's fine,' she smiled, taking his jacket and hanging it on the coat rack behind the door. 'A few glasses and who can tell the difference?'

Tom paused to inspect his face in the hallway mirror. 'Christ, I look shattered! Remember that scene in *The Hunger*, where David Bowie ages a thousand years in a few minutes? That's me now.'

Emma laughed. 'Stop being so melodramatic. Come on.' She led him through to the kitchen and poured him a glass of white from an open bottle she took from the fridge. Sancerre, Tom noticed.

He took the glass gratefully and knocked back a third of its contents in one slug. 'Thanks. I needed that.'

'At least it's all over now,' Emma said, watching him carefully.

'Aside from the small matter of the trial.'

'I meant, no more statements.'

'Until the trial. Then I'll have to go through it all again in court, while the defence try to trip me up.'

Emma smiled reassuringly. 'You'll be fine. You won't be the one on trial, remember. And if there was ever any chance of her being acquitted, she destroyed it the night she turned up at your flat.'

Tom's pulse quickened. The night Evie Stokes turned up outside his flat was less than a month ago. He still recalled the shock of seeing her – blatantly breaching her bail conditions, begging him to make it stop. He pushed the thought away. 'What's cooking?'

The table was already laid. Two large saucepans bubbled away on the hob, lids rattling, billowing steam.

'Thai green chicken curry.' Emma went over to inspect the pans. 'I wish you'd let me come with you. It's only just up the road.'

'It was kind of you to offer,' Tom replied, sneaking up behind her. 'But there was really no need.' He leaned over her shoulder and sniffed. 'Smells good. Who knew you were such a domestic goddess?'

Emma nudged him aside. 'Less of the domestic, if you don't mind. It might work for Nigella, but to me it just sounds like drudgery.'

She removed her apron and smoothed down her dress, fingers gliding over the sleek green fabric, which accentuated her narrow waist and skimmed her hips.

'New dress?' Tom asked.

Emma laughed. 'Don't flatter yourself. I may have worn it once or twice.'

'Very nice,' he nodded, approvingly. 'And presumably very expensive?'

'Let's not spoil things.' She tutted and turned her attention back to the stove.

Her flat had often struck Tom as rather small for a woman of Emma's means – one bedroom, a stylish but somewhat cramped living room and what estate agents would refer to as a kitchen diner, as if they were describing a loft apartment in New York and not a garden flat in south London. Through the kitchen window, Tom could see that the evening sky was still bright blue. He fished in his trouser pocket for the packet of Marlboro Green he'd bought at the off-licence.

'Okay if I pop out for a quick fag?'

She turned and frowned. 'I can't believe you're smoking again.'

'I know. Filthy habit.'

'I don't know how you can smoke and still go running.'

Tom grinned. 'I don't do both at the same time.'

'You know what I mean.'

'I do. But you'd be surprised at the number of guys I see leaving the gym and lighting up.'

'I don't care about them,' Emma said. 'I care about you.'

'I know. But it calms my nerves and helps keep the weight off. Those pills are making me balloon.'

Emma cast her eyes over him. 'Well it doesn't show. When can you stop taking them?'

'The doctor says I have to wait until after the trial.'

'I hope you included that in your police statement.'

'The pills? Of course.'

'And the cigarettes?'

'I may have mentioned them.'

'Well I hope you did,' Emma said. 'You know what I think about smoking.'

'It's a form of self-harm,' Tom replied, quoting her in a melodramatic voice.

She smiled. 'Well, it is. I know drinking isn't good for you, but at least it gives you pleasure. Smoking is just poison.'

'Oscar Wilde said that smoking was the perfect pleasure.'

'Didn't he also say that each man kills the thing he loves?'

'He did.'

'Well that's rubbish for a start. You're a man. You've never killed anyone.'

'Maybe I've never loved anyone.'

'You love me, don't you?'

'After a fashion.'

'There you go, then.'

'Right,' said Tom. 'And on that note I think I'll go and self-harm in the garden.' He grinned guiltily and slipped outside.

✻

The garden wasn't much to speak of – just a bit of decking, some shrubs in pots and a string of fairy lights along the back wall. Emma had many talents but green-fingered she certainly wasn't.

Tom had been spending a lot of time at Emma's lately. He didn't like to cook, and she was glad of the company. Like him, she lived alone. And like him, there hadn't been another man in Emma's life for quite some time. If asked, she'd have insisted that it didn't really bother her. But Tom knew her better than that. Behind that tough exterior was a woman who wanted nothing more than to meet Mr Right and settle down. Sometimes Tom wondered if he was the one preventing her from doing just that. Then he'd remind himself that she was a grown woman who was perfectly capable of making her own decisions. If she chose to devote herself to him, who was he to argue?

Back inside, he watched as she plated up the food and brought it to the table, gesturing for him to sit down.

'That cigarette didn't calm you, then.'

'Sorry?'

'You look tense,' Emma said, taking her seat.

'I was just thinking about the trial. Her defence do have a few things on me. The time I told her to drop dead, for example. Or the time I joked about her mental health.'

Emma reached for the wine and topped up their glasses. 'The woman was harassing you, Tom. What were you supposed to say – "Thanks for all the abuse but please stop bothering me"? I think you're allowed to lose your temper once in a while. You're only human. Nobody expects you to be a saint.'

'And I've just sent my halo off to be polished especially.' Tom smiled.

'You're probably right. It just feels as if I still have to prove myself in court, as if I'm the one who'll be on trial.'

'The police believe your story, don't they?'

He frowned. 'Why wouldn't they? It's not a story. It's what happened.'

'Don't be so defensive! I'm just saying that they're on your side. That goes a long way in court. And most judges aren't as out of touch as people imagine. They know that even saints lose their rag from time to time.'

'Indeed,' Tom nodded sagely. 'Look at Saint George. He slayed a dragon. Come to think of it, he probably had the right idea. There's a dragon lady I wouldn't mind slaying.'

Emma fiddled with the stem of her wine glass. Her face was deadly serious. 'Promise me something, Tom.'

'Anything.'

'Promise me you won't be like this in court.'

'Like what?'

She looked hesitant. 'It's just that, well, you can come across as being quite arrogant at times.'

'Arrogant?'

'Pompous, then.' She coloured slightly. 'I don't mean that in a bad way. I know you. I know what you're really like. But not everyone does. I'd hate for you to damage your case by giving the wrong impression.'

Tom weighed up her words as he considered his response. 'I won't,' he said finally. 'I promise.'

'Good,' she smiled. 'Now tuck in.'

He forked some curry into his mouth and declared it delicious.

She thanked him for the compliment.

'So tell me,' he said, playfully. 'What am I really like?'

❉

The first time Tom and Emma met, she'd told him he was vain and egotistical. 'But if I dig a little deeper, I'm sure I'll find some good qualities.'

She'd smiled when she said this, and he'd smiled back when he replied, 'What if those are my good qualities?'

This exchange took place eight years before, at a mutual friend's birthday dinner. To the casual observer, it might have looked as if they were sparring with one another, or possibly indulging in a strange kind of flirting. In fact, they were simply measuring each other up.

Tom had gone to the dinner out of duty, expecting it to be about as much fun as these things normally were. Finding himself seated next to a glamorous woman with shoulder-length expensively blonde hair and the biggest brown eyes he'd ever seen, he made polite conversation and was pleasantly surprised to find that there was far more to her than mere physical attractiveness. Still, he was disarmed when she looked him straight in the eye and said, 'I think we're going to be friends for a long time, don't you?' In Tom's experience, people only ever said things like that when they were drunk or high on something, and this woman didn't appear to be either.

But as he soon discovered, Emma Norton wasn't like most people. She was incredibly direct and never afraid to admit when she didn't know something. 'What does that mean?' she'd ask whenever Tom used a word that was intended to impress rather than communicate. Like many writers, he had the habit of deploying words as weapons, enjoying the power they afforded him. Nor was she intimidated by the fact that, whenever he took her to book launches or publishers' parties, she was often the least well-connected person in the room. It was a running joke between them that whenever some snooty PR or posh publisher's assistant asked her what she did, she'd respond by saying she had a proper job. Not that she thought a career in the financial sector made her any better than anyone else, but it certainly didn't make her any worse. And as she was well aware, a woman with her looks was never out of place and could get away with saying virtually anything – and often did. Coming from a world where everyone watched what they said and worried about how others perceived them, Tom found her physical confidence and lack of inhibition refreshing.

Theirs was one of those friendships that developed fairly quickly, based on mutual attraction and a shared sense of humour. In many ways they couldn't be more different. The room they were currently sitting in was a case in point. It was tasteful but lived in, whereas Tom's kitchen was all high-gloss units and gleaming marble work surfaces that had never seen a chopping board. Emma's warmth was one of the qualities he valued most in her. She had a career and a social life, but she was also a homebody who loved entertaining. His own flat was more like a show home. Tom rarely had visitors, and when he did they were more likely to be escorted straight to the bedroom than offered a place at his table.

Of course Tom was self-aware enough to know that he and Emma served a need in one another. Both single, neither of them getting any younger, they'd reached a point in their lives when they were the nearest thing either of them had to a significant other. He knew, also, that there were times when he'd taken her friendship for granted – abandoning her in strange bars when some handsome stranger caught his eye. But she took it all in her stride.

'We're just like an old married couple,' she was fond of saying. 'We know each other's darkest secrets and there's no sex.'

There was often an air of embarrassment when she said this, and Tom was reminded of a drunken fumble two Christmases ago, when they somehow ended up in bed together but came to their senses before things went too far. But he'd learned to cover any awkwardness by simply smiling at her and replying, 'Less of the old, if you don't mind!'

✷

Dessert was a home-baked blueberry cheesecake. It said a lot about Tom's current state of mind that when Emma set the plate in front of him, he immediately pictured the cream cheese clogging up his arteries. Even the blueberry coulis seemed sinister, pooling around the edge of the plate in a sticky half-circle the colour and consistency of congealed blood.

The revulsion must have shown on his face.

'That's not quite the reaction I was hoping for,' Emma said.

Tom blushed. 'Sorry. I was miles away.'

'You don't have to eat it if you don't want to. I know you said you've put on weight, but it really doesn't show.'

'Sorry. This looks wonderful.' With his dessert fork, Tom cut off a small piece of cheesecake, carefully avoiding the coulis, and popped it into his mouth. Feeling her eyes on him, he smiled and made suitably enthusiastic noises. 'This is really good, Em. I'd ask for the recipe but we both know I'm about as much use in the kitchen as a nun at an orgy. Just as well I have you, eh?'

Emma coloured slightly and changed the subject. 'So, how's the new book coming along?'

'Must we?' Tom reached for the bottle and sloshed more wine into his empty glass. 'You know I don't like discussing a new book until I've broken the back of it.'

'And are you any closer to breaking the back of it?'

He smiled enigmatically. 'Possibly.'

'Well, that's good, isn't it? At least the pills aren't clouding your mind. When my mum was on them she'd be lost in a fog for months.'

At the mention of her mother, Emma's voice faltered and her eyes glistened. 'Sorry,' she said, blinking back tears.

'Don't be,' Tom replied. 'I know how much you loved your mum. There are bound to be moments like this.'

Emma's mother had battled with depression all her life, before finally ending it two years ago with an overdose washed down with half a bottle of vodka. It wasn't the first time she'd attempted suicide, but it still came as a shock. It was Tom who supported Emma through the difficult months that followed. He helped with the funeral arrangements, listened as she struggled to make sense of her loss and held her as she cried. There was no father figure to help shoulder her grief. Emma's dad left when she was seven years old and moved in with his mistress and her teenage daughter. Emma hadn't heard from him since. It didn't take a genius to work out that this may have had some bearing on her trust issues where members of the opposite sex were concerned. Or that the loss of her mother may have contributed to what happened between Emma and Tom that Christmas.

'Anyway,' she continued brightly. 'I'm pleased you're still managing to write. Even with the antidepressants and everything you're going through.'

'You know me,' Tom said. 'Nothing gets in the way of the writing.'

'And it's okay for you to drink on them?'

'In moderation, yes.'

'I'd hardly call this moderation.' Emma gave him a questioning look. 'That's your sixth glass.'

'Who's counting?' Tom grinned. 'Well, you are, obviously.'

'Only because I care about you.'

'That's good to know. I care about you, too.'

He took a sip of wine and toyed with his cheesecake.

'That was great, Em,' he said finally, pushing the half-empty plate aside and reaching for his wine glass. Then, seeing the concerned look on her face, 'What's wrong?'

'I hate seeing you like this, Tom.'

'Like what?'

'Like this. The way you are now. Stressed. Smoking. Drinking heavily. I thought those pills were supposed to even you out.'

'They do.'

'Then why are you still so agitated? Is there something you're not telling me?'

'I'm fine, really.'

'This is me you're talking to,' Emma said firmly. 'You're not fine, and we both know it. So stop being so evasive and tell me what's wrong.'

He took a while to answer. 'It's the court case. What if she gets off? I'll never hear the last of it. I'll never be rid of her. She's relentless, Em. She'll just keep on and on and—'

'Tom!' Emma interrupted him. 'She won't get off. You've said it yourself: the weight of evidence against her is too strong. They wouldn't be prosecuting her if they didn't think they had a strong case. And she breached her bail conditions. That's bound to go against her.'

'I know. But the thing is...' Tom took a gulp of wine, avoiding Emma's gaze. 'I may have encouraged her. Just a bit, at the start.'

'Encouraged her in what way?'

He paused before replying. 'You know what they say – don't feed the trolls. Well, I did. I fed the troll. I replied to some of her tweets and emails. We had a correspondence, of sorts.'

Emma frowned. 'Whatever for?'

'I found her amusing, at first. I didn't know who I was dealing with. Not then. She seemed quite normal to begin with. Then, when she turned on me and started humiliating me on Twitter – well, I was angry. I said things. Things I regret.'

'What things?'

'Just stupid things. Insults. I called her names. I had a rant about her on Facebook, the night she turned up at my flat. I shared her address.'

Emma's eyes widened. 'You did what?'

'I know,' Tom said, shamefaced. 'But I was drunk and angry. I deleted it first thing the next morning. I don't think she's on Facebook, so I don't know if she's aware of it or not.'

'How did you get hold of her address?'

'The same way she got hold of mine, I imagine. I Googled it.'

'Have you told the police?'

'No.'

'Why not?'

'Because I don't want them to think badly of me. What was it you said earlier – that I need to make a good impression? That's what I've been trying to do. And you have no idea how hard it is, Em. Sitting there in the station, going over it all for hours on end. It wears you down. You even start to doubt yourself. What if the judge takes one look at me and decides I'm some overprivileged man abusing the criminal justice system to silence a poor innocent woman?'

Emma reached for his hand. 'They won't, Tom. The woman harassed you. She even turned up at your flat, for heaven's sake! This other stuff – the insults, the stuff on Facebook – I don't think it was very sensible of you, but it doesn't alter the fact that a crime was committed. It won't make any difference in court.'

'Are you sure?'

'I'm sure. Now, is that all?'

'That's all.'

'Good!' Emma stood and started clearing away the plates. 'Don't get me wrong. I know it's been a nightmare. But try not to dwell on it so much. Focus on your book. Stay strong. A few more weeks and this will all be over. She'll be found guilty and you can put this whole thing behind you.'

Tom sighed. 'You're probably right. It just feels like it's been dragging on forever. If I'd known it would take this long, I'd never have gone to the police in the first place.'

If Emma took this as a reproach for urging him to make the call, she didn't let it show. 'You don't mean that. If you hadn't gone to the police, there's no saying what would have happened. For all we know, she could be dangerous.'

Tom stiffened.

'Sorry,' Emma added quickly. 'That was stupid of me.'

'It's fine, really. I'm okay.'

'Are you sure?'

Tom puts his hand to his heart as if taking an oath. 'As God is my witness.'

'You're an atheist,' Emma reminded him. 'Now, why don't I make us some coffee?'

'Perfect,' he replied. 'I'll just pop out for another cigarette.'

✠

It was gone eleven when Tom finally left Emma's flat, refusing her offer to call him a cab and promising to phone her first thing in the morning. He'd said more than he'd meant to, and bitterly regretted those last few glasses of wine. The coffee had sobered him up just enough to let the remorse kick in.

The leafy side street was lined with parked cars, blank windscreens reflecting a bright half-moon in a cloudless sky. He set off at a pace and stopped as he approached a row of wheelie bins. Fumbling in his trouser pocket, he took out the packet of cigarettes and stared at it ruefully. Then he lifted the lid on the nearest bin and tossed the packet inside.

Traffic snarled as he turned onto Brixton Hill. There was a bus stop a few yards ahead, but Tom made it a rule to never take buses after dark. He'd lost count of the number of times he'd felt threatened on a night bus, low-level homophobic banter escalating into threats of violence while his fellow passengers looked the other way. You could be knifed on a night bus and nobody would intervene. He could always hail a black cab, but it was still mild and dry, and the walk would do him good. He hadn't been for his morning run today. A bit of exercise would help alleviate the guilt.

Crowds of people were milling around outside the Ritzy cinema, taking advantage of the warm night air. At times like this it was easy to forget that this area of London had more than its fair share of social tensions and that some streets weren't safe, especially for a man who didn't look as if he belonged here.

Tom straightened his shoulders and pushed the thought away. He walked purposefully and kept to the main thoroughfares, heading along the high street and past the police station where he'd spent the earlier part of the evening, then up Brixton Road to the Oval, where he veered left and followed the bus route around the cricket ground and on to Vauxhall. Passing the MI6 building, he felt the cool air coming off the river and turned up the collar of his jacket. It was probably just the chill in the air, but as he turned into his street he felt a shiver crawl over his skin.

Man up, he told himself. *It's all in your mind.*

But his sense of unease deepened as he approached his building, hand in pocket, fumbling for his key fob. He thought back to that night a little less than a month ago. He had been arriving home, just as he was now, when Evie Stokes suddenly emerged from the shadows

– hair unkempt, grey eyes glazed with alcohol, beseeching him in the half-light to let her in so they could 'talk things through'.

Tom shuddered at the memory. How many nights had she lain in wait for him like that? What did she expect him to do? Retract his police statement? Call the whole thing off? It was far too late for that.

He remembered the look on her face when he told her he was calling the police – confused, as if he was speaking a foreign language, or his words somehow didn't make sense. Here she was breaching her bail conditions and it didn't seem to have entered her head that she was doing anything wrong. And then the police arriving and her screaming blue murder as they dragged her away.

If Tom hadn't known what he was dealing with before that night, he sure as hell did afterwards. She was obsessed, unhinged, a basket case. As he informed the arresting officer and later confirmed in a further statement, the woman had threatened him with violence. The only comfort was in knowing that at least she wasn't armed. Not then. But what if there was a next time?

Stepping up to the brutal modernist block he called home – a fortress of concrete, steel and toughened glass, secured with a digital door-entry system – Tom half expected her to appear again, pleading with him or possibly even brandishing a knife. But all he saw was his own reflection in the glass. Heaving a sigh of relief, he swiped his key card and stepped inside, the door closing behind him with a satisfying click.

Later, in the silence of his vast living room overlooking the Thames, he felt the darkness pressing against the windows and wondered if he'd ever have peace of mind again.

7

DAY FOUR

I dreamed about you last night, Tom. In the dream, you weren't the monster you've become. You were the charming man who enjoyed my company and showered me with compliments – the one who said we were kindred spirits; the one who found me funny and fearless; the one who sought my advice on everything from dealing with critics to character development and ironing out plot holes in his latest book.

We were in a bar down by the river in Vauxhall, drinking ice-cold beer from tall glasses as the sun set slowly over Battersea Power Station. It was one of those rare, warm summer evenings in London, when everyone forgets about the pollution and the property prices and the misery of the Northern Line and behaves as if they're on holiday, flocking to the riverside in their linen shirts and backless dresses, ordering tapas and drinking al fresco.

And there we were, right in the middle of it all, barely aware of the crowds of onlookers craning their necks to see if that was really the famous writer who was rumoured to live nearby and whose latest book was receiving such glowing reviews in the weekend supplements. Little did they know how greatly the mystery woman at his side had contributed to that book's success, that without her input there wouldn't be a book at all.

You were wearing a short-sleeved white shirt, designed to show off your physique and drawing admiring glances from most of the women and quite a few of the men. But you only had eyes for me. We were deep in conversation, lost in a world of our own, finishing off each other's sentences and flitting from one topic to another with speed and ease, as only kindred spirits can. It was my idea of heaven, Tom. And from the way you acted – touching my wrist to emphasise a point, listening intently as I offered an opinion – I knew in my heart that it was yours, too.

But when I woke up this morning and logged onto my laptop, I was reminded that the man I once held in such high regard no longer exists, if he ever really existed at all. In his place is a petty, mean-spirited man who lies and twists the truth to fit his own agenda and is so driven by anger he seems hell-bent on my destruction.

Let me tell you a thing or two about anger, Tom. It's a perfectly justified emotion in someone committed to tackling social injustice. It's totally understandable in a situation where one is oppressed or rendered powerless. But when a man in your elevated position employs the full force of the law in an attempt to silence someone whose only crime was to say a few things he didn't like on social media – I think most people would find that rather questionable, to say the least. And any journalist worth their salt would be forced to wonder if perhaps that man has something to hide. Perhaps there's more to this than meets the eye. Perhaps a few pointers in the right direction would uncover a far bigger story than the one the media is currently being fed. The devil is in the detail, Tom. Did nobody ever tell you that?

Just as I predicted, there was no mention of my day in court in last night's *Evening Standard*. They were only ever interested in hearing your side of the story. But I did find a small item on the Court News website, together with an unflattering photo of me leaving the building yesterday. I don't recall seeing any photographers. The picture must have been taken surreptitiously, with one of those zoom lenses used to take candid shots of celebrities misbehaving on yachts or letting it all hang out on island hideaways. And as with those paparazzi shots, the photographer had gone to great lengths to make me look as unappealing as possible. I won't be wearing that blue dress again.

No doubt it will please you to know that there's such an unkind photo of me in circulation, but to me it feels like an invasion of privacy. Do you have any idea what it's like to have your face thrust into the full glare of the media without your consent? If that's not harassment,

I don't know what is. I feel violated – and no, I don't think that's too strong a word. I'm not like you, Tom. I don't crave attention the way you do. I'm not famous. I'm just an ordinary woman caught up in events beyond her control. I don't deserve any of this.

I checked my Twitter feed, but so far nobody had linked me to the offending news item, though I'm sure it won't be long before one of your many followers is encouraged to do your dirty work for you, the way I was once called upon to do. I searched for mentions of you, too, but there was nothing new to report – just that earlier *Evening Standard* article and a passing reference in the *New York Times*, one of those literary think pieces the Americans love so much, best summed up as, 'Whatever happened to Tom Hunter?'

What did happen to you, Tom? Did you lose confidence in your abilities? Did you run out of ideas? Is that what all this was about? You had no ideas of your own so you thought you'd steal mine?

I was about to log off and join my dad downstairs for breakfast, but then I came across something interesting – an article about ghosting. You know what ghosting is, don't you, Tom? It's when someone ends a relationship, but not in the way mature adults do – by sitting down with the other party and explaining why things aren't working – rather by simply going silent on them. According to the writer of the article, it's the most emotionally confusing and cruel way to terminate a relationship, and it's happening more and more. People meet, they hit it off, they might even fall in love, then one or other of them simply stops communicating. No phone calls. No texts or emails. No contact on social media. They just disappear as surely as if they'd died.

That's what you did, Tom. You worked your way into my life, took what you wanted, and then you dropped me without a word of explanation or a thought for my feelings. You became a ghost. It was as if you'd died. Maybe it would have been better for me if you had. At least then I'd have been spared the stress and indignity of this trial.

I was thinking about this on the way to court this morning, wishing I'd read this article sooner, wondering if it might have helped my defence. But of course it was too late for that now. And given the obvious difficulty the judge had understanding the way Twitter works, I dare say that she'd have found the whole idea of ghosting too confusing for her poor brain.

Again there was no sign of you in court. I can't say this came as a surprise. You have a talent for disappearing, matched only by your talent for telling tall tales and persuading people that there might actually be some truth in them. Nobody can say that you aren't gifted, Tom – though, as we both know, you didn't get to where you are today on talent alone. There's a ruthlessness there, too – a determination to put yourself first that some people might consider psychopathic. Without it you wouldn't be the arch manipulator you are. I suppose I should take some comfort in the fact that at least now I know the extent to which I was being manipulated. As became clear today, nobody else in that court room has even the faintest idea. They're as clueless now as they were on day one.

Your prosecutor was looking far less stern than usual. Her hair wasn't as tightly pulled back. Her eyebrows weren't knitted together. There was even the vague hint of a smile on her lips. If I didn't know better I'd have said she was almost being friendly. But we all know that appearances can be deceptive. And as recent events have served to remind me, it isn't wise to take people at face value, least of all when they're in the business of stitching you up.

She began by saying she would go gently with me.

'Go gently where?' I asked. 'Into that good night?'

I don't think she's familiar with the works of Dylan Thomas, because she didn't seem to get the reference. I'd have thought a man of letters such as yourself might have chosen a legal representative with at least a cursory knowledge of the literary world you inhabit, but evidently not.

She asked me if I needed a drink of water, or a moment to compose myself. I confess I sniggered at the suggestion. A number of people have composed themselves in court these past few days. Some have taken the whole idea of composing themselves to ridiculous extremes, putting on elaborate performances, spinning such wild tales, Wilde himself would have found them fanciful. But not me.

'I'm fine,' I said.

'I'm pleased to hear it,' she replied.

Quite honestly, it was all I could do to stop myself from making a barfing gesture right there in her face. We'd barely begun and already I was finding her saccharine sweetness nothing short of nauseating.

I won't bore you with every exchange that followed. Suffice to say that this little act continued for the best part of half an hour, by which time even the judge was starting to look unconvinced.

Finally, the prosecutor drew her cross examination to a close.

'I just have one last question for you,' she said, doing her best to disguise the note of contempt in her voice. 'Yesterday you told the court that Mr Hunter actively encouraged you to maintain contact with him. You said, and I quote, "He wanted this relationship to continue, just as much as I did." Is that correct?'

I said that it was.

'So can you please explain why, when Mr Hunter posted a tweet clearly asking you to stop contacting him, you continued to do so?'

Well, you know what they say, Tom: the truth will set you free. So I told the truth.

'I tried to stop,' I said. 'But by then we were so bound up in each other's lives, I just couldn't help myself.'

'Thank you,' she smiled. 'No more questions.'

And that was it. Case closed – and a pretty feeble case, at that. I don't know what a crown prosecutor is paid in a case like this, but I think I can safely say that the taxpayer isn't getting his money's worth. Put it this way – it wasn't like it is in the movies, or on TV. Where was the devastating summary? Where were the cunning questions and crushing one-liners that reduce the accused to a quivering wreck? I'd have expected a bit of grandstanding at least.

As the judge retired to consider her verdict, I saw my dad smiling at me from the public gallery. He looked relieved, which was a huge weight off my shoulders. I know this hasn't been easy for him, but at least I'd risen to the occasion and done him proud. I'd been open and honest, and unlike you, I hadn't resorted to name-calling or mud-slinging.

I was feeling pretty proud of myself, actually, and quietly confident that common sense would finally prevail and the judge would see this whole case for the travesty it was – one that should never have made it to court in the first place. I know we live in an unjust world. We're reminded of it all the time – all those tales of police corruption; all those miscarriages of justice we read about in the newspapers. But as a friend reminded me recently, most judges are pretty sensible, actually. It takes a lot to convince them that an innocent person is guilty of some heinous crime.

It was barely twenty minutes before she returned. Her face was expressionless. She might just as well have been an office worker returning from a coffee break. This, and the fact that she'd taken so little time to reach her verdict, made it pretty clear to me that I was going to be acquitted. As she began speaking, I thought of all the great literary heroines wrongfully accused or punished for crimes beyond their control – Tess of the D'Urbervilles, Jane Eyre, Dolores Claiborne. Then I thought of the femme fatales who got away with murder – Libby Parsons in *Double Jeopardy*, Linda Fiorentino in *The Last Seduction*, Sharon Stone in *Basic Instinct*. Naturally, I'm more inclined to identify with them. Who wants to end up like Tess?

'Ms Stokes!' the judge snapped. 'Do you understand what I just said?'

Oh, I understood alright, Tom. I understood perfectly. But that doesn't mean that I have to accept her judgement, not by a long way.

'You're to return to court in three weeks' time for sentencing,' she continued. 'In the meantime, your bail conditions still apply. If you break those conditions or you fail to appear in court on the day in question, you will be rearrested and may be sent to prison. Do I make myself clear?'

What's clear to me now, Tom, is that I never really stood a chance. You had me from the start. Right from the moment we met, you knew exactly how this would pan out. You knew which strings to pull, which cards to play. And you kept your hand well hidden. Of course you knew that I'd be taken in by your looks, your charm, that famous charisma. But you also had an ace up your sleeve, far blacker and more deadly than I could ever have predicted. Even when things turned sour, I never imagined for a second that you were capable of such deceit or that you could be so vindictive and stoop so low. I used to think I was pretty good at reading people. I used to think I was a good judge of character. How fitting that it took a writer to teach me otherwise.

Shortly after I was arrested, when I first felt the full weight of the legal system grind into gear, I used to have this image of us in my head. We were trapped in the back seat of a car, driven by a shadow man who refused to show his face. The doors were locked, the brakes had failed, and we were hurtling towards the edge of a cliff, certain in the knowledge that we'd go over but powerless to do anything about it. I used to picture us going down together, not in a blaze of bullets like Bonnie and Clyde, but in a Ford Thunderbird like Thelma and Louise.

Silly, I know. And it took me until today to realise just how ridiculous I was being. Because there was no shadow man. You were the one driving the car. The brakes didn't fail. You had your foot down on the accelerator the whole time. And the driver's door was unlocked, ready for the moment when you'd throw yourself to safety and leave me to plunge to my fate alone.

Did you honestly think that this would be the end of me, Tom? That the strain of the court case would tip me over the edge, and I'd crawl away and die somewhere? Was that part of your plan, too? That I'd lose the will to live? I wonder how you felt when you heard the news today. Pretty pleased with yourself, I imagine. Are you out now at one of your fancy members' clubs, surrounded by well-wishers and the popping of champagne corks, toasting my demise? 'Poor Evie. She was never that strong. All I wanted was for her to leave me alone. If I'd thought for one second that she was this unstable...'

Spare me the crocodile tears, Tom. And let's not get too far ahead of ourselves. I'm far stronger than you give me credit for. I have no intention of crawling away and dying anytime soon. I'm a survivor. And I'm sorry to disappoint you, but this isn't where our story ends. This was only the prologue. A lot can happen between now and the final chapter. You of all people should know that.

So here's my advice: enjoy your moment of triumph while you can. Savour the sweet taste of your champagne, just as I shall savour mine. Yes, I have a chilled bottle of bubbly in front of me right now. And while you're clinking glasses with your friends and admirers, I'll raise a toast of my own.

To us, Tom. And to our book. The one we're writing together. The book of us. I can't wait to see how it ends. Can you?

Always and forever

Evie

PART TWO

8

THREE WEEKS LATER

Female Blogger Guilty of Harassment

An internet 'troll' who sent a gay writer hundreds of abusive tweets and emails has been found guilty of harassment. Evie Stokes, aged thirty-four, from East Dulwich in south-east London, said the emails and tweets she sent author Tom Hunter were light-hearted and not intended to cause offence. But Camberwell Magistrates' Court heard that the messages called the recipient 'pansy', 'gaylord' and 'the AIDS generation'. After she was arrested, Stokes sent Hunter more threatening emails and even approached him at his home address, causing further distress. She was found guilty of harassment without violence. Sentencing is today.

'My treat,' Emma says. 'Now you're finally rid of that bloody woman.'

They're seated in a restaurant in Clapham. An hour ago, 'that bloody woman' was given a two-month suspended sentence, coupled with a restraining order prohibiting her from making any contact with Tom, either directly or indirectly, in person or through social media or a third party. As the sentence was read out, Tom's expression remained impassive. Inside his head he was screaming, *A suspended sentence? What good is that? She should be locked up!* He didn't utter a word of this. Not in court. And not to any of the reporters waiting outside. But there are no court officials here, and no prying reporters. Just two friends enjoying what's meant to be a celebratory lunch.

Tom doesn't feel much like celebrating, but Emma wouldn't take no for an answer, hailing a black cab and singing the praises of this fantastic new Peruvian-Japanese fusion place she'd heard about from a friend at the office. To be fair, the place does look rather impressive, helped in no small part by the fact that the waiters appear to have been recruited from a model agency – all square jaws, designer haircuts and buff physiques in short-sleeved, slim-fitting black shirts. Tom watches as they move expertly between the tables, snake-hipped and oozing testosterone, like male tango dancers.

It's still early for lunch, but the restaurant is already busy – a sure sign that Emma isn't the only one who's heard glowing reports, though whether these were about the food or the eye candy it's too soon to say. Tom wonders if he even has the stomach for food right now. His insides have been in knots all morning.

'Didn't you think the father was weird?' Emma looks over her menu.

'His daughter was being sentenced for harassment,' Tom says. 'I doubt it was his proudest moment.'

'Not just today,' Emma says. 'He was the same during the trial. Sitting there with his crossword, barely paying attention. His own daughter in the dock and he looked like he couldn't care less what happened to her.'

'Maybe he doesn't,' Tom snaps. 'Maybe he's had enough of her madness to last him a lifetime. I wouldn't blame him if he had. I know just how he feels.'

Emma looks as if she's about to say something, then thinks better of it. 'No, you're right. Anyway, it's all behind you now. She's not your problem anymore.'

'I wish I shared your optimism,' Tom replies. 'Did you know that of all the people issued with a restraining order, half breach it within the first few months? I read that recently. Of course nobody tells you this at the time.'

Emma's face falls. 'But she won't, will she? If she does, she risks being sent to prison.'

'Assuming of course that the judge doesn't decide that she's mentally unfit.'

'So what would they do then? Section her?'

'Never mind sectioning. I'd happily see her hung, drawn and quartered.'

A waiter approaches the table, and Emma dismisses him before he can even open his mouth. 'Sorry, we just need a few more minutes.'

Tom watches him retreat, taking in the boyish smile and manly physique – always a winning combination in his book.

'Try not to think about that now,' Emma says, and for a split second Tom thinks she's been reading his thoughts. 'The main thing is she's been found guilty. There's a restraining order in place. You'll probably never hear from her again. That's got to be worth celebrating, hasn't it?'

'So people keep telling me,' Tom replies, then softens his tone. 'Sorry, I'm not very good company.'

'Have you thought any more about seeing someone?'

On the far side of the room, the waiter is clearing a table. Tom watches as his broad shoulders strain against the cotton of his shirt, trousers clinging to his thighs and backside. 'I've told you, I'm not looking for a serious relationship right now.'

'Very funny,' Emma says. 'You know what I mean. Victim support.'

'I do, and yes I've thought about it.'

'So you'll go? ... Tom? Are you listening? This is important.'

Finally he tears his eyes away and looks at her. 'No.'

'Why not?'

Why not, indeed. Tom can think of a million excuses. He doesn't have time. He has a book to finish. He's thinking of leaving London for a while. But the truth is more complicated. It was bad enough, standing up in court and describing the various ways Evie Stokes harassed and humiliated him. Throughout the trial, Tom was torn between a loss of dignity, the desire to shut her up for once and for all, and the nagging sense that the scales of justice might tip against him. He hated every moment of it, but it served a purpose. It had to be done. Or so he kept telling himself.

But that's all behind him now. Seeking help from victim support would only make him feel more of a victim, and he isn't prepared for that. He was bullied at school and avoided telling his parents for fear they'd reject him, the way thousands of boys like him were rejected by their families. He still remembers coming home one afternoon with his shirt torn and his blazer covered in phlegm. The humiliation hurt as much as the bruises he hid from his parents. He vowed then that he'd never let anyone make a victim of him again. Yet here he is, struggling with a familiar sense of shame and twisted pride. And all because of a woman of all people.

'Tom?'

He feels Emma scrutinising him and shrugs. 'What?'

'You know what. Why won't you get help?'

'I'd just rather not.'

'You're being unreasonable.'

Is he? Perhaps he is. He certainly isn't himself, he knows that much. The case has taken its toll. It's left him feeling tired and irritable and something he can't quite put his finger on – a feeling of having suffered some kind of trauma, but none most people would recognise. Nobody died. There are no physical scars. Yet he feels as if a layer of skin has been stripped away, leaving him raw and vulnerable. His body is shot and his sleep patterns are all over the place. Some mornings he's awake as early as 5.00 a.m. and staring at his haggard face in the bathroom mirror. He must have aged a good few years these past eight months. If there was any justice in the world, today's sentence would have reflected that. But as he's found to his cost, there isn't much justice in the criminal justice system. Not really. Not when you consider the enormous impact a supposedly trivial crime like harassment can have on a person's physical and emotional wellbeing.

'Tom?' Emma says.

He shakes the thought away. 'Sorry.'

'I know this is naughty.' She leans towards him conspiratorially. 'But seeing as this is supposed to be a celebration, why don't we order some champagne?'

He feigns shock. 'At this hour?'

Emma gestures to the waiter, who appears at her shoulder but has his eyes firmly locked on Tom. Nice eyes, Tom thinks. And a tightly muscled body under that black shirt.

'The lady would like some champagne,' he says.

The waiter nods. 'And for you, sir?' He pauses slightly. 'What would you like?'

There's a definite hint of promise in that pause, a frisson of sexual tension that causes an immediate stirring in Tom's loins. With just a suggestion of a smile, he holds the waiter's gaze. 'Champagne will do for now.'

✖

Emma's colleague is right about the food. Everything they order is delicious. Emboldened by the champagne, Tom takes this as an invitation to flirt ever more outrageously with the waiter, complimenting him on each dish as if he's prepared it himself.

'That yellowtail sashimi was the best I've ever tasted,' he enthuses after the first course. 'And the scallops were superb.'

The waiter grins as he collects the empty plates. 'I'm glad you enjoyed them.'

And later, halfway through a second bottle, when Tom is even more effusive about the pan-fried shrimp and sea bass, the waiter positively glows with pride. 'That's my favourite thing on the menu.'

Tom thinks he detects a northern accent – Manchester perhaps, or Leeds. Drunkenly, he wonders what brought this fine young specimen of manhood to London, and begins filling in his back story: northern lad discovers he's gay, heads down south in search of gainful employment and sexual opportunity, meets mature writer who offers to show him the ropes. As the image forms, Tom feels his mood lift.

'I am still here, y'know,' Emma admonishes him as the waiter disappears in the direction of the kitchen. 'Honestly, I'd tell you to get a room if I didn't think you'd take it literally!'

'Don't be such a killjoy,' Tom replies. 'You can't begrudge me a bit of harmless flirting. I've had no sex drive for months. If anything's worth celebrating today, it's the return of my libido.'

'Fine, but at least try to keep your tongue in.'

Tom grins. 'I know where I'd rather put it.'

Emma rolls her eyes. 'You're terrible sometimes. Do you know that?'

'I do. But it's all part of my charm.'

'That's debatable.' Emma reaches for her champagne glass and takes a sip. 'So what next? Now this is all over? You should take a holiday. Go and lie on a beach somewhere.'

'Actually, I'm thinking of going to Hastings. I thought I'd rent a place on the seafront. St Leonards, perhaps. Or somewhere by the pier. I could really use some sea air. And a change of scenery will do me good.'

'I'll come with you,' Emma says. 'I'm due some time off, and it's years since I've been to the seaside.'

'Sorry Em, but I'd rather be alone,' Tom replies. 'I really need to crack on with this book.'

For a moment, Emma looks wounded, but she quickly rearranges her features into a playful smile. 'Fair enough.' She pushes her plate away and leans towards him. 'So are you going to tell me what this new book is about?'

'Absolutely.' Tom pauses. 'But not today. Sorry, it's just not at that stage yet. Maybe when I'm back from Hastings.'

'How long are you planning on staying?'

'A few weeks. Maybe a month. However long it takes.'

'And you'll be okay on your own?'

'Amazingly enough, I quite enjoy my own company. And there's always Grindr.'

Emma laughs. 'I don't think the pickings in Hastings will be quite what you're used to in London.'

'Possibly not,' Tom replies, eyeing up the waiter. 'But sometimes one must suffer for one's art.'

'I don't see why. Isn't that whole tortured-artist routine a bit old hat?'

'Aleister Crowley died in Hastings,' Tom continues, ignoring her question. 'There's even a rumour that he cursed the town, making it impossible for anyone to leave.'

Emma doesn't look very impressed. 'I have no idea who that is, but let's hope it's not an omen.'

'He was a famous occultist,' Tom explains. 'The press described him as the wickedest man in the world. He was openly bisexual, a total drug fiend and an admirer of Friedrich Nietzsche. David Bowie was a big fan. He used to refer to him in interviews. And Bowie's Thin White Duke persona was hugely influenced by Crowley's belief system. Homo superior. The superman. All that Nietzschean nonsense.' He pauses. 'He wrote a book called *The Book of Lies*.'

'David Bowie?'

'Aleister Crowley.'

Emma considers this for a moment. 'But isn't that what all novels are? Books of lies?'

Tom grins. 'Are you calling me a liar?'

'No. But you make it all up as you go along, don't you?'

'I think you'll find there's a bit more to it than that. But let's talk about something else. I can see I'm boring you.'

'Not at all. I'm just trying to picture you in Hastings. I've always thought it was rather shabby.'

'It's more shabby chic these days. It even won pier of the year.'

'It beats rear of the year, I suppose.'

Tom leers in the direction of the waiter. 'I don't think we need look too far for that.'

Emma slaps his wrist. 'Tom!'

'Sorry. Where was I? Oh yes, Hastings! It's the place to be, apparently. The papers are even describing it as Hoxton-on-Sea.'

'But you hate Hoxton!'

'No, I don't.'

'Yes, you do. You said it was full of pretentious twats with pretentious hairstyles pretending to be something they're not.'

'Did I really say that?'

'You know damn well you did.'

Tom shrugs. 'I was probably just saying it for effect.'

'You do that a lot: say things for effect.'

'Do I?'

Emma smiles. 'Didn't you once tell me you were bisexual?'

'I think everyone is, aren't they? In theory? We're all somewhere on the Kinsey scale.'

'But you've never actually been with a woman?'

Tom wonders if she's alluding to that night, then chooses to play dumb. 'I've been with plenty of women. I'm with one right now.'

Emma raises an eyebrow. 'That's debatable. But you know what I mean. Have you ever' – she lowers her voice to a stage whisper – 'been all the way?'

'If you're referring to sexual intercourse, this is neither the time nor the place.'

'Says the man who's been undressing the waiter for the past hour!'

Tom laughs. '*Touché*!'

'I'd like to propose a toast,' Emma says, raising her glass. 'To us!'

'To us!' Tom repeats, clinking his glass with hers and gazing over her shoulder at the waiter, who returns his look with a flicker of a smile.

❍

Emma doesn't want dessert. Neither does Tom, but he has no intention of vacating the premises just yet, not when there's the possibility of something off the menu.

'How about coffee?' he asks.

Emma shakes her head and empties the remains of the champagne bottle into her glass, sloshing a fair amount onto the table. Evidently, she's a lot drunker than he is. This may be because she's eaten far less, insisting that he sample everything she ordered and refusing to touch anything on his plate.

Tom smiles at her fondly as she leans towards him across the table.

'I'm pleased it went well today,' she says, reaching for his hand. 'You know how much I care about you.'

'I do,' he replies, stroking her fingers with his thumb.

'Let's ask for the bill,' Emma says. 'Then why not come back to mine? I have a surprise for you.'

'What sort of surprise?'

'If I tell you, it won't be a surprise, will it?'

Tom hesitates. 'Let's save it for another time. You've already spoiled me quite enough for one day.' He pats her hand and pulls away. 'I'll get you a cab.'

'Fine. I'll drop you off in Vauxhall on the way.'

'Thanks, but I'm not heading back yet. It's still early, and I've a few things I need to do.'

Emma sighs. 'What things?'

'Just ... things.'

'Oh.' She glances in the direction of the waiter. 'Those things.'

Tom grins. 'I'm celebrating, remember?'

Emma drains her glass. 'How could I forget?'

9

DAY 1

Today is the first day of the rest of my life. It's also the first day of my punishment for the crime of 'harassing' He Who Must Be Obeyed. The restraining order lasts for two years, or 730 days, which means there are another 729 days to go before I'm no longer legally prohibited from contacting you.

I hope you're satisfied, Tom. Somehow you managed to convince everyone that a serious crime had been committed and that it was incumbent upon the judge to pass the toughest sentence possible. She made this perfectly clear as she read it out. 'I'm warning you, Miss Stokes!' she thundered, peering at me over her spectacles. 'If you disobey this court order you will be rearrested and sent straight to prison!'

Here is a list of the things I'm currently prohibited from doing:

- Contacting directly or indirectly including through third parties TOM HUNTER, including but not limited to email or Facebook;
- Contacting directly or indirectly including through third parties TOM HUNTER, including but not limited to Twitter;
- Including Twitter handle @tomhunterofficial in any tweets;
- Editing any Wikipedia page of or related to TOM HUNTER or his work;
- Linking any blog and/or review and/or website to that of TOM HUNTER;
- Directly commenting on and/or about any blog and/or review and/or article written by TOM HUNTER.

I think you'll agree that this is a pretty comprehensive list. I'm also warned that if I fail to comply with any part of this order, I will be committing an offence and could be imprisoned for up to five years. I'm already on a suspended sentence, and that's pretty much how I feel: suspended. On hold. Can you imagine how that feels, Tom? Pretty shit, I can tell you.

Do you know what really pisses me off? I know what harassment is. Real harassment, I mean. Not the trumped-up nonsense I've been convicted of. There was a guy at college who wouldn't leave me alone. He'd wait for me outside lecture halls, lurking in corridors. He'd follow me around like a puppy, hoping I'd take pity on him or his persistence would grind me down. When that didn't work, he took it up a level. He'd turn up outside my flat, insisting that we were meant to be together. He'd say that if he couldn't have me, then nobody could. I don't mind saying it scared me – but not half as much as I scared him. I didn't go crying to the authorities, either. I have my own way of dealing with things. He got the message.

And you think this is harassment? A few emails? Some disagreements on Twitter? One foolish attempt to persuade you to stop being so melodramatic and taking things so far? You don't know you're born...

To add insult to injury, the judge called me homophobic. Me, who knows her Michel Foucault back to front. Me, who can quote Oscar Wilde until the cows come home. I'm not homophobic. I don't have a problem with gay people. The only problem I have is with middle-class wankers who are stuck up their own arses. But, of course, it suited your needs to play the gay-victim card – and like the idiot she is, the judge fell for it hook, line and sinker.

So yes, her ladyship was very tough on me. But was it tough enough for you, I wonder? I suspect not. I'm sure if you had your way I'd be locked in a prison cell already – one of the many women thrown under the bus by the great British legal system. Do you know there are currently more women in this country imprisoned for trivial offences like nonpayment of council tax than there are men serving time for murder? It's almost enough to make one a feminist. Almost, but not quite.

Thankfully, I'm not in prison. I'm back at home with my dad. He's upstairs now, having a rest before dinner. Poor man. This is the third time this week that he's been unable to get through the day without taking to his bed for a few hours. The stress and strain of this ridiculous charade has really taken its toll on him.

Not that I expect you to give a damn. I saw the way you looked at us today as we were leaving court. Gloating doesn't begin to describe it. And there was something else, too. It was a look of contempt, the kind people like you usually reserve for those paraded on Jeremy Kyle – for those they could so easily have been, were it not for a few A levels and a university degree. Oh yes, I see you, Tom. I know who you are and where you come from. I know the lengths you went to, to get as far away from that small suburban shit-hole as possible. I know how hard you studied, how diligently you worked to reinvent yourself and put your past firmly behind you. But it's still there, isn't it? It still lives inside you, eating away at you like a cancer. Self-improvement is a wonderful thing, but it can produce some truly toxic people.

I watched you today as you climbed into a taxi, barely glancing back at the destruction you'd left in your wake. Was there even a glimmer of sympathy for me, or has your heart hardened to such an extent that all human feeling is dead? My dad told me to turn away, to put you out of my mind. But how could I? There we were, Dad and me, publicly shamed, my life in tatters around me, while you drove off without a care in the world.

But what about your dear friend Emma? Was that a look of compassion I saw on her heavily made-up face today? If I didn't know better I'd say she was feeling ever so slightly sorry for me. Don't get me wrong. I don't want her pity. Not hers, of all people. I've seen the way she sucks up to you. I bet she's swallowed every lie you've ever told her. But when I caught her looking at me across the crowded courtroom today, she didn't seem too happy. I thought she'd be rejoicing in my downfall. Instead she looked rather sad and, dare I say it, confused. Are the doubts creeping in, do you think? Is she starting to wonder if perhaps you haven't told the truth, the whole truth and nothing but the truth? What I'd give to have a quiet chat with her one day, woman to woman. The tales I could tell!

The last three weeks have given me plenty of time to think about things. The judge told me to do this the last time I faced her, the day she delivered her verdict. 'I want you to think very carefully about what you've done,' she said, as if I'm the sort of person who never thinks about her actions. If anything, my problem is that I think too much.

Had I been given the opportunity to put my thoughts into words, I'd have told the court that there'd been a terrible miscarriage of justice, that the crime I stood convicted of is the same 'crime' ordinary, law-abiding people are actively encouraged to commit every day. We're all stalking each other online. All of us. We follow strangers on Twitter, comment on people's posts on Facebook, like their photos on Insta-gram. Sometimes we even send them private messages. And let's not forget all the times we Google each other, or search for people's profiles on dating apps. The whole online world is one big stalking exercise. If I'm guilty, then so are millions of others.

But I didn't get the chance to say this. 'You've had your opportunity to speak,' the judge snapped as soon as I opened my mouth. So instead I was left to ponder the absurdity of my situation – and I mean that in the theatrical sense. You're familiar, I'm sure, with the Theatre of the Absurd – all those post-war playwrights exploring the meaning of life in a world where God is dead and man is left to his own dark devices. This is what my life has become. It's a Beckett play in which I'm buried up to my waist for no apparent reason and slowly sinking. It's a play by Pinter in which every pause has the potential for violence and the punchlines leave bruises. It's a great big cosmic joke, darker and more twisted than anything Edward Albee or even Jean Genet could have imagined. It's Kafka's *The Trial* dragged, kicking and screaming, into the twenty-first century.

But you know all this. You know how unjust this whole episode has been, how absurd it is that I've been convicted of a crime I didn't commit. Despite what you said in court, you know that I'd never harm you, that words are my only weapons. Yet you managed to convince the judge that mere words caused you alarm and distress. And you, a celebrated writer. Hope you're careful when you sit down to write, Tom. Each time you open your laptop, I hope you wear protective clothing. We wouldn't want any of those nasty words leaping off the screen and causing you harm, would we?

How is the writing going, by the way? Are you still struggling? Or have you found yourself some other muse to exploit, the way you exploited me? I don't suppose Emma is much help. I can picture her flicking through a glossy magazine at the hairdresser's – that upmarket one in Bloomsbury, where she goes to have her roots done. But browsing a bookshop or scanning the shelves at her local library? She doesn't seem the type.

I know what you're thinking. Yes, I know where darling Emma goes to get her hair done. And no, I wasn't stalking her. If you must know, it happened quite by chance. It was last Tuesday evening. I'd left Russell Square Station and was on my way to see a film at the Brunswick Centre when there she was, hurrying across Woburn Place. I recognised her immediately from court, though I have to say she was looking rather more dishevelled than usual. I imagine it takes a lot of time and money to maintain that glossy image she aspires to; and it was the end of a busy working day, after all. But there was something more than that. She looked, I don't know, distressed. I confess my curiosity got the better of me. The film didn't start for another half hour, so I followed her, careful to maintain a discreet distance. I watched her enter the salon. The receptionist obviously knew her, and within minutes she was being ushered into a chair and surrounded by a team of stylists and offered coffee and a selection of magazines. She looked very much at home, and the grim face I'd glimpsed earlier on the street looked altogether more relaxed.

Later, when I got home, I took another look at her Facebook page and was astonished to find that she checks into this salon once every two weeks. Why on earth does she go so often, I wonder? How much maintenance can one woman need? I checked the price list for that salon. Your precious Emma spends more on her hair than my dad and I live on in a week.

It strikes me now that how we each spent that evening was a pretty good indication of the kinds of women we are. To use a hairdressing metaphor, it highlighted the difference between us. While I was busy broadening my mind at the Curzon, Emma was having all manner of chemicals plastered onto her scalp. Not that there's any crime in that, of course. But it does make me wonder what you see in her, what you get out of that 'special relationship' of yours.

As a wise man once said, there's more to life than books, Tom – but not much more. Is Emma a keen reader? Does she know her Jack Reacher from her Friedrich Nietzsche? Her Jean Rhys from her Jean Genet? Come to think of it, is she a fan of Bowie? Has she ever been moved by Morrissey or seduced by Suede? Does she know all the words to 'Life on Mars'? I doubt it somehow. So what on earth do you talk about? I can't imagine her work is very interesting. How excited can you get over a spreadsheet? And there's only so much interest a man like you can take in a woman's clothes, hair and makeup.

I'm starting to sound like I'm obsessed with her. And I'm really not. Honest, guv! I'm just … curious. We both know what a curious creature I can be. It's one of the things you used to say you liked about me. Until you decided you didn't.

But back to you and your book. If you're really stuck, it's worth remembering that Twitter is full of people offering tips for writers. Some are even published writers themselves! But you don't seem very keen on Twitter these days. You've hardly tweeted since this whole thing began. I know I shouldn't, but I can't resist sneaking a peak at your Twitter feed every now and then. There's nothing in the restraining order to say I can't.

My lawyer says I should steer clear of social media altogether, in case I'm tempted to try and make contact with you. I assured him I won't. These words I'm writing are for my eyes and peace of mind only. They won't be landing in your inbox any time soon, so there's no need for my legal pal to worry or for you to get your designer briefs in a twist. But I refuse to turn my back on Twitter and crawl away in shame. I'm not some troll you can banish from social media like the evil queen banished from the magical kingdom. This is not a fairy story (no pun intended) and you are not king of the world.

Incidentally, was it just my imagination, or were there far fewer reporters in court today? I was hoping for a few more newspaper cuttings to add to my scrapbook. Perhaps you're no longer as famous or as interesting as you like to think. Or maybe your media friends are feeling a teensy bit embarrassed for you – the man with the ego so big and so fragile he had to employ the full weight of the law to silence a poor woman.

But this woman won't be silenced. Like it or not, not everyone sees me the way you do. Thousands of people on Twitter enjoy my daily scribblings. My followers expect me to keep them entertained and I'm not about to let them down. I take my responsibilities seriously. I'm not one of those precious snowflakes who announces the need for a 'social-media detox' or flounces off Twitter whenever things don't go their way. I leave that to the cupcake feminists with their sugary sentiments and sick-inducing self-righteousness. I'm made of far sterner stuff than that.

It's good to remind myself of this, to remember that I existed quite happily before you came along. Sometimes I catch sight of myself in the mirror and I wonder what you did to me, how you drove me so far from myself that I became totally lost in you. You were like a black hole, sucking me into your orbit. The gravitational pull was like nothing I'd ever experienced, and I was powerless to resist. It was life, Tom, but not as I know it. Before you, I'd never felt so completely absorbed by another human being. I'd never been the sort of person who relies on someone else to complete their sense of self. I'd never been one of the 'we' people – the ones who draw attention to their relationship status with every word that comes out of their mouths: 'we think this' or 'we prefer that' or 'we thought we might try southern Spain this year'. Don't get me wrong. I know we were never a couple, you and I – at least not in the romantic sense. But there was a connection that went way beyond casual friendship, whatever lies you may have told yourself, the police and the Crown Prosecution Service.

Lying is an art, like everything else. You do it exceptionally well. And now that we live in an 'post-truth' age of 'fake news', I suppose it's only to be expected that the person with the greater media platform won. That's what impressed them all – your celebrity. What hope was there for me, a humble blogger, compared to a celebrated novelist like you? It wouldn't surprise me to learn that after the show trial was over, there was a queue for signed copies of your books. I can picture you at the bench, a stack of books beside you, wielding your pen and disarming them all with your smile. The same smile you used to disarm me.

I keep thinking back to that night in the pub, the night you denied all knowledge of. At the time of my arrest, several months had passed since that fateful night, our communication reduced to angry exchanges on Twitter. There were no photographs of us together, and if there were any witnesses, I had no way of tracking them down. It was so long ago, I doubt even the barman would have remembered me. My lawyer told me it would be my word against yours – and as I've since learned to my cost, my word counts for very little compared to the word of the great Tom Hunter.

Looking back, I don't think my legal representative was all that happy to be representing me. But that's what happens when you're forced to rely on legal aid. Had I been in a position to hire a lawyer of my own choosing, perhaps things would have turned out differently.

But there's no point in dwelling on what might have been. The important thing for me now is to look to the future. And I do have a future, whatever you might like to think. It might not be the future I'd have chosen for myself, but I'm extremely good at adapting to new challenges. I've had to be.

You see, Tom, I wasn't always like this. There was a time, not that long ago, when I was a fine, upstanding member of society. I had a job. I paid my taxes. I had hopes and dreams, just like you. But then something happened and all that was taken away from me.

Not that I expect you to understand. How could you? Your own life has taken a very different trajectory. In fact, this is probably the worst thing that has ever happened to you. Imagine that! Imagine being so blessed that the biggest complaint you have is that someone you were once friends with and later discarded refused to crawl away quietly and die. What a ridiculously privileged life you must have led. Aren't you even remotely embarrassed by your good fortune? I know I would be. But that's the difference between us. You have a strong sense of entitlement, whereas I've always been grateful for whatever slivers of success came my way. What was it Quentin Crisp once said? 'If we all got what we deserved, we'd be living in the gutter'. I'm happy to be in the gutter, looking up at the stars. But you? You want to own the stars.

Before I met you, I had a clear sense of my place in the world. I was under no illusions about how I was perceived by the people I encountered on a daily basis. I was someone's daughter, someone's neighbour, someone's student, someone's roommate, someone's work colleague. I was even, briefly, someone's girlfriend. But we needn't go into that now. It didn't last long and it didn't end well. But that's the risk you take, putting yourself out there. Life isn't a safe space. Life is wild and exciting and fraught with danger. That's what makes it so wild and exciting. Any fool knows that.

Which is why I feel so terribly disappointed in you, Tom. You're no fool. You're a writer, for fuck's sake. You know what life's about. You know the power of words – and you know their limits, too. I wouldn't expect the blunt brains of the criminal-justice system to appreciate the finer points of what we had together. To them, I'm just another fan who developed a crush and became obsessed with her favourite author. But we both know it was far more complicated and reciprocal than that. You fed my illusions. You encouraged me to dream. And now the dream is shattered, and I'm left to pick up the pieces while you swan off into the distance without a care in the world. It isn't fair, Tom. It isn't right. But I think deep down you know that, don't you?

Anyway, I think that's enough narrow introspection for one day. My world doesn't revolve around you, however much it might please you to think so. I still have a life to live, despite your best efforts to curtail it. I can hear my dad stirring upstairs. So no more words for now. Time for action. I'll be seeing you.

10

Tom's head pounds. He didn't sleep well – a combination of too much alcohol, too much tension in his neck and shoulders, and a nightmare he can't recall but which woke him early and with a profound sense of unease.

Climbing out of bed, he'd trodden on a used condom and very nearly slipped and fell on the hardwood floor. What a fitting end to yesterday's misadventure that would have been. His impromptu date had proved something of a disappointment. It wasn't the waiter's fault. He'd tried hard to please. Had Tom been in a better frame of mind, he'd have got off on his enthusiasm if nothing else. Instead he found the groans of pleasure off-putting and dedicated himself to speeding the other man along and getting him out of the flat as quickly as possible. The waiter had let it be known that he was free to spend the night, but Tom had made it clear that he preferred to sleep alone.

'I have an early start – and I'm the worst snorer imaginable after a few drinks. Trust me. You won't get a wink of sleep.'

The waiter, whose name was Luke and whose body showed no signs of abating, smiled and pulled Tom towards him. 'Maybe I don't mind.'

'But I do,' Tom replied, leaping to his feet and just managing to catch his champagne glass before it toppled to the floor. 'Sorry. But like I said, early start.'

The other man's face had fallen at that point. Tom felt a pang of pity, before reminding himself that rejection was character-building. A young man with Luke's physical assets wasn't used to being rebuffed. The experience would do him good.

It was barely 10.00 p.m. when Tom's guest left. He'd sat up for another hour or so, finishing off the champagne before cracking open a bottle of Grey Goose and smoking a few cigarettes from the pack he'd purchased on the way home.

Now, as he sits in the stillness of his open-plan kitchen, checking his phone and drinking his morning coffee, his eyes are drawn to the half-empty vodka bottle on the living-room floor next to the black leather sofa. At least it's upright – a bottle lying on its side would look far worse – but there's no escaping the fact that the bottle is half empty. Not for the first time, Tom wonders if his drinking is becoming a problem. And not for the first time, he tells himself that a real alcoholic would be reaching for the bottle now, just to stop the shakes.

Turning his attention back to his phone, he checks his email and social-media accounts. There's nothing in his inbox apart from the usual spam and nothing of interest happening on Facebook. He hesitates before checking his Twitter feed, afraid for a moment that the crazy bitch will have found a way to worm her way into his timeline, the way she has so many times before. But again, nothing. He debates searching for her Twitter account on Safari. He blocked her a long time ago, and at some point in the lead up to the trial, she retaliated by blocking him. But the last time Tom checked, her tweets were still public and could be viewed by simply leaving Twitter and using a search engine. It wouldn't hurt to see what she was saying, would it? He opens Safari and begins typing her name into the tool bar. Then common sense prevails and he places the phone face down on the kitchen counter.

Moments later there's a ping, so loud he almost drops his coffee. He glances up at the wall clock: 6.50 a.m. Nobody ever texts him this early in the morning. Anxiously, he reaches for the phone, half expecting a taunting message from his least favourite internet troll, telling him she knows he's been thinking of her. But no, it's last night's visitor, thanking him for a 'fun time' and suggesting they 'hook up' again soon. Funny, Tom doesn't recall giving the waiter his number. But he was pretty drunk last night, so he may well have done. He reads the message again, cringing at the faux Americanisms. He considers firing off a gently mocking reply, then decides against it. There's no need to respond now, if at all.

Draining his coffee, he feels the caffeine course through his veins and decides to go for a run. It'll help clear his head and burn off some of those empty calories. Decision made, he's feeling more positive already.

His mood darkens the moment he enters the bathroom. Catching his reflection in the mirror, he's dismayed at how rough he looks. His eyes are hollow, his skin ashen. Is it simply the hangover or lack of sleep or is this the cumulative effect of living the last year in a state of constant anxiety? Well, at least he can put all that behind him now. Assuming, of course, that Emma's assessment at yesterday's sentencing was correct.

Tom's whole body tenses as the thought of her brings last night's nightmare flooding back. He's in a strange room, in a house with floors the colour of dried blood. The walls are plastered with newspaper cuttings and hung with fairy lights, similar to the ones in Emma's garden. Against one wall there's a display case filled with framed family photographs, but on closer inspection Tom sees that all the photographs are of him. Here he is suited and booted at a book signing. And here he is in a vest and shorts, running beside the river. And the newspaper cuttings on the walls – they're all about him, too. The whole room is some kind of shrine. A chill runs though him. Is he dead or about to be killed?

There's a cold breath on his neck and suddenly Evie is there. He grabs her by both shoulders, shouting at her to stop. She laughs. 'I'll never stop, Tom. I'll never leave you alone. Never!' He pushes her against the wall, pinning her there with one hand and slapping her hard across the face. But she won't stop laughing. Blinded with rage, he hits her harder, first with his palm, then with the back of his hand, until his fingers sting and his knuckles are raw. And now it's no longer Evie he's hitting, but Emma. Her eyes are wide with fear and she's pleading with him. 'You have to stop this, Tom! Please! You're scaring me!'

Shaking the nightmare away, Tom runs the tap and splashes cold water on his face. What the fuck was that about? He's never hit a woman in his life. Did he fall out with Emma yesterday? He remembers that they were both pretty drunk, and that he was so eager for her to leave, he bundled her out of the restaurant and into a taxi as soon as she'd paid the bill. It's not just the hangover making him anxious. There's a pang of guilt, too. He shouldn't have sent her off like that, not when she'd been so generous.

Staring at his reflection in the mirror, Tom switches the water to hot and reaches for his shaving gel. Guilty feelings are another sign that a person's drinking is becoming a problem.

Lifting the razor to his face, he sees that his hand is trembling. That's another sign. Or maybe it's just tiredness.

A quick shave, a good run and he'll feel a whole lot better.

✳

Tom has been running all his life. As a small boy, he ran from the bullies who seemed instinctively to know there was something different about him, even before he did. As a teenager, he discovered the joys of cross-country running as a welcome alternative to the ritualised violence of rugby and other contact sports offered at school. And as a young man he ran as far from home as his exam results would take him, leaving the narrow confines of small-town South Wales and escaping to London, where the streets were paved with possibilities.

It was here that he finally gave himself permission to explore his sexuality. It was the mid-nineties. Bands like Placebo and Suede were channelling David Bowie and The Smiths, striking androgynous poses and singing songs about alienated outsiders and different kinds of love. Suede singer, Brett Anderson, even described himself as a bisexual who'd never had a homosexual experience. Tom had had no real sexual experience to speak of and rather fancied himself as someone similarly enigmatic. Yet despite his own claims of bisexuality, his brief period of experimentation soon led to the inescapable conclusion that he was gay.

Knowing this and accepting it were two different things, and for a while he struggled, alternating between periods of sexual abstinence and entire weekends lost in music and high on Ecstasy, rushing from one club to another in search of love or its nearest available substitute.

There was no Mr Right, Tom soon discovered. There was only Mr Right Now.

And then along came Aidan – the one-night stand who stayed for the best part of a year. Aidan was everything Tom thought he was looking for – tall, dark and handsome, with dazzling blue eyes and a smile that could charm the birds from the trees. He was also a compulsive liar who slept around, and left Tom humiliated and more heartbroken than he'd ever thought possible. The day he came home unexpectedly and caught Aidan in bed with another man, Tom lost all control and put his fist through the bedroom wall. He might have punched Aidan too had he not grabbed his things and beat a hasty exit.

Tom was never naturally trusting, even before Aidan. Growing up in a family where declarations of affection were rare, and resentments never far from the surface, Tom soon learned the value of self-reliance. What some saw as an air of superiority was actually a coping mechanism; one which had stood him in good stead – most of the time, at least. He dropped his guard when Aidan came along. After he left, Tom swore that nobody would ever hurt him like that again. He joined a gym and developed the kind of hard, ripped body he'd often admired and now wore as a kind of armour. He cleaned up his act and threw himself into his work. And still he ran. Sometimes it felt as if it was the only thing keeping him sane.

It was around this time that Tom's parents started alluding to his 'London ways' – meaning his love of culture and the air of detachment he assumes whenever they're forced together at family occasions. What they fail to have noticed is that he's been like this for most of his life. These days, communication between Tom and his parents is rare and strictly limited to safe subjects. They never enquire about his personal life and he never brings it up. He hasn't even told them about the court case. They wouldn't understand and he already knows what his father would say: 'Bullied by a woman? What the hell's wrong with you, man?'

If he only knew.

✦

Outside, the early-morning sun is bright and the streets are filled with rush-hour commuters, milling their way towards Vauxhall Station. Soon they'll be packed onto busy buses or crowded trains or sweltering on the underground with their face jammed against someone's armpit. Tom takes a moment to ponder his good fortune. He's never had a nine-to-five job, has always been his own boss. There's insecurity in being freelance, but there's freedom too. However challenging his day may be, at least he's spared the indignity of the daily commute.

Looking up, he watches a few clouds scurry across the sky, driven by a light wind coming off the river. He reaches into his shorts pocket for his earbuds and selects a playlist on his iPhone. A few stretches and he's off, heading down to the Thames, then turning right and following the path that leads eastwards, past the MI6 building and along the Albert Embankment towards Waterloo. It's not his usual route. Normally, he runs in the opposite direction, westwards towards Battersea. But for some reason, today he feels the pull of the South Bank with its theatres and street markets and concert halls. Maybe later he'll stop and see if they're still stocking his books in Foyles, then grab a coffee at Starbucks.

He settles into a familiar rhythm, feet pounding the pavement in time to the music, the anxieties of earlier lifting away. Tom has experienced many highs – the thrill of sex, the rush of drugs, the first flush of success – but nothing compares to the high he gets from running. He's addicted to it the way some people are addicted to cocaine, but with the added bonus of knowing it won't empty his wallet or turn him into an egocentric bore. He loves the Zen-like meditative quality of running, the way it makes him conscious of each breath, how it helps clear his mind. Even in a busy city street it's possible for him to zone out and focus. And there's nothing like the rush of endorphins to lighten his mood and chase the dark thoughts away.

There are surprisingly few other runners along today's route – just the odd one or two, who exchange nods as they go by, breaking the Londoner's code of conduct out of a shared sense of being not quite like other people. Tom pauses to take a quick drink from his water bottle. He can feel last night's cigarettes on his chest and promises himself there'll be no more. Then he's off again, the sweat trickling down the small of his back as he picks up speed.

More people start to appear as he approaches the Southbank Centre – fellow runners, tourists with backpacks, people in business clothes with styrofoam cups of coffee and tense expressions, barking into their phones as they elbow their way through the crowds. This is London in a microcosm – busy, diverse, frenetic to the point of rudeness. Tom dodges and weaves his way through knots of people, careful to avoid colliding with anyone, ignoring the frowns and tuts from those who think they own the pavement.

An old song begins to play on his iPhone – 'Pure Shores' by All Saints, from the soundtrack to *The Beach*. He glances to his left, sees the sunlight reflecting off the river, and immediately wishes he was in Hastings. He'd mentioned the idea to Emma – he remembers that now. He said he was going there to write. But he hadn't told her the whole story. Tom has an ulterior motive for visiting Hastings. It's not quite a plan, not yet. But he wants to consider his options. There are possibilities to be explored and decisions to be made – and Hastings may hold some of the answers.

He's visited the town once before – many years ago, on a school trip. He'd have been ten at the time. He remembers his history teacher explaining that the Battle of Hastings actually took place several miles away in a place known as Battle. But Tom wasn't really bothered about that. He remembers the oily, black fishermen's huts, and the brightly painted boats pulled up onto the gravel beach. He remembers the sky, all pinks and yellows, like an oil painting. And he remembers the sea, so much bluer and more inviting than the grey, choppy waters back home in Wales. It was like being abroad, or how his ten-year-old self imagined abroad to be.

He smiles to himself, lost in the memory. Then something catches his eye – a familiar face up ahead, half obscured by passersby. His skin prickles. It can't be, can it? But as he draws closer the crowd parts and he sees her. She's sitting on a bench at the side of the path, facing out towards the river, her hands folded neatly in her lap as if she's waiting for someone. She's dressed in a familiar pale-blue military-style jacket. Beside her on the bench is a large bag for life with the Foyles bookshop logo. Her head is bowed, but as he approaches she raises her eyes and stares straight at him. Evie Stokes.

Tom's breath catches in his throat. He feels a sharp stab of anxiety in his chest. All at once, the world seems to tilt away.

What is she doing here? It can't be a coincidence, can it? Did she follow him?

His rational mind tells him to keep running, look straight ahead, pretend she isn't there. But he isn't feeling very rational. His legs still move but his upper body twists as he cranes his neck to get another look. Then the wind is knocked out of his lungs, and the music stops as his earbuds are pulled from his ears and the ground comes hurtling up to meet his face.

11

For a few moments there's just blackness, shock and the burning feeling of humiliation. He's face down on the ground, one arm folded beneath him, numb with pins and needles. Then his vision clears and a voice echoes in his ear:

'Sorry, mate. Are you okay?'

Tom thinks he detects an accent – possibly South African, more likely Australian. He lifts his head and sees a pair of bright-red trainers. Then a man's hand reaches down to him. There's a Fitbit on his wrist and a muscular forearm glistening with sweat.

'I didn't see you,' the man says. 'I mean, I saw you coming towards me, obviously. But then you sort of dodged in front of me, and I wasn't expecting it and ... well, sorry.'

The man helps Tom to his feet. Automatically, Tom looks towards the bench. It's empty. Did he imagine seeing Evie sitting there? Is his mind playing tricks on him?

'Are you okay?' the other man asks. 'There's nothing injured, is there?'

'Just my dignity.' Tom forces a smile. He feels dwarfed by the other man's stature. He's well over six foot and has one of the broadest chests Tom has ever seen. Thick blond hair and sharp blue eyes complete the picture, putting Tom in mind of Chris Hemsworth as Thor.

'I'm fine, really,' he adds, ignoring the pain in his right knee. 'It's me who should be apologising to you. I don't know what's wrong with me today. I don't make a habit of bumping into strange men.' It's probably shock, or nerves, but the words blurt out before he can stop them. He feels himself flush with embarrassment and hopes it isn't visible.

Thor suddenly seems eager to get away. 'No problem,' he says quickly. 'So long as you're okay.'

'I am.'

'Right, well, see you around.'

Tom watches as he turns away and is soon neck deep in a sea of people, blond head bobbing above the crowd. He pats himself down. His keys are still in his zipped back pocket, together with the £20 note he always carries in case of emergencies. But his iPhone must have fallen when he lost his footing. Frantically, he scans the ground around him, panic rising in his chest. The whole of his life is on that phone – emails, texts, social media, even a banking app. Losing it would be a nightmare.

What if it isn't lost? What if Thor collided with him on purpose? Thieves often operate in areas like this. Anywhere there are crowds of unsuspecting people is a haven for pickpockets. And he was so distracted, he must have looked like the ideal target. He might just as well have had a sign written above his head. Tom cranes his neck to see if Thor's head is still visible, but of course he's long gone.

He feels a tap on his shoulder and spins round. Standing behind him is a bearded man in a filthy overcoat. By the looks – and smell – of him, he's one of the many homeless people who make their beds from cardboard boxes in doorways and under railway arches along the South Bank. He doesn't appear to be in too decrepit a state, though it's impossible to gauge his age beneath the caked dirt and fuzzy facial hair.

'Sorry,' Tom says, shaking his head. 'I can't help you today.'

The man looks wounded. 'I wasn't asking you for help.'

'So what do you want?'

'I just wanted to give you this.' He holds out his hand. The fingernails are long and yellow, and clutched in his palm is Tom's iPhone, the earbuds still attached. Relieved, Tom takes it and inspects the phone for damage. There's a slight crack on the top left-hand corner of the screen. But apart from that it appears to be in working order.

'Thanks,' Tom says, remembering his manners. 'And sorry for, y'know...'

'I saw it fly,' the man says. 'When you and the blond man collided. It landed right next to me. You're lucky it didn't land in the river. I've

seen a few things land in the river. Phones. Bags. No bodies, though.'
He gives a meaningful look, as if he's divulging some great secret.

'Right,' says Tom. 'So you saw all this happen. Where were you?'

'On my bench.'

Tom's skin prickles. 'Which bench?'

The man turns and points. 'That one.'

The bench where Tom thought he saw Evie.

'I sit there all the time,' the man continues. 'I like to watch the people go by.'

'Was there a woman sitting there?'

'Where?'

'On that bench. A few moments ago. Before I fell.' Tom feels his voice rising. 'Blonde hair. She was wearing a blue military-style jacket. And she had a bag, one of those bags for life. It had the logo for Foyles bookshop.'

The man considers this for a moment, scratching his bearded cheek with one hand. 'I haven't been in a bookshop for years. I used to love reading. Y'know, before.'

'And the woman?'

The man shakes his head. 'I didn't see any woman. Not on my bench. I think I'd remember. It's not often a young woman sits next to me. Most people act like I'm not even here.'

Tom feels a pang of social conscience and softens his tone. 'Well, thanks for returning the phone.'

The man shows no sign of moving. He smiles again and cups his hand. 'I don't suppose you could help me out, could you?'

Tom reaches into his pocket for some change, remembering too late that he only has a twenty-pound note. His fingers curl around it and he hesitates for a moment. But what choice does he have? 'Here,' he says, thrusting the note into the man's hand.

The man's smile widens, revealing black and broken teeth. 'Thank you. That's very kind of you.'

'You're welcome,' Tom replies. 'But please don't squander it on, well, whatever. Get yourself something to eat.'

The man winks. 'Course I will. Now you have a good day, and I hope you sort things out with your lady friend.'

Tom forces a grin and pockets his phone. Dusting himself off, he sees that both his knees are grazed and the heel of his right hand and much of his forearm is badly scraped where he reached out instinctively to break his fall. The skin on his hand is torn and there are already signs of bruising. He's lucky he didn't break his wrist. And all because he thought he saw that bloody woman!

He stretches and tests his knee. There's some pain, but nothing he can't handle. But there's no point in running any further, not if there's a chance of injury. All things considered, he escaped lightly. Really he should be counting his blessings.

As he starts walking back in the direction of Vauxhall, he wonders if he should phone the police. And tell them what exactly? That he thought he saw Evie. He can imagine what the response would be.

Tom sighs. He's had enough of police statements and court proceedings to last him a lifetime. Maybe he didn't imagine it. Maybe she really was there. But even if it's true, where does that leave him? Technically speaking, she might be in breach of her restraining order. If it can be proved that she'd followed him. If there's sufficient evidence of stalking. But what are the chances of that? And how long would it take to go to court? Another six months? A year? Tom doesn't want to put his life on hold for another twelve months. He just wants things to go back to normal, the way they were before he'd heard the name Evie Stokes. That crazy bitch has already taken up more than enough of his time. He needs to move on.

He feels a drop of rain and looks up. The sky has clouded over, though nothing too ominous. A passing shower, probably. His mind turns again to Hastings. The sooner he can get away, the better. The weather forecast for the south coast is promising, and it'll be good to put some distance between himself and the city he calls home but where so many things have gone wrong lately. He loves London, but it no longer feels safe. What if last night's dream was a warning? What if she never stops stalking him? He's afraid, not just of her but of himself – of what he might do.

Tom has only really lost his temper on two occasions. The first time was in his final year at school. One of the boys who'd bullied him since day one had a brother who was younger and slightly smaller than Tom but was keen to prove himself to the others by having a go at him. Tom was queueing for the canteen one lunchtime when the boy sidled up with a smirk, called him 'queer' and challenged him to a fight. Usually Tom would do anything to avoid a confrontation, but that day something in him snapped.

'Okay,' he said. 'You go first.'

The boy looked at him in surprise.

'Go ahead,' Tom said. 'Hit me.'

Grinning, the boy formed a fist and punched Tom in the face. And for the next few minutes Tom saw red. He has no recollection of what happened. The next thing he knew, the boy was flat on his back, and Tom was straddling his chest, pinning both arms to the ground with his knees and punching the boy's head repeatedly as a crowd gathered around.

A friend had grabbed him from behind, pulling him off with cries of, 'He's had enough!' After that, the school bullies left Tom alone.

The second time he lost his temper was with Aidan. He prefers not to think about it. Under the circumstances, his anger seemed justified. But later he was filled with remorse. He doesn't want there to be a third time.

And there needn't be, he assures himself. He just needs to unwind. A change of scenery will make a world of difference, and Hastings ticks all the right boxes. He'll find a place on the seafront, overlooking the ocean. He'll wake up early and go for his morning run along the promenade, filling his lungs with fresh sea air. Then he'll sit for hours over his laptop, cracking on with the new book. He'll enjoy a light lunch at some seaside café and spend the best part of the afternoon exploring the coastline or simply lying on the beach and reading. How long has it been since he's fallen asleep in the sun with a good book? Then back to his desk for another few hours writing before calling it a day and making plans for dinner.

The more he thinks about it, the more convinced Tom becomes. He needs to get away from London as soon as possible. And as if to prove the point, there's a sudden change in the air, followed by a crack of thunder and the first proper rainfall there's been in weeks. He's wet within minutes.

✼

By the time he arrives home, he's soaked to the skin. Approaching his building, he's struck how empty the wet streets are compared to a few hours earlier. There's not a soul in sight. But then the silence is shattered as a delivery van turns the corner and comes screeching to a halt outside his building. A spotty youth in a red-and-yellow branded T-shirt leaps out and runs to the door of the building, ducking his head as if that offers some protection from the downpour. Under one arm he carries a large cardboard box. He presses a buzzer and waits for a few minutes before turning and smiling hopefully at Tom.

'Alright, mate,' he says. 'I've got a package here for a Tom Hunter, only no-one's answering. You wouldn't mind signing for me, would you?'

Tom smiles back. 'Not at all. I'm Tom Hunter.'

He signs for the package, swipes his key card and hurries, dripping, through the marble-floored hall, up the first flight of stairs and into his apartment. As he closes the door firmly behind him and places the parcel on the kitchen counter, he has the distinct feeling that someone has been here in his absence. The air in the room feels different somehow, as if it has been displaced by the movement of another human being in a space usually occupied by one. But Tom's cleaner isn't due for another two days, and his dirty coffee cup is still in the sink. There's no sign of a break-in, no indication that anything is missing. One of the main selling points of the place was just how secure it is. Breaking in here would be like breaking into Fort Knox. If someone other than him has been here, they must have let themselves in. The only other person who has a key is Emma – and that's just for emergencies.

Tom fumbles in his pocket for his key card. Is it possible that someone could have cloned it, the way they use a hidden device to clone your bank card as they brush against you? He thinks again of the man he collided with at the South Bank. Was it all an elaborate set up? Then he remembers Evie. The woman who wasn't there. Never mind his key card. He's in danger of losing his mind.

He stares at the parcel and wonders who it's from. There's no card attached and no return address or company postmark. Sometimes he's sent proof copies of books in the hope of an enthusiastic quote, but the requests for endorsements have dwindled considerably since his last book bombed – and in any case the box is too big.

Gingerly, he picks at the packing tape until it peels away. Inside the box are layers of bubble wrap and foam peanuts. Buried deep inside is a bottle of Veuve Clicquot Yellow Label – the same champagne Tom polished off last night with the waiter. And there's something else, too – a familiar black box with the initials T.F. in silver lettering. Tom doesn't need to look any closer to know what it is – a bottle of his favourite cologne, Tom Ford Noir.

He searches again for a card, a note, anything to tell him who the parcel is from. Is it last night's sexual partner coming on too strong? First the early morning text message, now this. Luke would have spotted the cologne in the bathroom cabinet. Or could it be Evie Stokes, reminding him that she knows where he lives? Tom's heart races.

His phone rings and he almost jumps out of his skin. 'Hello?'

'Tom? Darling, are you alright?'

'I'm fine,' he replies, struggling to steady his nerves, inspecting the outside of the box for a return address.

'You don't sound it,' Emma says. 'You sound strange. You haven't heard from that awful woman again, have you?'

Tom thinks of the nightmare that woke him in the dead of night. 'No. But if she starts on me again, I swear I won't be responsible for my actions.'

'You don't mean that.'

'Don't I?'

'We're always responsible for our own actions,' Emma says. 'But I'm sure it won't come to that.'

'What if it does? What if she turns up at my flat again?'

'Tom, has something happened?'

He thinks before responding. 'No.' Tucking the phone under his chin, he makes his way into the bedroom, where he peels off his damp running gear and slips on his bathrobe.

'Tom?'

'Sorry, I'm just about to jump in the shower.'

'Then I won't keep you. I've had a text from the courier company to say my little surprise has arrived.'

Finally it dawns on him. 'It's from you? The care package?'

'Who else? I know your tastes better than anyone!'

Not all of them, Tom thinks. 'Of course you do!'

He wanders back into his bedroom and is surprised to see his laptop, open on his bedside table. Strange, he can't remember using it last night. Sometimes he'll wake in the middle of the night and write something straight onto the computer before it slips his mind – a telling phrase, a snatch of dialogue. It's quite possible that in his drunken stupor he did the same last night. He sits on the edge of the bed and taps the touch bar on the keyboard, bringing the screen back to life. The screensaver is a photo of him on the red carpet at Leicester Square for the premiere of the film based on his first book. He looks flushed – and he was. Flushed with success. Flush with excitement. Funny how things change.

'Em?' he says. 'You didn't pop over and let yourself in here earlier, did you?'

'What? No, of course not. Why would I?'

'To check I hadn't died of alcohol poisoning in my sleep?'

'I'm your friend, not your nursemaid. Besides, I was too busy sleeping off my own hangover to worry about yours. Why do you ask?'

Tom pauses, distracted by the ping of an incoming email. 'Forget it. My head's all over the place today.'

'Are you sure you're okay? You sound a bit odd.'

'I'm fine.' Tom opens the email and smiles to himself. It's from his mortgage provider, confirming an evaluation for tomorrow. 'Better than fine,' he adds, thinking of all the cash locked up in his property and how much easier life could be if he released some of it.

'I'm pleased to hear it. So when are you off to Hastings?'

'Soon.'

'I can keep an eye on things, if you like. Come and water your houseplants.'

'I don't have any houseplants. Everything I touch dies.'

Emma laughs. 'Not quite everything.'

'I'm fine, Em,' Tom says. 'Really. And thanks again for the gifts. That was sweet of you. But I really need to go now. I'll speak to you soon.'

And without waiting for her response, he ends the call.

12

DAY 4 (726 DAYS REMAINING)

My therapist thinks I should keep a journal. You have an agent – I have a court-appointed psychotherapist. I imagine they serve a similar function – at least in terms of encouraging us to write. She looked so pleased with her suggestion that I didn't have the heart to tell her I've been writing one for years. Or maybe I was just keeping my cards close to my chest. I guess she'll never know, will she?

My therapist is one of those hideously empathetic women who smiles a lot as she speaks, and tilts her head and nods slowly as you answer. I think I'm supposed to find this reassuring. In fact I find her patronising. She arrived at our first meeting carrying a small desk clock and a large mug of herbal tea and wearing open-toed sandals. I noticed that her feet were in dire need of a pedicure. As she talked, she kept dunking the teabag in her tea, which I found even more distracting than the state of her feet.

She introduced herself as Maria and asked if there was anything I wanted to say. There was a lot I could have said: 'Why are you making such a public display of those toenails?' or 'What does that teabag represent to you?' But as I'm here under duress and determined to volunteer as little as possible, I kept my thoughts to myself.

She offered me a cushion. I told her my chair was quite comfortable, thank you.

'I meant for you to hold,' she said. 'Some people find it comforting.'

How old did she think I was? Five? 'I'm not some people,' I replied and tossed the cushion on the floor.

'I understand that this can be difficult.' She opened a drawer and took out a box of tissues. 'Perhaps it would help if you were to think of these sessions as a safe space for you to explore your feelings. Anything you say here is completely confidential.'

That made a change from, 'anything you say may be given in evidence'. I thanked her for the vote of confidence and assured her that, should I ever decide to explore my feelings, she'd be the first to know. 'And we won't be needing those,' I said, indicating the box of tissues. 'Unless you have a cold, of course.'

'I'm sensing a certain amount of hostility,' she said, proving that her education wasn't entirely wasted.

'I'm not really a fan of safe spaces,' I replied. 'Life isn't safe. The best things in life certainly aren't safe.' I wanted to say that I wasn't really a fan of therapy either. That I was only doing this to keep the powers that be happy. But I didn't.

Maria gave me one of her smiles. 'And what do you consider to be the best things in life?'

'Ideas,' I said. 'Books.' Then, just to see her squirm, 'Sex.'

By now it was pretty obvious that this wasn't going the way she'd planned, so I suppose she's to be admired for sticking to her guns.

'Have you ever had any kind of therapy before?' she asked.

'No,' I lied, remembering the time my father dragged me along to see someone when I was twelve, and what a complete waste of time and money that turned out to be.

'And what about your parents?'

'I think they went for couples counselling a few times.'

'No, sorry.' Maria tilted her head. 'I meant, what's your relationship with them like?'

'There isn't a them,' I said. 'There's just a him. She fucked off years ago.'

'I see. And was that very difficult for you?'

'Not at all. We were never close.'

'Why do you think that was?'

I was tempted to say something flippant at this point: 'She'd have preferred a boy she could vent her feminist rage on' or 'she never forgave me for ruining her figure'. But instead I just smiled sadly, as if the memory was too painful to even think about. Therapists like to see pain. It makes them think they're getting somewhere.

We talked about my dad next. And even though I was far more forthcoming about him than I had been about my mother, and I noticed that Maria wrote things down in her notepad, I had the distinct impression that she was far less interested in him than she was in her. My mother would have loved that. She always liked to be the centre of attention. On the rare occasions that I think of my mother, she's always mid-sentence and happily holding court, oblivious to the fact that nobody else has spoken in quite a while. And if by some miracle some poor sod is able to get a word in edgeways, she'll allow them a brief moment in the spotlight before steering the conversation back to her favourite subject – herself.

'And what about you?' Maria asked.

I sniggered. 'I don't have kids.'

'Would you like to?'

'Not particularly.' It's sad, I think, that women still define themselves in term of their capacity to breed. All those yummy mummies and their cupcake feminism make me sick to the stomach. I see them in East Dulwich all the time, blocking the streets with their enormous buggies, meeting at Starbucks or Caffè Nero to get their caffeine fix and fill their empty days with inane chatter. But I didn't say so. I figured I'd said enough already. If my therapist wanted any more from me, she'd have to work for it.

To give Maria her due, she's not afraid of hard work. I don't know how many times she tried to crack me during that first hour we spent together, how many tactics she employed. I was exhausted just watching her. She asked about my relationship history. I told her it was none of her business. She asked about my work history. I told her to look on LinkedIn.

'Do you find that useful?' she asked.

'I never use it.'

'You use Twitter, though.'

'For my sins.'

'Tell me about Twitter. What do you use it for?'

'Killing time, mostly. Same as everyone.'

'And do you still use it now?'

I'd have been lying if I'd said 'no'. 'Sometimes,' I said. 'When I'm bored.' I reached into my pocket for my phone and made a show of checking the screen.

'Can I make a suggestion?' Maria asked.

'It's a free country,' I replied – graciously overlooking the fact that, thanks to you, my personal freedom has been somewhat curtailed of late.

'Sometimes a good way to deal with negative emotions is to write letters to the people who inspire them,' she said. 'And then burn them.'

'Great,' I replied. 'But what should I do with the letters?'

She looked rather alarmed at that, as if she truly thought I was some kind of pyromaniac. Immediately I pictured a bonfire of the vanities – not the satirical novel by Tom Wolfe but the actual burning of objects that might lead one into temptation, as sanctioned during the Renaissance. In my mind's eye, I pictured you strapped to a chair at the top of the pyre, flames licking at your skin as you begged for forgiveness. My kind of guy.

'Forget the letters,' Maria said. 'What about a journal?' To hear her speak, you'd think she was the first person ever to suggest such a thing. 'I think you'll find it helpful,' she added. 'It will help organise your thoughts.' As if thoughts need organising the way wardrobes do.

Here's a thought: I don't think Maria's wardrobe is very organised. Her look is arty charity shop, although as she's painfully middle class I'm sure this is merely an affectation. She could probably afford a personal shopper if she wanted one. But I don't get the impression that she takes clothes very seriously or looks after them particularly well. I don't think she assembles her outfits so much as throws them together from whatever items of clothing she finds strewn around her room. Maybe she thinks people are more likely to open up to someone who looks a bit of a mess.

I wonder what your wardrobe is like? Very organised, I imagine

– like Richard Gere's in *American Gigolo* or Christian Bale's in *American Psycho*. Interesting, isn't it, how popular culture's idea of taboo masculinity went from gigolo to psycho in just a few years? Even today, there's the suspicion that men who pay that much attention to their appearance aren't to be trusted – which just goes to show how clever you were in court last month. But then, as I think we've established, you're a particularly cunning kind of male narcissist.

I must have been slow to respond to Maria's suggestion, because that eager smile she wears started to fade and she began to look like a supply teacher I once had – a woman so meek and mild she once spent the best part of a lesson locked inside a broom cupboard by a class of unruly eleven-year-olds.

'Sorry,' I said. 'You were saying?'

Her face lit up a little at that. Evidently she thought she was getting through to me. 'A journal,' she said.

'Well, if it was good enough for Genet,' I replied.

She looked at me blankly, as I knew she would.

'Jean Genet,' I said. '*The Thief's Journal*. Widely considered one of the great transgressive texts of the post-war period.'

Still nothing. Truth be told, I felt a little sorry for her at that point, so I smiled and said a journal was a wonderful idea and one I would act on immediately.

Relieved, she glanced at her little clock, announced that our time was up and said she looked forward to seeing me again at the same time next week.

'I wouldn't miss it for the world,' I replied. As if I had any choice in the matter.

※

One thing I've learned these past few weeks. You don't have a lot of choices when you're a convicted criminal. Apart from the various restrictions placed on me by the restraining order, here is a list of things I'm currently obliged to do:

- Attend therapy once a week for a minimum of twelve weeks;
- Inform the police of any travel plans, including but not limited to holidays;
- Prove to the world that I'm a good girl and won't bother the poor, defenceless little man any more.

Okay, so I might have made that last bit up. Still. I'm sure you'll agree that a lot of people would be seriously pissed off at this level of state interference in their daily life. And I confess there have been days when I've woken up seething with rage. I've lain in bed, staring up at the ceiling, fantasising about all the ways I can exact my revenge on you. I don't think it's an exaggeration to say that, at times, my thoughts have bordered on the homicidal. This is what you've reduced me to. I hope you're proud of yourself, Tom. Not only have you destroyed our relationship; not only have you taken away my right to free speech and seriously compromised my chances of future employment, but, thanks to you, I'm also entertaining thoughts of murder. And all for the 'crime' of taking an interest in you and your work. What is it people say – no good deed goes unpunished? Isn't that the truth?

But as that other old saying goes, don't get mad, get even. And this is what I intend to do, Tom. The restraining order forbids me from making contact with you, which is why I'm writing these words down but you won't see them. This is just me organising my thoughts, as my therapist would say. These are letters I'll never send, postcards that will never make it to the postbox, diary entries nobody but me will ever see. But what if they weren't? What if, even now, I have a cunning plan up my sleeve? Think about it, Tom. The restraining order only lasts for two years. After that I'm free to do what I like. Maybe I'll sell my story to a newspaper. Or maybe I'll write a book about my ordeal. Wouldn't that be ironic? Me getting a book out of this while you continue to struggle with yours.

You see, I wasn't joking when I referred my therapist to Genet's magnificent book *The Thief's Journal*. It's the book that cemented his reputation. And like all great autobiographies, it's a blend of fact and fiction, with a large dose of what we'd now call 'self-mythologising'. But that doesn't make it any less true. In Genet's world, the normal rules don't apply. Traditional values are turned on their head. Moral codes are inverted. Truth and justice are merely concepts. The outlaw becomes the hero. Petty crime is raised to a fine art.

This is the thing I love most about Genet's writing. This, and the fact that he refused to let a little thing like a custodial sentence stand in the way of his creativity. The book widely considered his masterpiece, *Our Lady of the Flowers*, was written entirely from the confines of a prison cell. Imagine that, Tom. No morning runs by the river for him. No literary lunches at the Groucho. And no laptop either. He wrote with a pencil, on pieces of brown paper issued to prisoners to make bags as part of their daily punishment. One day, while he and his fellow inmates were out exercising in the yard, a prison guard entered his cell, found the brown-paper manuscript and burned it. A lot of people would have given up at this point. Not Genet. He simply started again. Why? Because for him, writing was an act of defiance.

I know it's bad form to compare oneself to one of the greatest writers of the twentieth century, but I'm beginning to understand how Genet felt. You know me, Tom. I'm not one to mince my words. But I do appreciate their power, and the freedom they offer. I'm like Genet, alone in his cell – writing because I have to and because nothing else matters.

And this will be it – my little book of sorrows, my voyage of self-discovery, my ultimate triumph in the face of adversity. All about Evie. I'm thinking of calling it *The Troll's Journal* – partly out of respect for Genet and partly as a big fuck-you for all those disgusting, dehumanising things you said about me in court. I wonder what Genet would make of you. There he was – a sexual outlaw who defied social conventions and regarded the petite bourgeoisie with nothing short of contempt. And here you are. Petty. Bourgeoise. A man so bound by convention he runs to the police at the first sign of trouble. A writer so afraid of criticism he'd see an innocent woman go to prison for the crime of daring to disagree with him. Quite honestly, I think he'd hate you. And who could blame him?

I'm going to stop now. I don't think this is quite what my therapist had in mind when she suggested that I start keeping a journal. She talked a lot about forgiveness and making amends. She used words like 'healing' and 'letting go'. She said that I should own up to my mistakes – only then would I be able to move forward. But maybe I'm not ready to move forward. Or maybe my idea of moving forward is very different to hers.

How much further forward are you, I wonder? Have you let go of the past, or are you still clinging onto it? The last time I saw you, the day I was sentenced, you looked just as consumed with anger as ever. Has this whole nasty business been a disappointment to you? Were you expecting more from your beloved criminal-justice system, a far greater punishment that the one meted out? We both know you have an exaggerated sense of your own victimhood. What would it take to make you happy? Would you rather I was placed before a firing squad? Or do you dream of seeing me hanged, drawn and quartered? Maybe it's you who should be seeing a therapist.

Joking aside, a therapist would probably do you more good than that agent of yours. If I heard you complain about her once I heard it a thousand times: 'She never calls me. She never takes me for lunch. She takes days to reply to my emails. I feel so neglected!' Poor you! But I bet she's still your agent, isn't she? You haven't moved on. You haven't dumped her the way you dumped me. And let's face it – I was far more use to you than she ever was.

Which reminds me. The other woman in your life – she of the high maintenance hair. The lovely Emma. I think I may have judged her too soon. I knew a girl a lot like Emma when I was at college. You know – expensive tastes; money to burn. One of those home-counties blondes. Her father was big in property and doted on her the way my dad dotes on me – but in a showy way, parading her around in designer clothes like she was an extension of his success. It was quite creepy, actually.

Anyway, one night I showed up at the student union in some outfit I'd bought on sale at Top Shop, and there she was – Miss Home Counties, surrounded with her usual entourage of girls cute enough to reflect well on her but not so good-looking that they posed a threat. She nudged the one nearest to her as she saw me approaching.

'You look great,' she said, flashing a smile that probably cost thousands. 'I wish I could carry off cheap clothes.'

Quick as a flash, I responded: 'I know. I'm very fortunate. Some people can spend a fortune on clothes and still look cheap.'

She weighed me up for a moment or two, then her smile widened. 'I like you,' she said, though I don't think she even knew my name at that point. 'I think we're going to be great friends.'

And the funny thing was, we were – for a while at least. Who knows? Maybe Emma and I will be, too. Stranger things have happened. Maybe I'll bump into her one day and she'll see the real me, not the person you made me out to be. People think chance encounters don't happen in big cities, that the odds against them are stacked too high, that there's safety in numbers. But they're wrong. When I moved to Manchester I thought I'd never see certain people again. I was wrong about that. And London's not that much bigger than Manchester, you know. Not really. It's just a series of villages. The same paths are crossed by people from all walks of life every day. And with social media it's easy to keep tabs on someone. All it takes is an enquiring mind.

So that's where I'm at, at the moment. I'm keeping an open mind, looking forward to new experiences, exploring new possibilities. These are qualities we should all aspire to, wouldn't you agree? I'm sure my therapist would. She's very big on personal growth is our Maria. It's good for one's wellbeing, she says. Only by breaking old habits and trying new things can we hope to move forward.

It isn't easy moving forwards, Tom. I know that better than most people. But sometimes you just have to put one foot in front of the other. You know how to do that, don't you?

13

As the train shudders to a halt and the automated voice announces that they've arrived at their destination, Tom leaps to his feet and reaches up to the luggage rack for his suitcase. Ten days after he told Emma of his plans, he's finally made it to Hastings. He dressed comfortably for the journey in cargo shorts and a polo shirt but the air-con is so strong that by the time the train was passing through Sevenoaks he had to place a zip top over his frozen knees, making him feel like an invalid and attracting knowing smirks from a group of workmen in paint-spattered overalls.

His mood wasn't helped by the woman across the aisle jabbering away on her phone at full volume, only pausing for breath when the train passed through a tunnel or the signal dropped out. At one point she complained that the journey was too bumpy for her to apply her makeup. 'I'm afraid I might poke myself in the eye!'

I think you'll find there's a queue, Tom thought, but said nothing.

Stepping off the train, he hoists his leather rucksack over his shoulders and pulls up the handle on his wheelie case. The rucksack contains his laptop, notebook and reading materials, and his case is filled with enough clothes and toiletries to last him a fortnight. If he decides to stay longer, he's been told the apartment is still available and has laundry facilities. The photos on the Airbnb website showed a stunning second-floor property, close to the pier, with sea views. He can already picture himself seated in the bay window, gazing out to sea, a cup of coffee at his side and his laptop open in front of him as the words flow from his fingers.

The remaining passengers disembarking the train at Hastings are a motley bunch. Tom spots several student types with arty haircuts and facial piercings, though most of their kind left the train a minute or two earlier at St Leonards Warrior Square. There are a few elderly couples in matching pastel outfits. And then there are the pirates. As the train pulled out of Tunbridge Wells, Tom heard someone say that today was Pirate Day in Hastings. Sure enough, by the time they reached Battle the carriage had filled with young men in pirate costumes. Tom watches as a group of fit-looking lads make their way along the platform and up the stairs ahead of him, laughing and jostling in their buccaneer boots, tight breeches, ruffled shirts and silk headscarves. If this is what Hastings has in store, he's confident he made the right decision.

Outside the station there are more people in pirate costume and others who are stubbornly refusing to enter into the spirit of things – grey-faced men in grubby sportswear, heavily made-up women in crop tops and Lycra leggings, all sucking furiously on their cigarettes.

Tom hasn't had a cigarette in five days. The craving is still there, together with the torment and self-loathing it brings. He hates himself when he smokes – really hates himself for it. Even as he tells himself that it's helping him to relax, he can feel the nicotine rushing though his body, making his pulse race. But he's determined to quit for good this time.

He reaches into his pocket for his phone – another addiction he needs to keep in check. The urge to check it every five minutes is always worse when he's away from home, as if the constant buzz of social media somehow makes him feel more grounded. In fact, the opposite is true. It only adds to his anxiety – much like cigarettes. Resisting the urge to check his Facebook and Twitter accounts, he slides the phone back into his pocket.

There's a bus stop and a taxi rank straight ahead, but the town centre and seafront aren't far and he feels like stretching his legs after the long train journey. He puts on his sunglasses and follows the flow of pedestrians past the picturesque fishing boat in the middle of the roundabout.

Crossing the road at the traffic lights, he heads past a Tesco Metro and a row of estate agents. Some of the names are familiar from the internet search he conducted before leaving London. He stops to take a closer look in one of the windows, and sees well-presented studio and one-bedroom flats for a fraction of what they'd cost in the capital. There's even a detached four-bedroom house for less than the price of a modest two-bedroom flat miles from the nearest tube. It's high on West Hill, with a landscaped rear garden and a sea view.

Tom's mind races. Until recently, he wouldn't have dreamed of leaving London. It's been his home for over two decades. But London today isn't the city it was twenty years ago. It's less forgiving and more violent. Knife crime is on the rise. Acid attacks aren't uncommon. Homophobia is ever present. Tom can feel the tension on the streets. How long before his luck runs out and he encounters an adversary far more dangerous than Evie Stokes? Maybe he should get out now while the going's good.

He could sell his flat in Vauxhall, pay off his mortgage, buy a house like this and still have enough cash left over for a small rental property or a decent-sized nest egg. But could he live in Hastings? He pictures himself at his writing desk in one of the upstairs rooms at the back of the house, overlooking the English Channel instead of the Thames; or sitting on the terrace at the end of a long sunny day, unwinding with a vodka and tonic. Sea views, fresh air and no more money worries. It sounds like a no-brainer. He makes a mental note to arrange some viewings as soon as possible.

By the time Tom reaches the seafront, there's not a cloud in the sky. The water glitters and stretches out before him, bottle green in some places and Mediterranean blue in others. The sense of being in a foreign country is accentuated by the light. You rarely see this quality of light in London. Maybe high up on Parliament Hill, but not down where Tom lives in Vauxhall. It has the golden luminescence he associates with places like the Italian Riviera or the Greek islands. Feeling the warm sun on his face, he heads right towards the pier.

What first strikes him is the sheer scale of it. A stark minimalist structure clad in reclaimed wood, it juts out over the sea like the deck of a great ship. Standing at what he imagines to be the ship's bow, Tom grips the handrail and gazes out across the water. Dotted here and there are windsurfers and small sailing boats, but compared to the hustle and bustle of city living, he might just as well be alone with his thoughts. He breathes deeply, filling his lungs with clean sea air, watching gulls glide effortlessly across the blue horizon. For the first time in months, he feels a weight lift from his shoulders. He could be anywhere. He could be anyone. King of the world! At least until the ship hits an iceberg and sinks.

Lowering his gaze, he watches the waves crash against the steel beams and enormous wooden supports left from the original structure. The beams are red with rust, the wooden piles rising up out of the sea, blackened and splintered with age. Some are studded with bent and broken metal bolts, like ancient weapons from some mythical battle or macabre totem poles for lives lost at sea. Tom spots a sign warning people not to jump off the pier and wonders what would possess someone to do such a thing. The average human body would die on impact long before it was dragged under by the tide, dashed against the steel beams or impaled on one of the wooden piles like some sacrificial offering to an angry sea god.

Memories of Saturday mornings watching Sinbad films flood Tom's mind as he reaches into his pocket for his phone. 'Guess where I am.'

'No idea.'

'I'll give you a clue. I'm all at sea.'

'Nope. None the wiser.'

'I've just taken a short walk on a long pier.'

Emma laughs. 'Lucky for you it wasn't the other way around. Unless you can walk on water.'

'Rumours of my divinity have been greatly exaggerated.'

'So how's Hastings?'

'Gritty. But not without its charms. The streets are littered with men dressed as pirates.'

'Poor you,' Emma says. 'It sounds perilous.'

'Nothing I can't handle. How about you? What are you up to?'

'Oh, you know – keeping busy. My life doesn't just stop when you disappear.'

'Ouch!' says Tom. 'You're not peeved with me, are you?'

'Why would I be peeved?'

'Because I'm beside the seaside and you're not.'

'Don't be silly! Anyway, I can't talk now. I'll call you later.'

'I'm busy later.'

'Tomorrow, then.'

'Fine.'

Pocketing his phone, Tom turns to face inland. Opposite the pier is the green-and-white awning of The White Rock Hotel. To his left is Warrior Square and further off in the distance he can make out Marina Court, the famous building that looks like a great cruise liner has crashed through the sea wall and up onto the promenade. His own home for the next few weeks is situated somewhere between The White Rock and Warrior Square.

He thinks he can see it from here – a tall terraced building painted a tasteful dove grey, sandwiched between two similar terraces in dark blue and pale yellow. It's only a five-minute walk at most. He grabs his bags and sets off.

✹

The apartment is even better than Tom imagined – high ceilings, huge rooms, flooded with natural light. Walking over to the enormous bay window, he stares down at the sea view below. The tide is out, revealing the wood and concrete groynes. They run down to the edge of the water at regular intervals, dividing the beach into sections, holding back the shingle and providing windbreaks for the lazy sunbathers who lie half buried, like birds nesting in the pebbles, or sit leaning back against the sun-baked wood.

There are fewer people than Tom was expecting, but then most of the tourists would be over by the Old Town, with its amusement arcades, fairground rides and crazy golf. This stretch of beach is fairly sparse in comparison – just the odd wooden kiosk and a concrete deco-style bus shelter, surrounded by palms. Tom watches as two young lads on skateboards speed along the promenade, dodging pedestrians and pursued by a small, overexcited dog.

Turning away from the window, he carries his bags into the bedroom, which is situated at the back of the property and is dominated by a large fireplace. Sash windows look out onto a small communal garden with a few plants in pots and a raised deck with a table and chairs. He unpacks his clothes and hangs them neatly in the wardrobe. Removing his shoes and spreading himself out on the king-sized bed, he wonders how many hours sleep he'll manage tonight. Four? Five? When Tom was studying English at university he read all about the creative benefits of sleep deprivation – Rimbaud and his 'derangement of the senses'; the romantic poets with their fanciful notions about insomnia being the gateway to new levels of consciousness. As he's discovered this past year, the reality is a little more prosaic. A life without regular, restorative sleep is a living hell.

The antidepressants his doctor prescribed might have helped regulate his sleep patterns, had he taken them. But despite what he told the police, the court and even Emma, he hadn't. The doctor had warned him that possible side-effects included headaches, nausea, weight gain and the loss of libido. For Tom, this was too high a price to pay. So each time he received a repeat prescription, he filed it away in his desk drawer, together with the unopened box of pills he'd collected from the chemist the day he broke down in his doctor's surgery. When it finally came to him giving his impact statement to the police, Tom did wonder if he'd be required to provide proof that he was actually taking the medication he'd been prescribed. But all they asked for was a letter from his GP.

Maybe he should have taken the pills. His anxiety levels rocketed in the weeks leading up to the court case, and he's still not quite himself. For months his mind has been turning in on itself, swirling around in an endless cycle of self-doubt and paranoia. Sometimes when he closes his eyes he's back in the witness box, being cross-examined by the defence. Contradictions trip from his tongue and beads of sweat break out on his forehead as the case against Evie Stokes falls apart and the judge tells her she's free to leave. Tom sees her trumpeting the news on Twitter, proclaiming her innocence, calling him a fraud and a liar. The words burn behind his eyelids – branding him, shaming him.

But none of this happened, he reminds himself. She was found guilty. There's a restraining order in place. She can't reach him now, even if she's willing to breach the order and risk a prison sentence. He's a long way from home, in a town where nobody knows him from Adam. His skin crawls at the thought. Adam and Evie. She'd love that.

The tightening in Tom's chest gives way to a yawn, catching him by surprise. It's his body crying out for sleep. But it's the middle of the afternoon. He's never been one for taking a siesta. On the rare occasion that he does nod off during the day – usually on holiday, usually on a sun lounger – he wakes feeling groggy and disoriented and lacking the motivation to do anything even remotely productive. Fine when you're on holiday. Not so fine when you have a book to deliver. Contrary to received wisdom, he doesn't find power naps the least bit empowering.

No, napping is for nanas, Tom thinks, swinging his legs off the bed and jumping to his feet. He'll sleep when he's dead. Time to take a shower and grab a bite to eat somewhere. Then he'll set off in search of a bar and possibly an adventure.

Well, it is Pirate Day, after all.

14

The website for The St Leonard describes it as 'gay friendly'. In Tom's experience, the chances of picking up in a gay-friendly pub are slimmer than in a good old-fashioned gay bar. On the other hand, it's fairly close by. According to Google Maps the pub is just ten minutes' walk from his current location. The St Leonard it is, then.

Heading along the seafront, Tom has the distinct feeling that he's on holiday. The sun has set but there are still people clustered around the beach bars at Warrior Square. Maybe it's the change of scenery or the moonlight reflecting off the water. Maybe it's the effects of the bottle of wine he polished off with dinner. But he feels more relaxed than he's felt in a long time.

The exterior of The St Leonard is painted a tasteful dark grey, with etched-glass windows. Entering the bar, Tom's eyes are immediately drawn to a large decorative anchor hung against an exposed brick wall – a little obvious perhaps, but in keeping with the general aesthetic, which is all shabby chic and quirky illuminations, reminiscent of similar venues in Hoxton.

The place is packed. There are more women than he was expecting or would prefer to see. Not that he doesn't enjoy women's company. He does, very much so. It's just that, contrary to popular belief, gay men and straight women don't always mix well. It's bad enough when gay bars are invaded by hen parties – as if gay men were some exotic species to be fawned over the way one might visit a petting zoo. But at least the hen parties are easily identifiable. Far worse are the lone women who take you by surprise, sidling up and assuming an intimacy that hasn't been negotiated and isn't welcome. Tom has come across these women before, back in his clubbing days – women who think that because gay men pose no sexual threat they can be treated as sex objects, with no thought for their personal autonomy. He even had a woman grab him by the balls one night at a club in Vauxhall. When he recoiled, she exclaimed scornfully, 'You're so gay!' 'Correct!' he replied. 'And this is a gay club. So show some fucking respect!'

Surveying the bar, Tom spots a number of rather alluring men dressed as pirates, seated with women who may or may not hold the keys to their hearts. Ah well, he thinks. Challenge accepted. Conscious of his own hypocrisy but confident that at least three pairs of eyes are quietly checking him out, he saunters over to the bar and orders a drink.

✘

An hour and three large vodka and tonics later, Tom's confidence is slowly ebbing away. Nobody has offered to buy him a drink, and not one of the men he spotted earlier has attempted to make conversation or even return a meaningful glance. They're too wrapped up in their female companions – quite literally, in some cases. Seated at the next table, one couple have their tongues rammed down each other's throats and are pawing at each other's clothing. The temptation to shout 'Get a room!' is overwhelming.

Surrounded by such blatant displays of heterosexuality, Tom begins to wonder just how gay friendly this place is. If there are any other gay men here, they're not exactly falling over themselves to make their presence felt. He drains his glass and is about to call it a night when someone catches his eye. A man dressed in full pirate regalia is standing alone at the bar, cradling a pint glass in one hand and staring intently in Tom's direction. He's well built and wears a red headscarf and tricorn hat with heavy dreads and thick black eyeliner, like Johnny Depp as Jack Sparrow. Snug breeches are topped with a large belt buckle and tucked into knee-high black leather boots, accentuating his sturdy thighs. A white ruffled shirt completes the look, open to reveal a muscular chest. There's something vaguely familiar about him, and it's not just the resemblance to a famous film character. His smile is knowing and, as he approaches, his walk reminds Tom of someone he knows.

'Can I ask you a personal question?' Johnny/Jack puts one heavily booted foot on the empty chair next to Tom and leans across the table with one elbow resting on his knee. He looks even better at close range, despite the ridiculous goatee.

Tom wishes he hadn't drunk so much and hopes it doesn't show. 'It depends how personal.'

The pirate pulls a cutlass from his belt and points it towards Tom's throat. 'Are you DFL?'

'You mean DILF?' Tom grins, eyeing the sword and reassuring himself that it isn't real. 'I'm not a dad. At least not as far as I know. But thanks for the compliment.'

The other man's expression is cold. 'I wasn't paying you a compliment. I know what DILF means – "dad I'd like to fuck". I asked if you were DFL – "down from London".'

Tom's smile freezes on his face. 'What makes you think that?'

The man doesn't answer the question. Instead he asks another. 'You're sure you're not FILTH? "Failed in London, trying Hastings"?'

Tom's skin prickles. 'What makes you think I'm from London?' He attempts a self-deprecating shrug. 'Is it that obvious?'

The man's heavily made-up eyes bore into him. 'You don't remember me, do you?'

Tom plays for time. The face is familiar but the setting is strange, and he's more than a little inebriated. 'No, sorry. Should I?'

'It's Luke,' the other man says. He lowers the cutlass and tugs at his beard, which comes away in his hand, leaving traces of glue around his mouth and jawline. 'We met a few weeks ago.'

'Of course,' Tom replies. 'Luke the waiter. I didn't recognise you under all that finery.'

The man smiles thinly. 'How many Lukes do you know?'

'One or two,' Tom says. Then, sensing his mistake, he adds quickly, 'But none as dashing as you. What are you doing here?'

'Visiting friends. You?'

'I'm here to write. How long are you staying?'

'I'm not sure yet. Maybe a week or so.'

Pleased at this sudden turn of events, Tom reaches to remove a glob of glue from the other man's chin.

Luke's hand shoots up and grabs his wrist. 'Not so fast!'

'You have something on your face,' Tom insists, and gently brushes it away, feeling the rasp of stubble under his fingers. 'There, that's better.' Suddenly self-conscious, he lowers his hand and changes the subject. 'So how have you been?'

'Since you kicked me out? Surviving.'

Tom feels his face flush. 'I didn't kick you out. Not exactly.'

'You did. But I may be willing to forgive you.'

'That's very big of you.'

'I've never had any complaints.'

'I'm sure you haven't.' Tom catches the other man's eye and feels a sexual charge pass between them. 'So, can I buy you a drink?'

'I'll have a tequila shot. But only if you join me.'

Tom shakes his head. 'I'm not good with tequila.'

'Who said anything about being good?'

'No, I know, but...'

'It's just a drink! It won't kill you!' Luke smiles. 'This is your chance to make it up to me, so stop being so difficult.'

'Right,' says Tom, and heads to the bar.

By the time he returns, Luke has his feet firmly under the table and is leaning back in his chair, legs spread, crotch thrust provocatively forwards, cutlass hanging at his side. He adjusts himself as Tom approaches and sits bolt upright with both elbows on the table, shirtsleeves rolled up to reveal muscular forearms.

'So what are you writing?' he asks after they've knocked back the shots.

Tom's throat burns from the tequila. 'A novel,' he croaks.

'What's it about?'

'I'd rather not say too much about it.'

'Why so cagey?'

'I'm not cagey. I'm just not ready to talk about it yet, that's all.'

'Fine,' says Luke. 'So what'll we talk about?'

'We could talk about why you called me FILTH just now.'

'It's just a thing people say down here. There's been a big influx of people from London, buying up property. Not everyone welcomes it.'

'I haven't "failed in London"', Tom says. 'I'm just here to—'

'Write,' Luke interrupts. 'You said. Message received, Mister Big-Shot Novelist.'

Tom frowns. 'What's going on?'

'I'm just messing with you. Lighten up.' Luke flashes a grin. 'You know what you need? Another tequila.'

Ignoring Tom's protests, he leaps to his feet and joins the throng of people waiting to be served at the bar, drawing admiring looks from most of the women and one or two of the men. For the first time since he arrived at The St Leonard, Tom is actually enjoying himself. He feels like the cat that got the cream.

'Listen,' he says as Luke returns and places the shot glasses on the table. 'I'm sorry about the other night. I'd had a bit too much to drink.'

'I remember. How are things with your lady friend?'

'Emma? She's fine. She knows what I'm like when the mood takes me.'

Luke gives him a meaningful look. 'If you say so. What's the deal with you two, anyway?'

'The deal?'

'Are you just friends? Friends with benefits? You're not married, are you?'

'Me and Emma?' Tom laughs. 'We're just friends.'

'Don't sound so surprised. It wouldn't be the first time a married man has come on strong to me at work.'

Tom smiles knowingly. 'Is that what I did? Come on strong?'

'You know you did.'

'I didn't hear you complain.'

'You didn't hear much of anything.'

'What's that supposed to mean?'

'Nothing,' Luke replies. 'Just a joke. Forget I said anything.'

But he doesn't look as if he's joking. Maybe it's the combination of wine, vodka and tequila sloshing around in his stomach, but Tom suddenly has the gut feeling that something isn't right. Did he mention to Luke that he was coming to Hastings? He can't remember. But him turning up like this seems like too much of a coincidence. And all those comments about failing in London. It's almost as if Luke knows more about Tom's personal circumstances than he's letting on.

'So where are your friends?' Tom asks.

'They went to buy cigarettes.'

'And left you here all alone?'

'I'm a big boy. I can look after myself.'

'But they live here?'

Luke frowns. 'Why all the questions?'

'Why are you being so evasive?'

There's a pause, then Luke says, 'You didn't reply to my text.'

'Didn't I?'

'You know damn well you didn't.'

'Sorry. I had a lot going on. But we're here now.'

'So we just pick up where we left off?'

Tom grins. 'That sounds like a plan!'

'I don't think so.' Luke stares at him for a moment. 'You don't remember, do you? The way you behaved that night. The way you spoke to me afterwards. You couldn't get rid of me fast enough. You made me feel like a piece of meat.'

Tom blushes. 'I'm sorry, I was—'

'Drunk? Yes, you said. That's still no excuse for the way you behaved.'

'Then why text me?'

Luke shrugs. 'I believe in second chances. I thought once you sobered up you'd realise what a dickhead you'd been. I was wrong.'

Tom's hackles rise. 'So what's all this about? If I'm such a dickhead? Buying me drinks. Flirting. Is this some kind of payback?'

Luke looks as if he's about to say something, then thinks better of it. 'Never mind. Enjoy the rest of your night.' He rises quickly from the table and disappears into the crowd.

As he watches the other man walk away, Tom is filled with regret – not only because he's no longer onto a sure thing, but also because he knows deep down that Luke is right. He did behave like a dickhead. He could have shown the man a little more respect, and would have done had he not been so drunk. Not for the first time, Tom asks himself whether his drinking is getting out of hand. And not for the first time, the nagging voice in his head tells him that it is.

Suddenly conscious of how drunk he is at this very moment, he takes a deep breath and is attempting to pull himself to his feet when a woman appears from nowhere and plonks herself heavily on his lap. Waving her glass at him, she sloshes white wine over his shirt. She emits a high-pitched giggle and pats the wet patch with one hand. 'Sorry, handsome!'

She places her wine glass on the table and turns in the direction of the bar. 'Chuck us a tissue,' she shouts to a group of men and women in pirate shirts and T-shirts. 'Lover boy has peaked too soon!'

Her friends cheer and laugh, egging her on like the chorus in a particularly bad musical.

'What do you think you're doing?' Tom snaps.

The woman adjusts her frilly white shirt, revealing a black lace bustier. 'What's it look like? I'm saying hello.' The lascivious look on her face suggests that she has more on her mind than a simple greeting. Her eyes are glassy with alcohol, her lips wet and puckered as if she's expecting a kiss.

'Get off me,' Tom says. 'I'm leaving.'

'But you can't leave now, darling,' the woman protests. 'We're just getting to know each other.'

She giggles again and drapes an arm around his neck.

'Do you mind?' Tom shrugs her arm away. 'I'm not your darling. And I'm not interested. I'm gay.'

'I don't mind at all, babes. I thought you were just, y'know, gay friendly.'

'Well, I'm not.'

'I can see that now, can't I? More of the gay, less of the friendly.' She roars with laughter at her own joke, displaying lipstick-smeared teeth.

'Would you please get off?'

The woman leers. 'Now you're talking!'

Tom looks around for some support, but all he sees are drunken faces delighting in his humiliation. The feel of the woman's backside on his lap makes him squirm with embarrassment, their intimate body parts separated by a few thin layers of fabric. A knot of anxiety tightens in his chest, pressing against his diaphragm and shortening his breath.

'Relax, mate!' a man calls out. 'Jenny's just being friendly!'

Pirate Jenny, Tom thinks. How bloody perfect.

'I'm not your mate,' he says and struggles to his feet, sending the woman sprawling. As she falls, her arm knocks over her wine glass, which rolls off the table and smashes next to her on the pub floor.

'That's not very nice, is it?' the man says, stepping forwards. He's bigger than Tom and wears an expression that says he's in no mood to be messed with. A bullet head sits on a thick neck with part of a tattoo creeping above his shirt collar.

'Sorry,' Tom says and reaches to help the woman.

She shrugs his hand away with a scowl. 'Fuck off!'

Her friends gather round. Two women help her to her feet while the man continues to stare hard at Tom. 'I think you owe the lady a drink.'

'What?' Tom gapes in disbelief. 'I didn't ask her to sit on me.'

Bullet Head glowers menacingly. 'Replace her drink, or I'll do a lot worse than sit on you.'

'You can't be serious.'

'Try me.'

'Leave it,' the woman snaps. 'He's not worth the trouble!'

It's clear from Bullet Head's face that he had no intention of leaving it. Tom feels a sharp pain in his chest. Is it heartburn from the tequila or is this what a panic attack feels like? He tries to speak but can barely catch his breath.

'It's okay,' a familiar voice calls out. 'I've got this.'

Tom is relieved to see Luke walking toward him, a glass of wine in one hand.

'White wine, wasn't it?' Luke says, and presents it to the woman with a smile and a courtly bow. 'Sorry about my friend,' he adds, shooting a warning look in Tom's direction. 'He's down from London.'

Tom smiles tightly.

Bullet Head hesitates, then rolled his eyes. 'That explains it. Your mate needs to learn some manners.' Still frowning, he ushers the women away, leaving Tom and his rescuer alone.

'You're back,' Tom says. 'My hero!'

'Just in time, by the look of things.'

'I don't think I've been so glad to see someone since, well, since I spotted you earlier.'

Luke doesn't react.

'What do I owe you for the wine?'

'Nothing. It's on me.'

'Some of it's on me.' Tom grins, indicating the wet patch on his shirt. 'But you're okay?'

'I am now. At least let me buy you a drink. Or come back to mine for a nightcap. I'm staying on the seafront, close to the pier.'

'Thanks, but no,' Luke says. 'Will you be alright getting home? Maybe you should call a cab.'

Tom tries to hide his disappointment with a playful smile. 'You can escort me, if you like. Make sure I'm tucked up safe and sound.'

Luke stares back at him for a moment. 'Can I give you a piece of advice?'

'It sounds like you're about to.'

'Try to treat people a little better. Trust me. These things have a habit of catching up with you.'

They already have, Tom thinks, but says nothing.

※

Outside, the air is surprisingly cool. Tom takes a few moments to get his bearings, his head cloudy from all the alcohol. Somewhere in the distance he hears raised voices and the screech of a car braking, but he sets his sights on the seafront and half walks, half lurches down the hill.

The need to urinate grows stronger as he walks, but he tries not to think about the pressure on his bladder, focussing instead on the road ahead. There's hardly a soul around. The seafront, where people made merry earlier, is deserted. The tide is high and a cool night wind is blowing off the black sea.

Crossing the road at Warrior Square, Tom spots a corner shop with the lights still on. Remembering that he needs milk, he pops inside and buys a pint, together with a packet of peanuts and a chocolate bar to satisfy his sudden sugar craving. The temptation to ask for a pack of cigarettes is strong, but he manages to resist. He pockets the peanuts for later and devours the chocolate as he walks, savouring the combination of fat and sugar, the satisfying, cheap sweetness. He'll make up for it in the morning with a good long run.

Something sparkles on the pavement up ahead – a piece of mirror, glinting in the moonlight. Immediately Tom's eyes are drawn to a parked car, its wing mirror smashed, the rubber casing hanging off. That must have been quite a clip, he thinks.

A little further on he sees another car in a similar state – and then a third, and a fourth. Clearly this was no accident. He pictures a drunken youth – or more likely a gang – cycling or skateboarding along the pavement at high speed with baseball bats, smashing car mirrors as they go. He imagines the damage a baseball bat can do – a broken mirror here, a fractured skull there. Suddenly the area doesn't feel so safe after all.

Tom plunges his hand deep into his pocket and bunches his house keys firmly in his fist. If someone jumps him, at least he'll be in with a fighting chance. Picking up his pace, he's back inside the flat within minutes.

15

DAY 11 (719 DAYS REMAINING)

So it transpires that last week's journal entries aren't quite what my therapist had in mind. I know this because she told me so. I didn't hand it in for her to mark, of course. It's not homework! But we talked about it at today's session.

I arrived early to show willing. It's only a short bus ride from my house to the ugly redbrick building where she practises, but I allowed plenty of time and was sitting patiently in the waiting room by 10.40 a.m. At 11.00 a.m. on the dot the door to one of the consulting rooms opened and there she was in her sandals and strange, mismatched outfit, cradling her mug of herbal tea. I hadn't seen anyone go in or come out of the room, so I can only assume she'd kept me waiting on purpose. I read somewhere that therapists like to impose structure, though if you ask me there's a fine line between imposing structure and being a control freak.

'How are you feeling today, Evie?' Maria asked as I sat down. 'You seem calmer.'

I wasn't feeling particularly calm but I played along anyway. 'Yes, I do feel calmer,' I said. 'Writing the journal has really helped.'

She looked pleased with herself, but as I reported back on last week's entries I saw her smile fade. 'I think there's been a misunderstanding,' she said. 'The whole point of you keeping a journal is for you to have someone else to direct your thoughts to. Someone other than him.'

By 'him' she meant you – or as I'm now obliged to write, You Know Who, or He Who Shall Remain Nameless. Then she started talking about transference.

I told her I thought that was when a patient developed a crush on their therapist, but she soon corrected me, explaining that transference has many meanings, including 'the redirection of feelings and desires unconsciously retained from childhood towards a new object'.

'I see,' I said. 'So what you're saying is that my feelings for, er, him are really about my father.'

'Not exactly.'

'Good. Because my dad is nothing like that.'

'Maybe that's something we can explore later,' Maria said, dunking her teabag. 'For now I'd like us to focus on your journal and why you feel the need to write as if you were writing to Mr Hunter. It's not as if he's ever going to read it, is it?'

'That depends,' I said.

'Does it?' Suddenly I had her undivided intention. 'On what?'

'On whether it becomes a bestseller or not.'

It took her a moment to realise that I was joking.

'I'm not a total idiot,' I assured her. 'I know I'm not supposed to have any contact with the gentleman in question.' I stressed the word 'gentleman' with a hint of irony, the subtlety of which seemed to escape her.

'Even so,' she said. 'I think it would be helpful if you were to address your thoughts to someone else. An imaginary friend, perhaps. Or your younger self.'

And there was I, thinking therapy was supposed to help straighten me out! 'Imaginary friend?' I replied. 'Talking to myself? I'm not a complete basket case!'

'I'm not suggesting that you are,' Maria said. 'How about "dear diary"?'

I laughed. 'I'm not an Edwardian lady either!'

But I knew what she meant. She doesn't want me writing to the architect of my destruction. She doesn't want me repeating the patterns of behaviour that got me into this mess in the first place. No more writing to He Who Must Not Be Named – even if I have no intention of sending my scribblings his way. No more thoughts directed at You Know Who. Fine. I get it. And I'll do as she says. I'll address my thoughts to my imaginary reader. But don't expect me to write like a neurotic teenager or some sad singleton. This isn't *Bridget Jones's Diary*. I won't be counting calories or units of alcohol. I won't be keeping a record of how many fags – sorry, cigarettes! – I've had. I may count the days since my sentence was passed, or the hours I spend thinking about He Who Did Me Wrong. I may list the more pertinent details of my daily existence. Dangerous thoughts – seven. Crimes committed – zero. Who knows? I may even share a secret or two.

But let's not get too far ahead of ourselves. If I'm to confide in these pages, the way my therapist would like me to, then first we need to be properly introduced, my journal and I. Before I fill these pages with descriptions of how I'm feeling now, it's important to establish who I was then. All stories have a beginning, and this is mine. Me before You Know Who. Me before there even was a me.

✳

My mother always felt that she married beneath her. Her father had spoiled her rotten, and she expected my father to do the same. She was an academic when they met – a lecturer in women's studies, no less. She'd even had a few papers published. As for my dad, he was the humble IT guy responsible for the computer systems in the college where she worked. I imagine she saw him as a bit of rough, like Lady Chatterley and her gamekeeper. But there was nothing ladylike about my mother. She was a game-player and a grasper. I think of her as the love object in Keats's 'La Belle Dame sans Merci' – a woman without mercy, whose main purpose in life is to entrap and enslave the noble knight who comes courting. And never was there a more devoted, love-sick knight than my dad. As soon as she realised that he was unable to provide her with everything her greedy heart desired, she left him. Then she discovered she was pregnant.

At this point, most expectant mothers would have stopped to consider what was best for the baby. Not my mother. As far as she was concerned, the new life in her belly was little more than an inconvenience, so she booked herself in for an abortion.

I grew up knowing this. My mother made no secret of it, insisting that it was in everyone's best interests to be honest about these things. I'm not sure how it served my interests to know that I wasn't wanted, but my dad did his best to soften the blow, assuring me that it can't have been an easy decision for her to make. Perhaps not, but she was a card-carrying feminist after all. I'm sure that whatever qualms she might have had were soon soothed away by her ideology. 'My body, my choice' is quite persuasive as slogans go, but it's not the whole truth. It takes two people to make a woman pregnant. I'm inclined to think that the father of the baby should have a say, too. Feminists are quick to complain when men walk away from their responsibilities. They're not so quick to accept that the father of an unborn child also has rights.

Needless to say, my mother wasn't of the same opinion. She didn't notify my father of her whereabouts or her condition. He found out the hard way, from a local gossip who'd caught the tail end of a conversation between my mother and her GP at the doctor's surgery some weeks before. Ever the dutiful husband, he tracked her down to a hotel in Brighton, where they resolved to give the marriage another go.

I don't know which of them saved me from the abortionist's forceps. When questioned, my dad always insists that my mother didn't take much persuading. But then, what else would he say? He's always been too kind for his own good. As for her, having planned my termination with a ruthlessness I was to witness many times during my early childhood, she apparently had a change of heart and embraced the idea of motherhood as eagerly as she had once embraced my father. I think of this as her Madonna 'Ray of Light' phase. Remember when the Material Girl suddenly went all Earth Mother on us? I have to say, this was my least favourite of Her Madgesty's reinventions. I preferred Madonna way back when she was a boy toy or now that she's an unapologetic bitch. But anyway, that was my mother. And like Madonna, she struck that particular pose for as long as she needed to, and no longer. It was all over five months later, from the moment I was born.

So that was it – my introduction to this unforgiving world. Barely out of the womb and already I'd had a narrow escape. I don't think it's insignificant that I was born six weeks premature. I'm sure my survival instincts told me to get out while I still could, before my mother's maternal instincts abandoned her and she reverted to her original plan, flushing me away without so much as a second thought. I think of my unborn self as rather like the creature from *Alien*, quietly biding my time but ready to burst through the host's stomach wall at the first sign of trouble.

Having got off to such an inauspicious start, I suppose it was inevitable that my mother and I would be at loggerheads from the day she brought me home from the hospital. I've seen the baby photos and I think it's safe to say that the woman holding the bundle of white cloth with a red face poking out of the top wasn't experiencing anything approaching joy. If anything, she looks rather repulsed. If these photos were to appear in one of those baby manuals you see in bookshops these days, it would be under the heading 'Failure to Bond with Your Baby'. My mother, of course, would never have admitted to any such failing. At the very least, she'd have insisted that the failure was mine and not hers.

It was her idea to christen me Eve – the first woman, she who succumbs to temptation, eats the forbidden fruit and brings about the fall of man. How very *Spare Rib* of her. I hated it and changed my name to Evie as soon as I could.

There was never any question of her breast-feeding. No, it was straight onto the bottle for me. Had it been possible, I'm sure she'd have had me feeding myself from a young age. Hers was the kind of feminism that placed a lot of emphasis on self-sufficiency. Astonishingly, she saw no contradiction between this political stance and her personal circumstances: depending on my father for everything from the roof over her head to the shoes on her feet. In the following years, I would take great delight in pointing this out to her. But for now I was forced to rely on her not-so-tender attentions, unable to put into words what I would later identify as her many shortcomings in the mothering department.

When I did develop the power of speech, I never cried for her. It was always my dad I called out for in the middle of the night, always him who would mop my fevered brow or soothe me back to sleep. He was the calming influence in our house, and when he wasn't tending to me, he was trying his best to please her. As the years went by, it became clear that all his efforts were in vain. Nothing seemed to please my mother. She was a woman who was permanently disappointed with life and was largely driven by resentment. I don't remember her ever smiling. Her features were always pinched, her brows knitted, her mouth a hard, red line.

I remember the day she told me my father was leaving us. I was eight at the time. We were in the kitchen, where moments earlier he'd pleaded with her to be reasonable, and she'd responded by grabbing a plate from the draining board and throwing it against the wall. 'He's leaving because of you,' she told me. 'He can't cope with the way you are!'

My therapist would probably have a field day with this, describing it as a childhood trauma. In fact, I found it funny. My poor mother, the proud feminist, unable to cope with the fact that her long-suffering husband didn't love her anymore, trying to pin the blame on her only child. Later she told the neighbours that the reason her husband walked out was because he had a terminal illness and wanted to spare her the agony of watching him waste away. I wonder what they thought when they saw him walk back in again a few weeks later, looking fit and healthy after a much-needed break from her constant complaints and incessant demands.

What was it Oscar Wilde said? 'All women become like their mothers – that is their tragedy. No man ever does – that is his.' Well, I'm pleased to say that Oscar was wrong. In fact, I'd say the opposite is often true. Lots of men become like their mothers – and I don't just mean the ones who like dressing up in women's clothing and having their bottoms spanked by a dominatrix in fetish gear. But few women ever do. I think we're better at avoiding it. Women tend to be more observant than men – we're more alert to the potential threat. This isn't to say that some mothers don't become like their daughters. We've all seen those middle-aged women desperately trying to compete with their twenty-year-old offspring. But that's a different kettle of mutton, and one I never had to contend with. By the time I posed any kind of sexual threat, my mother was long gone.

My mother and I share a few physical characteristics – enough to convince me that I must remind my father of her on some level. We have the same grey eyes, the same long neck, the same honey-blonde hair. But appearances can be deceptive. I'm pleased to say that I am nothing like my mother. When my father looks at me, I hope it's not her he sees. Because that would be horribly unfair – on him and on me.

✶

I had a nice long soak in the bath earlier, listening to the radio. The water had cooled, my fingers had wrinkled and I was just thinking about getting out when the DJ played 'Nothing Compares 2 U' by Sinead O'Connor. I'm sure everyone remembers where they were when they first saw that video. I remember reading somewhere that the single tear that rolled down Sinead's cheek was for her mother, who died in a car accident when the singer wasn't much older than I was when my mother left. But that's where the similarity ends. I didn't cry for my mother. Not a single tear.

Reading back over what I wrote earlier, it strikes me that this is precisely the kind of thing Maria is so keen for me to 'open up' about. Imagine if I'd said all this to her today! She'd have been over the moon.

'I think we've made a major breakthrough,' she'd have said, nodding at me and reaching for her box of tissues. Then she'd have talked about transference and role models and how people who suffer childhood trauma or rejection by a parent can grow up with a fragile sense of self, blah, blah, blah.

But we didn't talk about my mother. Instead she kept asking me about my 'living arrangements'. Have I always lived at home? Was it difficult, caring for my father? Did I have any kind of support? When was the last time I took a holiday?

I told her I was very happy with my living arrangements, thank you very much. And of course I haven't always lived at home. I went to college for three years, and worked in Manchester for a while.

'What did you study?' she asked, and immediately I regretted giving so much away.

'Does it matter?' I replied.

'It helps me to build a clearer picture,' she said. 'What interests you. What drives you.'

'What interests me is freedom of expression. What drives me is the desire to live freely.'

'And you were able to do that, were you? In Manchester?'

Truth be told, I haven't thought about what happened in Manchester for a long time. There's nothing to remind me. No police report. No contact with any of the people I hung around with back then. No way for them to track me down. I left quietly, without saying goodbye or making any fuss. I changed my number and left no forwarding address. I even changed myself. I'm not the person I was then. I left her behind and with each passing year the memory of that day and the girl I used to be fades further from view. What happened in Manchester stays in Manchester. My dad and I came to an unspoken agreement on this when I came back to live with him. Neither of us has spoken about it since. So why should I discuss it with my therapist?

Besides, I don't see why one event should cast such a long shadow. I won't allow it. We can't always control what happens to us but we can control how we deal with it, and I refuse to let one incident eclipse everything else or redefine me in any way. I had a great time in Manchester. In many ways, those were the best years of my life. I developed a real taste for freedom there. I learned to stand on my own two feet.

But try moving back to London without a foothold on the property ladder. It's impossible. House prices here are ridiculous. Rent is extortionate. Given the choice between a rented cupboard under the stairs in West Ruislip or my own room in a three-bedroom house in East Dulwich, why wouldn't I decide to move back home?

'Still, it must have been quite an adjustment,' Maria insisted. 'Giving up this life you'd carved out for yourself. Can I ask how old you were at the time?'

'I was twenty-three.'

I watched her write something down in her notebook, wondered if she was making some kind of judgement. I suppose some people might have been embarrassed – a woman my age with nothing to her name but bags of clothes and boxes of books. But we had already entered the age of Generation Rent. The age of adults forced to move back in with their parents was only just around the corner. I was simply ahead of my time.

'And were there relationships?' my therapist asked. 'Boyfriends? Girlfriends?'

I smiled knowingly at her political correctness. 'Boys to fuck and girls for laughs.'

She coloured slightly despite herself. 'Anyone serious?'

'Sex is always serious,' I told her. 'Even when it's casual.'

'I'll rephrase the question. Did the decision to move back home mean leaving someone special behind?'

'We're all special,' I said. 'Isn't that the received wisdom these days? Everyone is special in their own way?'

'And do you consider yourself special?'

I smiled again. 'I have my moments.'

She looked at me pityingly, and it was all I could do to stop myself from wiping the look off her face.

'I know what you're thinking,' I said.

'What am I thinking?'

'You're wondering if I'm a suicide risk.'

'And are you?'

'Not on your life!'

What my dear, hopeless therapist fails to realise is that some of us are made of far sterner stuff. We've had to be. Whenever I come across someone who claims to have had a happy, well-adjusted childhood, I pity them. They don't have the resources I have. They haven't developed the necessary life skills.

When I lived in Manchester, friends were always complimenting me on my culinary abilities. Most of them lived on takeaways. Even beans on toast was beyond their capabilities. And there was me, cooking up a storm. People always assumed that my mother taught me everything I knew, that the meals I prepared for my housemates were from family recipes passed on from one woman to another. I remember the pleasure I took in shattering their illusions, the looks on their faces when I informed them that my mother never taught me a thing.

Don't get me wrong. I learned a lot from my mother. But that's not the same as saying she taught me. That would imply some kind of personal investment on her part – and nothing could be further from the truth.

No, I learned from my mother the way a rabbit learns from a fox. I learned how to survive.

16

Maybe it's the change of scenery. Maybe it's the hangover from last night sharpening his senses. But the next day, in the stillness of his rented apartment, Tom finally finds the inspiration that's been eluding him for weeks. The words flow easily and he writes more than he's written in a long time, passing the thousand-word mark, then getting on for two thousand. Most days he's lucky if he can manage a thousand words tops, but today he's on a roll and it isn't long before he's completed another chapter.

He heaves a sigh of satisfaction, saves the document and copies a backup version to a memory stick before taking a short break and pouring a glass of Diet Coke from the bottle in the fridge. Returning to his laptop, he makes a start on the next chapter, sketching out the opening paragraph then pausing as he remembers something. He minimises the document and opens another untitled folder on his desktop.

When Tom first received the email from Evie Stokes with the zip file containing the manuscript of her book, he didn't know what to do. It stayed in his downloads folder for days, unopened and unread. Then one morning his curiosity finally got the better of him and he took a look. What he found was that she'd taken his first novel, *Boy Afraid*, and produced what some might call a work of fan fiction.

Initially, Tom was horrified. Not content with taking liberties with his book, the author had written herself into the story and included an intimate relationship between her character and a male character who was clearly based on him. Alarm bells rang as Tom read of their torrid affair, written in the kind of breathless prose normally associated with cheap romance novels or contenders for The Bad Sex Award. The whole thing was obviously intended as some kind of love letter, but there was nothing remotely flattering or heartwarming about it. It felt sinister. It unnerved him. It suggested that here was a woman with a fixation that went way beyond mere fandom.

It also told him that this was not a woman who would respond well under pressure. A slight nudge was all it would take to tip her completely over the edge.

Up until this point, Tom had found Evie's attention flattering and considered her a little eccentric but essentially harmless. He'd met her kind before – those often dowdy, somewhat shy women who usually sat at the back at author events, never raised their hand to ask a question but hung around afterwards, edging closer as the crowd thinned and they finally plucked up the courage to introduce themselves. He'd put her social awkwardness down to her being star-struck in his presence.

Having read some of her work, he saw that there was far more to her than that. She was clearly suffering from some kind of mental illness or personality disorder. But there was also a glimmer of talent there – raw and in desperate need of professional guidance, but a talent nonetheless. The question was, should he help to nurture it or distance himself from her as quickly as possible?

The answer was obvious. Evie Stokes wasn't a woman who took rejection well. He'd gleaned that from some of her interactions on Twitter. Any perceived slight could turn her from an adoring fan into an angry troll who was easily riled and refused to be ignored. And so it proved. By the time Tom reported her to the police, he'd gathered enough evidence to suggest that she was guilty of harassment. There were the copies of emails and the screenshots of tweets. There were the printouts of her blogs, her comments on Amazon reviews and her doctoring of his Wikipedia page.

The one thing he didn't mention was her book. That first night at Brixton Police Station, he'd come close to mentioning it, but something had held him back. He'd told himself that there was nothing in the book that seemed particularly pertinent, legally speaking. If writing fiction was a crime, there'd be a lot of people clogging up the criminal-justice system. All the book really showed was that Evie Stokes was obsessed with him – and there was already ample evidence of that. The sheer volume of tweets and emails indicated that hers was not a healthy obsession.

But there was another reason why he kept quiet about the book, and here Tom's motives were rather murkier. Despite its many weaknesses, the book ignited his imagination. The plot was compelling. It excited him in a way the book he'd been working on for the best part of three years never really had. Somewhere in there was the kernel of a good idea, and if anyone was entitled to run with it, he certainly was. Without his original work, her manuscript would never have existed. He was simply taking back what was rightfully his. So after meeting with his agent at the Groucho Club, and despite denying all knowledge of Evie's damn book, he took elements of her plot and developed them into a crime novel about a female blogger who becomes fixated with a male author and is charged with harassment.

Several months and sixty thousand words later, it's fair to say that the novel he's working on also contains a strong element of autobiography. Tom has never put quite so much of his personal experience into a book before. But as his creative-writing tutor at university never tired of reminding him, 'Write about what you know. It's all material!' What his tutor didn't say, but could very easily have said, is that writing can also be an act of revenge. Now whenever those writers' memes pop up on social media Tom feels as if someone is staring through his computer screen and inside his head, seeing every thought process and creative decision he makes – 'Don't mess with authors, we'll describe you'. Or better yet, 'I'm killing you off in my novel'.

He hasn't got round to killing her off yet. That's a pleasure he's looking forward to. But he has produced the best part of a book that is strikingly different to any he's written before – dark, gritty and really quite disturbing, perfect for today's crime-obsessed market. In other words, just the kind of thing his agent asked for.

Tom's stomach rumbles and he checks the time in the top right-hand corner of his computer screen; he's surprised to see that it's almost 3.00 p.m. He's loath to step away from the book when he's on such a roll, but hunger gets the better of him and, since there's nothing to eat in the flat, he has no choice but to venture out. He closes the laptop, grabs his keys and heads downstairs and out of the front door.

The beach is busy now. The groynes either side of the pier are lined with lazy sunbathers, shielding themselves from the sea breeze. Couples huddle together for warmth on the shingle. At the water's edge a fit young man in white swimming trunks is posing for photos, flexing his bulging biceps. He has dark cropped hair and a sleeve tattoo. He looks Eastern European – Polish, perhaps. Sometimes when Tom is out with Emma they play a game called 'gay or European?' where they try to guess a man's sexual orientation based purely on his physical appearance. Certain dress codes used to be a dead giveaway. Likewise the overuse of male-grooming products. But it's getting harder to tell these days, now that metrosexuality has gone mainstream and so many men aspire to look like the models on the cover of *Men's Health* – ripped bodies, tattoos, fake tans, even a piercing or two.

Tom stops and leans on the railings above the sea wall. He's glad he remembered to wear his sunglasses. All the better for watching people. The man has one of the best physiques he has seen in a while – a narrow waist, six pack, impressive chest and muscular thighs that complete the look rather than detract from it. This is not a man who goes to the gym and neglects leg day. He looks exotic and vaguely out of place among the hordes of pasty Englishmen with their pink faces and beer bellies. For a moment Tom entertains the possibility that he and this young man may have something in common.

The likelihood of this is somewhat reduced by the presence of the woman taking the photos, whose sense of ownership is clearly indicated by the way her hands travel over the man's body and by her peals of girlish laughter. Photo shoot over, she tucks her phone in the side of her bikini thong and grabs his hand as they head back up the beach. As they draw closer, Tom sees that the man's white swimming trunks aren't trunks at all but tight white briefs. Somehow, Tom doubts that this man has ever been to an underwear party. He's simply confident enough in his appearance not to worry about what's considered suitable beachwear.

Possibly sensing that he's being watched, the man pauses to embrace his female companion, pulling her body close to him and going in for a long, lingering kiss. As their lips lock together, he grinds his groin against hers, one hand stroking her shoulder as the other rests in the small of her back. Not for the first time, Tom wonders at the way straight couples take public space for granted, the complete lack of inhibition or fear that their displays of intimacy might result in anything more menacing than the odd raised eyebrow.

Finally, the man steps away, revealing a visible erection. Tom feels himself flush, embarrassed that he might be caught looking, yet simultaneously annoyed at himself for feeling that way when he's not the one making an exhibition of himself. Right on cue, the man turns his head in Tom's direction and flashes his teeth in a knowing grin. It's a grin that says, 'yes, I know you find me desirable'. But there's a hint of violence about it, too. Tom knows only too well how a situation like this can suddenly turn, how quickly a man can go from enjoying the attention to feeling threatened and lashing out.

He averts his gaze, turning away from the seafront and heading towards the town centre. He passes a parade of shops, bars, cafés and restaurants, most of them empty. A few people are sitting smoking outside a pub – the men in shorts and vests, the women in heels and full makeup, complete with heavy contouring and false eyelashes. At a neighbouring table, a couple are staring silently at their hotdogs with looks of deep disappointment etched on their faces. What were they expecting, Tom wonders – fillet steak?

The town centre is a flurry of activity. Market stalls selling everything from books and vegetables to army surplus, dream catchers and other assorted hippy paraphernalia. Tom watches as a small group of men and women snake their way quickly through the crowds – all pale, pinched faces and glazed, darting eyes. Hastings has more than its fair share of drug users. He remembers reading that somewhere. London boroughs move them here to save on housing costs. He braces himself as the group heads towards him, worried that one of their number might snatch his phone or wallet. But they hurry past without so much as a glance in his direction, eyes set on a different goal, bodies jerking like stick figures in baggy sportswear. Tom wonders how many of them still have a home to go to, how many are sleeping rough.

The smell of freshly baked bread draws him to the 1066 Bakery, where he buys a cheese-and-onion pasty. It's not the sort of food he'd normally allow himself, but what harm can it do? Stepping out into the street, he takes a bite and the warm pastry melts in his mouth, stomach grumbling as the digestive juices start to flow. There's a sudden rush of air behind him and something clips the top of his left ear. Startled, he looks up to see a seagull flap its lazy wings and soar high above the shops ahead. No sooner has it registered that the bird was going for his pasty than another gull swoops down and snatches it clean out of his hand. He watches them fly away, partners in crime.

Someone laughs – a loud, machine-gun rattle. One of the market traders gestures at him with a grin. 'Never mind, mate! At least it didn't shit on you!'

Burning with humiliation, Tom turns away, fumbling in his pocket for his phone as he starts to walk.

'You won't believe what just happened to me,' he says. 'I've been mugged.'

Emma's voice sounds panicked. 'What? Are you okay? Have you called the police?'

'By a seagull,' Tom says. 'Well, two, actually – working together. One acted as a decoy and the other snatched my pasty.'

'Sounds painful. I didn't have you down as a pasty sort of man.'

'I'm a man of many appetites.'

Emma laughs. 'Well, at least you weren't hurt. I'm glad you're okay.'

'I'm not okay,' Tom says. 'I'm far from okay. I'm literally starving and those bloody vultures just flew off with my lunch.'

'Isn't it a bit late in the day for lunch?'

'I was writing and lost track of time.'

'But that's good, isn't it? I'm glad it's going well. And how's Hastings?'

'Nice. Apart from the seagulls, obviously. They're enormous. And they're everywhere.' He spots a couple of fledglings on the pavement up ahead, fighting over a bag of chips. 'You think the pigeons in London are bad? These are like pigeons on steroids. No, worse than that: they're like pterodactyls!'

'Not that you're prone to exaggeration.'

'I'm not exaggerating in the slightest,' Tom says. 'Remember that scene in *Jurassic Park*, where the velociraptors work together to hunt and kill the gamekeeper? Imagine those with wings.'

'So tell me about Hastings,' Emma says. 'Where are you staying?'

'Close to the pier. I can see the sea from my front window.'

'And is it really like Hoxton-on-Sea?'

'Not really. Though I did spot a beardy hipster riding a penny farthing along the prom earlier.'

'You didn't!'

'No, I didn't. It hasn't reached that level of hipsterdom just yet. But I did see a man on the beach in his underwear.'

'Lucky you. Was he hot?'

'I assume so. Or maybe he's just an exhibitionist.'

'Very funny. You know what I mean.'

'I know exactly what you mean. And yes, he was hot. He was also painfully straight and shamelessly parading his heterosexuality for all the world to see.'

'How disgraceful! You'd think all the hot men would have got that gay memo by now.'

'My thoughts exactly. So how's London?'

'Warm. Sunny. And I'm stuck at my desk, staring out of the window at people making the most of the weather. Don't these people have jobs?'

Tom chuckles. 'Poor Em! Have you missed me?'

'Hardly. You've only been gone a few days.'

'A lot can happen in a few days. I could be abducted by pirates. Speaking of which, you'll never guess who I ran into last night.'

'No idea.'

'Guess.'

'Jake Gyllenhaal? Ryan Reynolds?'

'That waiter from the restaurant. He was dressed as a pirate. And I have to say, he wore it well.'

'I'm surprised you can remember him,' Emma says.

'I never forget a pretty face.'

'Really? I'd have thought they'd all merge into one after a certain point.'

'Ms Norton! Are you slut-shaming me?'

'As if!' Emma pauses. 'Have you heard from her?'

'Her?'

'You know who I mean.'

Tom's pulse quickens. 'Yes, I know who you mean. And no, I haven't. Why do you ask?'

'Just checking, that's all. I remember you saying you were worried she'd breach her restraining order.'

'Well, she hasn't. Not so far, anyway.'

'That's a relief.' Emma draws in her breath, like someone about to make a big announcement. 'Listen, I've been doing a bit of research, reading up on female stalkers.'

'Have you, now?'

'Apparently they all have certain characteristics in common. They tend to be single, heterosexual, highly educated women who suffer from some kind of mental illness or personality disorder.'

Tom sighs. 'Tell me something I don't know.'

'Hang on,' Emma says. 'Let me just pull up this article.' There's a moment's silence, then she's back. 'Right, so the thing I found most interesting is the way they select their victims. Male stalkers will stalk anyone. It might be someone they've had some kind of prior relationship with, in which case the stalking is an attempt to restore the same level of intimacy. Or it might be a total stranger – a woman they've only ever seen from a distance or on the TV. With female stalkers, it's different. They tend to latch on to men they already know – a work colleague or an acquaintance of some sort, someone they feel safe with. According to this psychiatrist, they're not trying to restore intimacy, they're trying to create it. Often they're driven by loneliness, jealousy, fear of abandonment and anger at what they perceive as some kind of betrayal by the object of their obsession.'

A familiar feeling of anxiety stirs in Tom's stomach. He scans the surrounding area, half expecting Evie to appear from behind one of the market stalls and walk towards him with that crooked smile on her face.

'Tom? Are you there?'

He lifts the phone closer to his mouth. 'I am.'

'I think she's suffering from de Clérambault's syndrome. Otherwise known as erotomania.'

'I know what de Clérambault's syndrome is. What I'd like to know is why you're telling me this.'

'Well, it helps explain her behaviour, doesn't it? And the thing is, people with her condition are rarely violent.'

'And you'd know, would you?'

Emma's voice falters. 'I'm just telling you what I read. I thought it might help.'

'Remember John Hinckley?' Tom says. 'He tried to assassinate Ronald Reagan. And do you know why? Because he was fixated with Jodie Foster. It was reported that Hinckley was suffering from erotomania and believed that shooting the president would somehow endear him to the object of his desire.'

'Oh.'

'Exactly. Oh. So please spare me the amateur psychology. I think I know who I'm dealing with, far better than you do.' Tom pauses. 'Sorry. I didn't sleep well last night.'

'That's okay,' Emma says hurriedly. 'I didn't mean to go on. I just found it interesting, that's all. I'm glad she's stopped bothering you. At least now you can get back to normal.'

Tom forces a laugh. 'Or as normal as I ever get.'

He begins to walk faster as he talks, scanning the road ahead, searching each face, each doorway. He feels the warmth of the late-afternoon sun on his face and is suddenly tempted by the thought of a chilled glass of wine and a bite to eat on the terrace at The White Rock. He hadn't planned on drinking today but he needs something to take the edge off. Besides, it's not every day a man is mugged by marauding seagulls, and he owes himself a reward for all the progress he's made on his book.

Emma must have read his mind. 'I'm glad the writing is going well.'

'Me too,' he replies, eager to draw the conversation to a close. 'Actually, I should probably be getting back to it.'

'Well, don't let me keep you.'

'Are you okay?' Tom asks.

'Of course. Why wouldn't I be?'

'You sound odd. You're not angry because I snapped at you just now, are you? I said I was sorry.'

Emma sighs. 'No. It's nothing to do with you. Long day at work. I can't wait to get home and put my feet up. I'm fine, really.'

'You're sure?'

'I'm sure. Now go and write.'

'I will,' Tom says. But he knows he won't. He pictures the chilled glass of wine waiting for him at The White Rock and can't wait for the comfort it will bring.

17

DAY 18 (712 DAYS REMAINING)

I've been thinking about something my therapist said. She wants to get to the root of my behaviour – as if I'm some plant which has failed to flower and whose roots must now be dug up and examined for signs of disease. Rose, thou are sick. Evie, thou art sicker!

I'm not convinced that I am sick. If you ask me, I'm pretty robust. Not entirely disease resistant, of course. But I'm no wilting, shrinking violet either. I'm more like a wildflower or a hardy perennial. I'll thrive anywhere. You could take cuttings from me and they would root easily, without the need for fertile ground or rooting powder. If I should ever go to seed – and looking at myself in the mirror these days, this seems a distinct possibility – little versions of me would spring up in the cracks between paving stones. I'll grow where others fail to germinate. Remember that song by Pulp, 'Weeds'? That's me. Invasive. Unstoppable. I would flower on wasteland.

As for the mother plant, that's a different story. I think of my mother as a hot-house flower, requiring perfect growing conditions and regular feeding. Liquid feed was her favourite, of course – especially the alcoholic variety. She demanded lots of loving care and attention. My poor father tended to her the way one might fawn over a tender fern or a rare exotic orchid. Though whenever I think of her I picture a Venus flytrap – vicious, snapping, deadly. She preyed on us the way a carnivorous plant preys on small insects.

Of course, I don't discuss my mother in these terms with my therapist. I know the drill by now. Keep it simple. Don't go off on flights of fancy. I think my recent eulogising about Genet sailed dangerously close to a celebration of criminality. Time to rein it in a bit. Time to make a good impression.

So when Maria enquired about my mother, I kept my answers short and to the point.

'We never really bonded,' I said. 'I think she found me a burden. We didn't have much in common, and she wasn't exactly the maternal sort. Parenting didn't come easily to her.'

'Do you think she may have been suffering from postnatal depression?' my therapist asked. As if this would explain my mother's actions during those early years. As if this would excuse the many crimes she committed and cruel things she did.

'She may well have been,' I replied. 'But the poor thing was already addicted to Valium by then, so it was hard to tell.'

This was a lie, of course. My mother's addictions were many and varied. Women who are addicted to Valium tend to be chilled out and pretty malleable most of the time. My mother was anything but.

'It must have been difficult, growing up with a mother like that,' Maria said.

'I didn't grow up with her,' I replied. 'She left when I was ten. First she drove my father away. Then when he came back, she fucked off. But you know what they say – what doesn't kill you makes you stronger.'

'Even so. It must have been difficult for you when she left.'

'On the contrary, the day she walked out it felt as if my life was just beginning.'

'And was that the last time you saw her?'

What could I say? Anything even close to the truth carried the risk of incrimination – not just for me, but for my dad too. So I lied. 'Yes,' I said. 'That was the last time I saw her.'

I hoped that this would draw a line under this particular subject, but Maria wasn't giving up so easily. She gave me one of her sympathetic looks and asked, 'When you think about your mother, what do you think of?'

What was I supposed to say? I know plenty of women have fond memories of their mothers. The mother-daughter relationship is one of those sacred bonds in our society. It's why the mother of Madeleine McCann is often given a hard time by the press and general public. What kind of mother would leave her precious daughter unattended? My own mother made Kate McCann look like Mother of the Year. Her maternal instincts were nonexistent. Her tongue was sharper than a razor. And she had plenty of other sharp objects at her disposal – a whole arsenal of them, in fact.

To return to my earlier analogy: when you take a cutting from a plant, it's important that the blade you use is sharp. I first began cutting myself at the age of twelve, the insides of my wrists and forearms a latticework of red lines. She was long gone by then, but I was simply continuing the work she'd started, managing my rage the only way I knew how.

'I never really think about my mother,' I said in answer to my therapist's question. 'To be honest, I haven't thought about her in years.'

'And is she still alive?' Maria asked.

'She died,' I replied. 'A few years ago. She fell down a piss-stained stairwell and broke her neck. She was drunk at the time. My mother was often drunk. The coroner returned a verdict of accidental death.'

My therapist's calm professional demeanour abandoned her for a moment. 'I'm so sorry,' she said.

'Are you?' I replied, all wide-eyed and innocent. 'I'm not.'

✳

In matters of great importance, style not sincerity is what really matters. Oscar Wilde said that, though it could just as easily have been me or a thousand others who learned from an early age that all people really care about is how things appear to the outside world. My mother never cared much for my dad or me. Not really. What she did care about was how our dysfunctional little family unit was perceived by the neighbours. It didn't matter what went on within those four walls, provided we kept up appearances. She was very good at this. So good, in fact, that my dad had no idea what went on half the time. He knew about her extramarital affairs. She made no attempt to conceal them from him, disappearing for the odd night or sometimes weeks at a time, forcing him to tell people that she was visiting a sick relative. I think she enjoyed humiliating him as much as she enjoyed the lavish gifts and illicit sex.

But he knew nothing of what went on inside that house when he wasn't at home. Had he done, I'm sure the marriage would have ended long before it did. But my mother was cunning. She knew how to cover her tracks. She knew how to silence me. 'Look what you made me do,' she'd say. And like the naïve fool I was, I believed her. It wasn't until after she left, when the dust had settled and the wounds had healed, that I began to put a name to her actions.

I never cried for my mother – and I never missed her, not once. How can you pine for something you never had? When my first period came, it was my dad who went out and bought tampons and sanitary pads. Everything I needed to know about female biology I'd already learned from sex education class at school. Dad taught me to cook and clean, though he never made me work for my pocket money. Not like her. She'd have had me running around after her day and night, had she stuck around long enough.

The day she finally left, I thought it would be a clean break, a new beginning, a chance for us to get our house in order. How wrong I was. My poor father grieved for months. Despite everything she'd done to him, despite all the humiliations she'd put him through, he still loved her. I couldn't understand it. How could I? I was only ten years old. But it seemed to me that the diseased branch had finally been cut away, giving our little family tree the chance to heal. I assumed that was the last we'd see or hear of her, and the thought filled me with joy.

How wrong I was. Even after she left, she refused to leave us alone. She Who Must Be Obeyed became She Who Must Not Be Ignored. People talk about harassment as if it's something peculiar to our day and age, a crime committed by isolated individuals who spend too much time online and latch on to people they barely know. They don't know what they're talking about. All the things I've been wrongly accused and convicted of, my mother was guilty of a thousand times over.

First there were phone calls demanding that I speak to her. Despite my father's protests, I refused to come to the phone. Then there were letters. I don't know what she wrote, because I never opened them, but I'd always know when one of mother's missives had arrived. I'd come home from school and my dad would greet me at the door with that hopeful expression on his face. I don't blame him. He only wanted what was best for me. He wasn't to know that the best had already happened. She'd finally fucked off, and I wanted nothing more to do with her. She was dead to me long before she drew her last breath.

The letter would be sitting on the kitchen table, addressed to me in her familiar handwriting – all bold strokes and extravagant flourishes, the self-conscious calligraphy of a woman who felt that the world should observe her every word.

'Why don't you read it?' my dad would say. 'She's still your mother, after all. There can't be any harm in seeing what she has to say.' Even then, he was determined to give her the benefit of the doubt, as if all the neglect and abuse amounted to nothing more than a misunderstanding.

So I'd take the letter from him, and smile and pretend I had every intention of reading it later, after dinner. We'd sit and eat, and all the while I would feel the envelope burning a hole in my pocket and picture her poisoned ink seeping through the paper, through my clothes and into my skin, branding me like a tattoo. After dinner, I'd help Dad with the dishes, insisting that as the woman of the house I wasn't above doing a bit of housework. Had I allowed him to, he'd have done everything for me. That's the kind of man he is. That's how deep his love for me has always been. It takes a particular kind of woman not to appreciate a man like that. It takes a woman so wrapped up in herself she's never satisfied with anything.

Later, when the dishes were washed and dried, and stacked neatly in the cupboard above the sink, I'd go to my room, take the envelope containing my mother's letter from my pocket and set fire to it with a cigarette lighter. I'd watch the paper blacken and the flames grow, and I'd wish it wasn't just her words I was burning but the fingers that held her pen, her hands, her hair, her blistering flesh. I'd think of witches being burned alive at the stake and wonder if maybe those witch-finders had a point. Oh, I know this makes me a bad feminist, but then I've never claimed to be anything else. I never swallowed my mother's doctrine, however much she tried to force-feed me. I've always followed my own path, which was one reason she hated the sight of me.

My father never enquired about the content of my mother's letters. Perhaps he thought they were too personal and didn't like to pry. They stopped after a year or so. There must have been fifty or more by then – all unopened, all reduced to ash as I sat in my room, fantasising about the things I'd like to do to her. Maybe she'd finally got the message. Or maybe whoever she was living off refused to cover the costs of all those sheets of writing paper, envelopes and postage stamps. My mother liked to make a good impression. She always chose the finest stationery – milled and watermarked paper folded into matching cream wove envelopes. I suppose it's easy to have expensive tastes when you're not the one footing the bill.

My father regularly sent her money. He never told me, but sometimes, when he was out working, I'd check his bank statements and see that transfers had been made to an account held in my mother's name – a few hundred pounds here, the odd thousand there. I never questioned him and I never really understood why he continued to help fund her lifestyle long after she'd left him. Even at a distance, she continued to wind him round her little finger.

I know he worried about me. He worried that I wasn't more outgoing, that I didn't mix well. I think he thought I was suffering from some kind of social handicap. But here's the thing about people like me: we make up for it in other ways, like a blind man whose hearing becomes more acute to compensate for his loss of vision. Those teenage years weren't wasted. Far from it. I read books and I learned how to read people. I developed computer skills and sharpened my understanding of information technology and human behaviour – faculties that would stand me in good stead when the world went online and masses flocked to social media. I didn't feel disadvantaged in the slightest. On the contrary, I felt as if I could take on the world.

After the letters stopped, I didn't hear from my mother for a long time. I didn't know where she was living or whether she was even still alive, and I honestly didn't care. She was no loss to me. I meant what I said to my therapist. The day my mother left was the day my life really began. But all good things must come to an end, and in due course my freedom from the woman who'd once been my prison would come to an end, too.

✄

Here's another thing my therapist said to me this week. 'I'm concerned about your obsession with sexuality.'

'Why's that?' I asked. 'Aren't women allowed to have a sexuality?'

'Of course,' she replied. 'But as I understand it, you're a heterosexual woman. Yet you seem overly interested in gay male sexuality. Why is that?'

You don't need to be a Madonna fan to know that straight women have been enjoying gay male sexuality for years. Mae West was a fag hag long before Elizabeth Taylor or Princess Diana got in on the act. Obviously I'm no Madonna. I'm no Elizabeth Taylor either. But to hear my therapist talk, you'd think there was something intrinsically wrong with women who happen to enjoy gay male company.

'Is it because you feel safer around gay men?' she asked. Clearly she's never been inside a gay club or heard the disgusting way some queers talk about women.

'Not particularly,' I said. 'Why do you ask?'

She paused before continuing. 'In my experience, people displaying the kind of behaviours you exhibit have often suffered some kind of trauma in early childhood.'

'Well I did fall on my head when I was five,' I grinned. Some people lie to please their therapist. I lie to test mine.

'And were you taken to hospital?' she asked.

'What do you think?'

'I think you're not being entirely honest with me.'

Full marks for that startling insight, at least.

'Abuse happens in lots of families,' she continued. 'It's far more common than most people think. It's estimated that one in four children suffers some kind of abuse within the family. Fathers and step-fathers are usually the ones responsible.'

I held her gaze for a moment. 'Are you suggesting that my father abused me?'

'Did he?'

I didn't know whether to laugh or cry. So I simply smiled and said, 'You couldn't be more wrong.'

✴

My mother tried to kill me once. It was before I was born, so I know most people wouldn't consider it attempted murder. But most people don't know what it's like to grow up knowing that you were never wanted, at least not by the woman who carried you inside her belly and would have ended your life before it had even begun, given half a chance. When you know this, it changes you. I knew from a young age, and I don't think it's an exaggeration to say that it made me the person I am today. The will to survive hardened in me like a protective shell or a coat or armour. I became a ticking time bomb, slowly biding my time.

I put up with the abuse. It hurt but it was never life-threatening. The bruises healed and the marks were easy to hide. I never confided in my father because he worshipped the ground she walked on. What child wants the responsibility of breaking up their parents' marriage? When she left, I was so relieved and saw no point in telling him what had happened. It was over now. She couldn't hurt me anymore, and he would only have blamed himself for somehow failing in his responsibilities as a father. I couldn't bear that.

So the years passed and the communication stopped, and by the time I left home for the great adventure of higher education I hardly ever thought of my mother. There were no photos of her around the house. My dad no longer mentioned her. It was an unspoken agreement between us, a shared silence that spoke volumes about how little she meant, this woman who had once been the centre of his universe and the horror at the heart of mine.

I moved to Manchester, where I studied English and graduated with a first-class honours degree, before landing a job on a local listings magazine. It wasn't my dream job, but it paid the bills. It was a start. I worked hard and made plans. Dad always said I was a dreamer. But now I started to dream big. I pitched ideas and book reviews to national newspapers and literary journals. I began working on that novel I'd always talked about. Life was good and the possibilities were endless.

Then, just when I thought I'd never see my mother's evil face again, she reappeared. So I did what any self-respecting survivor of abuse dreams of doing. I took back all the power she'd ever taken from me. Every hateful word, every hurtful action, every twisted thing that woman ever did – I took it all back in one fell swoop. I did what I had to do. I did what I should have done a long time ago.

I killed her.

18

Hastings is shimmering under a heatwave. It's barely noon and already the temperature is in the mid-twenties. Tom has spent the morning trying to write and achieving very little. But no matter. The important thing is that he's completed a further five chapters since arriving here a little under a fortnight ago. Just a few more and the book will be finished. Time to take a break and head to the beach. The sea air will help clear his head, and he can return to his writing later. He saves this morning's work to a memory stick, logs off his laptop and goes in search of his beach bag.

By now Tom has settled into a routine. He's awake each morning by 6.00 a.m., largely thanks to the seagulls, who begin their dawn chorus an hour or so earlier, and whose cries gradually filter into his dreams. He drinks his morning coffee, writes for a couple of hours, then goes for a run. This is followed by a few more hours writing, an early lunch, possibly another hour or so editing, and then he's done for the day. He's had a similar routine for years. He even wrote about it in one of those 'How I write' pieces for the *Guardian*.

Only now he's in Hastings and not London, the routine has changed slightly. He's swapped his morning run beside the river for a run along the seafront, up over the East Hill or through Alexandra Park. It's the best way to get to know a place, and he's discovered a lot in a relatively short space of time. He's aware of the rivalry between the Old Town with its boutique shops and the New Town, where much of the gentrification is now taking place. He's conscious of the positive impact the pier has had on the local area, the growth of new businesses and the steady influx of tourists and second-home owners. He's aware, also, that not everyone is as enthusiastic about the changing fortunes and demographics of the town.

Tom hasn't heard anyone refer to out of towners as FILTH and suspects this may have been Luke's idea of a joke. But he has heard the term DFL used in a disparaging fashion, as if people 'down from London' aren't to be trusted, and their investment in the local economy is something to be sneered at. A few days ago, he met his downstairs neighbour, an older chap named Colin, who's as deaf as a post and wears the least convincing toupee Tom has ever seen. If the thick brown thatch didn't look unnatural enough on his pale shrunken head, the tufts of fine white hair sticking out at the back and sides soon give the game away.

Cornering Tom in the hallway, Colin began by asking him where his car was parked, before launching into a tirade about the recent spate of vandalism on the seafront, something he attributed to the arrival of the nearby skate park.

'We never had any trouble here until they opened that park. Now you take your life in your hands the minute you open the front door.'

Tom nodded sympathetically. 'How long have you lived here?'

The old man cupped his ear with his hand and frowned until Tom repeated the question, slowly and louder.

'Too long,' Colin replied, eyes wide and watery behind thick spectacles. 'I'm ready to go, but the man upstairs has different ideas.'

It took Tom a moment to realise that the man upstairs wasn't him or a previous occupant but a higher being altogether.

For all of Colin's reservations – and Tom can see where the old boy is coming from, even if he doesn't share his belief in where he's going – it's hard not to feel enthused about a place going through a period of reinvention, looking to the future while retaining such strong links with the past. Tom loves the fact that the area known as the America Ground is so-called because this small patch of land was once declared an outpost of America, whose inhabitants flew the stars and stripes as a symbol of their independence from the crown. He finds it even more charming that this historical dispute is re-enacted in period costume in the run-up to Bonfire Night. Just one of the many quirks he's come to associate with the town – and proof of the local community's willingness to adopt fancy dress at the drop of a hat.

Hastings isn't quite the hipsters' paradise described in the weekend supplements. For every bearded creative in skinny jeans or crimson-haired woman on a butcher's bike, there are men in track pants and football shirts, and women with Croydon facelifts, pushing baby buggies. It may be on the up, but parts of Hastings are still very down at heel. And much to his surprise, Tom likes it that way. He likes the shabbiness, the grit in the oyster. But mostly he likes the fact that he's by the sea.

He's spent hours watching the tide coming in or going out, exposing the glittering stretch of sand below the shingle. He's even been swimming. The sea is warmer than he was expecting – hardly the Med, but not so cold you fear you might die of hypothermia. Swimming at Pelham Beach or diving off the groynes by the pier at high tide, he could almost convince himself that he's in another country.

It seems hard to believe after so short a time, but Tom is beginning to feel like a different person. It isn't simply that he's swapped his sharp suits and crisp white shirts for loose-fitting T-shirts and cargo shorts. It goes deeper than that. The heat has warmed his tired muscles and worked its way deep into his bones. He feels less on edge, more at peace with himself. It's as if the combination of sun, sea and sand has buffed and pummelled him into submission, easing away knots of anxiety the way a good massage might. He can feel the changes in himself – the loss of tension in his neck and shoulders, the relaxing of his jaw.

For years Tom has been attuned to the rhythms of London – the snarl of traffic, the rumble of the underground, the madness of the rush hour, the constant push and shove for which Londoners are infamous. Here, the rhythms are different. Most people appear to walk or cycle to work. There are no maddening crowds and far fewer exhaust fumes. The air is clean, and the only sounds are the cries of gulls, and the crash and drag of the sea – the waves hissing as they hit the shore, the suck and roll of pebbles as the water retreats. No wonder so many

Londoners are making a new home for themselves in Hastings. Based on what he's seen so far, Tom is seriously thinking of joining them.

✴

Heading downstairs, careful not to disturb his neighbour and risk another warning about the dangers posed by the skate park, it suddenly strikes Tom that he hasn't bumped into Luke once since Pirate Day. Not that it was inevitable. But Hastings is a pretty small town and Tom has seen every part of it. He's surprised they haven't crossed paths. Surprised and, if he's completely honest, a little disappointed. That night in The St Leonard, he'd felt there was a connection between them, even if Luke seemed wary after their previous encounter. He could look for Luke on Facebook, but he doesn't even know his surname. He could call the restaurant in Clapham and ask for him, see if he's returned to work. But he'd hate to come across as some kind of bunny-boiler. Tom has never chased after anyone in his life. He's not about to start now.

He's hardly been on social media. It's not that he's been avoiding it, simply that he's been so absorbed in his writing he's almost forgotten it's there. Every few months Tom promises himself a digital detox so he can clear his head and get more work done. He's seen other authors announce their breaks from Facebook and Twitter to complete their latest novel. It's always seemed like a good idea, like giving up smoking or not drinking for a year. And like many good ideas, with Tom it tends to get stuck at the ideas stage. But not this time. Whether by accident or design, this time he's been off social media for the best part of a week. And though it pains him to admit it, all the things the proponents of the digital detox say are true. His anxiety levels have dropped. He's sleeping better. He feels calmer and more focussed. If he'd only known it would make this much difference, he'd have done it months ago.

Still, there's no point dwelling on what might have been. The important thing is to keep moving forwards – the next day, the next page, the next chapter. But now it's relaxation time. The sun is high and there isn't a cloud in the sky. Time to hit the beach.

There aren't many sunbathers today. Down by the shore, a man is teaching his small son to fly a kite, barking orders at him while the boy struggles to keep control, the kite barely rising a few feet above the ground before dive bombing back down again. Tom is reminded of his own father, who never had any patience with him, making every shared activity a source of dread.

A short distance away, a male school teacher with a strong Geordie accent is leading a field trip, explaining the principles of sea erosion and longshore drift to a class of largely uninterested teenagers. Tom listens as the teacher enthuses about the varieties of rigid hydraulic structure – rock groynes, wooden groynes, concrete groynes – and how they interrupt water flow and limit the movement of sediment, preserving the beach from erosion by the tide. He then divides the class into four groups and sets them each a task – taking measurements, inspecting the groynes, collecting sand samples. 'And try not to disturb the man who came here for a bit of peace and quiet.'

Feeling self-conscious in his swimming trunks, Tom reaches for his phone and pretends to be checking something as a group of teenagers draw nearer, the girls giggling excitedly and the boys laughing and jostling each other as they approach. He thinks he hears one of the boys say 'queer' but he can't be sure. His body tenses. People who joke about men having sand kicked in their face seem to think that it ends there, that kicking sand is never a precursor to something more violent. He keeps his head up, reminds himself that there's a teacher present, that it's the middle of the day on a public beach and not some remote corner of a park in the dead of night. Nothing bad can happen to him here. He fumbles in his bag for his earbuds and selects some music. The opening strains of 'Aerial' by Kate Bush fill his ears.

After a few minutes, the teenagers leave, reassembling at the top of the beach, where the teacher is gesturing towards the sea wall, no doubt explaining its function and construction and not the meaning of the graffiti scratched or spray-painted onto the concrete. Tom lies back, enjoying the warm sun on his body. His eyelids grow heavy and he can feel himself drifting off to sleep, when the music cuts out and his phone's ring tone cuts in. There's no name displayed on the screen and the number isn't one he recognises. His first instinct is to decline the call but curiosity gets the better of him.

The caller gives her name as Ruth Freeman. She's a freelance journalist and she's writing a piece about online harassment for the *Guardian*.

'Can I ask how you got this number?' Tom asks.

She sounds surprised. 'It's on our database. I think you've written for us before?' There's an upward inflection at the end of her sentence, making the statement sound more like a question. Tom immediately puts her age at around thirty.

'Of course,' he says. 'How can I help?'

'I was hoping to ask you about what happened with Evie Stokes. I read about the case on the Court News site.'

'Then you'll know what happened,' Tom says. 'She was found guilty.'

'Yes, I know,' the journalist replies. 'Sorry, I wasn't very clear. This piece is really about the impact harassment has on the victims. Most of the people I've spoken to are women. It would be really good to get a male perspective on this, to give it more balance? Obviously a lot of the hate online is directed at women but I think it's important for people to know that men can be on the receiving end, too.'

'I see,' Tom says. Part of him wants to end the conversation here. What's the point in going over it all again? What's to be gained? Unless of course it's to publicise the fact that Evie Stokes is a convicted criminal who obviously can't be trusted.

'Mr Hunter?' the journalist says. 'Are you there?'

'I am. Sorry, could you tell me your name again?'

'Ruth Freeman.'

Tom makes a mental note. 'Now's not a very good time,' he says. 'Could you call me back later, around six o'clock?'

'Can we make it six-thirty? I have another interview at half-five and it might run over.'

'Six-thirty it is,' Tom says. That'll give him more time to run a background check on Ruth Freeman and see what kind of journalist she is.

The sun glares off the screen of his phone, making it difficult to read. He sits upright with his back to the sun and leans forwards, shielding the screen with his upper body. It takes him a few minutes to confirm that Ruth Freeman really does work for the *Guardian*. She has her own profile, complete with a photograph and links to various pieces she's written for the newspaper. The photo shows a young blonde woman with a determined expression and just a hint of a smile. The pieces are mostly opinion columns of the kind the paper specialises in – feminist slants on popular culture, angst-ridden takes on environmentalism, trans politics and class privilege. There are a few longer, more investigative pieces, too – one about knife crime in inner city schools, another about grooming gangs. She has a head for crime, then. That's something.

Next he checks her Twitter profile, sees that there's a blue tick next to her name and she has more than sixty thousand followers. The numbers are meaningless, of course. There are plenty of people on Twitter with larger followings, most of them paid for or acquired on the basis of fellow nobodies shoring up each other's egos. But the blue tick means her account has been authenticated. Someone, somewhere has decided that Ruth Freeman is exactly who she says she is. In light of his recent experience, Tom wishes he'd always been so circumspect.

He's about to put down his phone when his thoughts return to Evie Stokes. So far he's resisted the urge to check her activity on Twitter. But with her fresh in his mind the temptation is too strong. It won't hurt to know what she's up to, especially now he has an interview lined up. He types her name into the toolbar and her Twitter account appears immediately. It's still set to public. He knew it would be. Protecting her tweets would mean limiting the number of people who can see them, and she's all about playing to the gallery.

He taps the link with his forefinger and there it is, pulling him back to all the times he checked her profile, all the hours he spent taking screenshots for the police. It's changed since he last saw it. Her profile picture used to be a shot of Bette Davis in *All About Eve*, complete with poised cigarette and mad staring eyes. It was her idea of a joke, a play on her name and the relentless narcissism of social media – All About Evie. Now the image has been replaced with one of Kathy Bates in *Misery*.

The header has changed, too. Where there used to be a photo of Marilyn Monroe surrounded by hordes of adoring men in *Gentlemen Prefer Blondes*, now there's a picture of a starry sky and a quote from Oscar Wilde: 'Always forgive your enemies – nothing annoys them so much.'

Tom's pulse races, the soothing sound of the sea drowned out by the rush of blood in his ears. This is all for his benefit. The film reference, the quote, the twisted sense of martyrdom and sly little digs – they're all aimed at him. There's nothing here that breaches the terms of her restraining order, just enough to let him know she's thinking of him.

But what really makes his heart pound is the tweet pinned at the top of her feed. It reads simply, 'I'm not the kinda girl...' and includes a link to a music video on YouTube. The song is 'The Tide Is High' by Blondie.

'"Who gives up just like that"', Tom thinks, completing the lyric as the sky darkens and a cold shiver runs across his skin.

19

'Tom!' Emma snaps. 'Slow down. You're not making any sense!'

'Don't you see? The Blondie video. It's her way of telling me she's not giving up, she's not going to stop.'

'Or maybe she just likes Blondie.'

'This is her we're talking about,' Tom says. 'Evie Stokes. You saw her in court. You know what she's like. Nothing she posts online is ever entirely innocent. It's all designed to provoke a response. It's all calculated. This is what she does. Troll people. Harass people. It's her whole pathetic little life.'

He's walking as he talks – shifting and sliding over the shingle, barely looking where he's planting his feet. His beach things are in a bag slung over his shoulder. It bumps against his rib cage as he walks.

'I think you need to spend less time on social media,' Emma says.

'I haven't been on social media. Go and look if you don't believe me.'

'Who said anything about not believing you? You just said you'd checked her Twitter feed. What am I supposed to think?'

Tom reaches the top of the beach and climbs the wooden steps to the promenade. 'I told you,' he says, pausing for breath as he leans against the railing, gazing down at the sea. 'I only looked at her feed because I'd spoken to that journalist. She's calling me back in a few hours.'

Emma sighs. 'Are you sure that's a good idea?'

'Why wouldn't it be?'

'What's the point of reliving it all again? Let it lie. Move on. Finish your book. Get on with your life and leave that poor pathetic woman to get on with hers.'

'She doesn't have a life,' Tom says. 'That's why she latches on to those of us who do. She's a parasite. And if I didn't know better I'd say you were feeling sorry for her.'

There's a pause before Emma replies. 'Well, don't you think she's been punished enough?'

'Hardly, if she's still messing about on Twitter.'

'But you have no way of knowing if this is even about you. You're reading into things. And why risk antagonising her?'

'Whose side are you on, Em?'

'What? Yours, obviously. But this isn't about sides. I'm simply saying you should leave it alone. Why do this? What do you stand to gain from it?'

'It's a chance to tell my side of the story.'

'You've done that already. You did it in court. And the judge believed you. You won the case. Surely that's enough? This just makes you look vindictive. And it could lead to people harassing her online the way she harassed you.'

'Tough. I'm not responsible for anything that happens to her as a result of her actions. She is.'

'You're being very hard, Tom.'

'Am I? Maybe I am.' He stares at the sea. The water is rising. The stretch of sand where he lay only a few minutes ago is now fully submerged, the waves lapping at the pebbles and crashing against the wooden groyne, sending up spray. At high tide, all that will be left visible of the groyne is the wooden post set in concrete at the top of the beach. A thought crosses his mind and a knot of anxiety tightens in his stomach. 'You don't think she knows I'm here, do you?'

'What?' says Emma. 'Of course not. How would she?'

'It could be a message – 'The Tide Is High'. It could mean she's here in Hastings.' He looks around, scanning the crowds for her face. 'She could be watching me as we speak.'

'Now you're being ridiculous. It's a summery song. It's summertime. And Hastings isn't the only seaside town in the world. Maybe she's lying on a beach somewhere. Maybe she's simply wishing she was. It doesn't always have to be about you.'

'Ouch,' says Tom.

'You know what I mean,' Emma says. 'We all do it sometimes – think the world revolves around us. The things other people say or do aren't always about us. Sometimes it's just about them.'

'She's not just "other people" though, is she? She's obsessed.'

'I know. But you obsessing about her isn't helping anyone, least of all you.'

'I saw her,' Tom blurts.

'What? When?'

'A few weeks ago, in London. I was out running and I thought I saw her, at the Southbank.'

'Hang on. You saw her, or you only thought you saw her?'

'I was sure I saw her, but when I looked again, she'd gone.'

'Oh, Tom,' Emma says. 'Is that why you were in such a hurry to get away?'

'Partly,' he replies. He doesn't have the heart to tell her that part of the reason he left so quickly is that he wanted a break from everything, her included. 'I needed a change of scenery. I thought the sea air would do me good. And it has. I'm sleeping better and writing more.'

'Well, then,' Emma says. 'Try to focus on that. Don't waste your time worrying about her. And please don't do this interview. Cancel it. Tell them you've changed your mind. Say you've been advised not to talk to the press. Tell them I told you.'

'I will,' Tom says. But he's lying, even to himself. Evie Stokes is like the scab on a wound. He knows he shouldn't pick at it but he can't help himself.

✳

Arriving back at his building Tom sees his downstairs neighbour, sitting on a kitchen chair on the front terrace. He's dressed in a pale-yellow short-sleeved shirt, olive-green knee-length shorts and the curious combination of sandals and grey socks often sported by men of a certain age. His lower legs are far paler than the rest of him, the sun turning the mottled skin the pink of raw sausage meat. Beside him, on a small table, are a newspaper and a jug of water. His head must be sweltering under that wig, Tom thinks, wondering why he doesn't just swap it for a sun hat. It's not as if he's fooling anyone.

'Hello again,' Tom says, smiling as he approaches. 'Lovely afternoon, isn't it?'

'I'm glad I've seen you,' Colin replies. 'I'd like a word.'

Tom's face falls. 'I hope I haven't disturbed you. I've been trying to keep the noise down but I tend to be up pretty early.'

The old man snorts. 'You call that early? Wait till you're my age. I'm lucky if I can stay in bed till five. No, you're not disturbing me. Why don't you sit down for a minute?' He gestures towards a second chair a few feet away. 'You're not in any hurry, are you?'

'No,' says Tom, pulling up the chair and placing his beach bag on the paved floor beside him.

'Good,' says Colin. 'Only you look like someone who's always in a hurry. Believe me, life happens fast enough, without all this rushing about.'

Tom feels a prickle of indignation but decides to humour the old man. 'So you didn't fancy the beach today?' he asks, speaking slowly and enunciating each word like a foreign-language student.

'I prefer to sit and watch the world go by. Stay in one place long enough and it all comes to you eventually.'

Great, Tom thinks. A philosopher in our midst. 'You must have seen some changes,' he says. 'Living here all this time.'

'I have,' Colin replies. 'And there's no need to talk like that. I can hear you perfectly well.'

'Sorry, I thought you were—'

'Deaf? Yes, I am.' The old man grins, revealing startlingly white, even teeth. Crowns, Tom thinks, or possibly dentures. But good ones, not the kind you normally see on British men of a certain age. Either Colin is rich or National Health dentistry has come a long way. 'I've got my hearing aids in,' he adds, still smiling. 'The doctor says I'm to wear them all the time, but sometimes it pays not to hear half of what's going on. There's so much noise nowadays. All that constant chatter. I'm surprised people can find time to think. Or maybe they don't. Maybe that's why the world is in such a mess.'

Tom nods, wishing he was anywhere but here. 'So you said you wanted a word. Can I help you with something?'

Colin frowns. 'You help me? Not unless you can have a word with the man upstairs, ask him to speed things up a bit. No, I'm more concerned about you.'

'Me?' Tom feels himself flush. 'You needn't concern yourself about me. I'm fine.' He's about to add, 'and you don't even know me' but manages to hold his tongue. He's still the outsider here. He doesn't want to cause offence and have to live with unnecessary tension.

'Are you?' the old man asks, staring intently with his watery blue eyes. 'Tell me to mind my own business, but I've lived a long time, and if there's one thing I've learned it's how to tell when someone isn't happy. Looking at you, I see a man who isn't happy.'

Sensing Tom's obvious discomfort, he falters, then changes tack. 'I know we've hardly spoken, and you probably think I'm a foolish old man. But I still have eyes and I still have ears.' He grins. 'Just about.'

'I don't know what to say,' Tom replies, though he can think of a few things – 'mind your own business' being one.

'I can see I've embarrassed you,' Colin says. 'I'm sorry if I've overstepped the mark. My late partner was always telling me off for that.'

Partner? Tom thinks. 'Was she?'

'He,' the old man corrects him. 'And yes, he was.'

※

The telephone interview goes well until the journalist, Ruth Freeman, asks Tom to describe how he feels now the court case is behind him. A spike of anxiety shoots through him and suddenly he's lost for words.

'Fine,' he says at last. 'The troll got what she deserved.'

'I mean, how do you feel within yourself,' the journalist says. 'Victims of crime often experience a kind of post-traumatic stress disorder. And stalking is a very intrusive crime. It's deeply personal and it usually occurs over an extended period, which means it can have a profound effect on the victim.'

'I see,' Tom says, rising from his chair and walking over to the window. On a bench overlooking the beach he sees a man gazing out to sea, smoking. Right now he'd give anything for a cigarette. 'I don't see much point in dwelling on the past,' he says. 'I'm a great believer in moving forwards.'

'Of course,' Ruth Freeman replies. 'But often these crimes can have lasting effects. I suppose what I'm really after is a sense of how this has impacted on you long term.'

'Impacted on me in what way?'

'Some of the people I've spoken to experience feelings of anxiety and symptoms of depression. Some have had flashbacks or panic attacks. Some people have difficulty sleeping or concentrating, or self-medicate with drink or drugs.'

'None of the above,' Tom says, more glibly than he intended. 'Sorry, it sounds serious.'

There's a pause before the journalist continues. 'Well yes, it is. Other people have spoken of feelings of guilt, embarrassment, humiliation or self-blame. Often there's a fear that the perpetrator will reoffend. As I'm sure you're aware, many do. Over forty percent of people convicted of stalking go on to breach their restraining order. The effects on some-one's mental and physical health can be truly debilitating.'

'I see,' Tom says. 'Well, I certainly don't feel guilty or blame myself for what happened.'

'Good. And there's been no further contact from the perpetrator?'

He hesitates. Does that recent tweet count as contact? Or the apparent sighting at the Southbank? Or will he just sound mad? 'No,' he says. 'No further contact.'

'That's good to hear. And what about the other symptoms I've described?'

'I don't really see myself as having symptoms,' Tom replies, though he knows damn well he does. But it's one thing admitting it to himself, quite another broadcasting it to readers of a national newspaper. How's that supposed to help with feelings of embarrassment or humiliation? Sharing his humiliation publicly. Letting the whole world in on it. The last thing he wants is for that bloody woman to know she's still affecting him. He doesn't want to give her the satisfaction.

'You were prescribed antidepressants, weren't you?' the journalist asks.

How does she know that? Tom wonders, then remembers it was discussed in court. The judge even referred to it in her summing up. 'I was.'

'How did that make you feel?'

'I wasn't exactly jumping for joy.'

'Your GP must have thought you needed them.'

'Obviously, or he wouldn't have prescribed them.'

'Do you remember what the symptoms were? How were you feeling at the time?'

'I was having trouble sleeping. I went to my doctor to ask for sleeping pills. It was him who suggested antidepressants.'

'So you were depressed.'

'I was suffering from lack of sleep.'

Another pause, then Ruth Freeman says, 'I was thinking about your first book, *Boy Afraid*.'

'People really seemed to like it,' Tom says, adopting his professionally modest tone, happy to be on more familiar ground. 'Though inevitably some prefer the film version.'

'I was thinking more about the title.'

'What about it?'

'Well, in light of what happened, don't you think it's rather prophetic?'

✶

After the interview, Tom finds it hard to settle. He didn't give a good account of himself and he knows it. He was prickly and defensive. The journalist probably wondered why he agreed to talk to her in the first place. Hopefully she has another male interviewee lined up and won't need to rely on his responses to provide the gender balance she was looking for. He wonders if he should call her back and ask, but decides against it. He's wasted enough of her time already.

Checking his phone, he sees that it's almost time for dinner, but he isn't remotely hungry. His stomach is in knots. A glass of wine would help him unwind, but he questions the wisdom of drinking on an empty stomach. Besides, he doesn't have any wine in, and the thought of venturing outside fills him with dread. Is this what he's reduced to now? Some strange kind of agoraphobia? He's surprised this wasn't one of the symptoms discussed during his interview.

He wanders into the kitchen and fills a glass with water from the tap, gulping it down like he's just returned from a run. He recalls a quote from somewhere – 'The body knows things about which the mind is ignorant' – and wonders what his body is trying to tell him. Is he thirsty? Dehydrated? Or is this its way of trying to drown the feeling of unease? He rinses the empty glass and places it on the draining board.

Returning to the living room, he sees his laptop on the table and reminds himself that there's more to him than this. He's not simply the victim of a crime. He's achieved things his stalker can only dream of. He's been published. He's had a bestseller. And with his new book very nearly finished, he has the means and the opportunity to do it all again. As for motive, what better motive could there be than the need to prove the doubters wrong? Not to mention the thought of her reading his book, knowing he's made good use of her. Whatever disruption and distress she may have caused him, there's comfort in knowing that he's turned their association to his advantage, whereas all she's got out of it is a criminal record.

He sits at the computer and tries to write, but the words won't flow. Staring blankly at the screen, he sees only her – her face, her Twitter profile, her snarky tweets and abusive comments, cluttering up his timeline. He's about to close the laptop when a pinging sound alerts him to an email arriving in his mailbox. For one awful moment he imagines it's her. She's somehow aware that he's been thinking about her and talking about her on the phone, and is emailing to taunt him. He's doing it again – investing her with a power she doesn't have. She's just a sad woman with no life, hiding behind her computer screen.

The email isn't from her. It's from a man claiming to be a private investigator. He introduces himself as David Rees and explains that he has a client who is being targeted by Evie Stokes.

'I hope you don't mind me contacting you,' he writes. 'I read about your case and I'm hoping you might be able to help. I'd rather not go into detail in an email, but if you could please call me on this number I'll be happy to explain.'

Tom checks the email address against the company website and confirms that the man calling himself David Rees does indeed run a firm of private investigators in Swansea. Then he dials the number.

David Rees certainly sounds genuine. 'Thanks for calling,' he says. 'I hope I'm not disturbing you.'

It's a bit late for that, Tom thinks. As if he had any option but to call after receiving an email like that. 'It's fine,' he says. 'How can I help?'

The investigator explains that his client was first befriended by Evie Stokes on Twitter around eighteen months ago. 'Things were fine for the first six months. They exchanged pleasantries and even began emailing each other. Apparently, she seemed perfectly normal.'

'Yes,' says Tom. 'She hides it well.'

'Sorry, I thought you told the court you'd never met her?'

'Just the once,' Tom replies, kicking himself. 'She came to a book signing.'

'I see. Well, as I said, she seemed perfectly okay at first. Then, around a year ago, my client started to receive emails and tweets of an increasingly aggressive nature.'

Tom's pulse quickens. 'That sounds familiar.'

'I thought it might. Stokes never mentioned you to my client, but she saw some of the more offensive tweets Stokes posted, and she backed off.'

'So your client is a woman.'

'That's correct.'

'And can I ask if she's a writer?'

'She's an artist. And between you and me, I'm not sure how reliable she is. She has a history of mental-health problems. She's convinced herself that Stokes has planted some kind of spyware on her computer. She came to me because the police weren't taking her complaint very seriously.'

'So you think she might be paranoid? About the spyware?'

The investigator takes a sharp intake of breath. 'We deal with a fair number of harassment cases. In my experience, the perpetrators tend to be rather inadequate individuals. I've yet to come across any criminal masterminds.'

'And your client is in Swansea,' Tom says, recalling the company address.

'No, she lives just outside Cardiff.'

'That's close to where I grew up.'

'Yes, I know.'

Tom's mind races. 'What's her name? Perhaps I know her.'

'I'm afraid I'm not at liberty to disclose that information. But she assures me that she doesn't know you. She's a different age group, went to an all-girls school. So the case doesn't appear to be related.'

'How can you be sure?'

'I can't. Not one hundred percent. But it seems unlikely.'

'So where do I fit into all of this?'

'I'm trying to build a clearer picture of Evie Stokes and work out how much of a danger she poses. I know she likes to play mind games. In your dealings with her, was there ever any threat of violence?'

Tom's chest tightens. 'You think she's capable of violence?'

'I honestly don't know. Did you ever fear for your physical safety?'

'Not really,' Tom says.

He does now.

20

DAY 19 (711 DAYS REMAINING)

The circumstances surrounding my mother's death are not something I like to think about very often. Not out of a misplaced sense of guilt or even a modicum of grief or pity. I felt none of those things. Any familial feelings I have are reserved for those deserving of my sympathy – namely, my father.

To this day, I'm not sure how much he knows about what happened. He's never asked me and I've never volunteered any information that might incriminate him or tempt him to perjure himself, should I ever be found out. If he has his suspicions, he has always kept them to himself. It's better for both of us that way.

The facts are as follows. She found me. I don't know how, but she did. My first thought was that it was a terrible coincidence, but I refuse to believe in coincidences, certainly not where that scheming bitch is concerned. As Blondie once sang, 'accidents never happen'. And as they also sang, 'rip her to shreds'. Growing up, I must have played that last song a thousand times, the venom of it flooding my veins. It sounded like an exhortation, though I know Debbie Harry wasn't singing about her mother. She was adopted as a child and grew up not knowing the woman who gave birth to her. I wish I'd been as lucky.

Picture this: it was early January. I'd gone to the Arndale Centre to browse the sales, and suddenly she appeared – my estranged mother, no longer out of the picture but in Manchester, in TK Maxx and in my face. I saw her before she saw me, her disembodied head bobbing above a clothes rail a few feet away. I barely recognised her at first. Her jaw was slacker than I remembered and her eyes less bright. Her hair had thinned, and her skin was as pale as parchment. Something told me she'd been drinking, which would explain her lack of focus and the air of irritation as she riffled through the sale items, failing to find what she was looking for. Then our eyes met across the cut-price clothing racks and I saw a flicker of recognition pass across her face.

It's hard to say what I felt at that precise moment. Shock, I suppose, though this quickly gave way to that most basic of human instincts – fight or flight. I ducked behind a clothes rail hung with assorted unsold Christmassy tat and made my way hurriedly to the exit, hoping to lose her in the crowds. The sales had only just started, and the shop was heaving with bargain hunters hoping to come away with the best of the discounts. Nobody took any notice of me as I wormed my way towards the door. They were too busy fighting over clothes they would probably hate when they got them home and never wear.

More people milled around outside. I pushed my way through them towards the escalators, finally breathing a sigh of relief. I thought I'd lost her, when suddenly the crowds parted and there she was – not the woman I remembered from my childhood but a pale facsimile, thinner and frailer than I would ever have expected. She tried to smile, and even from a distance I could see that her teeth were discoloured. She looked old enough to be my grandmother.

Over the years, I've read a lot of self-help books and visited various online forums where survivors of childhood abuse share their stories and generally have a bit of a pity party. They all talk about the need to cut their abuser down to size. The theory goes that abusive parents are not the towering monsters we remember them as, but small, weak individuals who vent their frustrations on those they perceive to be smaller and weaker than themselves. Seeing them for what they really are is all part of one's 'recovery', apparently.

Seeing my mother again after all these years, I didn't need to shrink her down to size. The years and the lifestyle she'd chosen had already done that. Or perhaps she was ill, her body ravaged by cancer or some other wasting disease. I don't know, and to be perfectly honest I don't care. All I remember thinking is how small and feeble she looked, so light I could probably have picked her up and held her above my head, had the urge taken me. I could have thrown her down the nearest escalator or from the top of a high building and watched her puny body fall to the ground below.

That's when the idea came to me. I knew this wasn't the place for what I had in mind. There were too many people and too many cameras. I don't just mean security cameras. There are companies who design elaborate CCTV systems especially for large shopping centres, not to monitor shoplifters but to measure the footfall at various entrances and exit points, all the better to sell advertising space and premium-priced retail units. Our shopping footprint is mapped out daily so some corporation or other can make even more money out of our insatiable desire for conspicuous consumption.

I was wearing my winter coat, so I pulled up the hood and lowered my head to obscure my face. Then I took the escalator up to the third floor. As I reached the top, I glanced back to check that she was following me. Sure enough, she was. Stepping off the escalator, I kept my head down and made my way towards the door marked 'Emergency Exit'. I knew there'd be far fewer cameras in the fire escape. Another quick glance back to confirm that she was still in pursuit, and I slipped through the door.

The top of the stairwell smelt faintly of piss, as if someone had lost control of their bladder before making it to the toilets, and the cleaners had neglected to do their job properly. Neglect can take many forms, as I've known since the day I was born. It also leaves its mark. The Human Stain isn't simply the name of a best-selling novel by Philip Roth. The capacity for evil lurks in the hearts of many of us, and all actions have their consequences. It may take weeks, months or even years, but the stains we make catch up with us eventually. Just as my mother had finally caught up with me, so her sins were about to catch up with her. What a stain on humanity she was – and what a stain she would become.

There was no sound from below, no indication that anyone was making their way up the stairs. Why would they? The lifts from the car park served each floor of the building. Why would someone too lazy to walk to their local shopping centre suddenly decide to take the stairs? I checked for the nearest security camera, stood well out of its view, with my back pressed firmly against the wall, and pulled on my woollen gloves. My mother could come through the door at any moment, and I needed to be prepared.

Minutes passed. I looked at my watch. Where the hell was she? I was just about to lose hope, when the door swung open. She stepped out onto the landing in front of me, oblivious to the fact that, unlike Elvis, Evie hadn't left the building but was standing right behind her.

'Hello, Mother,' I said. The sound of the word stirred something deep in my stomach as she turned to face me.

'Evie,' she replied. 'What a pleasant surprise.'

She was even drunker than I thought, her eyes glassy and unfocussed. As she turned, she stumbled slightly, unsure of her footing but too inebriated to sense the danger she was in. The heels of her shoes were inches from the top step. Behind her, the light on the empty stairwell flickered ominously.

'Well?' she said. 'Aren't you going to give your mother a hug?'

My skin prickled in anticipation of her touch. Holding me. Hurting me.

Suddenly I was a child again, performing the part of the loving daughter for the benefit of visitors.

I didn't say anything. I simply went to her and folded my arms around her skinny frame. I swear there was nothing of her. She was all skin and bone. I could smell the booze on her now. And there was something else, too – the smell of decay. Whatever shred of pity I may have felt turned to disgust. I gripped her firmly by the shoulders, looked her straight in the face and pushed. A moment in my arms and she was gone.

I'd love to say that I saw the panic in her eyes or smelt the fear coming off her as she plummeted to her demise. I wish there'd been a blood-curdling scream. But there was none of that – none of the horror-film clichés. Even in death she was a dreadful disappointment. A gasp of surprise escaped her as she fell. Hands that used to enjoy inflicting pain reached out helplessly, grasping at air. Seconds later, there was a dull thud as her body landed on the stairwell below. I didn't need to inspect my handiwork to know she was dead. There's no way a woman in her condition could have survived a fall like that. I pictured her head cracking open like an egg. I imagined I could hear every bone in her brittle body break, and it was music to my ears.

There's a scene in *Nausea* by Jean-Paul Sartre in which the protagonist is so overcome by the sickly-sweet sense of alienation, he is unable to recognise his own hands. I had no such problem. The hands that killed my mother were the same hands that fought her off as a child. They were mine and I felt no disassociation from them whatsoever. If anything, I felt more attached to them than ever before.

An icy calm descended on me as I took the lift down to the ground level, left the shopping centre and made my way to Piccadilly Station, where I bought a return ticket for the first train to London. I needed to be with my dad. I needed an alibi.

✠

A few days later, the police knocked on my father's door and informed us that a woman matching my mother's description and with a purse containing a credit card bearing her name had been found dead. My father turned white with shock. I did my best to comfort him, placing a reassuring arm around his shoulders as he heaved and wept. I'm sure our reactions were those of any normal family. I'd already disposed of the coat I wore that day at the Arndale Centre, tying it up in a black bin liner and dumping it in a skip half a mile away on the borders of East Dulwich and Peckham. It was pretty nondescript, but I wasn't taking any chances.

I needn't have worried. As far as the police were concerned, the day my mother died I was in London visiting my father. There were no witnesses or CCTV footage placing me at the scene. The camera on the stairwell wasn't even working, so there was no record of her fall, no film clip to capture her final moments. Someone found her shattered body on the stairs and called the police.

Their questions to us were pretty perfunctory. When did we last see or hear from her? Were we aware of her history of drug and alcohol abuse? Did we know of her last known address? Had she tried to contact me when she was in Manchester?

I pleaded ignorance on all counts but the first, saying I hadn't seen or spoken to my mother in years. They seemed satisfied – and why wouldn't they be? Twelve thousand people die in accidents every year in the UK. Traffic accidents account for around a quarter of these, but the number of fatalities from falls is even higher. Add to this the fact that there are almost nine thousand alcohol-related deaths per annum, and it's easy to see why my mother's demise failed to arouse much interest or suspicion. The coroner's report showed high levels of alcohol in her bloodstream, and after a brief investigation the cause of death was recorded as accidental. She was drunk. She tripped, fell and died. End of story. For me, there couldn't have been a more fitting ending.

My mother's funeral was a quiet affair. There are no prizes for guessing who footed the bill. Savings my father could have spent on home improvements or a well-earned holiday were squandered by a woman who never showed him the slightest appreciation or even a modicum of respect. I attended as a show of support for my dad and to avoid any suspicion that I was somehow implicated in my mother's untimely demise.

Though it bothered me that my dad was paying for her sendoff, the one consolation was that her will stipulated that she wished to be cremated. Not only was this cheaper than a burial, finally I had the satisfaction of knowing that her flesh was really burning, the way I'd fantasised about all those years ago. Sitting in the crematorium, I pictured her skin blackened and blistering, and had to bite the insides of my cheeks to stop myself from grinning. It isn't the done thing to smile at someone's funeral, however little kindness they may have shown you during their lifetime. And I was the grieving daughter, after all. A certain level of solemnity was expected. I couldn't fake tears. I'm not one of those women who can turn on the waterworks at the drop of a hat or an unkind word. But I retained my composure and sat stoically, with my father sobbing gently beside me. Whether his tears were for her or me I never found out.

Something in me changed after my mother died. I stopped cutting myself. I no longer felt the need to manage my rage the way I'd been compelled to when she was alive. We all have our own coping mechanisms and this was mine. A small incision, a moment of pain, a little blood-letting and the pressure was off. But now there was the possibility of a new beginning, free from her and all the damage she caused. Watching my broken skin heal, I could almost convince myself that my body was regenerating, that I was somehow on the verge of being reborn. I would rise like a phoenix from my mother's ashes and take on the world.

Remember how, in *Now, Voyager*, Charlotte Vale blossoms after she escapes her tyrannical mother? I love that film. Given my name, people often assume that my favourite Bette Davis film must be *All About Eve*. But *Now, Voyager* gets me every time, especially when the mother has a heart attack and dies, finally releasing poor Charlotte from her evil clutches. I thought that would be me. I didn't expect Claude Rains to come and sweep me off my feet and onto a luxury cruise liner. I didn't wish for the moon or the stars. But I expected a newfound sense of freedom, a feeling of liberation.

Instead the opposite was true. My world seemed to shrink. I lost my job on the magazine in Manchester. They said I failed my three-month probation, that I wasn't really the kind of person they were looking for, that I lacked focus. Six weeks after my mother's death, I started having nightmares – vivid dreams in which her blackened, blistered corpse kept rising from the dead and crawling under the bed covers to torment and torture me. I'd smell her burning flesh and wake up choking, with blood on the sheets and wounds on my wrists where I'd scratched the skin raw during the night.

It was my father who suggested that I move back home, 'so we can keep an eye on each other'. I thought he was humouring me at first, until it became apparent that he needed my help as much as I needed his. He wasn't the man he used to be. I don't know when the decline had set it, but he wasn't looking after himself properly. He lived on takeaways and microwaved ready meals and frequently fell asleep in front of the TV. I'd hear it burbling away late at night and either wake him gently and show him to his bedroom or simply cover him with a blanket and leave him to sleep on the sofa. I made it my mission to get some decent food down him and would welcome him home from work with healthy stir fries, fresh fish and plenty of vegetables and salad.

I also gave the entire house a much-needed spring clean – dusting, vacuuming, shampooing the carpets, cleaning the oven, scouring the bath and removing years of grime from the kitchen tiles and work surfaces. Some days I'd start straight after breakfast, forget to stop for lunch and still be hard at it when Dad returned home from work. He'd say I was overdoing it and urge me to slow down a bit. But if a job's worth doing it's worth doing well – and the harder I worked, the sooner we'd both benefit. Sorting out the room Dad once shared with my mother, I was horrified to find some of her personal possessions still tucked away at the back of one of the bedside drawers. Nothing of any value, of course – just a balled-up pair of tights and a necklace he once gave her, which she never wore and obviously saw no point in selling. I bagged them up and put them where they belonged – out with the rest of the rubbish.

My own room was exactly as I'd left it. The mattress still had the indent of my teenage self, but a new mattress topper made all the difference. My books were still lined up neatly on the shelves – Penguin classics rubbing shoulders with Michel Foucault and Jean Genet, old Stephen King novels next to my well-thumbed copy of *Sexual Personae* by Camille Paglia. My posters still hung on the walls – Suede, Placebo, The Libertines, Radiohead, an old image of Madonna channelling Marlon Brando in a biker's cap during her gender-fucking 'Justify My Love' phase. Madonna is everything my mother's generation of feminists hated about female empowerment. It didn't take me long to justify my love for her.

The desk where I'd once studied for my exams still stood next to the window. But my studying days were over. I had no need for my books on film theory, cultural studies, poststructuralism and all that queer theory bollocks. But I still had my computer. I still had my novel. I know a lot of people say they have a novel in them, and for most it's just a way of making themselves sound more interesting. But mine was no longer simply in me – it was down on paper. I'd completed the first draft and was busy working on the second. I was buzzing with energy and ideas. I may have been out of work, but I still had plenty of reasons to get up in the morning.

Remember when people used to sneer about bloggers? Some still do, of course. But as the traditional media has shrunk and the opportunities for professional book reviewers have become fewer and far between, publishers have embraced the blogging community like never before. By the time I started my blog, most of my former colleagues on the magazine in Manchester had been made redundant, their jobs lost to a brave new world of automated systems and user-generated content. One day you're a journalist, the next you're replaced by a 'content provider'. How fucking insulting is that?

I blogged daily, mostly about books but sometimes about music or whatever else took my fancy. Some mornings a particularly smug feminist column in the *Guardian* would set me off, and since they'd blocked me from commenting on their website, I'd respond by writing a column of my own, demolishing their argument paragraph by paragraph and posting it on my blog. I'd tag the offending columnist when I shared my blog on social media. My reputation soon spread.

I increased my social-media presence mainly as a means of promoting my writing. I never really took to Facebook. It's far too cliquey for my tastes. But I found a natural home on Twitter, where pithy comments are rewarded and shared, and you can create your very own Twitter storm if you know how to play the game correctly. I was never looking for anything so petty as approval. I wanted to provoke thought and spark debate. My computer became a window into a world far wider than any I'd inhabited before, filled with unlimited opportunities for dialogue and the exchange of ideas. I made more friends on Twitter than I ever made in what some people refer to as 'real life', as if social interaction is only ever 'real' if it's experienced face to face.

I laugh when I think of how my therapist suggested that moving in with my dad was some kind of step backwards. On the contrary, it was a step forward. It gave me opportunities I never thought possible. Writing my blog gave me daily discipline. It gave me a voice, unmediated by the personal prejudices of commissioning editors or the tyranny of political correctness. It gave me the freedom to write, which is the one thing every writer truly needs.

And ultimately, of course, it gave me you.

21

'I'm afraid there's not a lot I can do,' Detective Inspector Sue Grant says. 'There's no proof that what Ms Stokes posted on Twitter is directed at you. She hasn't named you or tagged you, so legally speaking it can't really be described as harassment. Unless she's in breach of her restraining order, she hasn't broken any laws.'

'I appreciate that,' Tom says. 'But statistically speaking, there's a strong possibility that she will, isn't there? Plenty of people do.'

'There's always that possibility, yes. But we can't go around arresting people for crimes they might commit at some point in the future. That's not how the law works.'

More's the pity, Tom thinks. Judging by the tone of the detective's voice, he strongly suspects that she feels the same way – though of course she's hardly going to say so. 'But what about the woman in Wales?' he asks. 'Surely that shows that she's still harassing people?'

'That's for the local police to decide. And from what you've told me there's some doubt about the reliability of the witness.'

Tom falters. He's not sure what he was expecting, but he'd hoped for better than this. He hardly slept a wink last night, and it's taken him the best part of the morning to get Sue Grant on the phone. Now that he has, he thinks he detects a note of irritation in her voice.

'Is there anything else, Mr Hunter?' she asks briskly, confirming his suspicions. 'Only, I am rather busy.'

'I think I saw her,' Tom blurts.

'By "her" I take it you mean Ms Stokes? And was this in Hastings?'

'It was in London, before I left. I was out for a run.'

'And you say you think you saw her?'

'I was pretty certain at first,' Tom says, knowing how unconvincing this sounds. 'But when I looked again, she'd gone.'

'So it's possible that you were mistaken?'

Grudgingly, he agrees. 'It's possible, yes.'

The detective's voice is muffled, as if she's placing her hand over the receiver. Tom hears her call out to someone, telling them she won't be long. Then she's back. 'I'm sorry, Mr Hunter. It's not uncommon for people who've been harassed to continue to experience a sense of being followed. The after-effects of a crime can last for quite some time.'

'So I keep hearing.'

'Sorry?'

'Nothing. Could you at least speak to the private investigator?'

'I'll have a word with my colleagues at South Wales Police,' Sue Grant says. 'And if you are approached by Ms Stokes, or she tries to contact you in any way, please don't hesitate to call me. Now, I'm sorry but I really have to go.'

Tom knows there's no point in arguing. He can tell when he's being palmed off, but without sufficient evidence he has no further claim on the detective's time. He thanks her and ends the call.

Standing at the window, he gazes down at the seafront. The tide is out and the morning sun is high in the sky. A small group of men and women in steam-punk outfits are walking in the general direction of the pier. Tom watches them as they pass – the men in silk waistcoats, tall hats and motorcycle goggles resembling giant fly's eyes, the women in leather corsets and lace petticoats over skinny jeans, or long ruffled skirts with fishnets or striped leggings. As they disappear from his line of vision, his eyes are drawn to a young lad crouched on the concrete groyne directly opposite his building, taking pebbles from a carrier bag he obviously filled earlier and arranging them to spell out the words, 'I love you, Karen'.

Tom wonders if Karen feels the same way and whether she's staying in the apartment next door and will see this declaration of affection when she comes to the window. Maybe she and the lad are lovers and have recently had a tiff. Perhaps her parents disapprove. Even from this distance, Tom can see that the lad is shabbily dressed. A lock of thick black hair hangs low on his forehead, glistening in the sunlight. Tom's imagination runs riot, conjuring up romantic images of Juliet and her Romeo, of Cathy and her Heathcliff.

Then another interpretation presents itself. What if Karen barely knows this lad? What if he's taken a shine to her and won't leave her alone, following her back to the apartment she and her parents have rented for the week and insisting on making his presence felt? What if this is a clear case of harassment? Tom pictures Karen holed up in the apartment next door, peering nervously through a gap in the curtains, her parents hovering protectively behind her, afraid of being seen or leaving the building lest she's accosted by some lovestruck loser she only spoke to out of politeness a few days ago but who hasn't left her alone since. He imagines her fractured state of mind, the sense of self slowly unravelling, constantly looking over her shoulder, anxiety levels spiking. He hears her father threatening to call the police, her mother pleading with him not to overreact and make matters worse. What if the boy is mentally unstable? What if this tips him over the edge?

That's quite some story, Tom thinks, and one which probably says far more about his current state of mind than someone he hasn't even met.

He tears himself away from the window and strides purposefully into the kitchen, where he fills a glass with Diet Coke. Returning to the living room, he sits down and opens his laptop. One last push and the book will be complete. Time to channel his wild imaginings into something creative.

There are days in every writer's life when the words flow and every-thing falls into place. Today is not one of those days. Try as he might, Tom can't get the thought of Evie Stokes out of his mind.

He wonders what she's doing now and whether it's worth checking his phone to see if she's posted anything else on Twitter. He wonders if

Sue Grant is right and he's experiencing some kind of aftershock where he imagines he's being followed or that Evie is waiting for him around every corner. That day at the Southbank he was so sure he saw her. But when he looked again she'd vanished into thin air. Either she possesses supernatural powers, or he's in danger of losing his grip – not just on his writing but on his sanity.

Frustrated by his lack of progress, Tom slams the laptop closed and rises from his chair. He's damned if he'll let that bloody woman take up another moment's headspace, not when he's this close to finishing his book. Time to walk it off and come back to it later.

Outside the sun is scorching and the beach is packed with people thankful they didn't fork out for a foreign holiday when it's so warm at home. News reporters are saying it's the hottest summer since 1976 and that temperatures are expected to last until September. With any luck, the forecasters will have got it right for once.

Scanning the beach, Tom sees that the message in pebbles is still visible on the groyne, though a few stones have been dislodged and the messenger is nowhere to be seen. He wonders if Karen has spotted it yet, and glances up at the windows. They stare back at him: blinds drawn or shiny and blank. He remembers Evie's eyes the night she turned up at his flat – the blankness of them, the moment it dawned on him that the lights were on but there was no-one home. And he'd invited this. Not then, but before. What the hell was he thinking?

A thought surfaces, and something the private investigator said echoes inside his head. 'Most internet stalkers pose no real physical threat. Put them in a real-life situation and they fall apart – ninety percent of them, anyway.'

Great, Tom thinks. But what about the other ten percent?

22

The *Guardian* article appears the next day. Sitting at the kitchen table with his morning coffee, Tom opens his laptop to find a Google alert with his name and a link to the webpage. A knot of anxiety tightens in his stomach as he clicks on the link and waits for the page to load.

'The Danger of Female Stalkers' screams the headline. Beneath it, there's the writer's byline and a subhead that reads, 'Most internet trolls are men. But that doesn't mean men can't be victims of harassment too'. Already this sounds like a very different article to the one Ruth Freeman told Tom she was writing. He distinctly remembers her saying she was looking for a male perspective to provide some gender balance to the piece. Instead she seems to have focussed entirely on male victims of stalking, talking to a handful of men about their experiences and explaining that, while women account for only a small proportion of stalkers – twelve percent, according to the latest research – the impact they have on people's lives is no less harmful.

'Nearly forty percent of cyberstalking victims are men', Freeman writes. 'As with male rape and male victims of domestic violence, it's possible that these numbers are just the tip of the iceberg and the actual numbers are far higher. Many experts believe that cases of cyberstalking against men are underreported due to social stigma and men's reluctance to come forward lest they be perceived as weak. Previous studies have identified women as much more at risk from face-to-face stalking, but in the case of online harassment and cyberbullying, the gap between the sexes is far narrower.'

She then quotes a female psychologist and author of a recent study into cyberstalking, who stresses the widespread lack of understanding of the impact of this kind of behaviour. 'People have a tendency to dismiss or belittle the impact of stalking on men. One of the questions we asked ourselves was, "Is there psychological harm?" Worryingly, a third of the men sampled experienced this. We're not just talking about stress but everything from acute anxiety and depression to full-blown panic attacks. There's a clear clinical record of serious psychological harm.'

Tom's pulse rate increases. He's used to seeing his name in print, just not in this context. And there it is. 'One man who knows all about the impact of stalking is author Tom Hunter', he reads. 'Hunter was stalked for months by a woman he met online. The perpetrator was Evie Stokes, who sent hundreds of emails and tweets to Hunter and on one occasion even turned up at his home address. Two months ago, Stokes was found guilty of harassment without violence. Last month she was given a suspended custodial sentence. Recalling the events that led to her conviction, Hunter says, "It was a living hell. I couldn't sleep. I ended up on antidepressants. There were days when I thought I was losing my mind."'

Tom's stomach churns. He never said those words, not exactly. It was Freeman who brought up the subject of antidepressants, not him. He's aware that journalists often paraphrase quotes for clarity. He's done it himself. But there's paraphrasing and there's putting words in someone's mouth.

Alongside the offending paragraph is his author photo and a pull quote that reads simply, 'Tom Hunter – victim of stalking'. So that's who he is now – a victim. As if all his achievements have been eclipsed by this one experience. He scrolls down the page, scanning the text for further mentions of his name. Halfway down the first column, a chunk of text jumps out at him. 'Hunter admits that he delayed reporting the crime for as long as possible. "The decision to go to the police wasn't any easy one," he says. "But by that point I didn't feel I had any other choice."'

He remembers saying that, or words to that effect. What he doesn't appreciate is Freeman's use of the word 'admits', with its implication that he's somehow at fault, that it was some misplaced sense of male pride that prevented him from reporting the crime earlier. If she was going to suggest that, she could at least have put it to him first.

The next paragraph addresses the way male victims are treated by the criminal-justice system. 'Hunter describes the police response as "sympathetic and supportive", but is less enthusiastic about the Crown Prosecution Service, complaining that the time delay between him first reporting the crime and the case finally reaching court was "unnecessarily long and enormously stressful". Had he known that it would take this long to get justice, Hunter says he might never have gone to the police in the first place.'

Tom has no real issue with this, though seeing his words in print gives them an added weight. He wonders what the investigating officer and crown prosecutor will think. That he's ungrateful for all the support they gave him? Finally the journalist asks him about the sentencing and he says simply, 'The troll got what she deserved.' He remembers saying that and doesn't regret a single word. His only regret is that the sentence wasn't more severe. If he'd had his way she'd have been locked up.

Having satisfied himself that his quotes are mostly accurate, Tom returns to the top of the page and reads the article again from start to finish. There are three other men interviewed, all using pseudonyms. 'Pete' describes how his life was ruined by a female coworker who became fixated with him, making false claims of sexual harassment when in fact it was she who had harassed him. The subsequent stress forced him to resign from the job he loved. Tom feels for him. He knows what a solace work can be.

Next there's 'Joe', who was stalked by an ex who refused to accept that their relationship was over – turning up outside his house, posting love notes through the letterbox and sending threatening messages to the new woman in his life. They've since split up. Again, Tom feels for the poor man, remembering how alarmed he felt the night Evie Stokes turned up outside his apartment building. Plenty of people think men have nothing to fear from women. But plenty of people can be wrong.

This point is proved by the case of 'Alan', who was stalked online and then in real life by a woman he'd never even met but whose behaviour escalated to the point where he feared for his safety. One night he arrived home to find that she'd broken into his flat and was waiting for him with a kitchen knife. He was stabbed twice in the chest and spent ten days in intensive care. His attacker is currently serving a prison sentence for harassment with violence. Tom can only begin to imagine what he must have gone through. It's his own worst nightmare.

All three men state that their lives have been seriously affected by the crimes committed against them. 'Alan' suffers from acute anxiety and depression. 'I keep reliving it all in my head,' he says. 'I'm finding it very difficult to move on. I keep seeing her everywhere I turn.' Tom knows the feeling, though it's not one he'd readily admit to – certainly not to a journalist. Towards the end of the article it's revealed that Joe's stalker has since breached her restraining order and is currently awaiting trial. Finally Tom reads the depressingly familiar statistic – that more than forty percent of offenders convicted of stalking or harassment breach their restraining order.

He now knows why the journalist was so keen to talk to him. He's the only person in the article who's properly identified – the only one named, the only one whose photograph appears. As much as Tom sympathises with these men – and he does, very much – it's easier to say these things when it's not your name and photo in the paper. He's the one people will think of when they read this – not 'Pete' or 'Joe' or 'Alan' or whatever they're called. Him. Tom Hunter – bestselling author turned victim of harassment, reduced to a case study by some crazy woman hiding behind her keyboard. How the mighty are fallen!

As he closes the webpage, a prickling sensation creeps around his hairline and tightens across his skull. He's picturing his nemesis poring over the same article. Knowing how obsessed she is with the *Guardian*, the likelihood of her not seeing it is pretty minimal. In fact, knowing her, she probably has Google alerts set not just for her own name but for his too.

He opens a new window on his search engine and locates her Twitter account. There's hardly any activity. She hasn't interacted with anyone or posted anything new in days. It's not like her to be this quiet. Tom is reminded of a pet saying of his mother's – 'It's the quiet ones you have to watch out for.' It's something people say without very much thought, and he doubts there's much truth in it. There are plenty of people who announce their bad intentions loudly and persistently – are they really any more trustworthy? But in this case it seems fitting. Why is Stokes suddenly piping down? Unless of course it's finally sunk in that her online behaviour is a problem and she's decided to rectify it. Tom doesn't believe that for a second.

He's still staring at her Twitter profile, wondering if perhaps she's ill or away for some reason, when something appears. A new tweet. It says simply, 'LYING FUCKING QUEER PRECIOUS SNOWFLAKE!' There's no name, no tag, nothing to identify him. But it can't be about anyone else, can it? Then a second tweet appears. 'DON'T BELIEVE WHAT YOU READ!!!'

She's seen it, then. He can picture her now, staring furiously at her computer screen, fingers hovering over her keyboard, unable to comment on the *Guardian* website for fear of breaching her restraining order. Or maybe the temptation will prove too great and she'll respond, laying herself open to further charges and a possible prison sentence.

Go ahead, Tom thinks. *Do your worst*. If she ends up in prison there's no saying what will happen to her. She'll probably crack up and either top herself or finally get the help she so obviously needs. Either way, she'll be out of his life for good. Pushing the thought away, he closes the laptop and changes into his running gear.

✳

There's a change in the air, a mugginess that feels as if it might bring rain. But the sky is blue and there's hardly a cloud in the sky. Tom crosses the road to the promenade and heads westwards along the sea-front towards St Leonards, picking up speed as he goes, then settling into a steady rhythm as he runs past Warrior Square and on towards Marina Court.

The tide is low and there's hardly any wind. Small waves nag at the shoreline like a dog with a bone. A group of people in wetsuits are paddleboarding. Tom watches as they glide across the surface of the sea as if it were a millpond. The light bouncing off the water lifts his spirits – so much so that he hardly notices the few drops of rain that begin to fall as he approaches the bowling green. The sun shower is over before it's really begun, but by the time he reaches the beach huts with their cheery pastel stripes his mind is racing. There's nothing like a good run to get the creative juices flowing. Time to head back and crack on with his book. Writing novels is what he does. It's what gives him the greatest satisfaction and his sense of identity. Nobody can take that from him, least of all some angry little keyboard warrior whose only claim to fame is a criminal record.

It's as he's making his way back along the seafront that the dark thoughts begin to resurface. He thinks of the man in the article whose coworker prompted him to resign from a job he loved. He thinks of the man whose ex caused him so much aggravation, his subsequent relationship buckled under the stress. 'It was impossible to move on,' he was quoted as saying. 'She wouldn't let me. She still won't.'

Tom wonders if this will be his fate, too – tied forever to a woman he wishes he'd never met.

❊

Arriving back at his apartment building, Tom sees his neighbour seated outside, a copy of the *Guardian* folded on the table next to him.

'I saw you in the paper,' Colin says. 'Sounds like you've had quite an ordeal.'

Tom pauses to catch his breath. He's glad his face is flushed from the run, so Colin can't see his embarrassment. 'It could have been worse,' he says, then immediately imagines all the ways in which it could still get worse. Maybe Emma was right. Maybe Stokes will see the interview as some kind of provocation. He forces the thought away. 'The important thing is it's all behind me now.' He wipes the sweat from his forehead with the back of one hand, hoping the older man will take the hint.

He doesn't. 'Have a seat,' Colin says, gesturing to the chair beside him.

'I'm okay standing, really.'

'I didn't ask if you were okay standing. I should think you are, big strong lad like you. I asked you to sit with me.'

Reluctantly, Tom does as he's told.

'It makes you wonder what's wrong with people,' Colin continues, 'spending all their time on the internet, harassing people like that.'

'The wonders of modern technology,' Tom says, trying to lighten the mood and failing miserably. Just the thought of it is enough to set his pulse racing.

'Mentally ill then, is she?' Colin says. 'She'd have to be, I suppose. I don't see how she can be anything else. I'm surprised they didn't just section her.'

Tom smiles tightly. 'It's not as simple as that, or so I'm told.'

'Not much comfort to you, though, is it? Her still at large when she's already put you through such an ordeal. They should have locked her up and thrown away the key.'

For a *Guardian* reader, Colin sounds like he'd be more at home with the *Daily Mail*. Tom wonders how old Colin is exactly. He takes in the man's tanned skin and freshly laundered sportswear. Late sixties, maybe? Then he sees through the tan to the sunken cheeks and broken capillaries and adds another five to ten years. He tries not to stare too hard at the pink neck, the flesh puckered and hanging in folds. This will be him one day. Assuming he lives that long.

'It was her first offence,' Tom says, sounding far more charitable than he actually feels. 'People rarely get locked up for their first offence. Not unless they kill someone or there's violence involved.'

'In my day people got locked up for a lot less,' Colin replies. Tom expects him to launch into an angry tirade about petty criminals and liberal politicians, but instead his face softens and his eyes mist over. 'They used to lock men like us up just for being ourselves. Hardly bears thinking about now, but the first few years we were together, my partner and I slept in separate beds. It was against the law, being queer. And even after the law changed you had to watch yourself. All it took was for some nosy neighbour to catch you showing affection in your own home and you could be had for gross indecency.'

'It must have been awful,' Tom says.

The old man nods. 'It was. One chap I knew killed himself. Lots of men did in those days. Things are a lot better now, of course. But old prejudices die hard. You still hear about people being attacked in the street – or on the internet.'

'I didn't have you down for a silver surfer,' Tom says, and immediately regrets his choice of words. The hair colour Colin chooses to present to the world is anything but silver. Is it just Tom's imagination, or does the old man's toupee look even less convincing today?

If Colin is offended, he doesn't let it show. 'I don't use it much. I have a niece in Australia. We talk on Skype sometimes. And I have a Facebook account I barely use. But I see what goes on. And we didn't go through all the battles of the last fifty years so some crazy woman can go around attacking people just because they're gay.'

Tom's face burns. 'There was a bit more to it than that.'

'It says in the paper that she called you queer and pansy and made jokes about AIDS.'

A vein throbs in Tom's left temple. 'She did.'

'And you didn't even know her?'

'Not really, no.'

'She should count herself lucky you didn't take the law into your own hands. Some men would have gone round and taught her a lesson she wouldn't forget.'

'I don't believe in hitting women.'

'Me neither,' Colin says, though the look on his face suggests that he might be willing to make an exception. 'I knew there was something wrong the first time I clapped eyes on you. I said to Graham, "that man's got the weight of the world on his shoulders".'

'Graham?'

'My other half.'

'Sorry, I thought you said your partner was—'

'Dead? Yes, he is. He passed away in 2014. It doesn't stop me from talking to him, though. He always said I talked too much. I'd hate to disappoint him now.'

Tom forces a smile. 'How long were you two together?'

'The best part of sixty years. He held on long enough to see the equal marriage bill passed. That's something we never thought we'd see in our lifetime. What about you? Are you spoken for?'

'I'm not in a relationship.'

'I'm surprised. Good-looking chap like you. I'd have thought you'd be fighting them off. Or is that it? You'd rather fight them off than let someone get too close?'

Normally, an enquiry like this would prompt Tom to clam up or tell someone to mind their own business. But the conversation has taken him by surprise, and for some reason he feels he's talking to someone who deserves an honest answer. 'You're probably right,' he says. Then, feeling the old man's eyes burning into him, 'There was someone, once. It didn't end well.'

'I see,' Colin replies. 'Well, far be it from me to tell you how to live your life. But if you were thinking of giving it another go, my advice would be not to leave it too long. It doesn't get any easier with age, I can tell you.'

'No,' says Tom. 'I don't suppose it does.' And then the most alarming thing happens. He feels something churning inside him. It starts deep in his stomach and rises to his chest. His breath shortens and his rib cage heaves. He can't remember the last time he cried, but suddenly there's the unmistakable sting of tears in his eyes.

Don't cry, Tom tells himself. But he already is.

Colin's face creases with concern. 'Oh dear,' he says, rising to his feet and gesturing to Tom to follow him. 'Come along. I think we'd best get you inside.'

I see you've taken time out of your busy writing schedule to tell your sob story to the newspapers. Honestly, Tom. Anyone would think you had nothing better to do. Or is this who you are now? A professional victim determined to milk this experience for the rest of your life? Reading the article, I hope you felt a stab of shame when you compared yourself to the other men interviewed. What happened to them was truly terrible. Perhaps there's a part of you that wishes you'd had it as hard as they did. It wouldn't surprise me. Victimhood is a competitive sport these days, and people like you seem determined to take it to a whole new level.

There was that word again – 'troll'. You just can't let it lie, can you? I confess I spent a few minutes composing a comment from one of my online aliases to post under the article, pointing out the hypocrisy of such a self-righteous organ as the *Guardian* resorting to such dehumanising name-calling. But then I decided I had better things to do than risk another visit from your friends on the police force. What a charmed life you lead. Enforcers of the law at your beck and call. Friendly journalists waiting to be fed your version of events. And still you lay claim to being a victim.

According to Wikipedia, 'a troll is a person who sows discord on the internet by starting arguments or upsetting people, by posting inflammatory, extraneous or off-topic messages in an online community with the intent of provoking readers into an emotional response, or of otherwise disrupting normal, on-topic discussion, often for the troll's amusement'.

Of course the same could be said of half the journalists who complain of being 'trolled' on Twitter before flouncing off and suspending their accounts – only to reappear a few days later and applauded for their bravery in returning to the fray. Such courage! Such hypocrisy! Such is the life of the commentariat – those precious snowflakes who troll their readers one minute and scream blue murder the next. Consider me suitably amused.

I don't know if your new friend at the *Guardian* has ever complained of being trolled, but she certainly seems to have swallowed their editorial line. I can't say I'm familiar with the work of Ruth Freeman, though with a name like that she probably considers herself some sort of liberal firebrand – Ruth the Truth Sayer, speaking truth to power from her lofty perch at the nation's least favourite broadsheet.

And you, feeding her the lines. For someone who claims to want nothing to do with me, you seem to spend a lot of your time thinking about me. Do you miss me, Tom? Only you do seem rather obsessed. Perhaps it isn't me who needs a therapist, but you. Aren't you a bit old for name-calling? I do have a name. It's Evie. Not 'the troll' as you seem so intent on calling me. Not a nice way to describe someone, is it? Though I suppose I should be flattered that I'm worthy of the definite article, at least. It shows that I matter, that I'm not just any old troll in your eyes, as I apparently am to some.

Even before the Google alert appeared in my inbox, I'd had several of your most ardent admirers attack me on Twitter. I suppose you see that as some kind of justice – 'the troll' gets trolled. Did nobody ever tell you that two wrongs don't make a right? It's a funny kind of justice – not the kind most *Guardian* readers would ascribe to.

I'm reminded of a recent conversation I had with my therapist, who seems to have lost interest in my family history and keeps steering me back to more recent events.

'What does the term "troll" mean to you?' she asked, as if I didn't know exactly where she was going.

'There are many varieties of troll,' I replied. 'You need to be more specific.'

'I'm thinking specifically of people who abuse and harass others on the internet.'

'Again, you need to define your terms,' I said. 'Abuse and harassment are both relative. One person's abuse and harassment are another person's fair and reasonable sustained critique.'

Maria raised her eyebrows at me. 'Not according to the law. You were found guilty of harassment under the Malicious Communications Act. The case against you was based on behaviour widely recognised as trolling.'

'I haven't trolled in my life, ducky,' I said. 'I leave that to the rough trade down the Dilly. You should vada the lallies on some of those omee-palones. Bona doesn't begin to describe them!'

I don't think Maria is familiar with the old Polari, because she stared at me blankly.

'I was speaking in Polari,' I explained. 'It's gay slang. "Trolling" means looking for sex.'

'I see,' she said. 'Then allow me to rephrase my next question. When did you first become aware that people perceive you as an internet troll?'

I smiled at her knowingly. 'That's a bit like asking a homosexual, "When did you first realise you were gay?" Like "gay", "troll" is a social construct and one I categorically refuse to accept.'

It was Foucault who said that living in San Francisco he felt like a homosexual in a city full of gays. I know the feeling. I'm a champion of free speech in a world full of trolls.

'Nonetheless, you were found guilty of online harassment,' Maria said. 'If we're to make any progress in these sessions, it would help if you would at least acknowledge the crime of which you were convicted.'

Hark at her, I thought, but said nothing.

'I know this isn't easy for you,' she continued. 'But if you can't admit that your behaviour was wrong, I don't see how you can possibly hope to be rehabilitated.'

'Is that why I'm here?' I asked her. 'To be rehabilitated? I thought this was just part of my punishment.'

'Is that how you feel?'

'Oh, am I allowed feelings?'

Maria tilted her head in that sympathetic fashion she has. 'How are you finding these sessions, Evie?'

'Simple,' I said. 'I take the bus. It stops right outside.'

She gave me one of her tight smiles. 'I meant, do you find them difficult? Are they helping you?'

'Is that what you're trying to do? Help me?'

'Of course. But for me to help you, you have to help yourself.'

'The Lord helps those who help themselves,' I said. 'You sound like an evangelist! But I suppose this is your religion, isn't it?'

She didn't respond. 'And what about your journal? Are you finding that helpful?'

'Oh, *yes*,' I said. 'One should always have something sensational to read on the train.' I grinned at her. 'It's a quote. Oscar Wilde.'

'I'm well aware of that. It's a line from *The Importance of Being Earnest*. Cecily Cardew, if I'm not mistaken?'

'Well done,' I said. 'Full marks.'

Maria nodded. 'Perhaps it would be more helpful if you quoted less and talked more about how you're feeling. Otherwise there's not really much point in you being here.'

'Come now,' I replied. 'Let's not play games. We both know I'm not here through choice.'

Maria gave the tiniest of shrugs. 'I'm just trying to help.'

'Of course you are. But maybe I don't need help. Or at least not the kind you're advocating.'

I felt her stifle an exasperated sigh. 'Okay. So what kind of help do you need?'

'Where do you want me to start?'

'Start wherever you want.'

So I gave her a list. Maria wasn't to know this, but I was quoting from Madonna's infamous 'rap' in 'American Life', the one where she catalogues her various employees, from her agent and her manager to her chef, gardener and bodyguards. Only I wasn't quite that demanding. I wanted an agent, a publisher, an editor, a publicist – all the help one needs to launch one's literary opus on an unsuspecting world.

'That's quite a list,' Maria said when I finally ran out of steam.

'There's a few people I forgot. I also need the help of other authors.' I paused. 'You know, for puffs.'

Maria frowned. 'Puffs?'

I smiled, sensing that she thought I was being offensive to oversensitive homosexual types. 'Puffs. Those quotes you see on book covers urging you to buy this book immediately, telling you how truly wonderful the author is.'

'I see. And is that what you were hoping to get from Mr Hunter?'

I paused for a while before answering, knowing we were nearly out of time. 'Oh, no,' I said finally. 'I got a lot more from him.'

✠

I first discovered the great white hope known as Mr Tom Hunter when his debut novel, *Boy Afraid*, was published. To fully appreciate the book's impact, you have to consider the context. For years, bookshelves everywhere had groaned under the weight of Bridget Jones and all her Chardonnay-soaked sob sisters. Now, finally, some critics were calling time on chick lit. For me, the end couldn't come soon enough. I hated Bridget with every fibre of my being – a neurotic, calorie-counting child woman we were all supposed to identify with, in a tale lifted straight from the pages of Jane Austen. How backward-looking is that?

After chick lit we had dad lit – Nick Hornby, Tony Parsons and all those famously sensitive male authors eager to demonstrate that men had feelings too. Like chick lit, dad lit suffered from an overdose of sentimentality. The formula was simple: take one small family unit consisting of a hapless but lovable father figure and his troubled young son. A toddler will do, but a boy aged around eight is best. He has to be prepubescent as teenage boys bring their own problems and a whole other weight of expectation. Add a beautiful and much-loved mother figure who is spoken of with great reverence but is no longer in the picture due to a messy divorce or untimely tragic death. Watch the male characters bond as they struggle through the trauma of grief and a diet of takeaways. Then introduce a mother substitute who fills the woman-shaped gap in their lives, bonding with the son and providing the dad with someone to share his bed and his love of some revealingly sensitive hobby, such as plant husbandry or nature photography. Failing that, a shared passion for exotic cookery will do.

Hunter's book wasn't like that. It was bold. Original. It dared to go where no dad lit had gone before. Here at last was a contemporary writer I could identify with. His hero is a man who struggles to raise his only daughter after his wife leaves him – rather like my own dad. The wife isn't the saintly figure of so many dad lit novels, but a hard-bitten bitch – rather like my own mother. The father-daughter relationship is explored in a way I hadn't seen done before, which led me to assume that the author must be a dad himself. The discovery that he wasn't only made his achievement all the more remarkable. I won't give away the plot, but suffice to say it doesn't end well. Again, this was not only brave but honest. We live in a world where men are three times more likely than women to commit suicide. If women were killing themselves at the rate men are, we'd never stop hearing about it. It took an author of Mr Hunter's calibre to give those men a voice.

As the book rose up the charts, he became quite the celebrity. One minute he was chatting on the sofa with Lorraine Kelly, the next he was on the cover of the *Sunday Times Magazine*. And much to my amazement, he looked every bit as good as his author photo. How often have you come across a celebrity in real life only to find yourself bitterly disappointed? I saw Orlando Bloom at the BFI once. I'm afraid to say he looked rather runtish. Not so our Mr Hunter. He was taller, more handsome, with an impressively full head of hair. No wonder my own head was turned.

The book was so successful they even made a film starring Ryan Gosling. He wouldn't have been my first choice, and the film's ending was a total cop-out, but that's Hollywood for you. At least it ensured that sales of the book continued to rise. To say that I took an active interest in Mr Hunter's career would be putting it mildly. I blogged about his work. I attended book readings. I even had him sign my copy of his second, less successful novel, the one he seems to be mildly embarrassed by, though to my mind it's every bit as good as his first. We became pen friends shortly after that night – and the rest, as they say, is history.

But here's the thing about history. It's always told by the winners. Just because Mr Hunter won his court case against me, that doesn't make my account of what happened between us any less true.

※

I spent a few hours at the library yesterday. I like to support my local library, and it's handy to have access to a computer with an IP address that can't be traced directly back to me. Not that I was doing anything illegal, but sometimes it pays to err on the side of caution. If only I'd learned this lesson sooner.

I arrived home mid-afternoon to find my dad sitting quietly at the kitchen table, a load of papers spread out in front of him. It was barely three-thirty, so I was rather surprised to find him sitting there.

'Is everything okay?' I asked him. 'You're never normally back this early.'

'I'm fine,' he insisted. 'It was a slow day so I decided to come home and catch up on some paperwork.'

He wasn't fine – I could see that. But there was no point in pushing it. He's as stubborn as a mule when he wants to be. I take after him in that respect. I take after him in lots of ways. If I hadn't been untimely ripped from my mother's womb, I'd question whether I had any of her DNA in me at all.

'I bought some of those salmon fishcakes you like,' my dad said. 'I thought we'd eat around six, if that's okay. I quite fancy an early night. I'll give you a shout when dinner's ready.'

Something told me he wasn't telling the whole truth, but I left him to his paperwork, went up to my room and logged onto my computer. I had a blog to write and some social media stuff to catch up on. I'm writing a blog about all the people who've blocked me. It's a bit playful and tongue-in-cheek, but makes a number of serious points about censorship and freedom of speech. I'm not allowed to mention Mr Hunter by name and I'm not allowed to follow him on Twitter. Not that I need to. I have other ways of keeping tabs on people of interest.

There were a number of emails, mainly related to a new project I'm working on concerning a woman artist in Wales. And there was another email, too – a most surprising email from someone I wouldn't have expected to hear from in a million years. At first I thought it was some kind of joke or possibly even a trap. I hesitated before replying, but my curiosity got the better of me. Life can take such unexpected turns sometimes, can't it? People you thought were friends turn out to be enemies – or 'frenemies' as we're now required to call them – and people you considered enemies can turn out to be potential allies. To say I was pleased by this sudden turn of events would be putting it mildly. By the time Dad called me for dinner, I was positively bubbling with excitement.

My bubble soon burst. Seated at the dining table, I'd barely taken a bite out of my fishcake when I sensed something was wrong. 'What's the matter, Dad?' I asked. 'What is it?'

He took a few moments before answering. 'I need to ask you something. It's about your mother.'

I crammed in another mouthful. 'Must we? I'm eating.'

'It's not a joking matter, Evie. This is important. It's about the day she died.'

I chewed thoughtfully and swallowed before replying. 'That was years ago. I think it's time we moved on, don't you?'

Dad set down his knife and fork and stared across the table at me. 'But we've never really talked about it, have we? Not properly.'

'Why drag it up now? Let sleeping dogs lie.' I couldn't help but smirk slightly. Referring to women as 'dogs' was one of my mother's pet hates.

Dad pushed aside his untouched plate. 'Your mother wasn't the easiest of women, Evie. I know that. But she loved you in her own way.'

I hate it when people use that expression – that someone loved you 'in their own way'. As if love is such a nebulous concept it can be stretched to encompass virtually anything. As if abuse, cruelty and neglect can all fall under the banner of this wonderful thing we call love. As if you can stretch a rubber band and it won't snap back in your face.

'And in what way would that be?' I asked.

'She had a very difficult childhood. Her own mother never showed her much love, so she didn't have a good role model.' Dad smiled sadly. 'Children don't come with a user's manual, more's the pity. But she did care for you.'

I nearly laughed at this point. Never was there a less caring woman than my dear departed mother. The only person she ever cared about was herself.

'She wasn't a well woman, Evie. She had mental-health problems.'

'Alcohol problems, more like.'

'She wasn't always like that. Her illness … it hid itself for a long time.'

'It didn't stop her running off with other men though, did it?'

'It wasn't as simple as that. We both made mistakes. I wasn't the perfect husband, not by a long way. I didn't handle things as well as I could have. I let her down. I let you both down.'

'Don't make excuses for her!'

'I'm not. It's the truth.' He looked at me meaningfully. 'Things are never as simple as they appear to us when we're children.'

I didn't like the way this conversation was going, so I tried to close it down. 'I don't know why you're bringing this all up now,' I said. 'It's ancient history.'

He leaned towards me across the table. 'It's not though, is it? You were there the day she died. In Manchester.'

'I wasn't. I was here with you.'

'No, you weren't. You arrived later that evening. I remember the way you were – so agitated. Why did you turn up like that? So suddenly?'

'Can't a girl choose to visit her own father?'

'Of course you can. You're always welcome here. But I need to ask you something. And I need you to be honest with me. Can you do that for me?'

I smiled. 'Of course.'

'Only you haven't always been entirely honest with me in the past, have you?'

'What's that supposed to mean?'

'This business with the writer. I was there, remember. In court. I heard the evidence against you.'

'So now you're on his side. Is that what you're saying?'

'I'm saying I need you to be completely honest with me. Can you promise me that?'

I nodded, feeling about ten years old again.

'The day your mother died,' Dad said. 'You were in Manchester. Did you have anything to do with what happened to her?'

'Of course not. You remember what the police said. It was an accident.'

He stared at me for a few moments, before gathering up our plates and taking them through to the kitchen. I heard the tap running.

'Don't wash up,' I called. 'I'll do it later.'

The sound of the water stopped but he didn't return to the table.

'Dad?'

Moments later, he re-entered the room, his face still serious. 'This thing with the writer – that's all over now, isn't it? You haven't breached your restraining order, have you? Because you know what'll happen if you do.'

'Of course not,' I replied. 'And that whole thing was just one big misunderstanding. I told you that.'

'And is the therapy business helping?'

I thought carefully before replying. 'It's helping me put things in perspective. So on the whole, I'd say yes.'

'Good.' There was another long pause. 'I worry about you, Evie,' he said eventually. 'I've seen the marks on your wrists. The ones you try to cover with long sleeves and those bracelets you wear.'

Immediately my right hand went to my left wrist, where a few small scratches were concealed beneath a cotton weave wristband. 'It's just eczema,' I lied. 'I've made an appointment to see the doctor for some steroid cream.'

It would take more than steroid cream to salve the anger that produced those marks – marks that have your name written on them, as clearly as if you'd carved it there yourself.

'And you're having nightmares again,' Dad said. 'I heard you crying out in the night.'

'Everyone has nightmares from time to time. It's not against the law, is it?'

He smiled at me kindly. 'No, it's not against the law.'

'Well, there you are, then.'

He held my gaze for a while. Finally he said, 'I worry about what would happen to you if I wasn't here.'

'You're not planning on going anywhere, are you?'

'No, but...'

'Good,' I said. 'Then we're all fine, aren't we?'

✼

After dinner we watched a film. My dad is a big fan of Sean Connery. I think he's the kind of man Dad always hoped he'd be, had he not been emasculated by my mother. One of the film channels was showing *The League of Extraordinary Gentlemen*. I don't think even Connery's most ardent admirers would argue that it was his finest hour – and if they did I'd be forced to say 'surely shum mishtake?' in my best Connery voice – but Dad seemed content enough.

During the first of many ad breaks, I fixed us both a drink – a gin and tonic for me (heavy on the gin) and a whisky on the rocks for him. I finished my drink pretty quickly and poured myself another. Dad's remained virtually untouched. By the time the film ended, he was half asleep in his armchair.

'Come on, Dad,' I said. 'Time for bed.'

He looked at me strangely, as if he was waking from a dream or seeing me for the first time.

'I meant what I said earlier,' he said. 'You need to take better care of yourself. Get out more. Spend less time on the internet.'

'I will,' I replied. 'I promise.'

I kissed him goodnight and went up to my room, where I looked to see if anyone had commented on my latest blog post. Nobody had, but it was still early. Most of my loyal followers log on in the morning, before work. I opened the Facebook account I'd created a few weeks earlier using a false name and a stock photo, and scoured a few profiles of interest before opening another tab on my browser. I have a new anonymous Twitter account, too – several, in fact, linked to various email service providers. Neither Facebook nor Twitter seem particularly keen to divulge information or help the police with their enquiries, but it pays to be cautious. I was checking my Twitter account when I remembered my conversation from earlier. I opened my mailbox and there it was – the email I'd been waiting for. Finally I had an appointment with someone I'd been dying to meet for a long time.

24

Colin's flat is very different from how Tom imagined it. He expected wall-to-wall carpets, a three-piece suite and rooms crammed with enough clutter and soft furnishings to fill a small department store. In other words, the kind of decor his parents would have chosen. Instead there are polished floorboards and a minimalist look that borders on the austere.

While the old man disappears into the kitchen to make tea, Tom follows his host's instructions and waits in the living room. There's a large oatmeal sofa and two wingback leather armchairs in different shades of green. Next to the sofa is a standing lamp with a sandy shade and a stem fashioned from driftwood. A smaller matching lamp sits on a large glass-topped coffee table alongside a stack of magazines. The overall effect is of the waiting room in a private doctor's surgery, albeit one where the doctor is only qualified to dispense tea and sympathy.

The wide bay window looks out onto the main road, the lower half of the frames filled with etched glass for privacy. Tom wonders how many nights the old man has spent sitting here in this room, watching silhouettes pass the window, thinking about his own mortality. Loneliness can be a killer, or so people say. Tom can only begin to imagine what it must be like to have spent the best part of your life with someone only to suddenly find yourself alone. No wonder Colin insisted on inviting him in. He must be glad of the company.

In the alcove next to the fireplace is a large TV. In pride of place on the mantelpiece is a silver-framed photo of a much younger Colin with a full head of hair and a bushy moustache. Standing next to him is a handsome man with floppy blond hair. They're both smiling at the camera, looking relaxed and tanned. Behind them, an olive tree is silhouetted against a deep-blue sky, and a bright-pink bougainvillea climbs against a white-washed wall.

'Mykonos,' Colin says, entering the room with a tray laden with mugs of tea and a plate of biscuits. 'Nineteen eighty-four. Our first time there. Of course it was different back then. Not like today.' He sets the tray down on the coffee table. 'I forgot to ask if you take sugar.'

'No, thank you,' Tom says. He's never seen the appeal of places like Mykonos. A gay party island is his idea of hell.

'Good,' says Colin. 'I've never understood people who put sugar in their tea. Totally destroys the taste. They say it's good for shock, but personally I've always found brandy hits the spot far better. I have some if you like?'

'Tea is fine. Thank you.'

'Well, don't stand on ceremony. Sit yourself down.'

Tom glances at the sofa, conscious of the fact that he's still in his running gear. 'I'm afraid I'm a bit sweaty.'

'I can fetch you a towel if you like. Or there's an old dog blanket somewhere.' The old man grins. 'I'm just messing with you. A bit of sweat never hurt. Please. Sit yourself down. You're making the place look untidy.'

Not wishing to risk sitting in his host's favourite armchair, Tom chooses one end of the sofa and lowers himself carefully onto it, perching as far forwards as possible. He can feel the sweat pooling in the small of his back and wishes he'd taken up Colin's offer of a towel.

'That's better,' the old man says. 'And help yourself to biscuits.'

Tom takes one, more out of politeness than appetite, and is surprised and somewhat embarrassed when his stomach responds by gurgling gratefully.

'Sounds like you needed that,' Colin smiles. 'Feeling better?'

Tom nods and speaks through a mouthful of digestive biscuit. 'Thank you. You're very kind.'

Colin waves one heavily veined hand. 'Nonsense. It's no trouble at all.' He sits in the nearest of the two armchairs and reaches for his tea.

Neither of them speaks for a few minutes. The only sounds are the rumble of traffic on the road outside and his host slurping his tea. Tom has never been in therapy or gone to confession but he can't escape the feeling that Colin is waiting for him to unburden himself. And for some strange reason, Tom feels the urge to do just that. Maybe it's the freedom of knowing that he and Colin are practically strangers and may never see each other again, so anything he says now will probably be forgotten. Or maybe it's guilt. Guilt that he was so quick to dismiss Colin as some ridiculous old man in a bad wig. Guilt that he hasn't been completely honest. He's already cried in front of Colin, and the old man has shown him such kindness.

'I lied,' Tom says suddenly. 'In court. I lied.'

Colin raises his eyebrows so high, they disappear into his unnaturally low hairline. 'Lied about what?'

Tom thinks carefully before continuing. 'I said I didn't know her, that we'd never met. We did. She came to a book signing, and then a few weeks later I met her for a drink.'

'I see,' Colin says. 'What on earth did you do that for?'

'I felt flattered, I suppose. I was having a hard time. I'd taken a bit of a hammering from the critics, and she was so full of enthusiasm for me and my work.'

'I meant, why did you lie?'

'Oh.' Tom lowers his eyes. 'I was embarrassed. I felt as if I was somehow to blame for what happened, that I'd brought it on myself. I'd allowed my ego to get in the way of my common sense, and I was too ashamed to admit it. And once I'd lied to the police I thought I'd better stick to my story.'

'Weren't you worried that you'd be found out?'

'At first, yes. I already had a story in place. I was going to say that she must have followed me there. It's a pub I never normally go to. I took a chance that nobody would remember seeing me with her. It would be my word against hers. I thought it would come up before the case reached court, or her defence would suddenly spring it on me under cross-examination. But it was never mentioned.'

'Why not?'

'I don't know. Because she's mad? Or maybe her lawyer advised against it. Maybe the evidence against her was so strong, they thought it wouldn't have made any difference. I honestly don't know.'

'I see,' says Colin. 'Well, maybe they're right.'

'About what?'

'About it not making any difference. She's still guilty of stalking you. Whether you met her for a drink or not. Some people are stalked by ex-husbands or people they once had a relationship with. It doesn't change the fact that they were stalked.'

Tom lifts his head. 'I guess not.'

'So stop being so hard on yourself. You're not the first man to make a mistake and you won't be the last.'

'I suppose I'm worried that it'll catch up with me.'

'That's just your guilty conscience talking. Do what I do.'

'What's that?'

'I turn my hearing aid off.'

Tom smiles. 'What have you got to feel guilty about?'

The old man winks. 'Let's just say I've had my moments.' He points at Tom's mug. 'More tea?'

'I'm afraid it's gone cold.'

Colin reaches for the mug and rises to his feet. 'Then you'd better wait here while I make us a fresh pot.'

✳

Left alone with his thoughts, Tom casts his mind back to that night. If he'd only known then what he knows now, he'd never have agreed to meet with her. But at the time it seemed so innocuous. A friendly drink with a woman who admired his work – where was the harm in that?

In retrospect, he must have had an inkling that something wasn't right; why else choose a pub he never visited? On some level, he was maintaining a safe distance between her and the world he inhabited on a weekly basis – a world where pubs rarely featured. It was a bit like going on a blind date with someone you're not too sure about and want to avoid bumping into again, should things go spectacularly wrong. The last place you agree to meet them is at your favourite bar or restaurant. The one thing Tom hadn't done was arrange for someone to call him on some pretext, should he need to make a quick getaway. Because that someone would have been Emma, and he'd already taken the decision not to tell her about his new Twitter friend. Emma could be a little possessive at times – something he attributed to her upbringing – and he had no desire to hurt her feelings or risk an argument.

Evie Stokes was waiting at the bar when Tom arrived, sipping a drink and looking smarter and more groomed than when they'd first met at the bookshop. She wore a tight black skirt and a metallic-blue top with long sleeves that flared slightly at the wrists. Her hair was sleek and glossy, as if she'd just been to the hairdressers. She was wearing rather a lot of makeup and Tom remembers thinking she seemed quite agitated. He'd put it down to nerves. It never crossed his mind that a few nervous tics might be a sign of something more serious.

She had a way of absent-mindedly tugging at the sleeves of her blouse or the hem of her skirt, as if they weren't quite long enough or she wasn't used to the feel of the fabric against her skin. She reminded Tom of the girls he knew at school, who'd shorten their skirts by hitching them up and folding over the waistband, then spend half their time fiddling with the hem and making adjustments. Like them, Evie looked as if she was trying out a new look and wasn't quite comfortable with it yet. Tom had to remind himself that she wasn't a schoolgirl but a woman in her mid-thirties. For one awful moment he wondered if she'd bought the outfit especially. Some men would have been flattered. Instead he felt a stab of anxiety – was she expecting more from this encounter than he was willing to give?

'Sorry I'm late,' Tom said, though a quick glance at his watch confirmed that he was actually dead on time.

'I was early,' she replied. 'I was in the area.' Why, she didn't say, though Tom later wondered if she already knew his address and had been busy familiarising herself with his part of town.

He bought her another drink – a white wine spritzer – and they found a table at the rear of the pub.

'Thanks for meeting me,' she said as they sat down. 'I wasn't sure you'd come.'

'I always keep my promises,' Tom replied, though he was already beginning to doubt the wisdom of his decision. He took a mouthful of his pint of lager – not his usual drink of choice but one that seemed more fitting for the situation. This was a pub where men drank pints and women drank wine from enormous glasses on long stems. At the next table, two men appeared to be involved in a drinking contest, knocking back pints and belching their appreciation.

'You look nice,' Evie said, and Tom replied almost without thinking, 'So do you.' Then, eager to steer the conversation onto less personal ground, he asked her if she'd read any good books lately.

'I'm giving Bret Easton Ellis another go,' she said, as if she and the author were a couple who'd been through a rocky patch and had agreed by mutual consent to go to couples counselling and work through their differences.

'Rather you than me,' Tom replied, remembering the time he shared a platform with Ellis at the Southbank Centre. He felt Evie watching him and added quickly, 'I always preferred Jay McInerney.'

The conversation was stilted at first, but after his second pint Tom started to relax. He enquired about her blog and complimented her on her outspoken and often provocative opinions. She asked about his writing and told him again how much she loved his last book. Then she mentioned that she was working on a novel of her own. Alarm bells rang as she asked Tom if he'd mind taking a look at it, and he mumbled something about being extremely busy right now but maybe at some point in the future he could read a couple of chapters. If Evie knew she was being palmed off she didn't let it show. For a few minutes it looked as if any awkwardness or social embarrassment had been avoided. Until she changed the subject.

'So have you always fancied men?' she asked suddenly. She was on her third drink by now, which may have accounted for the sudden rise in volume and the directness of her question. Still Tom found it impertinent, not to mention embarrassing. Already he could sense the two men at the next table exchanging smirks and meaningful glances in his direction.

'Not exclusively,' he replied, as if a few fumbles with the opposite sex were enough to save face and make him more of a man in their eyes. 'There are plenty of women I find attractive.'

If Evie sensed his discomfort, it didn't prevent her from labouring the point. 'But you don't sleep with them.'

Tom gritted his teeth. 'On the whole, no. But there've been a few.'

'Was your friend Emma one of the lucky few?'

It may have been the drink talking. It may have been bravado. But it was then that Tom said something he should never have said. Something he's been quietly regretting ever since.

✻

'Here we are,' Colin says, entering the room with two fresh steaming mugs of tea and placing them on the table. Settling down in his armchair, he takes a sip of tea and smiles reassuringly. 'I was just thinking about something while I waited for the kettle to boil.'

'What's that?' Tom asks.

'Tell me to mind my own business, but I just wanted to say, there's no shame in admitting weakness. You were the victim of a crime. It's bound to affect you.'

Tom's face burns. 'I think I'm embarrassed by the fact that it's a woman.'

'I don't see why. Remember that gay chap who was beaten to death in Trafalgar Square?'

'Ian Baynham.' Tom nods. Of course he remembers. The case made the national news. There was even a candlelit vigil at the scene of the crime.

'One of his assailants was a young woman,' Colin says. 'Tough as nails, some of them. There's nothing for you to feel embarrassed about.'

'I hate to be thought of as a victim.'

'You're only a victim if you let it define you, and I'm sure you're far too clever for that. But if you try to deny your feelings, they won't go away. They'll just become all twisted up inside.' The old man smiles knowingly. 'You wouldn't want that, would you?'

'I guess not.'

They sit in silence for a while. The hot tea warms Tom's throat and he holds the mug close to his mouth, grateful for something to focus on and to occupy his hands. That was always half the attraction of cigarettes, though he's not entirely sure his smoking days are completely behind him. The craving is still there – more psychological than physical, but no less powerful. He could use a cigarette right now.

Finally Colin sets down his mug and fixes Tom with his milky blue eyes. 'I'd like to show you something,' he says. 'If I may?'

'Of course,' Tom replies, expecting another old photo or a memento of some kind. Instead the old man gently removes his wig, revealing a bald head with fine tufts of white hair at the sides. But that's not what grabs Tom's attention. What shocks him is the large crescent-shaped scar on the top left-hand side of the old man's head; it's about the size of a clenched fist. The scar tissue is paler than the rest of his scalp and raised slightly, like the ridges of a fossil. At the centre of the scar is an indentation, as if someone has taken a blunt instrument to the old man's skull.

'What happened?' Tom asks, though he already has a pretty good idea.

'I was attacked,' Colin replies. 'It must be over thirty years ago now. It was when I lived in London, near Clapham. I'd gone to the gay pub down by the common, The Two Brewers – perhaps you know it?'

'Otherwise known as The Two Sewers. Yes, I know it.'

The old man smiles. 'Not quite your scene? No, it was never quite mine, either. But it was someone's birthday. I can't remember whose. My memory is a bit hazy. But I do remember that Graham wasn't well, which is why I went on my own. The last thing he said to me before I left was "be careful". They were dangerous times, you see. More so than now. Anyway, it was late – around one o'clock or so. And I'd had a few, as you do. I was walking across the common to my bus stop and they just came out of nowhere. Two men with baseball bats. By the time I realised what was happening, it was too late. I called for help but there was nobody around, or if there was they didn't want to know. I tried to run, but they were too fast for me. The last thing I remember is a blow to the head, and that was it. I was out cold.'

'Oh my God,' Tom says. 'That's awful.'

Colin shrugs. 'It could have been worse. I could have died. I very nearly did. Some man found me an hour or two later. The police said he was out walking his dog, though I've often wondered. Who walks their dog in the middle of the night? But he couldn't have told them what he was really doing there. They might have charged him. The doctors told me my head was the size of a watermelon. Blood everywhere. I was unconscious for days. They had to reconstruct part of my skull. That's why there's that bloody great dent at the top. Poor Graham. I'll never forget the look on his face that day at the hospital. "I thought I'd lost you," he said. And the truth is, he very nearly did.'

'Did they ever catch them?' Tom asks. 'The men who did it?'

Colin snorts. 'Did they hell! I don't think it was high on their list of priorities. And it was no good the police appealing for witnesses. People didn't trust the police. They were worried that they'd be arrested, or exposed at work and lose their jobs. It was a different world back then. The night I was attacked, the police arrested three men they caught cruising on the common. That's where their priorities lay. Never mind the poor bastard who'd just had his head smashed in.'

'How did you cope?' Tom says. 'Afterwards?'

'I was shaken, obviously. I was afraid to leave the house for a while. I kept seeing men with baseball bats on every corner. But what can you do? Life goes on. You have two choices: you either get on with it or you give up. I chose to get on with it.'

Tom nods. A wave of emotion washes over him and he struggles to maintain his composure. He's already broken down crying once in front of Colin. The last thing he wants is a repeat performance.

'I'd better be going,' he says, rising to his feet. 'Sorry to rush off but I have work to do and I really ought to take a shower.'

'Well, you know where I am,' the old man says. 'Any time you fancy a chat, my door is always open.'

'Thanks,' Tom says. 'And thanks for the tea, and the conversation. It's been humbling talking to you.'

'Humbling? Why?'

'It's not often I meet a man like you.'

'A man like me? What am I like?'

Tom blushes. 'A survivor.'

Colin grins, flashing his too-white teeth. 'We're all survivors, aren't we? Until we die.'

25

It's almost 10.00 a.m. when Tom leaves Colin's apartment and heads upstairs. By the time he's shaved, showered, dressed, has eaten a quick breakfast and is finally settling down at his computer to work, it's closer to 10.45 a.m. The *Guardian* article has been live for a little over three hours. But when he checks his Twitter account he sees that it's already caused quite a stir. More than fifty people have retweeted the link from the newspaper's Twitter feed, including the journalist herself. Tom knows this because he's been tagged. His notifications show that dozens more have liked, retweeted or commented on the original post.

The first comment says simply, 'Brave of these men to speak out' and has already attracted a number of responses. Most are pretty innocuous. 'Some crazy bitches out there', writes one woman. Some are plain stupid. 'Scared of a woman? LMAO!' says one man. Others are more aggressive. 'Women like this need to be taught a lesson', says one. Another reads, 'Bitch tried this shit with me she'd be dead!'

Tom swallows. It's not that long ago that he wished Evie Stokes dead. But there's a difference between wishing it and threatening it. Seeing it spelt out like this leaves a nasty taste in his mouth.

Further down the thread, he sees that someone has tagged her, adding 'Pleased to see this pathetic troll finally got what's coming to her'. Several others have liked the comment or responded with further insults. 'No wonder she hides behind stock photos', says one. 'Imagine the face on it!' Someone responds, 'Never mind the face. Imagine the twat! #shudder'. Another says, 'Mad bitch wants locking up'. A fourth man suggests a hashtag, #FuckEvie and calls for people to hound the 'evil cunt' off Twitter. 'No place for hate', he adds, with no apparent sense of irony.

If Stokes has seen these tweets, she hasn't responded – at least not so far as Tom can see. He feels a pang of pity tinged with guilt and has to remind himself that she brought all this on herself. The online abuse she's getting now is nothing compared to the abuse she dished out to him. He recalls some of the tweets she sent – the ugly words, the way she'd tag as many people as possible to maximise his humiliation and increase the chances of him seeing what she'd written when someone replied. He isn't comfortable with what he's seeing now. The misogyny makes him squirm, and the bullying way people are ganging up on her sends shivers of recognition down his spine. But he isn't responsible for any of this. Twitter can be a real viper's nest. She of all people should know that. She thrives on it. Didn't she like to boast about the number of people who'd blocked her? Wasn't she thrilled when one of her blog posts caused a Twitter storm, attracting an avalanche of hostile comment? 'Writing should provoke people', she used to say. 'Everything else is just PR.'

Tom keeps telling himself this as he watches the number of retweets rise sharply and other Twitter users pile in with further insults. People are calling for her blood now. Men are competing to see who can come up with the most offensive putdowns. She's a 'stupid cunt', a 'pig ugly troll', a 'mad bitch' who should be 'put out of her misery'. A few women try to challenge some of the language used and are shouted down, dismissed as 'feminazis' or lesbians who 'need a good seeing to'.

A coil of anxiety tightens in Tom's stomach. He wishes he wasn't tagged in these posts, but short of muting or blocking everyone who shares or comments, there's not a lot he can do. At least most people seem sympathetic to his situation. Though knowing Twitter, it won't be too long before the tide turns and the storm changes direction. He's seen it happen a thousand times. Unless of course it all blows over by lunchtime, eclipsed by the latest terror attack, natural disaster or celebrity sex scandal. Here's hoping.

He logs off Twitter and quickly checks his emails before turning off the Wi-Fi on his laptop and putting his phone on silent. With a bit of luck he may even finish his book today. Time to focus on what really matters. Time to write.

✻

Maybe it's the welcome distraction from all the crap on Twitter. Maybe it's the relief at having unburdened himself to Colin, and the reminder that life is short so he should stop messing about and just get on with it. Maybe it's that mystical state of mind every writer longs for but few are able to describe in terms that don't make them sound like a total wanker. But upstairs in his rented flat, Tom finally pushes through whatever's been holding him back these past few days and experiences that rare sensation of being possessed by the spirit of a story he's been chosen to tell – words he would never repeat to a third party, for fear of ridicule. He writes quickly, the words falling over themselves, faster than his fingers can type. All the pent-up emotion he's been storing for months pours into his writing. He loses all track of time until suddenly he's at the end of the last paragraph to the final chapter of the book.

Tom sits back in his chair, hits the return key twice and types the words 'THE END'. There are few things in life more satisfying than this, and he pauses to savour the moment before the usual doubts start creeping in. He has a sudden craving for a celebratory cigarette – but that would mean going to the shop and committing to a pack of twenty, and he knows his lungs won't thank him for it. What he needs is a new ritual, one that won't fill him with carcinogens and self-loathing. The clock at the top of his screen says the time is just past 2.00 p.m. It's a bit early for a drink. and there's not much fun in cracking open a bottle of champagne on his own. The celebrations will have to wait.

He closes the laptop and rises from his chair. For now at least, the book is complete. He can reread the final chapter later and make any necessary adjustments. Reaching for his phone, he turns it on and sees that there are two missed calls and two voicemails. The first is from Emma and was left shortly after 11.00 a.m.

'Tom, it's me. I've seen the article. Look, I know you think you're justified in doing this, and I've tried to see it from your point of view, I really have. But I'm your friend and I have to tell you I think you're making a big mistake. I've got a bad feeling about this. I'm assuming you've seen what's happening on Twitter, so you'll know what I'm talking about. If not, go and take a look. But please, don't respond. Don't make this any worse. Just stay out of it, please. Call me when you get this message. Okay, bye.'

Great, Tom thinks. His best friend, and she's more concerned about the woman who harassed him than with his personal welfare. How can Emma be so disloyal? He thought she had his back. Evidently he thought wrong.

The second call is from his agent, and the contrast couldn't be more striking.

'Tom, darling! It's Lucinda. Great piece in the *Guardian* today. I've had *Woman's Hour* on the phone. They'd like you on the show tomorrow. Call me.'

He hits the call-back button and is surprised when he's put through to her immediately. 'Tom! Just the man I want to speak to. How's that wonderful new book coming along? You know I'm dying to read it.'

'It's finished,' he replies, and immediately wishes he'd played for more time. What if he reads over it later and decides it still needs work?

'Wonderful news!' Lucinda says. 'So you'll send it to me this afternoon?'

'I'd like a day or two to go over it one last time, if that's alright.'

'Of course. Why don't you do that, but send it to me today anyway. I'm out of the office for a few days, and I can't wait to get stuck in. Besides, you'll be too busy tomorrow with *Woman's Hour*.'

'About that,' Tom says. 'Are you sure it's a good idea?'

'It's a great idea. They loved the *Guardian* piece, and you're obviously the go-to man on this.'

'But that's just it. I'm not sure I want to be.'

Lucinda pauses. Tom is sure he can hear her fingernails tapping on the phone. This is not a good sign. Lucinda tapping her nails is like a cat whipping its tail or a dog baring its teeth. Warning sign. Danger approaching. Then she laughs – a deep, throaty chuckle that contains very little warmth. 'Tom, darling. This is a great opportunity. The BBC haven't exactly been beating a path to your door lately. Do this and it might lead to other things. It's time we got you back in the saddle.'

Immediately Tom pictures himself being thrown from a horse. 'Yes, of course,' he says, imagining cracked ribs and a broken collar bone. 'Tell them I'd be happy to go on.'

His agent practically coos her approval. 'Wonderful! I'll have the researcher call you. And I look forward to seeing the book.'

'I'll get right onto it,' Tom replies, but she's already gone.

✳

He doesn't get right onto it. For the next ten minutes he sits and stares, wondering why on earth he has allowed himself to be coerced into doing something he'd rather not do. He's not a regular listener to *Woman's Hour* but he has a feeling they'll be far more interested in Evie's side of the story than his. What would drive a woman to behave the way she did? How does it feel to be on the receiving end of so much abuse from misogynistic trolls on Twitter? What's the feminist angle on this? Is the patriarchy somehow to blame?

A loud bleep snaps him out of his reverie, announcing the arrival of a text message. Tom glances at his phone, sees Emma's name flash up.

Where r u? the text reads. *Call me.*

A surge of irritation lifts him from his chair and marches him into the kitchen. The craving for a cigarette is stronger than ever, but he takes a few deep breaths and pours himself a glass of water. Returning to the living room, he snatches up the phone and calls Emma's number. She answers on the second ring.

'Great news,' he says. 'I've finished the book.'

'Good for you.'

'That doesn't sound very sincere. I thought you'd be pleased.'

Her tone softens. 'I am pleased. Seriously. Well done. That's great news.'

'I sense a but.'

Emma sighs. 'I assume you've seen what's been happening on Twitter?'

'I glanced at it earlier.'

'Well?'

'Well, what?'

'Are you happy with your handiwork? All those men bullying her like that?'

'Hang on a minute,' Tom says, pacing the room as he talks. 'I'm not responsible for any of that. She's the one who committed a crime, not me. All I did was tell the truth.'

'Is that all you did? Really?'

'What's that supposed to mean?'

Emma pauses. 'I wish you hadn't spoken to that journalist. I tried to warn you, Tom. I told you it wasn't a good idea.'

'Yes, you did. But I'm a free agent and I make my own decisions. I happen to think it was the right decision. And just so you know, I've been asked to go on *Woman's Hour* tomorrow.'

Emma's tone is despairing. 'Oh, Tom. Why?'

'Why do you think? To talk about what happened to me. To share my experience with their listeners.'

'I meant, why do it?'

'I know exactly what you meant. You'd rather I just shut up about it. But I won't. Why should I?'

'Stop it, Tom. Please, just stop it. Before things get any worse.'

'What's that supposed to mean?'

'You're devoting so much of your time to this. You're letting it take over your life. You're letting *her* take over your life. Is that what you really want?'

'Don't patronise me, Em!'

'I'm not!'

'Yes, you are. You're talking to me like I'm a child. I'm a grown man. If I decide to talk about my personal experience with a journalist or discuss it on the radio, it's nobody's business but my own.'

'Is that right?' Emma's tone is brittle. 'I'll bear that in mind in future. In the meantime, your personal experience is splashed all over the internet, and now a vulnerable woman is being harassed as a result of it.'

Tom's temper flares. 'Vulnerable woman? You've changed your tune.'

'I haven't. But it is possible to feel sympathy for both parties in a situation like this. She clearly isn't well, and what's happening now could be enough to tip her over the edge.'

'So the troll gets trolled. You live by the sword, you die by the sword. What do you expect me to do about it?'

'Two wrongs don't make a right, Tom.'

'I never said they did. But I haven't done anything wrong.'

'Are you sure about that?'

'I am.'

'In that case, I don't think there's anything left to say, is there?'

'No,' Tom snaps. 'I don't suppose there is.'

He ends the call and stands at the window, waiting for his anger to subside. Then, when his breathing has returned to normal, he opens the Twitter app on his phone. A shiver of unease creeps across his skin. There are hundreds of notifications, all in the space of a few hours – more than he's seen since the days before Evie Stokes was first arrested. Experience tells him that they can't all be friendly mentions. A feeling deep in his gut says it's worse than that.

It is. The Twitter storm has turned. The main focus of people's outrage is no longer Evie Stokes. It's him.

'What's the matter, Tom?' asks one man. 'Nasty woman calling you names? Diddums!'

Tom's throat tightens. The tweet has been shared more than twenty times and liked by dozens of people. Of course it's possible that one or more of the people adding fuel to the fire is Stokes herself. Fake profiles aren't exactly unheard of on Twitter. But would she really risk these tweets being traced back to her?

Tom checks the profile page for the author of the tweet. 'Terry Teaches' seems legitimate enough. There's a photo of a heavyset man with a goatee and a history of interactions suggesting that the account is genuine. Tom wonders what Terry's problem is. Is he connected to Stokes somehow? Then he checks a few of the profiles who've shared the tweet. Again, they look pretty authentic.

Returning to his long list of notifications, Tom sees that his name has been mentioned and tagged dozens of times. 'Typical male cry-bully', says one woman. 'Pick a fight with some vulnerable woman then go running to the police.' Another asks, 'What's your problem, Tom? Think men are the real victims? Think again!' A third says, 'Tom Hunter makes up stories for a living. What do you expect?' A fourth reads, 'Glad you've found another way to get your name in the paper. That last book didn't do so well, did it Tom?'

There's even a hashtag – #IBelieveEvie – where he stands accused of everything from censorship to encouraging the kind of misogynistic abuse that gives Twitter a bad name.

Tom's pulse races. Is this really how people see him? He's not a misogynist. He loves women. Just not all women – and not in the romantic sense.

Then his eyes fall on a tweet from a woman calling herself 'Avenging Angel'. It reads, 'You might have fooled the court but you don't fool me. I saw you post that poor woman's address on Facebook. Shame on you!'

Tom's throat tightens. He thinks back to that night all those months ago when he drunkenly took to Facebook to vent about Stokes turning up outside his flat and stupidly included her name and address. It seemed reasonable at the time. He was simply playing her at her own game, hoping to publicly shame her into leaving him alone. But in the cold light of dawn, with a raging hangover threatening to crush his skull, he realised what a terrible mistake he'd made and deleted the post. There'd been no mention of it during the court case, which led Tom to conclude that Stokes was unaware of his error of judgment. But if it escaped her attention then, she's sure to read about it now.

He can always deny it, of course. 'Avenging Angel' hasn't attached a screenshot of Tom's original Facebook post. Either she doesn't have one or she doesn't want to give Evie's enemies more ammunition by revealing her address. There's nothing to prove that what she says is true. But Tom knows that trial by Twitter doesn't require much in the way of hard evidence. Now that the allegation is out there, there's no knowing how many times it'll be shared or who'll read it and judge him accordingly.

Pushing the thought away, he closes the app on his phone, breathes deeply and then opens it again. He knows he shouldn't read further, but he can't help himself. It's as if he's reading about another person. People he's never met are forming opinions of him, and most of them are far from flattering. According to Twitter, he's a bully and an abuser of women, 'a gay chauvinist pig' and 'a precious snowflake faggot who can't stand the heat of grown-up debate'. This last tweet comes from someone called 'Child of Genet', though it sounds suspiciously like the kind of thing Evie Stokes would say.

Tom pockets the phone and rushes over to his computer. Still standing, he opens his search engine and locates her Twitter profile. It's changed since the last time he looked. The header image shows a pebble beach, not unlike the one he can see from his window. Even as he's considering the implications of this, his attention is drawn to her profile picture. It takes a few seconds for the image to register. It's a detail from the Bayeux Tapestry. King Harold with an arrow in his eye. The battle of Hastings.

Tom's stomach churns. She knows where he is. Somehow, she's keeping tabs on him.

Then he sees her latest pinned tweet. It's another YouTube link. 'The More You Ignore Me, the Closer I Get' by Morrissey. A song for stalkers everywhere.

Heart pounding, Tom fumbles in his pocket for his phone, fingers shaking as he searches for the number. Finally he finds it. 'Hello? Yes, I need to speak to Detective Inspector Sue Grant. It's urgent!'

26

DAY 24 (706 DAYS REMAINING)

I didn't go home last night. I know it's wrong of me. I knew my dad
would be worried. He left several messages. But I needed time to clear
my head. I couldn't bear to see that look on his face. The disappointment. The shame. It's too much. So I checked into a budget hotel in
Camberwell and waited for him to leave for work this morning. That's
the great thing about London. There are plenty of places to hide. A girl
can just disappear.

Things haven't been the same since we had That Talk last week. He's
tried to hide it, but sometimes I catch him watching me and I know that
something has changed. He tries to smile but the smile never extends
to his eyes. He's keeping something from me. He's biting his tongue.

Take the night before last. He arrived home over an hour later than
usual. Nothing wrong with that in itself. I'm not my father's keeper.
But he didn't phone to say he'd be late, and when he did finally arrive,
he offered no apology or explanation as to why he'd been held up or
where he'd been. I'm sure plenty of wives and girlfriends are used to
this kind of behaviour from their menfolk and complain bitterly about
it whenever they get together. But I'm not his wife or girlfriend. I'm his
daughter. And I'm not complaining, either. I'm just concerned.

When I haven't been worrying about my dad I've been thinking back to my last therapy session. I've been doing this a lot lately
– looping back to recent events and conversations, going over them
again in my head. Some days it feels like I'm unravelling. The feeling
starts at the top of my head and creeps around my hairline, corkscrew-
ing its way down and around my face, like someone peeling an orange.
I picture my skin coming away, revealing the fruity pulp beneath. Then

I pull myself together, remind myself that I've survived far worse than this before and I'll live through this, too.

I'll say one thing for my therapist: she isn't afraid of a challenge. I don't know how well versed Maria is in literary criticism, but she doesn't let a lack of education stand in her way. We talked a lot about books and authorship. I don't know which of us brought the subject up – it can get confusing at times – but as soon as it was mentioned she was like a dog with a bone, referring to my case file and questioning me about the book I'm alleged to have written and sent to you.

'Alleged to'! I did write that book and I did send it to you. I thought that much had been established in court, despite my lawyer's insistence that it wouldn't strengthen my case and may even play into the hands of the prosecution. What a world we live in, when the act of writing a book and sharing it with the man who helped inspire it can be seen as an act of harassment! What a twisted, unthinking, anti-intellectual world! How long before we start burning such books and those who have the audacity to write them?

I didn't say this to my therapist. In fact, I didn't say very much at all, keeping my answers short and to the point, the way I was advised to do in court.

'You told me that you got a lot from Mr Hunter,' my therapist said. 'What did you mean by that?'

I replied that I found your work inspiring.

'Inspiring in what way?' she asked.

Poor Maria. It's not her fault she lacks imagination.

'Inspiring in many ways,' I replied. 'I could go through them all one by one, but we'd be here all day.'

'Why not make a start, and we'll see how far we get?' she smiled. Have I mentioned how annoying she can be sometimes?

I thought of all the inspirational quotes and platitudes people post on Twitter along with the usual hashtags about books and writing. 'Books are windows into other worlds,' I said.

Maria nodded. Whether she was humouring me or agreeing with me, I couldn't say for certain.

'Books encourage us to think outside ourselves,' I said.

Again she nodded. Again I wasn't sure why. But I was starting to enjoy this game now.

'Books are a girl's best friend,' I said and immediately saw from her reaction that the game was up.

'This is all very good, Evie,' she said. 'But I asked you about Mr Hunter's books in particular, and so far you haven't really answered my question. What is it about his work that you find so inspiring?'

'His characters,' I replied. 'He gives a voice to men who don't have a voice, who are often silenced.'

Maria raised her eyebrows. 'You think men are silenced?'

'Some are, yes. Or they're only presented in certain ways – cheating husbands, abusive fathers, serial killers.'

'So you're talking about crime fiction.'

'I'm talking about most fiction. Film. Television. Men are usually the villains, rarely the victims.'

'I don't think that's strictly true,' Maria said. 'But even if it were, isn't that because men generally commit more crimes than women? The vast majority of violent crimes are committed by men.'

'But that's not the same as saying that the vast majority of men commit violent crimes, is it?' I countered. 'For every man who does commit an act like that, there are millions more who don't. Men are also the victims of violent crime. Men are raped. Men are the victims of domestic abuse.'

She nodded. 'And men can be the victims of stalking.'

'If you say so.'

'It's not a question of whether I say so,' Maria insisted. 'It's a fact. Significant numbers of men report being stalked, often by women they barely know but who feel connected to them in some way. Do you know what erotomania is, Evie?'

'Of course,' I smirked. 'It's an album by Madonna. Widely considered one of her best recordings, though overshadowed at the time of release by her infamous *Sex* book.'

'Very funny. But I can see you're deflecting. Erotomania is a type of delusional disorder in which the affected person believes that another person is in love with him – or her. This belief is usually applied to someone with higher status or a famous person. Mr Hunter, for instance.'

I smiled tightly, although at that precise moment in time I wanted to grab Maria by the hair and slam her smug face against the nearest hard surface. 'I didn't stalk Mr Hunter,' I replied. 'Nothing on my record says that I did.'

'No, you were found guilty of harassment. But it's a thin line, isn't it? Between harassment and stalking?'

'It's a thin line between love and hate,' I smirked, recalling an old Pretenders song.

'And do you hate Mr Hunter?'

'No,' I lied. 'And I never loved him, either. I loved his work. It is possible to separate the two, you know.'

'I wonder how easy it is, though. For you, I mean. Because your criminal record tells a different story.'

'We all have a story to tell,' I replied. 'It's simply a question of how we choose to tell it.'

✶

I had a creative writing tutor back when I was at uni – a woman called Jan. She had been published once, a long time ago – before she was reduced to teaching undergraduates for a living. The resentment oozed out of her like the copious amounts of red wine she was rumoured to drink when she was alone in her office between tutorials, supposedly marking. On one occasion, at a staff and student social, I saw her knock over a full bottle and attempt to scoop the spilled wine off the table top and back into her glass with the cup of her hand. Catching me looking at her, she smiled and said, 'I'd rather see a church burn!'

Jan's favourite teaching method was to encourage us all to write and read aloud our personal stories – the more personal, the better. 'All writing is therapy,' she'd say, though I often wondered who was benefiting from this particular form of therapy – us or her.

I once watched her tear a fellow student to shreds, a young woman whose best friend had committed suicide a year earlier and who she'd written about at Jan's behest.

'Sentimental and cliché-ridden!' Jan remarked, as the poor girl's eyes filled with tears.

Had I ever entertained the possibility of becoming a truly confessional writer, it was driven out of me at that precise moment. Instead I tried my hand at various forms of fiction, working on short stories and finally developing the idea for a novel. I shared as little as possible with Jan. Instead I would churn out pieces especially for her classes – pieces I had no personal investment in but would knock out the night before and claim came from direct experience. I wrote about the time I was mugged, despite never having been the victim of such a crime. Similarly, I wrote about surviving a car crash as a child, about the time I nearly drowned and the time I was wrongly arrested for shoplifting. None of these tales contained even a glimmer of truth, and it pleased me no end that Jan was unable to tell when I was lying and would judge my work accordingly, often harshly but without denting my confidence the way she delighted in destroying the dreams of my fellow students. In her own mean-spirited way, I think Jan prepared me for the reality of becoming a writer.

I'd started working on my novel long before I left the cosseted world of academia. But it wasn't until the untimely death of my mother and my subsequent return to London that I was able to give it my full and undivided attention, rising early to write a few hundred words before breakfast and returning to it for the best part of the day. There was no pressure on me to find a job. My dad earned a decent wage, the mortgage was paid off and, as he kept insisting, 'two can live just as cheaply as one'. In many ways I was extremely advantaged. But I also had a mountain to climb. For every novel that gets published there are thousands more that never see the light of day. I had no connections and no celebrity, no fast track past the gatekeepers of the publishing world. All I had was self-belief and a story that needed to be told.

It's often said that a writer's first novel is really just a thinly disguised autobiography. This may well have been true of my first draft. The main character, Sylvie, is a lot like me. She doesn't dream of getting married. She isn't looking for a man to complete her. She's independent, a bit of a dreamer, a little on the kooky side. I'm aware, of course, that some people consider me kooky – and that's fine with me. I'd rather be seen as kooky than not seen at all.

But there the resemblance ends. Sylvie isn't as tough as I've had to be. She doesn't have my strengths. She's really quite an innocent – and by that I'm not suggesting that I am in any way guilty, merely that she lacks my resourcefulness. She isn't a survivor, the way I am. She isn't a freak like me.

But as I was saying, this was only my first draft. By the second draft, I'd realised where I was going wrong. There wasn't enough of me in my book. I was hiding behind my characters. What's that great Oscar Wilde saying? 'Man is least himself when he talks in his own person. Give him a mask, and he will tell you the truth.' But I wasn't being truthful. The mask I wore wasn't working. And that's where you came in. You inspired me. More than that, you freed something in me. You gave me another mask – not to hide behind, but through which I could reveal my true self.

I'd been writing daily for the best part of a year when the idea struck me. I know how averse to risk the publishing world can be. It's more like the Hollywood film industry these days, isn't it? They love a good franchise. They want a ready-made readership, a sure thing, the same but different. And while they're all waiting for the next *Gone Girl with the Dragon Tattoo on the Train*, originality is passing them by, and the likes of me end up on someone's slush pile.

But I knew the power of the internet. I'd seen the fan forums. I knew there was another way. Do it yourself. Seize control. Self-publish and create a stir. It worked for E.L. James. Why shouldn't it work for me too? So here's what I did: I wrote myself into your book. I carved you up and filleted you like a fish. I took the bare bones of your story and fleshed them out with the blood, guts and beating heart of mine. I took my characters and inserted them into your narrative. Then, when I'd breathed new life into your book, I wrote you into mine. I added a character called Tom in homage to the man who'd helped inspire me. The scene where he and Sylvie first meet simmers with sexual tension.

There's a name for this, of course. Some call it fan fiction. I prefer slash fiction. It's more evocative and reminds me of Williams Burroughs and his famous 'cut up' technique, where he'd literally cut up pages of text and rearrange them in random chunks to reignite his imagination. To me, this sounds far more creative and less fawning than mere fan fiction.

Besides, the book I wrote was nothing like *Fifty Shades of Shite* – to date the most successful fan fiction ever, despite its complete lack of literary merit. I was channelling the great Mr Hunter, not churning out dodgy porn inspired by sappy tales of teenage vampires. It was a meeting of minds. Remember how, in David Cronenberg's *The Fly*, Jeff Goldblum and the fly enter a teleportation pod and re-emerge as one living organism? That's how it was with us. You were the visionary. I was the fly in the ointment. Together we became a wild mutation, a hybrid. Two became one.

Had I said this to my therapist, she'd have probably taken it literally. As I write these words, I'm seeing her reaction in pure eighties body horror movie terms. I'm picturing her in a lab coat, staring in shock and awe as my physical self mutates into something half woman and half monster – the monster, of course, being you. Had I only known your true nature at the time, I could have spared myself a lot of grief. What can I say? I was blinded by your talent. I was dazzled by your charisma. I saw only what I wanted to see.

Because here's the truth of the matter: if I was the fly, then you were the spider – and soon you had me trapped in your web of lies.

✹

I didn't tell my therapist I was worried about my dad, but I think she sensed it somehow.

'How are things at home?' she asked as our session was drawing to a close.

'Fine,' I replied.

'And your father? How's he?'

'He's fine, too.'

She paused before continuing. 'You can talk to me about anything at these sessions, Evie. Anything you like. So if there's something troubling you at home, you can tell me. You do know that, don't you?'

'There's nothing troubling me at home,' I said. 'My home life is good. Couldn't be better, in fact.'

Maria smiled professionally. 'I'm pleased to hear it. But if there ever was anything, I hope you'd feel comfortable bringing it up.'

'I'm never more comfortable than when I'm discussing my personal life with strangers,' I replied, archly.

Maria didn't miss a beat. 'Is that why you spend so much time on social media?'

'If an idea's worth having, it's worth sharing. I rarely discuss my personal life on social media.'

'But you posted a blog about people blocking you on Twitter. That sounded quite personal.'

'So you're reading my blog now, are you? I'm honoured.' I grinned at her. 'And for the record, that blog wasn't remotely personal. It was just a bit of fun, that's all.'

'Really? So it doesn't bother you when people block you on Twitter?'

'I consider it a compliment.'

Maria frowned. 'Why?'

'It shows they can't hold an argument. Nothing says you've lost an argument like blocking someone. It's like shoving your fingers in both ears and shouting, "I can't hear you!" It's pathetic.'

'But what if someone has blocked you, and you keep tagging them and their followers in your tweets? Why would you continue to do that?'

Of course I saw exactly where she was going with this. 'By "someone" you mean Mr Hunter,' I said. 'That was a special case. I don't make a habit of that kind of thing.'

'Are you sure?' Maria asked. 'Only that blog you posted suggests that you do. You even include the Twitter handles of people who've blocked you. Some might argue that you have difficulty accepting that people don't wish to communicate with you. They might see it as an inability to cope with rejection.'

'Some might argue that the world is flat,' I replied, flatly.

Maria widened her eyes. 'That's hardly the same thing.'

'Isn't it? I don't see why not. For years, people thought the earth was flat. Scientific fact is only what the majority of scientists hold to be true at any given time. And time itself is a relative concept, as I'm sure you're aware.'

I could tell I'd stumped her then, because she looked at the little clock on the table beside her and could barely disguise her relief.

'And that's all the time we have today,' she said with a smile. 'I'll see you at the same time next week.'

'I wouldn't miss it for the world,' I replied. 'Assuming I don't wander off the edge of the earth between now and then.'

✺

I'm sure it will please Maria to learn that I haven't wandered off the edge of the earth. But I have become rather elusive. I had another message from Dad a short while ago, demanding to know where I am. I suppose the honest answer is that I'm alone with my thoughts. Not every writer needs a room of her own. A table in a cafe or at the local library will suffice. We don't all have the luxuries Virginia Woolf enjoyed. We can't all afford to sit around in our seaside retreats, waiting for the muse to strike. For me, writing is a lot like physical exercise. The longer I leave it, the harder it gets. Words wither and waste away like unused muscles. But having put the hours in today, I'm pleased to say that I've made a major breakthrough.

Remember when I sent you my manuscript? I was so excited. I thought I'd hear back from you the following day. I expected you to write and tell me you'd been up all night reading and how honoured you were to have helped inspire such a novel. We'd already talked about it. You'd already taken such an interest. You were my champion and here I was, paying you the highest compliment possible. I even dedicated the book to you. How could you be anything but flattered?

When I didn't hear from you, the elation I felt on finally completing my first novel began to drain away. With each passing day my insecurities deepened. Slowly but surely, I lost all confidence. My book was rubbish. My manuscript was unpublishable. As days turned to weeks, it felt as if a part of me had died. I pictured my words twisting and crawling over the pale pages like insects on a rotting corpse. Sickened at the thought, I locked the manuscript safely away in a drawer. Still it wouldn't leave me alone. In my fevered imagination, the drawer became a coffin. I pictured my characters shaking their heads sadly at me like mourners at a funeral, mortified at the way I'd failed them. I imagined them whispering together behind my back, out there in the darkness. Sometimes I swear I could even hear them.

But today I decided to face my fears. I crept back into the house while Dad was at work and retrieved my manuscript from my desk drawer. I was half expecting to find it reduced to dust and ashes. But there it was, as solid as the day I last saw it. Reading it again, I'm pleased to say that it's far better than I remembered.

There's just one problem, one element that isn't quite right. For the life of me I couldn't work out what it was. And then it finally hit me. It's you. Your character isn't working for me anymore. And you know what they say, Tom. Sometimes you have to kill your little darlings. So I've decided to kill you off.

27

'I was told she'd be back at work today,' Tom says to the impatient-sounding woman on the end of the phone. 'Yes, I called earlier. Yes, I know she's been away. I see. Well, if you could ask her to call me back as soon as she gets this, I'd be very grateful.'

It's just after 10.00 on Monday morning. Five days since he rang the police and was informed that Sue Grant was on annual leave. Four days since he risked his agent's wrath by pulling out of *Woman's Hour* at the last minute, pleading an upset stomach but secretly fearing that any further mention of Evie Stokes would only add fuel to the fire. Three days since he received a text from Emma telling him he'd made the right decision. Two hours since he last checked Twitter, hoping the storm will have finally blown over and disappointed to find that it hasn't. At least the hashtag #IBelieveEvie is no longer trending. On Thursday it reached a point where he felt as if the whole world was against him. At least now it seems to have died down a bit.

God knows he's tried his best to avoid social media. He knows it isn't good for him, not in his current state of mind. But it's been impossible to ignore it completely. He's scrolled through his recent Facebook posts, looking to see if there's something there that reveals his whereabouts. He's not in the habit of 'checking in' on Facebook, the way some people seem compelled to do each time they visit a new city or some swanky bar or restaurant. He hates the thought of someone tracking his every move. But perhaps he inadvertently gave away the fact that he's in Hastings, and this is where Evie Stokes gleaned her information. But no, there's nothing. There's nothing on his Twitter feed either. This leaves two possibilities: either she's a mind reader or she's been talking to someone. Only two people knew of his plans to come to Hastings.

Tom doubts very much that Stokes would have gained access to his agent. Which leaves Emma.

He hasn't responded to her text, and there's been no further communication from her since. Is she still angry with him, or is her prolonged silence evidence of a guilty conscience? Come to think of it, he hasn't heard from Lucinda either. He wonders if she's been too busy to find time to read his manuscript. Maybe she hates it. Or maybe she's still smarting about *Woman's Hour* and is making him suffer. If that's her plan, it's working.

Tom reaches for his coffee cup, drains it and rises from his chair. There's no point sitting here in his bathrobe, waiting for his phone to ring, going round in circles. Too much introspection can drive a man insane. He needs to clear his head. Time to face the day and get some fresh air.

※

Half an hour later, shaved and showered, Tom heads downstairs and opens the front door to what he assumes will be another sunny morning, perfect for lazing on the beach. But his hopes are dashed the moment he steps outside. It's like walking into a cloud. A thick fog has rolled in, so dense he can barely see the far side of the road. A string of cars passes by, travelling at well below the speed limit, hazard lights on.

'Sea mist,' a familiar voice says. 'It gets like this sometimes. Even in high summer.'

Tom turns to see Colin perched on his usual chair on the front patio, a newspaper open on the table beside him.

'How long will it last?'

His neighbour shrugs. 'Hard to say. Could be a few hours. Could be a few days. I hope it clears by tomorrow or we'll miss the blood moon.'

Tom looks at him blankly.

'The lunar eclipse,' Colin says, jabbing a finger at his newspaper. 'They've been going on about it all week.' He looks at Tom. 'Are you okay, son? Only you don't seem quite yourself.'

Tom forces a smile. 'You know us writers. Head in the clouds.'

The old man studies him for a moment, then rises from his seat. 'Well I'm going back indoors. You can join me if you like, only I should warn you I'm not great company today. It's the anniversary of my Graham's passing.'

'I'm sorry to hear that,' Tom says. Then, for want of something else to say, 'You must miss him.'

'Every day. But we'll be together again soon. It won't be long now.' Colin must sense Tom's discomfort because he changes the subject. 'If you're stuck for something to do, I can recommend the aquarium. I don't think this mist will clear any time soon. It's a thick one. What we used to call a real pea-souper.'

⋈

The old man isn't wrong. Crossing the road to the seafront and heading in the general direction of the Old Town, Tom is amazed at just how thick the mist is. It rolls around him like the famous London fog he's only ever seen in photographs. It's hard to believe that yesterday the beach was packed with people sunbathing. He knows the sea is still there. He can hear the crash and hiss of waves on the pebbles. But the water is no longer visible, the shoreline shrouded behind a wall of white.

The pier is closed. Tom stops and peers through the wrought-iron gates, imagining the empty wooden deck as the setting for some gothic melodrama. He pictures shadowy figures in oilskins emerging from the mist, the vengeful ghosts of ancient mariners, come to claim the lives of innocent townsfolk. He recalls some slasher film with photogenic teens being ripped apart by a fisherman with a meat hook.

There's a chill wind blowing along the seafront. Even the gulls are feeling it. They shiver on the shingle at Pelham Beach, hunched and watchful as cats. Heading along East Beach Street, Tom wishes he'd worn a zip top over his T-shirt and cargo shorts. But he's almost reached his destination and can't face the thought of turning back now.

The Blue Reef Aquarium is situated past the Jerwood Gallery at Rock-a-Nore, close to the Fisherman's Museum and the Shipwreck Museum. Tom smiles to himself. Only in Hastings. The outside of the building is rather shabby. A window display promises more than forty naturally themed habitats, 'from the shoreline of Hastings to the tropical waters of the deep ocean' complete with 'fascinating sea-horses, pulsating jellyfish, amazing pufferfish and graceful rays'. The main selling point is a 'giant ocean exhibit where an underwater tunnel offers incredible views of reef sharks, stingrays and shoals of colourful reef fish'.

Tom has seen his fair share of exotic fish, snorkelling in the clear blue waters of Sharm el Sheik back in the days before it became a no-go area for tourists. He's also cage-dived with great white sharks in far murkier conditions off the coast of South Africa. He recalls the thrill of seeing an enormous great white emerge from the gloomy depths and nudge the cage with its snout. Somehow he doubts that the aquarium's resident black-tip reef sharks, 'Razor and Elsa', will live up to that adrenaline-pumping experience. But he hands over his tenner to the bored-looking girl at the front desk and pockets the change before following the signs down to the exhibits.

Inside, it's busier than expected, presumably on account of the bad weather. Groups of teenagers are milling about – the boys laughing and jostling for position, the girls issuing squeals of protest that barely disguise their delight in all that male attention. 'That's disgusting!' one girl cries, pointing at the glass where a striped, spiny fish is fanning its pectoral fins and gazing blankly, open mouthed.

'Actually, that's a lion fish,' Tom feels like saying, but keeps his own mouth firmly shut. He can already feel the boys eyeing him with suspicion, that sixth sense they have for singling out men not quite like themselves.

In another part of the aquarium, a small child is shouting excitedly to his parents, pointing at a clown fish and announcing that he's found Nemo. The mother catches Tom's eye and gives a little shrug as if to say, 'you know what they're like'. He smiles back, though he has only the vaguest idea of what they're like. He barely knows his young nephew and niece, and has never considered the possibility of having kids of his own. He likes small children, but they're as alien to him as the creatures housed behind the glass.

Later, walking through the underwater tunnel beneath the ocean tank, Tom spots one of the black-tip reef sharks and begins to feel a sense of wonder. It's not the same as seeing these magnificent creatures in their natural habitat, but the sight of any shark this big carries a certain level of excitement and comes laden with cultural reference points, from *Jaws* to *Open Water*.

Tom stops and stands, staring up at the four-foot long fish passing above his head, marvelling at the muscular, streamlined body with its white belly and black-tipped tail and dorsal fin. Though smaller than the mighty great white, reef sharks are apex predators and one of the most commonly sighted of all sharks. They prefer shallow water and can often be seen swimming close to shore with the dorsal fin exposed – the classic 'shark shot' so beloved by filmmakers. They feed mainly on smaller fish, though Tom recalls reading somewhere that people wading through shallow water have been known to be attacked. The key, apparently, is to submerge your body and swim rather than wade, so the shark is less likely to mistake you for food. But wasn't *Open Water* based on a real-life incident? And weren't the killer sharks featured in that film members of this species?

He senses a sudden movement behind him as a huddle of tourists pass by, their reflections dark and squat, distorted by the curve of the glass tunnel. Moments later, they're gone, voices echoing as they disappear from view. Tom returns his gaze to the sea world above his head, lost for a moment in memories of Sharm el Sheik, the morning a couple of reef sharks suddenly appeared in the hotel's off-shore swimming area and everyone was urged to get out of the water.

Something catches his eye – a shadowy figure hovering behind him, the face a blur framed by long hair. Abruptly, the woman steps forwards, her reflection sharpens and her features come into focus. Tom's heart stops. It's Evie Stokes. He spins round, arms raised to defend himself.

'What the—'

The woman facing him isn't Evie Stokes. She's a lot younger and wears a shirt emblazoned with the logo for the aquarium. She smiles nervously. 'Sorry to startle you, sir. I just came to say we'll be feeding the rays and sharks in a few minutes. You're welcome to stay here, but I could see how interested you are in the sharks, so...'

Tom's face burns with embarrassment. 'Yes,' he says. 'Yes, of course. And sorry about that. I thought you were ... someone else.'

Outside, the sea mist shows no sign of lifting. If anything, it seems thicker than when he arrived, swirling in dense clouds around him, making visibility poor. The moist air clings to his face, clammy and claustrophobic. Tom checks his phone, sees there've been no missed calls. He considers trying Sue Grant again, then decides against it. What would she think if she could see the state of him? Would she hear the tremor in his voice? For a moment back there, he was convinced that Stokes had tracked him down. She'd come seeking revenge for all the things he'd said about her and all the abuse she was receiving on Twitter. She's obsessive, relentless, mentally unstable, capable of anything. And somehow she'd found him. Tom thinks of the man in the *Guardian* article whose stalker stabbed him in the chest. His blood runs cold.

He tries to shake the feeling off, but it stays with him as he heads back towards the main road, breath catching in his throat at the slightest movement. The mist is so thick he can barely see more than a few metres in front of him. Familiar landmarks are reduced to vague shapes – a towering cliff face here, a squat building there. The famous fishermen's huts loom around him like giant tombstones, the air thick with the smell of fish guts and the cries of seagulls. For a moment, Tom loses all sense of direction and looks around helplessly, before his eyes are drawn to the glow of a street lamp.

Cars crawl by so slowly, it's as if he's in a dream – one of those nightmares where everything goes into slow motion and you try to run from the horror but your feet refuse to move, paralysed with fear or gripped by some invisible force. *A Nightmare on East Beach Street*: 'One, two, Evie's coming for you!'

He pushes the thought away and hurries along the seafront, struggling to contain the panic rising inside him. Sounds carry on the wind – a car horn, a woman's laughter, a police siren. Blinded by the fog, it's hard to tell which direction they're coming from or how close they are. Gulls squall overhead, as if he's wandered into a scene from Hitchcock. A dog barks and Tom flinches, half expecting some snarling hound from hell to leap out in front of him, jaws dripping with drool. Clouds of mist shift and part, shadowy figures appearing as if from nowhere.

A man suddenly materialises inches from Tom's face – eyes glazed, breath thick with alcohol. 'Awright, mate?' he slurs. 'Got a spare fag?'

'Sorry,' Tom says and pushes quickly past, ignoring the man's protests and stumbling as his right foot comes into contact with something unexpected and skims along the pavement. He looks down and sees the remains of someone's lunch – a mess of greasy paper, chips and ketchup. Gritting his teeth, he scrapes the mess from his shoe and glances back over his shoulder. The man has gone, enveloped by the mist like some ghostly apparition.

It's then that Tom sees her for the second time. There's a flutter of recognition in his chest and then his whole body jolts, heart pounding. She's no more than six metres behind him, shrouded in fog, but unmistakably the woman who has plagued him for so long he can barely remember a time when she wasn't there. She's wearing the same coat she wore at court – pale blue, double-breasted with military buttons. He'd know that coat anywhere. As she narrows the gap between them, he wonders what she has hidden in those inside pockets, concealed under those folds of fabric. He pictures her pulling out a knife and his mouth goes dry, pulse racing.

He walks faster, his breath coming in short, shallow gasps. Footsteps echo behind him. She's picking up speed, the heels of her shoes tapping out a staccato rhythm on the pavement. He looks back over his shoulder, sees that she's gaining on him. She's barely a few metres away. He freezes, feet rooted to the spot.

Then the mist parts, and he sees that it's not her. Of course it's not her. This woman is older and has darker hair. She catches Tom staring at her and gives a quizzical look as she passes by. He smiles and nods, wishing the ground would swallow him up. He's being ridiculous. Seeing her at every turn. Frightened of his own shadow. He needs to pull himself together. He can't go on like this, living on his nerves, seeing threats where none exist. He's an idiot. He's a mess. He's a man in need of a stiff drink and a cigarette. Sod his good intentions.

Hurrying on, he hasn't gone far when he senses a sudden movement in his peripheral vision. He flinches, bracing himself for an attack. But it's just his mind playing tricks on him again. Why can't he get her out of his head? God knows, he tries, but each time he does she worms her way back in. Taunting him. Haunting him. Turning a trip to the aquarium into a psychological assault course. He really needs to get a grip on himself. Failing that, a large vodka and tonic will do nicely.

He crosses the road at the America Ground, dodging the slow crawl of traffic near the pedestrian crossing. There's a shop close to the True Crime Museum with its door firmly closed against the swirling sea mist but a sign saying open for business. He goes in and exits the shop a few minutes later with a bottle of vodka, two bottles of tonic, some Diet Coke, a packet of Marlboro and a disposable lighter. The bag is heavy, the cheap blue plastic stretched thinly and digging into his fingers. He stares down at it, half expecting it to snap at any moment and the bottle of vodka to fall and smash on the pavement. But the bag holds. Not far now.

He's still tense when he arrives back at the flat. Fumbling in his pocket for his keys, he feels a sudden rush of air behind him and they slip through his fingers, hitting the ground with a sharp crack. Tom curses under his breath and kneels to retrieve them as a mountain bike speeds by, its rider already lost to vision in the mist, no lights to warn pedestrians of their approach.

Angrily, Tom slides the key into the lock and slips through the door, his heart pounding.

A shadowy figure looms at the foot of the stairs and he practically jumps out his skin.

'Are you alright, lad?'

'Colin! You startled me.'

'So I see. I was just looking to see if there'd been any post. Didn't think much of the aquarium, then? You've hardly been gone five minutes.'

Embarrassed, Tom forces a smile and searches for an excuse. 'I remembered there's something I need to do.'

The old man glances at the blue carrier bag. 'Are you sure you're alright?'

'I'm fine, thank you.'

'Only you look like you've seen a ghost.'

If you only knew, Tom thinks but says nothing and hurries upstairs.

28

DAY 26 (704 DAYS REMAINING)

I'm at the hospital. There's a fly buzzing. I don't know where it is but I can hear its wings vibrate. It sounds angry, or desperate. Maybe it's looking for somewhere to lay its eggs. Maybe it knows something I don't.

The only other sound comes from the clock on the waiting-room wall. It's working but appears to have slowed to such a pace it bears no resemblance to real time at all. I wonder if hospital minutes are like minutes on the underground – not fixed periods of time but elastic, so they stretch on for longer than the usual sixty seconds. It's so warm in here that as I stare at the clock I picture that painting by Salvador Dali, the one with the melting pocket watches. I think of the ants crawling over the face of one of his famous timepieces. I remember my art teacher at school telling us the ants were a symbol of decay.

Outside, the long day is dying. It's been one of those hot summer-in-the-city days when people flock to the nearest park or lido, or dine al fresco by the river, grateful for the breeze coming off the water. London in summer is another country, and you rarely hear anyone complain. I can picture them now in their short sleeves and summer dresses, sipping Pimm's or G&T, or returning from the bar with tall glasses of lager, the chilled amber liquid foaming down the side of the glass. What I'd give for a drink right now.

In here, the only drinks available come from the water fountain or the vending machine. The air is thick with worry and smells of death and disease and disinfectant. The floral tang catches in the back of my throat and burns my sinuses, making me think of things I'd rather not – lilies, wet earth, endings. There's another smell, too – the sharp stench of stale sweat. I wonder if it's coming from me, but it's too strong for that. It's the smell of someone who has night terrors, who sweats alone in a narrow bed in a roomful of strangers and hasn't bathed properly in weeks. It's the smell of someone who's been institutionalised.

I shouldn't be here. It must be past dinnertime by now. I should be at home with Dad, finishing our dinner. I'd be clearing the plates away and then I'd fix him a drink and we'd sit together, my dad and me, watching an old film or just talking about things.

But we're not. Instead I'm sitting here on this plastic chair in this awful place that smells of death – and as for my dad, well, I don't know where he is. They won't let me see him. Each time I ask, I'm told to wait and someone will be with me soon. But I wait and nobody ever comes. I'm beginning to think there's something they're not telling me. We all have secrets, don't we? Even people who work in hospitals. We're supposed to be able to trust them with our lives, but how far can you trust anyone, really? We've all heard tales of medical negligence, how overstretched doctors are, how they cover up for each other.

If I'm to believe the clock on the wall, it's almost 9.00 p.m., which means I've been here for the best part of five hours. Nobody will tell me anything – or if they do, it's to reassure me that they're doing everything they can. But I know when people are trying to pull the wool over my eyes. I ought to by now.

'Can I see him?' I ask the stern-faced nurse when I finally manage to grab her attention.

'Not just yet,' she replies, all brisk voice and tight smile. 'Maybe you should go home and get some rest.'

Home and rest are the last things I need now. I'm too tired to sleep, and to go home without my dad would feel like giving up hope. Without him, I can't rest. Without him, I have no home. So I'll sit and wait, and hope that my gut instinct is wrong and he isn't going to die.

✹

Tonight was supposed to have been a celebration. I came home this morning with a plan to surprise Dad and make up for my brief period of absence with a special dinner. He'd already gone to work when I let myself in, so I had a good soak in the bath and sat down to write. By lunchtime I had another chapter complete; the inspiration I'd felt all those months ago had finally returned. I printed off the pages to proofread later and poured myself a celebratory gin and tonic. Had my dad been at home, he'd have disapproved of me drinking so early in the day, which is one reason I keep a bottle of gin hidden in the filing cabinet in my bedroom. All the best writers appreciate the benefits of alcohol, and what he doesn't know can't hurt him.

By the time I'd finished my gin, washed and dried the glass, and placed it back in the kitchen cupboard, where it belongs, it was so warm my face was damp with sweat and I knew I had to get out of the house. I walked to the Portuguese fishmonger and stood admiring the variety of fish on their bed of ice before selecting two large sea bream, so fresh their eyes were as clear as if they were still alive. People go on about sea bass, but for my money sea bream is the far finer fish. There are fewer fiddly bones, and the cooked flesh isn't flaky but comes away in thick white chunks. It's a fish you can really sink your teeth into.

I watched as the fishmonger dropped them onto the scales and scribbled the price on a piece of paper, all without saying a word. I asked him to gut and scale them for me and continued watching as he slid his knife expertly through their bellies and removed their innards with a flick of his finger. I wondered how long it took him to develop skills like that, whether gutting fish is as easy as he made it look. He wore latex gloves, which lent him an air of surgical authority and were in stark contrast to the grubbiness of his apron, which put me in mind of Sweeney Todd.

When the fish were ready, he rinsed them thoroughly under the tap and wrapped them in a plastic bag and newspaper before tying the bundle inside a carrier bag and placing it next to the till, where his unsmiling wife completed the transaction without even making eye contact. She simply pointed at the piece of paper with the price written on it and held out her hand. I know she's capable of speech. More than once, I've heard her talking to her husband in a mixture of

Portuguese and English. I also know that her rudeness isn't directed at me personally. She's like this with everyone. Still I couldn't resist the urge to unnerve her by thanking her profusely and grinning like a maniac, much to the amusement of her husband, who stood wiping his knife with a knowing smile playing on his lips.

Next I went to the greengrocer, where I bought some fresh thyme and lemon for the fish, along with some baby new potatoes and a bundle of asparagus. I'm not a big fan of asparagus but I wasn't thinking of myself. I was thinking of my dad and how much I owed him.

The greengrocer is called Kay. She's one of those salt-of-the-earth Londoners loved by the makers and viewers of soap operas – big, blonde, brassy, knows everyone's business. I assume she knows about my recent run-in with the law, but if she does she didn't let it show.

'Cooking something nice?' she asked, nodding at my shopping bag as she totted up my bill on her old-fashioned cash register.

'Sea bream,' I replied.

'Very nice. Who's the lucky fella?'

I don't know why people automatically assume that if a woman is preparing a fancy meal it must be for her latest love interest. As Madonna would say, it's so reductive. Suddenly I had a vision of myself dressed in an apron in your shiny new kitchen, cooking up a storm while you sweated over your latest opus.

'My dad,' I said.

Kay didn't bat an eyelid. 'You're a good daughter,' she smiled. 'I hope your dad appreciates just how lucky he is.'

Her words were still echoing in my ears when I arrived home. I wished Dad had been there to hear them. Because no sooner had I opened the door than my whole world came crashing down.

⋇

I knew Dad was home early because the front door was no longer double-locked. I removed my mortice key and slid the Yale into place.

'Dad?' I called out as I closed the door behind me. He didn't reply.

I pictured him collapsed on the bathroom floor and fear gripped my chest.

'Dad?' Again, there was no response. Panicked, I dropped my shopping in the hall and ran to the foot of the stairs. I grabbed the bannister and was about to haul myself up when something caught my eye. The kitchen door was wide open and there he was, bathed in sunlight, dust motes circling in the air around his head.

My first thought was that he looked lifeless, like a waxwork. He was seated at the kitchen table, completely motionless, staring into space. In front of him on the table was a laptop. My laptop. What was he doing with my laptop? I walked towards him and it was as if he woke from a trance.

'Evie,' he said. 'It's time we had a talk.'

Suddenly it was if all the air was sucked out of the room. I noticed that the kitchen window was closed and wondered why he hadn't opened it, given the temperature in the room.

'It's like a furnace in here,' I said, walking over to the window.

'Sit down, Evie!' he snapped. 'Leave the window. I don't want the neighbours hearing what I have to say.' Still he refused to look at me.

I pulled out a chair and did as I was told. 'What are you doing with my laptop?' I asked.

He didn't respond. Then, after a long silence, he started talking. 'I've tried my best with you, Evie. I know it hasn't always been easy for you, but I've done my best.'

'I know you have—' I began, but he cut me off.

'You lied to me,' he said. 'When I asked you about your mother, you lied.'

'I don't know what you're talking about.'

'The day she died. You were there.' Finally his eyes met mine. 'You killed her.'

My mind raced. The laptop. My journal. He'd worked out the password and he'd read it. What else had he seen? I forced a smile. 'Of course I didn't. Where on earth did you get a silly idea like that from?'

He didn't reply.

I gestured towards the laptop and rolled my eyes. 'Don't tell me you've been reading my novel.'

I saw a shadow of doubt flicker across his face. A shadow was all I needed. A shadow can conceal almost anything.

'You shouldn't go around reading people's work in progress,' I said. 'You're liable to jump to the wrong conclusions.'

'But why would you write that?' he asked, aghast.

'There are no limits to the imagination, Dad,' I said. 'A writer has to give herself absolute freedom.'

'So is that all this is? The product of your imagination?'

'Of course.'

I don't know if I convinced him that what he'd read was a work of fiction, but after a few minutes of intense cross-examination he seemed to falter.

'There's some other stuff on here, too,' he said, patting the laptop. 'Files on people. That Tom Hunter, for one. You promised me that was all behind you.'

'It is,' I lied. 'Those are just notes I kept from the court case.'

He looked doubtful. 'Why would you keep notes from the court case?'

'I'm a writer. Keeping notes is part of the job. Maybe they'll come in handy for something one day. A character in a novel.'

'Another novel.'

'I think I have a few good novels in me.'

'I don't think it's good for you to be dwelling on these things so much,' he said. 'What does your therapist think?'

'She encourages me to write about it. She says it will help me gain perspective.'

Still he looked sceptical. 'There's something else,' he said. 'The search history on your laptop.'

My pulse quickened. 'You looked at my search history?' Usually I'm so careful. I make a point of clearing it before logging off. But I'd been so absorbed in my book I'd forgotten. 'But you can't do that,' I said, meeting my father's gaze. 'It's an invasion of privacy!'

'Funny you should say that,' he replied. 'I saw the words 'ghost

IP' and 'keystroke recorder'. And there's a software package on your hard drive that looks suspiciously like spyware. That's an invasion of someone else's privacy, not to mention a crime.'

'Spyware?' I laughed. 'What on earth would I want with that?'

'That's what I was wondering. What would you want with that?'

'It must have downloaded automatically when I was watching a film on some file-sharing site.'

He frowned. 'Are you lying to me?'

I felt my skin prickle and my voice rise. 'I told you. I don't know what you're talking about. I wouldn't risk infecting my computer with viruses. I'm not a complete idiot.'

My father sighed. 'I can't keep protecting you, Evie. Not if you're engaged in criminal activities.'

'I'm not,' I insisted. 'It's not what you think. Honestly.'

A strange look crossed his face. 'I need to phone the police.'

'The police? What for?'

'I reported you missing. I didn't know where you were.'

'I'm home now. That's all that matters.'

'Where were you?'

'Out and about.'

'But where did you sleep?'

'Around.' I smiled meaningfully. 'Like mother, like daughter.'

'Stop it, Evie. I'm calling the police.'

'Don't do that, Dad!' My voice was louder than I'd intended.

He looked at me warily. 'If I find out that you've lied to me – about this, about your mother.'

I know I shouldn't have, but I couldn't help myself. I pictured my mother falling to her death, and the corners of my mouth twitched.

'Oh my God, Evie!' My dad's eyes hardened as the truth finally dawned. 'How could you?'

I could have lied, but there was no going back now. The cat was out of the bag. In some ways it was a relief. My lip curled and my smile became a snarl. 'What does it matter? She was an evil bitch. She got what she deserved.'

But Dad wasn't listening. 'This is all my fault,' he said. 'If I'd only protected you more, none of this would have happened. She only hurt you to get back at me.'

I couldn't believe my ears. 'What did you just say? You knew what she did? How could you know and not do anything?'

Dad's mouth opened, but whatever he was about to say next, I may never know. The words seemed to catch in his throat. His left arm flinched, and he grasped it with his right hand. Then his eyes bulged and his hand went to his chest. His face paled and a slick of sweat formed on his top lip. I could see he was short of breath. He tugged at his shirt collar, mouth gaping as he gulped for air.

'Call an ambulance,' he rasped.

I stared at him, my mind racing. I needed time to think.

'Evie!' He slid down in his chair, his voice practically a whisper. 'Help me!'

I reached for my laptop and rose from the table. My shopping was where I'd left it, in the hall. I pictured the eyes of the fish turning milky in the heat, but there was no point worrying about that now. My rucksack was hanging at the bottom of the stairs. I put the laptop inside, took out my phone and made the call.

✳

Later, in the ambulance, while the paramedic explained that my dad had likely suffered a heart attack, I thought back to our earlier conversation, Dad's and mine, and felt a fire growing in my belly. I've seen my dad angry before. Raising me wasn't always easy. I don't need anyone to tell me that. Teenage girls can be a nightmare, and I wasn't immune to the usual temptations – drink, drugs, boys. More than once he was required to collect me from some teenage party where I'd drunk too much and made a show of myself. The hangovers were skull-crushing and usually accompanied by a stern talking-to as I lay in bed, riddled with remorse and barely able to move.

But I've never seen him as angry as he was today. Actually, no. It was worse than anger. It was despair. I saw it in his eyes and heard it in his voice. I've never had any doubt that my dad's love for me is unconditional. Until today. But I know we can pull through this. If he can forgive me my wrongdoing then I can forgive him his. There's no reason to let my mother come between us. He was as much a victim of her cruelty as I was.

When we arrived at the hospital and they rushed Dad off to theatre, I vowed that if he pulls through this I'll change. I'll come off social media. I'll even abandon my book if that's what it takes. I'll do whatever's necessary. All I ask is that he doesn't die. My dad is all I have left. Without him, I'm all alone in the world.

That was hours ago, and now my hope is dwindling. Has Dad survived the operation? Has he spoken to the doctors? Sitting here in this soulless waiting room, a familiar, nagging voice whispers in my head. I close my eyes and count my breaths. But it's no use. The pressure builds. Rage burns through my veins. I scratch at my wrist, drawing blood.

Then my thoughts return to you. This is all your fault. The court case. The stress and strain it placed on my poor dad. Without you, none of this would have happened. It's your actions that have led me here. You were like the Pied Piper, leading me a merry dance. You'd have lured me to the nearest river and drowned me if you could. In court, on Twitter, with all the lies you told, not once did you show even the slightest compassion. I was just a plaything to you – someone to be toyed with and then not so much tossed aside as thrown into the path of an oncoming juggernaut. Anything to shut me up. Anything to silence me.

You think you've won now, don't you? You think this is all over. Well, I hate to burst your self-congratulatory bubble but you're wrong. This isn't over by a long way. How can it be? How can I go down without a fight? You've taken so much from me already. You've had your pound of flesh. Any normal, decent person would think that's enough. But it's never enough for you, is it? You and your appetite – never satisfied, always wanting more. You took from me and you stole from me and you kept on taking. Soon I'll have nothing left to lose. And you know what they say, Tom – never leave someone with nothing left to lose. They're capable of anything.

I see a movement up ahead. There's someone heading towards me. I sit bolt upright in my chair and there he is – the surgeon. He's wearing a lab coat and has one of those tight-lipped expressions. My throat tightens and my stomach lurches. I know what he's going to say before he even opens his mouth. He's standing over me now. He looks down at me with a mixture of professional concern and pity. But he doesn't tell me that he's sorry for my loss. Instead he says, 'The police are here. They'd like to ask you a few questions.'

And then I run.

29

Tom's head pounds. His throat is dry and his mouth tastes like something crawled inside during the night, curled up on his tongue and died there. How much vodka did he drink yesterday? Half a bottle? More? And how many cigarettes did he smoke? He dreads to think. One thing he knows for sure: those men's magazine articles are right – smoking makes a hangover a thousand times worse. He can't remember the last time he felt this rough.

Hauling himself out of bed and staggering into the kitchen, he puts the kettle on, pours a glass of water and gulps it down. He refills the glass and begins opening and closing cupboard doors in search of painkillers. He knows they're here somewhere. Where the hell did he put them? Yanking open the cupboard above the sink, he leans forwards too quickly and catches his head on the corner of the door. 'Fuck!'

Lurching into the bathroom to inspect the damage, Tom studies his reflection in the mirror. A visit to A&E won't be necessary. There's a large bump on his forehead. A bruise is forming, purple against his pale, tired complexion. The skin is broken, revealing a small pink gash. But there's no blood. Just as well – there's enough of that in his eyes, the whites yellow and veined with red. He tests the bump with the top of his finger. *Ouch*. Then, satisfied that it doesn't need a plaster, he heads into the kitchen.

Waiting for the coffee to brew, he struggles to piece together yesterday's events. He remembers getting home and pouring himself the first of many drinks. He remembers stepping outside for the first of many cigarettes. He knows he ordered a pizza, because the leftovers are staring him in the face, congealed in the box and making his stomach cramp and gurgle ominously. And at some point during the evening he had a sudden craving for a different kind of takeaway, opening the Grindr app on his phone and checking out the local talent. After that, it's all a bit of a blur.

He didn't invite anyone over for sex. He knows that much. The pickings weren't particularly tempting, consisting mostly of young men still claiming to be straight and older couples looking for a third person to spice up their flagging love lives. There were very few face shots and some profiles had no photos at all. The feelings of angst and frustration dating apps invariably brought him were compounded by the fact that he hadn't had sex in quite some time. How long has it been exactly? A few weeks? Hardly a drought by most people's standards, but he can't recall the last time he went so long without getting his rocks offs.

He pours his coffee and takes it into the living room. The curtains are drawn, the sunlight bleeding around the edges of the fabric. He pulls them open and looks up at the sky. No sea mist today, just sunshine and blue skies as far as the eye can see. Then he lowers his gaze to the beach. At first glance, it looks as if the lad with a crush on the girl next door has been back, leaving love notes written with pebbles on the concrete groyne. But something isn't right.

Tom squints and his stomach lurches. 'Fuck!'

◆

Moments later he's hammering frantically on Colin's door, shirtless in his boxer shorts, muttering impatiently under his breath, 'C'mon, c'mon!'

After what feels like an eternity, the door cracks open and the old man appears. 'Alright! What's the emergency? Oh, it's you. Are you okay, son? You look awful. What happened to your head?'

'The groyne,' Tom says, ignoring the question and waving his hand in the general direction of the beach. 'Have you seen anyone out on the groyne this morning?'

'What?'

'The groyne opposite. That concrete thing on the beach.'

Colin rolls his eyes. 'I've lived here for over twenty years. I think I know what a groyne is.'

'Right. But have you seen anyone there this morning?'

The old man looks at him as if he's mad. Maybe he is. 'I can't say I have. Should I? What's going on? Why aren't you dressed?'

'Come with me,' Tom says, turning towards the front door. 'I'll show you.'

'Shouldn't you put a shirt on first?'

'Never mind that now. Please, hurry.'

Agitated, Tom waits for Colin to find his keys, then leads him across the road to the promenade.

'There,' he says, gesturing at the concrete groyne, where an arrangement of pebbles spells out the words 'Hello Tom' in large letters.

Colin smiles. 'It looks to me like you have an admirer!'

'A stalker, more like!'

The old man's face falls. 'You don't think it's her, do you? That woman who was bothering you?'

'Who else would it be?'

'It could be anyone. It could be kids. You haven't broken any hearts in Hastings, have you?'

'Of course not,' Tom says. Then he remembers the pirate. The waiter from London. What's his name? Luke! But there's no reason to suppose he even knows where Tom is staying. Maybe it's one of the men he chatted with last night on Grindr. They could have tracked him down using the app. Did he chat with anyone? He can't remember. He reaches into his pocket for his phone but hesitates. He doesn't want to open the app with Colin standing right next to him.

'What are you doing?' the old man asks.

'What does it look like? I'm calling the police.'

Colin looks doubtful. 'What will you say? That someone's written your name in pebbles on the beach? I don't think they'll take you very seriously. I mean, it's just a few pebbles. There's nothing to say it's even her. There's nothing threatening.'

Tom runs his hand over his head, flinching as it comes into contact with the sore spot. He blows out his cheeks and takes a deep, steadying breath. His mind is all over the place, anxiety levels spiking with the effects of the hangover. 'What should I do?' he asks, gazing around as if the answer could be found hanging somewhere in the sky.

'Honestly? I think you should go back to bed. You look terrible. Go and sleep it off. Things will look better after a few hours' rest.'

◆

Tom takes Colin's advice plus a couple of painkillers from the blister pack he finds in the bathroom cabinet and sleeps for a further four hours. When he wakes again it's late afternoon, the hangover has receded and he's feeling almost human. Reaching for his phone, he checks his emails and Facebook account and resists the temptation to see what's happening over on Twitter. Whatever it is, it won't be pleasant.

He puts the phone down and immediately there's a pinging sound. He has four notifications from Grindr, all from men he has absolutely no interest in. One looks young enough to still be at school, and the remaining three are either too old, too plain or too out of shape. Tom knows from experience that the less attractive some men are, the more persistent they can be. He goes to each of his admirers' profiles and hits the block button.

He's in the shower when the phone rings. Wrapping a towel around his waist, he sprints into the living room, leaving a trail of wet footprints.

It's his agent. 'Tom, darling, you're a genius!'

Instantly, his spirits lift. 'You like it, then?'

'Like it? I love it! It's dark and twisty, and just what publishers are after. Sylvie is a really compelling character. Readers will love to hate her. Honestly Tom, it's the best thing you've written. And I'm not the only one who thinks so. I've shown it to a few readers here and we're already in talks with editors. I think we're looking at a bidding war.'

'That's wonderful news,' Tom says. He's already picturing the book jacket, the book launch, the displays at all the big bookshops. This could be it. His second big break. He won't need to sell up and leave London after all.

'When are you back in London?' Lucinda asks.

'Later this week.'

'Let's make a lunch date soon. You must be getting tired of all that fish and chips.'

Tom chuckles. 'They do have other restaurants here.'

'Of course they do, darling. Of course they do. But isn't it all a bit shabby?'

'Shabby chic,' Tom corrects her.

Lucinda audibly shudders. 'Two words that should never go together. Anyway, enjoy the rest of your week and we'll speak soon.'

'You too,' Tom says, but she's already hung up.

All this talk about food and restaurants has made him hungry. He takes a shower, dresses quickly and heads downstairs.

'You've resurfaced, then,' Colin says from his usual spot out front. 'You're looking a lot better, I must say. How's the head?'

'Fine, thank you,' Tom replies and tells his neighbour the good news.

'What are you doing here?' Colin asks. 'You should be out celebrating. I'd come with you, but my knees aren't what they used to be and I'd only cramp your style.'

'Maybe a toast later?' Tom says. 'I could bring back a bottle of champagne?'

'That sounds very civilised. But see how you get on. No need to rush back on my account.'

'It's a date,' Tom says. 'I'll see you later.'

Colin smiles. 'I'll see you when I see you.'

✶

When Tom signed his first book deal, his agent took him for dinner at The Ivy. He still remembers the excitement at being welcomed into that hallowed space and served by briskly efficient waiters who'd seen more famous faces than he'd had hot dinners. It felt like he'd arrived.

Today, two hours after the same agent rang to say she thinks she can sell his new book for rather a lot of money, he's sitting in a pub on the seafront in Hastings, finishing off a large plate of scampi and chips. He'd like to think that this is a sign of how much earthier and unpretentious he's become. Still, he can't help but notice that he's the only person here whose choice of drink to accompany his meal is a chilled bottle of champagne. Not a particularly good bottle of champagne, it has to be said. But champagne, nevertheless – a fact that hasn't been lost on the family at the next table, who keep staring over as if they've never seen a man dining alone before.

The bottle is already half empty. Tom wishes he'd insisted on bringing Colin with him. They could have taken a taxi. But then he wonders what this lot would have made of the pair of them – him with his champagne tastes, Colin in his dodgy wig. Perhaps it's for the best that he came alone.

His phone vibrates in his pocket and he slides it out. Emma's name flashes up. He hesitates before answering.

'I can't hear you. I'm in a pub on the front. The signal's a bit dodgy here.'

'This can't wait. It's important.'

'Hang on, I'll take the phone outside.' He rises from the table and heads for the door. Outside the sun is low in the sky, and people are making their way back from the beach, laden with bags, windbreaks and inflatables. A group of foreign-language students with backpacks are filing onto a coach by the Jerwood.

'Tom. Are you there?'

'I'm here and I'm celebrating. My agent loves the book. She's already had lots of interest, so she's confident of a decent advance. I'm back, Em. Tom Hunter is back!'

'Good for you. Look, I'm sorry to rain on your parade but she's missing.'

'Who?'

'Who do you think? Evie Stokes. I'm at Charing Cross Station and there's a bloody great digital-display poster with her face on. Christ! She's a missing person, Tom.'

'What are you doing at Charing Cross?'

'What? I had a client meeting. What does it matter? That's hardly the point. The point is, she's missing.'

'So?'

'So she's probably in some kind of trouble. For fuck's sake, Tom! I know you're not her biggest fan, but she's clearly vulnerable and under a lot of pressure right now.'

'Not my problem,' Tom says. There's a feeling of unease in the pit of his stomach, but he refuses to give in to it. Not today. He had enough of that nonsense yesterday. Today he's on the up. Nobody's going to take this away from him. He won't let them.

'My mistake,' Emma says sharply. 'I forgot who I'm talking to. The man who's never in the wrong. The man who bears no responsibility for all the abuse she's suffered on Twitter.'

'You haven't put anything on social media, have you?'

'What? About her going missing? I've only just found out.'

'About me being in Hastings.'

'Of course not. Why would I? You sound paranoid. Are you okay?'

'I'm fine, thanks. Never better. Anyway, it's been great talking to you, but there's a chilled glass of champagne here with my name on it.'

'Tom!'

'Not now, Em. I told you. I'm celebrating. If you can't be happy for me, the least you can do is not bring me down. I'll talk to you soon. Bye.'

He ends the call and heads back inside. Moments later his phone vibrates in his pocket. It's Emma again. He declines the call and switches the phone to silent.

✴

When the waitress comes to clear his plate, Tom asks for another bottle of champagne. 'And make sure it's chilled, please.'

She looks at him as if he's asking for the moon, then rearranges her features into a professional smile. 'Yes, of course.'

It takes a while to arrive – Tom begins to wonder if it's being flown in especially – but when it does the bottle is perfectly chilled and presented in an ice bucket. As he tops up his glass, he feels several pairs of eyes boring into him. Let them look. It's not the first time he's felt out of place, and it won't be the last.

He's still pondering this thought when the pub doors swing open and a man enters and strides over to the bar. He's dressed in khaki shorts and a fitted white T-shirt that shows off his physique. His hair is cropped shorter than usual, with the tell-tale ruddiness around the back of the neck indicating a recent visit to the barber. Tom recognises him instantly. Luke hasn't seen him and is busy ordering a drink. Confident that he's unlikely to turn down the offer of a glass of champagne, Tom rises from his chair, raising a hand to catch his eye. Suddenly it looks like this won't be such a lonely celebration after all.

Luke's face breaks into a grin. For a split second Tom thinks it's directed at him. Then another, younger man appears, greeting Luke with a bro-hug and a pat on the back – the kind gay men give each other when they're avoiding public displays of intimacy. But Tom isn't fooled for a moment. These two are an item. He'd bet his life on it.

He's still standing, feeling increasingly awkward, when Luke finally spots him.

'Tom Hunter,' he says, walking over. 'I heard you were still hanging around Hastings.'

'Really?' Tom replies. 'Who's been talking about me?'

'My friend Adam. He's an estate agent. He says you're looking to move here. So I was right about you, after all. You're not just down from London. You're proper FILTH.' Luke grins to show he's just teasing.

Tom smiles back, determined to save face. 'Actually, I'm keeping my place in London. I'm looking for a second home. And how are you? Who's your friend?'

Luke turns and gestures to the younger man. 'Kyle, come over here. This is Tom. The guy I was telling you about.'

Kyle comes over – blond hair, blue eyes, too much space between his nose and upper lip. 'Pleased to meet you,' he says, every word dripping with insincerity.

'Pleased to meet you too, Kyle,' Tom says, stressing the name with an amused grin that suggests some private joke.

'Drinking alone again?' Luke asks. 'Are you okay? Only, if you don't mind me saying, you look a bit rough.'

'Charmed, I'm sure,' Tom fires back. 'If you must know, I'm celebrating. I've finished my new book. My agent thinks it's my best yet.'

'What's it about?'

'A female stalker.'

Luke frowns. 'Didn't you recently have one of those?'

'Word certainly gets around.'

'So it's, like, art imitating life?'

'Something like that.'

'Good for you,' Luke says. Then, turning to Kyle, 'Tom's an author.'

The younger man doesn't look remotely impressed. 'We should go.'

'You have time for a quick drink, surely?' Tom hopes he doesn't sound too desperate.

Luke and Kyle exchange a meaningful look. 'We'd better be off,' Luke says. 'It was good to see you. And go steady on the champagne.'

Tom wants to ask him about the message on the beach this morning, but with the other man present it feels awkward and even less likely that Luke had anything to do with it. 'Good to see you too,' he says and watches them both leave, the disappointment bitter on his tongue.

No sooner have they gone than he's reaching into his pocket, reminding himself that there are plenty more pebbles on the beach. He opens the Grindr app on his phone. The profiles are displayed in order of proximity, with the person physically closest to Tom's current location in the top left-hand corner of the screen and the one furthest away in the bottom right. The distances range from a few hundred metres to several miles. One man's profile has an arrow pointing left with the words 'He's closer!' which makes Tom smile. It's rare to find someone with a sense of humour on the dating apps. Sadly, a good sense of humour isn't high on Tom's list of priorities right now, and the man's profile pic doesn't excite him in the slightest.

He tops up his glass and scans the bar at the top of the screen showing 'fresh faces'. Most of them look anything but fresh, but there's one that grabs his eye. The photo shows a handsome, muscular man in his early thirties, standing shirtless in front of a bathroom mirror, iPhone in one hand, the waistband of his Calvin Klein underwear visible above his lowrider jeans. Hardly an original pose, but you can't have everything. According to the app, 'Regular Guy' is less than a kilometre away.

What's more, he's interested. A private message arrives: *Hi sexy.*

Tom feel a rush of excitement. He takes a gulp of champagne before replying. *Hi there. What's up?*

Not much. Been to the gym. Horny. Looking for fun. You?

The phone vibrates in Tom's hand and Emma's name appears. Why won't she leave him alone? He declines the call and returns to the app, his fingers fumbling over the screen as he types.

Sounds good. Where are you? I can accommodate.

Prefer to meet first, comes the reply. *Make sure you're not a serial killer!* There's a smiley face to show he's half joking at least.

OK, Tom writes. *Where?*

At the pier.

Be there in 10 mins.

See you then.

Not if I see you first, Tom types. He pauses and deletes each word before he screws things up and scares the lad off. *On my way*, he writes, and hits send.

✳

The pier is closing as Tom arrives. The sun has set, and a full moon hangs heavy in the sky, casting white light onto the black water. A cool wind blows in from the sea. The temperature has dropped considerably.

A few people are still milling about on the promenade, huddled in hoodies or wrapped in scarves. None of them looks remotely like the man Tom is looking for. Great, he thinks. It's going to be one of those guys using a photo from ten years ago or – worse – one they've stolen from another man's profile.

His phone chirps as another message arrives: *I'm under the pier*.

Descending the wooden steps to the beach, Tom hears the crash and drag of waves on pebbles. The tide is rising. Another hour and there'll be hardly any beach left. Not that he plans to be here then. He's never resorted to public sex before, and he's not about to start now. A quick introduction and he'll take his prize catch home.

Crunching across the shingle, he passes a couple of drunks sheltering against the sea wall. Engrossed in some incoherent argument over a can of lager, they barely notice him. He hurries on, catching his foot on one of the concrete groynes but managing to regain his balance despite all that champagne. So what if he's had a few too many? He can still hold his drink.

There's a slight incline up ahead, and then the pebbles give way to a steep slope leading down to the base of the pier. Tom treads carefully, arms out to his sides for balance, feeling the stones shift and roll beneath him. He half walks, half slides down the slope and is relieved when the terrain finally levels off and he's back on firmer ground. He steps across another groyne, narrowly avoids tripping over a chunk of driftwood and then he's under the pier.

Thick steel pillars rise up out of the shingle, supporting the enormous structure high above his head. The air is damp and smells of seaweed. Clusters of mussel shells cling to the pillars, glinting in the half-light. Stepping forwards into the gloom, Tom ducks under one of the cross struts joining the steel posts, steadies himself and looks around. There's not a soul in sight.

'Hello,' he calls.

There's no reply, just the sound of the waves and the whistle of the wind. Frustrated, he reaches for his phone. Then a sudden movement catches his eye, and a familiar figure steps out of the shadows.

He starts, his eyes still adjusting to the darkness. It can't be. But it is. She smiles. 'Hello Tom.'

30

Her appearance has deteriorated since the last time he saw her, outside the magistrates' court. At least then she'd looked presentable – all part of her attempt to convince the judge that she was a fine, upstanding member of the community. Now she's a mess, as if she just doesn't care anymore. She's wearing the blue military-style coat Tom remembers from court and thought he saw on another woman yesterday. But that's where the resemblance ends. Her hair is lank and clings to her skull, as if it hasn't been washed in weeks. She's lost weight – her face gaunt, the eye sockets dark and hollow. Only her eyes remain the same. Pale and grey, they bore into him, barely blinking.

'Evie,' Tom says. 'What are you doing here?'

She grins. 'What's the matter, Tom? Expecting someone else?' She reaches into her coat pocket and takes out her phone. Swiping her finger across the screen, she holds it up for him to see. 'Him for example?'

Tom sees the photo of a man that drew him here. It takes a moment for things to click into place, and he shakes his head ruefully.

She laughs. 'Honestly, Tom. You'd think you'd have learned your lesson by now. You can't always trust people you meet online.'

'Very funny.'

'Do you think so? I don't think it's funny at all. Not even remotely. Take you, for example. You're nothing like the man you pretend to be. We both know it. Only the police and the judiciary were too thick to work it out. But we know the truth, don't we? You and me. We know who you really are.'

Tom swallows. 'I don't know what you're talking about.'

'I think you do. Pretending you didn't really know me. Acting like there was never anything between us.'

'But there wasn't,' Tom says. 'Not really. It was all in your head.'

'What about that night in the pub? Was that all in my head, too?'

'That was a mistake. I'm sorry if I gave you the wrong impression. I tried to let you down gently but you wouldn't listen.'

'Let me down gently? By reporting me to the police?'

'That was later. You wouldn't leave me alone. I was at my wit's end. I didn't know what else to do.'

Her eyes flash. 'You think you're so special, don't you? You with your fancy flat and your photo in the paper. You're far too good for the likes of me.'

'It wasn't like that,' Tom protests.

'Wasn't it? So tell me, what was it like?'

'I liked you. I found you interesting. But then things got out of hand. You wanted something I couldn't give.'

Her lip curls. 'You think I wanted you for sex? We're not all like you, y'know. We don't all go around using people for a little warmth and then dropping them as soon as we're done. Some of us are a little more evolved.'

'That's not what I meant.'

'So what did you mean? What did you mean when you said we were kindred spirits? What did you mean when you agreed to read my book?'

'I was being polite.'

She snorts. 'Liar. You're lying now like you lied in court.'

'No, I'm not.'

'Yes, you are. You told the court you hadn't read my manuscript. You said you hadn't even opened the email. I know for a fact that you did.'

'Okay,' Tom says. 'Maybe I did. What difference does it make?'

'It makes a world of difference. We both know I sent that manuscript to you in good faith. What you don't know is that I also included a little insurance policy.'

He stares at her, uncomprehending. 'What kind of insurance policy?'

'The kind that allows me to keep tabs on you. A little bit of software, automatically downloaded onto your hard drive when you opened that zip file. It allows me access to all kinds of things – your desktop, your webcam. I've been monitoring you for months. I see you've stolen my book. Does your agent know you've been a naughty boy?'

Finally it sinks in. Tom's skin crawls. All those times he felt her presence, all the times he felt as if he was being spied on – he was, just not in the way he thought.

'I've been watching you,' Evie says. 'Every keystroke. Every word. Poor Sylvie. You killed her off, like you'd have killed me given half a chance.'

'That's not true,' Tom says, though he wonders if there's at least an element of truth in what she's saying. 'I've never wished you harm!'

She laughs. 'Never wished me harm? You've wished me dead!'

'You need help,' Tom says. 'Seriously. When the police hear about this they'll have you locked up.'

She steps forwards, the corners of her mouth twitching as if she's on the verge of laughter. 'I'm not the one who needs help. And don't even think of calling the police. The signal is terrible down here. They can't help you now.'

'We'll see about that.' Tom fumbles in his pocket for his phone.

'Look at me when I'm talking to you,' Evie snaps. 'I'm in charge now. I've lost everything thanks to you. Did you honestly think I'd let you get away with it?'

Tom watches in horror as she pulls a kitchen knife from inside her coat, the blade glinting in the half-light. A voice in his head screams at him to turn and run, but his feet are rooted to the spot.

'You can't be serious.'

'Oh, but I am. Deadly serious. Ask your old friend Colin.'

She raises the knife and Tom sees that the blade is stained with something dark and sticky. He clears his throat. 'What about him?'

She smirks. 'Who'd have thought the old man would have so much blood in him?'

'What?'

'*Macbeth*. Lady Macbeth to be precise. Women are often the worst, aren't they? I'm sure your friend Colin would agree.'

'What have you done to him?'

Evie laughs. 'Old Wiggy. Full of spirit, he was. He's not so full of it now.'

'Tell me you haven't hurt him!'

'Why do you care? Oh yes, I forgot: you're close, you two. At least that's how it looked this morning. I saw you stepping out of the front door together – and you barely dressed, too. Was that the walk of shame? Because, let's face it, there's a lot you should feel ashamed of.'

'The message on the beach. It *was* you.' Tom's gut tightens. He should have listened to his instincts.

'Bingo! Not so stupid, after all. Though looking at you now I'd say you're pretty drunk.'

He can still feel the effects of the alcohol. It blurs his vision and dulls his senses, making everything seem unreal. He forces himself to stay focussed. She's right here in front of him – and she has a knife.

'Don't do this, Evie,' he says, glancing around, biding for time. 'Whatever you think I've done, let's just sit down somewhere and talk about it. I'm sure we can work this out.'

'Like we worked it out before? I don't think so. Remember that night I pleaded with you to drop the charges against me but you wouldn't listen? The shoe's on the other foot now, isn't it?'

'It wasn't up to me,' Tom says. 'The police, the CPS, they were the ones calling the shots.'

'Bullshit. You could have withdrawn your statement at any time. You chose not to. Then you went ahead and lied about me in court. You dragged my name through the dirt. All I ever wanted was to be close to you, but you twisted everything. You lied about me and humiliated me. Thanks to you I have a criminal record. I've had death threats on Twitter. And to top it all you robbed me of the only person who ever truly loved me. My dad is dead, and it's all your fault.'

Tom pictures the man he glimpsed briefly outside court. 'I don't know what you think I've done,' he says, struggling to process the information being thrown at him. 'And I'm very sorry to hear about your father. But I'm not responsible.'

'You totally destroyed my life. Why should I spare yours?'

For the first time in a long time, Tom feels physically afraid. Not just afraid. Terrified. He can feel it in his stomach and taste it in the back of his throat.

'Please don't do this, Evie,' he says, his voice pathetic even to his own ears. 'You don't want to do this.'

'Oh, so it's Evie now, is it? Not troll or stalker or madwoman? Why the sudden change of heart? Anyone would think you were scared.'

'I'm not scared,' Tom says, as confidently as he can. But he is – and not just of her but of what he might do.

'Don't worry,' she says, taking another step towards him. 'It doesn't hurt for long. It's really just a question of mind over matter.'

She pulls up the sleeve of her jacket and drags the tip of the blade across the inside of her wrist.

'I've got scars you wouldn't believe, Tom. Real scars. Not the wounded looks you faked for the police. See?'

As the blood wells up, Tom sees the marks she's already made there – a crisscross of white lines against the pale skin. He stares at her in disbelief. 'What are you doing to yourself?'

'You did this to me, Tom. You and her. But that was a long time ago. She can't hurt me anymore. I've seen to that. Now I'll see to you.'

'I don't know what you're talking about.'

'My mother,' she says. 'I killed her. My own flesh and blood. So you see, killing you will be easy.'

'You're bluffing,' Tom says. But somehow he knows she isn't.

She points the knife at him. 'I want to hear you say it.'

'Say what?'

'Admit you lied about me. To the police. In court. You said I threatened you with violence.'

Tom glances at the blade. 'You're threatening me now.'

'Now, yes. But not then. Not when I came to your flat. All I wanted was to talk. That's all I ever wanted.' She raises the knife. 'Admit you lied. You fabricated evidence against me. Those emails. The death threats. You set me up. Say it!'

'This is insane!'

'Say it!'

Tom drags the words up from the pit of his stomach. 'Okay. I admit it. I lied.'

'Now say you're sorry.'

'I'm sorry. Now please—'

'Too late!' There's a flash of silver as she lunges at him.

Tom raises his arms to block her, and seconds later there's a searing pain as the blade slices across his left palm. 'You fucking bitch!'

Suddenly he doesn't feel so drunk anymore. The adrenaline has kicked in. He feels it coursing through his body, sharpening his senses.

He stares at the blood dripping from his hand.

Evie smiles. 'What's the matter? I thought you'd be pleased. You always said I was violent. Now you've been vindicated.'

'You fucking mad bitch!' Tom manages to take several steps backwards, not seeing where he's going but afraid to take his eyes off her for even a second.

She charges at him again, but this time he's too quick for her, dodging behind the nearest steel pillar as she stabs furiously at the empty air. She loses her balance and stumbles. Then, before she can find her footing, he grabs her from behind, pinning both arms to her sides and wrestling with her writhing body until his hands are locked firmly around her wrists. He squeezes until she cries out in pain and pulls the knife from her grasp. It slips through his fingers and clatters to the ground. He kicks it with his right foot, sending it skidding across the shingle, disappearing into the darkness.

She twists and turns, hissing and spitting like something possessed. Tom tightens his grasp and blood oozes between his fingers. He can't tell if it's his or hers. He pictures their blood mingling in some perverse bonding ritual, and it sickens him to his stomach. He imagines the satisfaction she'll derive from it. Her and him, exchanging bodily fluids.

She's stronger than she looks. It takes all his strength to hold on to her as she bucks and squirms, elbows and shoulder blades digging into his chest. Her heels kick back against his shins as she heaves and groans, her voice as wild as the wind whipping around them.

Finally it's as if all the fight has gone out of her. Her shoulders relax and her chest heaves as she starts sobbing gently.

'It's not my fault,' she whimpers. 'I didn't mean for any of this to happen. All I ever wanted was to be close to you.'

Alarmed by her tears and the feel of her body against him as she shudders, Tom releases his hold on her. She pulls away and spins around to face him – her eyes dry, lips stretched thinly into a mocking smile.

'I'll never stop, Tom. You know that, don't you? I'll never leave you alone. You're all I have left now.'

She raises her arms as if to hit him, and he grabs her by both wrists. There's a brief struggle, then she pulls one hand free and swipes at him. A bone hard smack lands on the side of his face, making the blood bang in his ears.

Anger bubbles up inside him as he tries to warn her off. 'Stay away from me!'

She laughs. 'Or what? You'll go running to the police? Or are you ready to teach me a lesson? You said you wanted me dead. Here's your chance. There's no-one here now. Just you and me. It's always been you and me, Tom, from the day we met. And it always will be, until one of us dies. So what's stopping you? Not man enough?'

'Stop it Evie, or I'll—'

'Or you'll what? Hit me? Go on, then. You know you want to!'

Grabbing her by the throat with one hand, he raises the other above his head, fist clenched, shaking with rage. The fear of losing control flashes like a warning sign inside his head.

'Come on!' she taunts. 'Do it! You know you want to. If not for yourself then for poor Colin. He didn't deserve to die.'

Tom feels a stab of anger in his chest, as surely as if she'd knifed him. He pictures Colin alone in his apartment, lying in a pool of his own blood. And then in his mind's eye Tom sees how this all plays out. Him constantly looking over his shoulder. Her always on his case, never leaving him alone. What's a few years in prison to her? What use is a restraining order? She'll only breach it. She has no intention of stopping. He'll never be free of her. Not now. Not ever.

He looks at her now, laughing at him the way that bully at school laughed at him before Tom took his power away, pinned him to the ground and punched him so hard he nearly knocked him unconscious.

He can't go on like this. He can't let her destroy his life, his reputation, everything he's ever worked for.

He feels his temper rise and tries to push the thought away.

But it's no use. The blood rushes to his head. It bangs inside his brain.

He sees red.

PART THREE
SIX MONTHS LATER

31

AUTHOR ACCUSED OF MURDER

Bestselling author Tom Hunter stands accused of the murder of Evie Stokes, the woman previously convicted of harassing him. Stokes was found guilty in June last year, after sending Hunter hundreds of emails and tweets, calling him 'queer' and 'gaylord'.

A restraining order was in place at the time of her death in Hastings, where Hunter was spending the summer. He denies the charges. As previously reported in this newspaper, the *Boy Afraid* author recently signed a major deal for two new books. His publisher was unavailable for comment. The trial begins today.

I didn't mean to kill her. I must have gone over this a thousand times in my head. There are so many small decisions that led up to that moment, so many things I wish I'd done differently. But this much I know for certain: it wasn't intentional. I'm not a murderer.

I tried reasoning with her. I tried telling her this wasn't good for either of us. But I swear she went completely mad. It all happened so quickly. One minute we're talking and the next she's right up in my face, spitting obscenities like something possessed.

She struck the first blow. I want to make that clear. She slapped my face so hard, I saw stars. I stumbled backwards – disoriented, not seeing where I was going. Then just as my head cleared and I managed to regain my footing, she launched herself at me.

The next thing I know, I'm flat on my back and she's straddling my chest, her hands locked around my throat. I see the look in her eyes – angry, demented, murderous. Fear turns to panic. She has every intention of killing me. There's no doubt in my mind. If I don't stop her, she'll choke me to death.

I claw at her hands, but her grip is too strong. I can't breathe. My vision blurs, and my head feels like it's about to explode. Desperately, I reach around, scooping up handfuls of shingle and sand. Then my fingers close around something larger – a stone as big as my fist. I swing it upwards, striking the side of her head. Then again, and again – until the grip on my throat loosens and she slumps forwards, the full weight of her body on mine.

I wriggle out from under her and kneel on the shingle, struggling to get my breath back.

'Evie?' I say finally. 'Are you okay?'

She doesn't answer. She doesn't move a muscle.

What the hell have I done? I try telling myself that she's simply unconscious. I wait for her body to stir, like someone waking from a deep sleep. But she just lies there, face down, her hair fanned around her head, darkening against the wet shingle. Blood oozes from her shattered skull, soaking into the sand. A cold feeling hits me in the pit of my stomach. I know she's dead.

I think I'm going to be sick. I clasp one hand over my mouth and climb unsteadily to my feet. Fumbling in my pocket for my phone, I try to dial 999, but my fingers are shaking so much, I keep pressing the wrong buttons. Then I stop. What will I say? I just killed someone. I didn't mean to but I did. I could go to prison for this. At the very least, I'll be charged with manslaughter. What sentence does that carry? A few years? I wouldn't survive a few months.

I panic. You think you know what you'd do in a situation like this. But you don't, not really. Not until it happens. I tell myself to breathe, calm down, think it through. But my nerves are jangling and my head is all over the place. The coppery smell of her blood pricks my nostrils. My heart races. The wind howls and it's like a wake-up call. I need to get away, before anyone sees me. I look around. There's no-one else in sight. It's just me and her. Or what remains of her.

The stone I used to fight her off is lying next to her body. I pick it up, walk down to the water's edge and throw it as far as I can. It hits the water with a loud plop. If someone sees me I'll be just another tourist tossing pebbles into the sea. I picture it sinking to the bottom, lost among a million others. I wonder how far the current will carry it, what the likelihood is of it being found and identified as the murder weapon.

Another wave of panic hits me, and I turn and run up the steep bank of shingle towards the top of the beach. I say 'run'. Have you ever tried running over shingle? You can't. Your feet slip and slide, making progress slow. I feel the ground shift beneath me, and my whole world seems to tilt on its axis. It's like that feeling you get when you're so drunk the room starts to spin – sky, sea, moon, stars and shingle all kaleidoscope together. My stomach heaves and my breath comes in short, shallow gasps. But somehow I make it up to where the shingle levels off and the lights from the promenade cast deep shadows along the sea wall.

I stay close to the wall, edging my way towards the wooden steps, listening carefully for voices or footsteps from above. But no sound carries down. The adverse weather has driven everyone away. The promenade is deserted.

When I reach the top of the steps, I stop and look back towards the pier. The tide is rising. I tell myself that the water will wash everything away – the guilt, the evidence, the body. The tide will rise and fall, and by the morning she'll be gone, dragged out to sea by the current, never to be seen again.

I was wrong about that. As it turns out, I was wrong about a lot of things.

✹

I remember the first time I saw her in court. I remember thinking how fragile she looked, how unlike the monster you'd described to me so many times. I remember thinking back to all the other little things that didn't quite add up. I'd had my doubts, Tom. Something wasn't right. There was something you weren't telling me. I'd had this feeling for months.

I recalled the way you rejected my offer to accompany you to the police station the day you first went to give a statement. I'd never known you to refuse my support before. I couldn't think why you'd want to do this alone. It wasn't until later that it struck me: you were like an actor preparing for a role. You needed to get into character, rehearse your lines, get your story straight. Of course you didn't want me there. I know you better than anyone. I'd have seen through your performance.

That day in court, when you were giving evidence and practically broke down in the witness box – you were acting then, weren't you? And the story you told, about how this woman had wormed her way into your life and refused to leave you alone – that wasn't entirely true, was it? I'm not saying you made the whole thing up. There was some truth in what you said. But a lot of it was embellished. I believed you when you said she wouldn't stop contacting you. But when you described the impact her actions had on your quality of life and told the court how fearful you were, I had my doubts.

You said you'd had friends who'd died of AIDS, that her tweeting about you as 'the AIDS generation' brought back painful memories. Yet you've never mentioned these friends to me, not in all the years we've known each other. Not once. Why is that? At the time, I told myself that I wasn't being fair, that you had every right to play for sympathy if that's what it took to win the case. The judiciary love a good victim, after all.

Besides, I'd seen for myself the state you were in. That night you came for dinner at my place after giving your impact statement to the police, you seemed so stressed. You were drinking heavily. You barely touched your dessert, despite the fact that it was your favourite – blueberry cheesecake. I'd gone to a lot of trouble baking it. Not that I minded; not really. What bothered me was that you were smoking again. You said it helped keep the weight off, that the antidepressants were making you balloon. But you didn't look overweight to me. If anything, I thought you looked rather gaunt.

We talked a lot that night. You told me things you hadn't mentioned before, like the time you posted her address on Facebook. You were worried about some of the things you'd said on Twitter and the fact that you'd exchanged pleasantries with her before things turned nasty. You thought the defence would use it against you, that you'd lose the case. I remember asking you if that was all. You assured me it was.

And still it kept nagging away at me. Something wasn't right. Call it woman's intuition, but something didn't quite add up. I didn't know what it was. I just knew that something was wrong. Why were you acting so strangely? Was it all down to her? Or was there something else you weren't telling me?

That first day in court, she barely spoke, and when she did she was ordered to stop. 'You'll have your chance to speak!' the judge scolded her. But I wondered if she would, really. I never told you this, but the day after you gave evidence I went back to court to hear what she had to say. I wasn't able to stay long. I had a client meeting at noon. But I heard and saw enough to convince me that she wasn't fit to stand trial. She kept incriminating herself. Even her defence lawyer looked embarrassed to be there. It seemed to me that her fate had already been decided. Nothing she said now would make a blind bit of difference.

What rankles me is that I also gave a statement to the police, describing the impact she'd had on you, the stress you were under, the various ways in which her actions had been detrimental to your health. I did it because you asked me to. You said it would help strengthen your case. How could I refuse? But you misled me like you misled the police and the court. Had the prosecution felt it necessary, I'm sure you'd have let me take the stand and lie on your behalf. You'd have let me perjure myself. Because, by the time the trial was over, I knew that what you were saying wasn't the truth, the whole truth and nothing but the truth.

✶

It's hard to say when exactly the nagging voice in my head became impossible to ignore. I supported you throughout the court case, despite my misgivings. I was there for you when the judge delivered her verdict and when the sentence was passed. I might have had my doubts, but you were still my friend. I hoped that now, finally, things would go back to normal, and you'd put the whole sorry business behind you.

But that's not what happened, is it? If anything, you seemed more obsessed with her after the trial was over than before it began. I started to wonder if you were suffering from some kind of post-traumatic stress disorder. I urged you to seek counselling. I even made the mistake of mentioning victim support.

'I'm not a victim,' you replied, sharply.

It was then that I began to seriously ask myself who this person I'd been supporting all this time really was. Because if you weren't the victim in all of this, what exactly were you?

After you left for Hastings I went to your flat. I let myself in with the spare keys and I had a good look around. What else was I supposed to do? You were definitely hiding something and I wanted to know what it was. I wanted to know who you were. For years I thought I knew you, but apparently that was just wishful thinking on my part.

So there I was, a loyal friend who thought she'd earned your trust, reduced to snooping around your empty flat. I'm not sure what I was looking for. Something to prove me right? Something to prove me wrong? I think I was hoping, somehow, that my suspicions were unfounded. I wanted to think the best of you, not the worst. I always have.

And then I found them, going through your desk drawer – the anti-depressants you were supposed to be taking. But you never took them, did you? The boxes were unopened. The repeat prescriptions were never handed in. I counted half a dozen of them, going back months and months. All those times you told me the pills were making you sluggish, all the side-effects you described to me in such detail – it was all a pack of lies. And if you'd lied to me about that, what else were you hiding from me?

The answer was staring me in the face. A letter from your bank, confirming an evaluation on your flat and the release of a substantial loan, secured against the value of the property. The letter was dated a week earlier. At the bottom were a few calculations in your handwriting and the word 'Hastings', followed by the names of what I assumed were local estate agents. You hadn't mentioned any of this to me. Had I known you had money worries, I'd have been happy to tide you over. And what was all this about Hastings? You told me you were going there to write, not to look at properties. Surely you weren't thinking of moving there? When were you planning to tell me?

But that wasn't all. Beneath the letter was a bundle of A4 paper secured with a rubber band – around three hundred pages in all, covered in text, neatly double-spaced. At first I thought it was a draft of the book you've been working on, the one you'd been so cagey about. But when I looked again I saw that it wasn't your manuscript. It was hers. The one you'd denied all knowledge of. Her name was printed on the first page, below the title – *The Book of Us*. On the next page was the dedication – to you, of course. I didn't read much beyond that. I didn't need to.

I was placing the papers back in the drawer when I noticed it – the watch I gave you for Christmas a few years ago. The Christmas we ended up in bed together. The one we never talk about. It was an Omega Seamaster – as worn by Daniel Craig in the Bond films we'd both enjoyed so much. You've always had expensive tastes, but I figured you were worth it. I even had it engraved, 'To Tom, love Emma'. You told me you loved it at the time, though I've rarely seen you wearing it. There was no sign of the presentation box. It just lay there with the paperclips and old biros. So much for you loving it. So much for you valuing our friendship.

I didn't act immediately. But when you insisted on giving that interview and I saw the misogynistic abuse Evie was getting on Twitter, I knew I had to do something. That's when I decided. I needed to speak to her face to face, and find out what really happened between the two of you. I'd heard your version of events, but I hadn't heard hers, not properly. She was such a mess in court, rambling on and going off at tangents, incriminating herself at every opportunity, it was no wonder the prosecution ran rings around her. But that doesn't mean she made the whole thing up, does it?

32

I found her on Twitter and sent an email via a link on her blog.

She must spend most of her time online because the response came back within a few minutes: 'I'm not supposed to contact you. The restraining order forbids it, or have you forgotten?'

'But I'm the one contacting you,' I replied. 'I need your help.'

'With what?'

'With finding out why Tom lied in court.'

There was a delay of ten minutes before she responded again. I pictured her staring anxiously at her computer screen, wondering if I was being honest with her or if this was some kind of trap.

'How do I know I can trust you?' she asked.

'Because I believe you. I believe what you said in court. I know Tom lied.'

I didn't believe everything she said in court, of course. She was obviously infatuated with you, and her fixation led to harassment. Legally speaking, a crime was committed. But I didn't believe it was as straightforward as you'd made out. I believed her when she said that you'd encouraged her, at least in the beginning. I had doubts about some of the allegations you'd made.

'I don't want to discuss this via email,' she wrote. 'I don't want my emails coming back to bite me. I've been there before.'

'I know you have,' I replied. 'And I want to hear your version of events. We can do this whichever way you want. No emails. No phone numbers. Just suggest a time and place, and I'll be there.'

Finally she agreed to meet me.

✶

We met at a dive bar on the edge of Chinatown – one of those places I assumed had closed down years ago, like most of the old Soho I used to know. A bit dingy and seedy, to be honest. I'd expected her to choose somewhere like a café at the Southbank or the National Gallery. But she was obviously paranoid about being seen with me. She was wary and watchful. She kept looking over my shoulder. When I asked her why, she said she was checking to see if there was anyone else with me. She meant you, of course. I could see how obsessed with you she still was. I could even picture her face lighting up at the sight of you. Even then. Despite everything.

She looked worn out. Her face was thinner than when I'd last seen her in court. There were dark circles under her eyes. Her skin was sallow and dotted with pimples. It was as if she'd stopped taking care of herself. I asked her how she was feeling and she laughed bitterly.

'How do you think?'

'I don't know,' I said. 'Why don't you tell me?'

So she did. She told me how you'd first met, at that book signing. She described how you flirted with her – laughing at her jokes, pocketing her business card and referring to her as a kindred spirit. And I believed her, Tom. I believed every word. We both know what a flirt you can be, how you use your charm to get what you want from people. I'm not saying she didn't harass you afterwards. I heard the evidence in court and it was strong – strong enough to have her convicted. But it wasn't the whole story, was it? There was more to it than that.

'But you went to his flat,' I said. 'After you'd been arrested. When the police had warned you to stay away from him. Why?'

'To talk,' she said. 'I pleaded with him. I begged him. I didn't threaten him. And I didn't send him those threatening emails, either.'

'He said you did.'

'He lied. He lies about a lot of things.'

So it seems. She described meeting you for a drink – the clothes you wore, the smell of your cologne. In court you denied ever arranging to meet her socially, but deep down in my gut I knew she was telling the truth.

'When was this?' I asked.

She smiled. 'A few weeks after we first met.' I could see the hypnotic effect the thought of you still had on her. Her eyes shone. She was miles away.

'Where?'

'The Red Lion. It's a gastro pub in Kennington. Do you know it?'

I didn't. I couldn't picture you in a gastro pub. I still can't. All those real ales and dark wooden beams – they're just not you. But as I was quickly discovering, I don't know you half as well as I thought.

'Did you mention this to the police?' I asked.

'What do you think?'

'But there must be some way of proving this meeting took place. How was it arranged?'

'He called me,' she said. 'I knew he would.'

'Then there'll be phone records.'

'He withheld his number. He's good at withholding things, or haven't you noticed?'

'But surely your defence could have found some evidence to prove he was lying?'

She smirked at that. 'Let's hope you never have to depend on legal aid. Not that it would have made any difference. They all had it in for me. The police. The crown prosecution service. Even the judge. And my only crime was to love someone. That's what I am, you know – a prisoner of love.'

I couldn't help myself. 'It's a pretty fucked-up kind of love.'

She glared at me. 'Well, you'd know all about that, wouldn't you?'

I tried to pretend that I didn't know what she meant. But I knew alright. She was toying with me. It was written all over her face.

'Did he ever talk about our time together?' she asked.

I told her that no, you hadn't.

She smiled knowingly. 'He talked about you.'

Then she told me things – things she could only have known if you'd confided in her. She knew about that Christmas. The Christmas after my mother died.

'Did you think you'd finally snared him?' she said, and as she spoke it felt like a dagger in my chest, twisting and turning with every word.

What happened that night was between us. Nobody else. Why would you tell her? I've never told anyone. It's none of their business. Why would you share something so personal with someone you claimed you hardly knew?

'Poor Emma,' she added. 'It was just a pity fuck. It didn't mean anything, not to him anyway. He just felt sorry for you.'

You told her we fucked? I know you're prone to exaggeration, but chalking me up as another of your sexual conquests is really taking the piss. What happened between us that night was certainly intimate, but it wasn't intercourse. I think I'd have remembered.

'You don't know what you're talking about,' I said.

'Don't I?' she replied. 'It must have been a difficult time for you, after your mother took her own life like that.'

So you'd even told her about my mother. How could you?

'You know he's planning on selling up and leaving London,' she said then. 'He wants to cut his emotional ties and start a new life in Hastings.'

I told her I didn't believe her. But how did she know you'd had your flat valued? How did she know you were in Hastings?

'It looks to me like he's played us both for fools,' she said, grinning triumphantly.

I really didn't have an answer for that. You'd betrayed my confidence. You'd shared the intimate details of our friendship with a stranger. There was nothing I could say that would alter the fact.

Can you imagine how I felt at that precise moment? Hurt doesn't begin to describe it. I was devastated. I'm not like her, Tom. I'm not some little fangirl with a crush who you can toy with whenever it suits you. We have a history, you and I. We're friends, for fuck's sake! Friends are supposed to look out for one another. Whatever happened to loyalty? Whatever happened to trust? I thought you respected me. Evidently not.

I didn't think it could get any worse, but then she said you'd raped her.

At first I thought I was hearing things. You may be many things, but a rapist? Never. Then she explained. 'Artistic rape', she called it. She described how you'd stolen her ideas, how the book you were writing could never have been written without her input. You'd always been so cagey with me about your new book. Now I knew why. It wasn't entirely your own work. No wonder you were so determined to discredit her. After being convicted of harassment nobody would take her claims seriously.

'Have you read it?' she asked.

I told her that no, I hadn't.

'Has he ever asked you for feedback on his work? Has he ever sought your advice?'

'Of course,' I replied, though in reality you never have.

'You're lying,' she smirked. 'You're as big a liar as he is. No wonder you get along so well.'

And then she said that you'd stolen her life. Thanks to you, she had a criminal record. Thanks to you, she was being trolled on Twitter. Thanks to you, her beloved father was under enormous strain. She described how his health had deteriorated rapidly since the court case. I can only begin to imagine what his subsequent death did to her. I think it's what finally tipped her over the edge.

I tried to defend you, tried telling her it wasn't your fault, that you would never knowingly hurt anyone. But my words sounded hollow even to myself. You encouraged her, Tom – at least in the beginning. And when things got out of hand, you twisted the truth to suit your needs. You lied to everyone, including me. You had me believing you were on antidepressants and on the verge of a nervous breakdown – knowing what I went through with my mother. How could you? After the trial, when you said you'd seen Evie at the Southbank, I thought you were suffering from some kind of post-traumatic stress disorder. Now I realise it was just your guilty conscience.

Finally the words died in my throat.

'Poor Emma,' she said, shaking her head. 'You're still under his spell, aren't you?'

She left pretty abruptly after that, looking around one last time and thanking me for the drink with what sounded like genuine gratitude. Maybe it wasn't the drink she was grateful for. Maybe it was the fact that someone had given her a fair hearing.

She didn't say anything else. She didn't need to. Her point had been made. You're quite capable of using someone, then dropping them when their services are no longer required. I of all people should know that.

33

The day she was sentenced, I took you for a celebratory lunch at that restaurant in Clapham. The truth is, I didn't feel much like celebrating. In fact, I felt sorry for her. She looked so broken – and the lack of interest on her father's face made me wonder what kind of childhood she'd had, whether the reason she craved attention was because she'd never had it. I know how damaging a distant father can be for a young woman's self-confidence. It's not unusual for a girl raised in those circumstances to repeat that pattern well into adulthood, chasing after men who are emotionally unavailable. I should know.

Lunch was a disaster. You barely listened to a word I said. You were too busy flirting with the waiter. I tried to engage you in conversation, but when you weren't cruising him, you were cracking jokes or being evasive. You didn't ask a single question about me, my work or how I was feeling. From the moment we sat down, the only person you had eyes for was him. I left the restaurant knowing I wouldn't be missed, that the two of you would hook up as soon as he finished his shift. I knew you'd get what you wanted. You usually do.

That was supposed to have been our celebration – yours and mine. Just for once, couldn't you have focussed on me? A friend who's always been there for you. Someone who has stood by you, cared for you, cooked for you and, yes, loved you.

I know we're not supposed to talk about what happened at my place that Christmas – though obviously you have no problem discussing it with others. It was a moment of madness, you said, one of those silly things that happens and is best forgotten. I was still grieving at the time. My emotions were raw and my head was all over the place. All I wanted was a little comfort – though if memory serves me correctly, it was you who made the first move.

We'd been drinking heavily all day – Bucks Fizz at breakfast, wine with lunch, vodka and tonic as we curled up on the sofa watching *It's a Wonderful Life*. I started to get a bit weepy and you put your arm around me, told me not to cry, started nibbling at my ear. I turned to face you and suddenly we were kissing.

I pulled away. 'Tom,' I whispered. 'What are we doing?'

'Shh...' you replied, putting a finger to my lips. 'Where's the harm?'

Maybe you've forgotten that part, but I haven't. I've always found you attractive, always known that you were off limits. Sex between friends is rarely a good idea. But because I'd drunk too much and my judgement was clouded, I cast my doubts aside. The next thing I knew, we were naked in bed together. I was gripping your broad shoulders, and you were kissing my neck, your penis semi-erect against my thigh.

But that was as far as it went. The spirit was willing but the flesh was weak. A quick fumble and you realised your mistake.

'Sorry,' you said. 'This isn't going to work. Too much booze.' Embarrassed, you climbed out of bed and pulled on your clothes.

'It's fine,' I replied, and at the time I truly believed it was.

More fool me. From the way you reacted afterwards, it was as if I was the one who'd initiated it. What do you take me for, Tom? Do you seriously think I was trying to convert you? I know the nature of your desires. I know what really turns you – and I know it isn't me. All I expected from you afterwards was a little respect. Is that too much to ask? Apparently so.

I thought what happened that night would bring us closer. But I was wrong. The closer I get, the more distant you become. And the more I realise how little I really know you after all.

That day in the restaurant, I tried not to let it bother me. But as I watched you flirt shamelessly with the waiter, I couldn't help but think of all the other times you've taken me for granted. I was never part of your world, Tom. Not really. Not where it mattered. I was always on the periphery. I was there for you when you needed me. That was a given. I was the one you invited to parties and book launches when you needed someone to support you in the all-important business of being Tom Hunter. But I was never your equal. I was always your plus one.

And though we arrived together, we seldom left together. There was always a more important or more attractive proposition. I've lost count of the number of times you've abandoned me, left me stranded, being pawed by some sweaty man who's big in publishing or well connected in the media and unhappily married to a woman who doesn't understand him. Do you have any idea how often this happens to women? How many times in a woman's life she's subjected to unwanted sexual advances? The world is full of men who think that our bodies are theirs for the taking. And where were you when this was happening to me? Off with some random guy you'd just met and would probably never see again. So much for loyalty. So much for friendship.

But despite all this, despite everything I now know – the lies, the betrayal – I couldn't just switch off my feelings for you. I still cared. When I saw that missing-person display at Charing Cross station, I felt sick to my stomach. I feared for her welfare – but I feared for yours, too. I knew how obsessed and unstable she was. I didn't know then that her father had died. But I'd seen the abuse she was getting on Twitter. Rape threats. Death threats. Threats you shrugged off when we spoke about it. The kinds of threats women are subjected to every day, and men can only begin to imagine. She had every reason to be angry. Perhaps if you'd taken my advice and thought twice before agreeing to that interview we wouldn't be in this situation now.

I tried to warn you, but you wouldn't listen. You were too busy celebrating the fact that your agent loved your new book – the one you've never even discussed with me. Maybe I should have made myself clearer. But it was hard to know what to say when there was so much I had to avoid saying. You sounded paranoid on the phone. It wasn't just the drink talking. There was a tone to your voice I barely recognised. What had become of you? I couldn't tell you I'd met with her, not after everything that had happened. You'd have hung up on me. You hung up on me anyway. When I tried calling you back, you ignored my calls. I tried several times and each time it went straight to voicemail.

So I did something I've been quietly regretting ever since. I jumped on the first available train and came looking for you.

34

I didn't expect to find you so easily. I tried calling you again from the train, but you still weren't responding and by the time we reached Hastings the battery on my phone had died. I left the station wondering what the hell I was doing. But Hastings isn't a large town and when we last spoke you were in a pub on the seafront. I knew from our previous conversations that the place where you were staying was also on the front, close to the pier. So I followed the signs and arrived at the seafront just in time to see you heading west along the promenade.

I stood at the pedestrian crossing, waiting for the lights to change. You were on the far side of the road. There were four lanes of traffic between us, but even from this distance I could tell you weren't yourself. Your movements were erratic; you even looked a bit crazed. It was also clear from the way you walked that you were more than a little drunk. I called out to you but you didn't seem to hear. Then a bus passed and I lost sight of you. When I looked again, you'd gone.

The lights changed, and I walked briskly across the road. Where were you? Then I saw you, about a hundred metres ahead, swaying slightly as you navigated the pavement, sidestepping a stream of people heading away from the pier and towards the Old Town. I followed you, slowly closing the gap between us. As you approached the pier, you stopped and pulled out your phone. What were you doing? You didn't speak to anyone, just stared at the screen before stuffing the phone back in your pocket.

When I saw you descend the wooden steps to the beach, I knew something wasn't right. It was already getting dark, the tide was rising and a bitter wind was blowing in off the sea. This was no time to be taking a leisurely stroll on the beach. Then it hit me. I'd never had you down as the type to go cruising for sex in public spaces, but what did I know? I held back, wishing I'd brought a jacket but grateful for the warmth of my cashmere sweater. The wind whipped my hair and made my eyes water.

What now? Should I wait to see if you reappeared or follow you down? If I stumbled across you having sex with someone I'd be mortified. If I stayed where I was I might lose track of you altogether. I gazed up at the stars, as if they somehow held the answer.

There was a full moon – not the blood moon I'd heard about on the radio that morning, but a big fat moon, hanging low over the horizon, as bright as a searchlight. I don't know how long I stood there for. Ten minutes, perhaps? But then some other instinct drove me forwards. Call it morbid curiosity. Call it the desire to see things through. I'd come this far. Why turn back now?

A yellow warning sign greeted me at the top of the steps – 'Danger. Do not walk under pier'. Next to it, another sign advised, 'Caution. Beach levels may change. For your own safety keep off groynes and other structures'. I wondered how unsafe it was, really.

As I stepped down onto the pebbles, I spotted a couple of drunks huddled against the sea wall. Apart from them, there didn't appear to be a soul around. Then I heard your voice cry out, 'You fucking bitch!' You sounded furious.

Ignoring the warning signs, I followed the source of the sound towards the pier. The shingle crunched and shifted as I walked across the groyne and down the steep bank to where the ground levelled and the pebbles finally gave way to sand. There were no stars now. The night sky was obscured by the enormous wooden deck high above my head, casting everything into deep shadow. Steel supporting pillars rose up out of the gloom, as thick as tree trunks – a forest of steel. It felt as if I'd entered an alien underworld – a strange, forbidden place where anything could happen.

The only light was the cold glow of the moon, reflecting off the black water. Then, as my eyes adjusted to the gloom, I saw you. At first I couldn't believe what I was seeing. You were wrapped around each other in some kind of embrace. Is that what it had been all along? You and her – lovers? But surely she'd have told me? Then I saw you pull her hands away and hold her by the wrists as she struggled. I couldn't hear what you were saying. Your words were carried away on the wind. But I could tell from your body language that you were arguing.

I watched as she managed to free one hand and slap you hard across the face. There was a moment's delay – shock, I imagine. Then you raised your right fist while your left hand reached for her throat. I've never seen you so angry. I didn't know if you were going to choke her or punch her. When I opened my mouth to shout 'stop!' I gasped as a rush of cool air filled my lungs. I hadn't realised I'd been holding my breath. I watched as you threw her roughly to the ground and stood over her, clenching and unclenching your fists.

Then you turned abruptly and stormed off in the opposite direction, still visibly shaking with rage.

I should have followed you. How I wish I had. We could have talked and sorted this whole thing out. Instead I made the fatal mistake of trying to talk to her. By the time I reached her she was back on her feet and staring longingly after you.

'Are you alright?' I called out as I approached.

Startled, she turned to face me. 'You again. What's the matter? Can't leave him alone for five minutes?'

'I think it's you who can't leave him alone,' I replied.

'He cut me,' she said and held up her arm, showing me the gash across her wrist. 'He had a knife. Look what he did!'

I didn't know what to think. I hadn't seen any knife. Of course you could have had one concealed about your person as you headed for the pier. But that would mean you'd gone there planning to use it, and that didn't sound like you at all.

'Tom would never do that,' I said, though I was beginning to have my doubts.

'You think you know him so well, don't you?' she sneered. 'You don't know him at all. It's thanks to him that my dad is dead.'

'What?'

'A few hours ago. They called me from the hospital.'

I stared at her, not knowing whether to believe her or what to say.

'What's the matter?' she said. 'Cat got your tongue?'

'Oh, Evie,' I said. 'I had no idea. I'm so sorry.'

Her eyes glistened, and for a moment I thought she might break down and cry. Then it was as if a mask slipped. Her face changed, hardening into a look of pure hatred. 'I don't need your pity,' she spat. 'You of all people.'

'This has to stop, Evie,' I said gently. 'It's not doing you any good. You need help.'

'Don't fucking patronise me! You condescending bitch!'

And that was it – she launched herself at me.

I thought I'd be able to get through to her. I thought she'd listen. After everything she'd been through, I didn't think there'd be any fight left in her. How wrong I was. But let's not go over all that again.

It wasn't until afterwards, as I hurried back to the station, that the full magnitude of what I'd done really sank in. I kept seeing her face and hearing the sound of her skull cracking. I pictured her lying there under the pier, lifeless. It was a high price to pay for getting involved with a man like you.

※

The last train from Hastings to Charing Cross leaves at 9.50 p.m. I caught it with minutes to spare. The station toilets were locked, so as soon as I boarded the train I made straight for the toilet, where I took out my compact and checked my reflection. There was a red welt with signs of bruising around the base of my throat. I covered it by turning up the collar of my shirt.

It was then that I saw the blood stain. It wasn't large, but it was noticeable – a blot of red on my right shoulder, blossoming darkly against the cream cashmere of my sweater. I pictured her head against my shoulder. My stomach spasmed, and I vomited into the sink. I rinsed my mouth before taking off the sweater and stuffing it into my handbag. When I looked in the mirror I barely recognised myself. I was altered in a way I would never have thought possible. It wasn't my face staring back at me but the face of a killer.

I found a window seat in a quiet carriage and sank into it. As the train lurched forwards, I watched the town slide away and wished I'd never set foot in the place. The air-con was on full blast, so it was hard to tell if I was shivering due to the cold or from shock. A prickle of sweat broke out on my upper lip. When the guard came to inspect my ticket I almost jumped out of my skin. Gradually the carriage filled and the hum of conversation drowned out the hammering in my chest. A couple of transport police boarded the train at Battle, and I shrank down in my seat, convinced that they'd come looking for me. I needn't have worried. They made their presence felt for a few stops and left the train at Tonbridge.

As we passed through Kent and the familiar stations of outer London, I weighed up my options. It wasn't too late to confess. Leaving the scene of the crime would count against me, but at least my conscience would be clear. On the other hand, what was the point? You'd already destroyed her life. Why should I allow you to destroy mine? I thought of all the times you'd abandoned me, all the times you've taken me for granted – and now I was the one left to clear up your mess? Panic turned to fury, and I struggled to get a grip on myself. I needed to stay calm and think clearly.

By the time I reached my destination, I'd made my decision. As I left the train at Charing Cross and crossed the concourse to the underground, an automated voice warned that 'CCTV is in operation at this station'. Fair enough, I thought. If the police came for me, I'd confess. If not, I'd wait and see how this played out.

The missing-person digital poster I'd seen earlier was displayed on the southbound Northern Line platform, her face staring back at me accusingly. I had to avert my eyes until the train came screeching and rattling into the station, obscuring her from view. The carriage was crowded and for once I was glad of it, as if the presence of all those living, breathing, sweaty Londoners drew me back from the brink and into a world I knew.

Sleep eluded me that night. At 4.00 a.m. I climbed out of bed, went out into the garden and stared up at the sky. And there it was – the lunar eclipse we'd been promised. The moon was no longer white but steeped with red – a blood moon.

I thought of that bloodied stone on the beach in Hastings and wondered if I'd ever sleep again.

35

I didn't expect them to find her so quickly. But then, she'd always said you wouldn't get rid of her easily. It seems she was right about that. The next morning, a man was walking his dog down by the pier and there she was – no longer missing but soon to be the subject of a murder investigation. She hadn't been swept out to sea as I'd anticipated. Her body was caught on one of the wooden piles.

The first few hours of any crime scene are the most critical. Everyone knows that. And the body had been submerged in sea water, making forensic analysis more difficult. But the police had a lead. A man fitting your description was seen leaving the scene of the crime on the night in question. One witness recognised you from that newspaper article and described you as looking 'extremely agitated'. Another said he'd seen you earlier in the pub, behaving erratically.

Face it, Tom. You were bound to be the first person they'd want to speak to. You had motive, means and opportunity. She wouldn't leave you alone. You'd wished her dead on several occasions. You were in the Hastings area at the time the crime was committed. You'd even called the police to say she was still stalking you. Of course you'd be their prime suspect.

What I didn't know then was that you had another motive for killing her. You'd made a new friend in Hastings – an old man who lived in the flat downstairs. You went back that night expecting to find him dead, murdered by the woman whose murder you're now charged with. Instead you found him somewhat alarmed by your dishevelled state but very much alive.

Why didn't you call the police there and then? Was it shock? Were you still drunk? The way you described it, it was your neighbour's idea to leave it until the morning, when you'd sobered up and could give a better account of yourself. Perhaps he thought there was more to this than you were letting on, that you'd done something you shouldn't have and were in danger of incriminating yourself. The police came soon enough anyway – not in answer to your call but to take you in for questioning.

The day you were arrested, I was at work. The call came through just before lunch.

You sounded panicked. 'It's me, Em. You won't believe this, but Evie is dead, and the police think I killed her.'

Oh, I believed it alright. How could I not? Though, naturally, I feigned surprise. 'Christ, Tom! That's awful. But try to stay calm. And don't say anything until you've seen a solicitor.'

Your voice shook. 'What am I going to do, Em?'

'It'll be okay,' I assured you, knowing full well that it probably wouldn't. 'If you're innocent, you have nothing to worry about.'

'What do you mean, "if"? Of course I'm innocent!'

'Of course you are,' I said. But we both know you're not. Not entirely.

I came to the magistrates' court the following morning and to the first Crown Court hearing two days later, where the judge granted your application for bail based on your previous good character and with certain conditions attached. You were ordered to hand over your passport, remain at your registered address and report to the police station once a week.

'Fail to comply with these conditions and you will be rearrested and remanded in custody until your trial.'

A few days later, back at your flat, I watched as you tried to make sense of what was happening to you. It was less than a week since you were first taken into custody, but the difference in you was shocking. You looked lost. We were sitting in your living room overlooking the river, but already you had the air of a man condemned to a prison cell.

'She killed her own mother,' you said, leaping up from the sofa and pacing the room. 'She was going to kill me.'

I said the first thing that came into my head. 'So it was self-defence.'

You turned on me then, your face ashen and unshaven, eyes blazing. 'I didn't kill her, Em! Christ, if you don't believe me, what hope is there?'

What hope indeed? The witness statement isn't the only evidence they have against you. Forensics came back with a partial thumbprint on her wrist where your hands had gripped her, and they found a gay dating app on her phone. No prizes for guessing what that was doing there, or how she lured you to the pier that night. Typical man, always thinking with your dick. The messages you'd exchanged with 'Regular Guy' that night were still on your phone, confirming the time and place of your hook-up. The same technology that led you to her that night led the police back to you.

They also found a kitchen knife with your fingerprints, and hers. There was blood, too – mostly hers and a trace of yours from the wound on your hand, the kind easily inflicted during a struggle. The stone that broke her skull was never found. But even without the murder weapon, the prosecution seem confident they have enough to convict. It's their contention that you intended to kill her. She'd harassed you, humiliated you, injured your male pride and lured you to the scene of the crime under false pretences. You don't deny any of that but insist that she pulled the knife on you, that you have no knowledge of how she died, that she was still alive when you left the scene. But we only have your word for that, don't we?

As news of your arrest spread, your ex, Aidan, crawled out of the woodwork to say you had a history of violence, that you raised your fist to him on more than one occasion. I'm pretty sure he's lying, but his testimony suits my purposes. All in all, it's not looking too good for you.

'You believe me, don't you?' you asked me that day at your flat. 'You know I didn't kill her?'

'Of course,' I replied. 'I know you're not capable of killing anyone.'

I wonder how true that really is. If there's one lesson I've taken from all of this, it's that we're all capable of things we never thought possible. Even me.

Don't think these past few months have been easy for me. They haven't. I think about her often. I think about what you said: that she killed her own mother. I wonder what would drive someone to commit such an unspeakable act. Behaviour like that doesn't just come from nowhere. She was clearly damaged – a broken, twisted thing. I have nightmares about that night under the pier. I remember her fingers closing around my throat and that crazed look in her eyes. Then I picture the blood oozing from her shattered skull and I wake up gasping for air.

I've had more than my share of sleepless nights. I took time off work. I even bought sleeping pills on the internet. I didn't want my GP knowing, in case questions were ever asked. I don't think it's very likely, not when the police and prosecution already have their killer. But you can't be too careful, not when there's so much at stake.

Watching you suffer has been unbearable. I do feel for you, Tom. I guess that's part of the problem. I feel for you too much. I always have. But I can't take the fall for this. We did this together, you and me. Between us, we destroyed her. But it was mostly your doing. You created the monster. You set this whole chain of events in motion. All I did was try to tidy up your mess.

I'll see you in court. They're calling me as a character witness. Of course I'll tell them there's no way on earth you could be guilty of such a heinous crime. Not you. Not my Tom. And when you're found guilty, as I'm sure you will be, I promise I'll visit you in prison. I'll come as often as you like – and on the day you're finally released, I'll be there waiting for you. It's what you'd expect, after all.

Good old Emma. You can always count on me.

ACKNOWLEDGEMENTS

Thanks to my agent, David H Headley, for finding me a new home, and to Karen Sullivan and all at Orenda for making me feel so welcome.

Thanks to my publicist, Sophie Goodfellow, and all at FMcM Associates for their support.

A number of people helped bring this book closer to the one you hold in your hand. For their encouragement and feedback, I'm indebted to Matt Bates, Jane Gregory, Paulo Kadow, V.G. Lee and Rebecca Lloyd.

Thanks to Angus Hamilton for advice on court procedures, Ed Hall for information on spyware and Gareth Evans for help with other legal queries. Any mistakes are entirely my own.

Thanks also to Susie Boyt, Marina Brasil, Elaine Burston, Alexis Gregory, Lorna Lloyd, Karen McLeod, Sarah Sanders, Paul Watson, The Hastings Gang and The Polari Posse.

The crime writing community is famously supportive – and none more so than my criminally savvy author pals on Facebook. Hardly a day goes by when I'm not encouraged, entertained or inspired by your posts and comments. Thank you, one and all.

Thanks also to the booksellers, bloggers, event organisers, librarians and reviewers who work so tirelessly to support authors.

Last but not least, thanks to you, my readers. Without you, I'm nothing.

Paul Burston, *Hastings, March 2019*